AGE of SHAME

Karl Manke

author of *UNINTENDED CONSEQUENCES*
SECRETS, LIES AND DREAMS
& THE PRODIGAL FATHER

Karl F. Manke
2019

Alexander Books

Alexander, N.C.

To my beautiful wife: Carolyn,
for her immitigable patience and...

To my parents:
Richard and Aristine Manke

Publisher: Ralph Roberts
Cover Design: Ralph Roberts
Interior Design and Electronic Page Assembly: WorldComm®

Editor: Pat Roberts

ISBN 978-1-57090-276-5

Alexander Books—an imprint of *Creativity, Inc.*—is a full-service publisher located at 65 Macedonia Road, Alexander, NC 28701. Phone 1-828-252-9515, Fax 1-828-255-8719. For orders only: 1-800-472-0438. Visa and MasterCard accepted.

This book is also available on the Internet at **Amazon.com**

CONTENTS

PROLOGUE

As the plane descends into the airport at Miami, Florida, an elderly passenger returns an aged, yellowed piece of paper to his pocket. He has a shock of white hair and a small goatee. He is gracious to all on board, sporting a ready smile and twinkling blue eyes and it's apparent that he speaks with a German accent. Throughout the trip he has read and re-read the paper. Between reads he spent time with his head back against his seat as if deep in thought or memories.

In the past year he has been widowed and through the Internet has found and agreed to meet an old friend in the lobby of a fine hotel in downtown Miami. This well-dressed, stately-looking gentleman walks through the airport with the aid of a cane as he contemplates their upcoming meeting.

An older lady is escorted by a male driver about twenty years younger than herself. In appearance, she possesses a steady gaze as someone who has spent her life as a professional person. It's not hard to imagine her as the CEO of a top-flight company. She possesses an assurance that is hard to set aside despite her advanced age.

The driver has been around this lady long enough to see beyond appearances. He wonders about the man they are to meet. Who is he that this normally very controlled lady is alternating between anticipation and anxiety?

CHAPTER 1

REINIE

BOOM! BOOM! The percussion of several-hundred-pound bombs is not merely deafening it's also deadly, especially for those who never hear them coming. Those who die are free from the savagery of man's wars; those who survive spend much of their lives tortured by the meanness of an uncompromising vexation to their spirit. Some are able to overcome these devastating experiences using the most ingenious methods. As fate will have it, these horrible destinies life dealt have nonetheless led to a multitude of unusual success stories.

It is 1943. This is the beginning of an economic boom in the United States. This is not so in Eastern Europe. Secret political boundaries are already being drawn by the Allied and Axis Powers dividing the spoils. The German people don't know it yet but their fate will be systematically ripped from their hands and redistributed among the Allies. In the end, the western sectors will be divided between the United States and Great Britain with the eastern sector going to Russia.

Reinhardt Ludwig Koehler, a German teenager, is a survivor of everything life has thrown at him. Hoping to escape the ravages of their war-torn country, his parents moved to their summer cottage on the Baltic Sea in German-occupied Lithuania. At first they found a solace there. Now, the Allies have destroyed the shipbuilders along with the ports supporting supplies coming in and out of the country while the Russians only remain a distant threat. But without notice this all changes. Between the German military advancing into Russia during the war and the Russians destroying everything behind them in order to prevent their retreat, Russia has been decimated. They, in turn have begun a calculated revenge against Germany to punish them for their war crimes. There is no discrimination between innocent German citizens and Hitler supporters. Germans are Germans and to the Russian, they are all to be punished alike.

Being placed under the control of the Soviets, the Germans are expected to automatically become communists. The full force of this maneuver hasn't been felt by this family until this day late in the war when a Russian stake truck stops in front of the cottage. Two armed soldiers walk unannounced through the door followed by an officer who speaks German. What quickly becomes apparent is that they are here to remove the family from the home.

"Was machst du?" ("What are you doing?"), are the only words Herr Rudolph Koehler and his wife Katrina are able to utter before being loaded into the waiting trucks, leaving with only the clothes on their back. In a predictable Russian fashion, these soldiers move quickly, brutally and decisively removing people from their homes often with nothing more than what they may carry in their pockets. Raping the woman, regardless of age, is the norm of these soldiers. If a husband, brother or son objects, it becomes the only excuse necessary for the soldiers to brutalize them before shipping them off to labor camps, often somewhere in Siberia.

It soon becomes apparent that they are being dispossessed and all this region is being given to Poland. Along with other Germans in the realm, they are taken to the city of Klaipeda. From there they are loaded into cattle cars, to be relocated. Some are selected to be shipped to labor camps while others are dropped into the interior industrial centers of Russia and ultimately forced into their factories as laborers.

Reinhardt, affectionately nicknamed "Reinie" by his parents is the only surviving child in this Koehler family. His older brother Stephen has been killed last year while serving in Hitler's brown shirt brigade. Reinie has been working in a neighboring village helping a peat farmer at the time of his parent's abduction. Not yet aware of this travesty, he returns home to find the cottage vacated and padlocked with a legal notice nailed to the wall warning trespassers to stay away. Everything is in place including the wooden furniture on the porch along with his mother's sewing basket indicating this may have been the last place his mother had been. He knows she would never have willingly left it unattended like this.

In one way this is all strange, in other ways this young teenager has come to expect the unexpected. In his short years he has witnessed Jewish children he played with snatched by German SS agents never to be seen again; homes and lives destroyed by incessant bombing. He has witnessed the hopelessness of children who have lost their entire families to war. The latest travesty, to be somehow endured, is the expulsion of the German people from their homes by the Red Army.

The sun is low in the western sky casting a golden glow across the landscape. Its beauty soon turns to a somber brown and then to the gray of evening. The feeling of desperation has replaced the good tiredness of a week's hard work with the peat farmer. Reinie finds himself forced to form decisions that most adults have trouble making.

He has a fairly good grasp of what "self-respect" expects of him. His entire upbringing has been one where control of his emotions was a plus; now it's become a necessity that he can ill afford to lose. A good portion of his young life has been dominated by some form of mental, physical, or spiritual testing and now due to the war tearing his homeland apart, he's being tested on these fronts more often than one would expect of one so young.

A large part of his everyday experiences, including this day, have found him forced into a survival mode. Breaking a window is his first thought. If it were not for the locked shutters prohibiting that thought from becoming an action, he'd be in the house. His second thought comes rushing through the abyss of his memory. *"The root cellar! I must get to the root cellar!"*

The remembrance of how this haven of safety provided as good a protection as any underground military bunker during the period that allied forces systematically bombed the neighboring ports, draws him toward it. It's some distance behind the cottage, reinforced deep into the side of a hill with the entrance hidden behind an overgrowth of ivy. Visually sweeping the area until he's satisfied he's alone, he carefully makes his way to this hidden tactical fortification.

Forcing open the door creates a screech from these rusted hinges and then the all too familiar damp, musty, still air of the cellar greets him, enveloping his nasal passages, drifting its way into his lungs. But now all of this ill-smelling foulness is quickly minimized as it also carries with it a comfortable feeling of refuge.

This unexpected change in his life has him yearning for a break. *"I wish I could stay here forever,"* is his first thought. He releases a long sigh and lights the lantern left behind for just such an occasion as this. The light casts a warm yellow freshness to the otherwise gray cedar poles that dominate the structure. The shelves are bordered with home-canned beets, fish and berries along with a covered wooden bin of potatoes. Bunk beds built with the ever plentiful cedar poles line the opposite side of the narrow room. Reinie, not yet full grown, finds that he is still able to stand upright in the center of the dirt floor on the spot where his father would have to stoop. It leaves him feeling an awareness of his insignificance.

Opening a can of fish along with a can of beets, hardly able to eat it all, he nonetheless fills himself. Satisfied that the darkness will conceal him, he opens the cellar door and makes his way to the back yard water pump. Once there, he quenches his thirst and fills an old canteen left hanging on a bed post for this purpose.

Fully aware that something clandestine has happened to his parents and from the signature left on the warning nailed to the door, he knows the Russians are behind it. The only thing left to do for this precocious teenager is to begin to plot his next move.

Thanks to the wife of the peat farmer, he has a couple changes of freshly laundered clothing and from the farmer himself a week's worth of currency. All this can easily fit into his nap-sack along with a can of fish and another of beets and just for good measure a half dozen raw potatoes. With this larder he envisions a sense of well being; possibly a carry over from these war years when his father would assure him this was a safe place for anything that was thrown at them.

It proved to be just that until he opened the door the following morning and found himself face to face with a Russian officer and three armed soldiers. What had not been obvious to him was the Russians had questioned his parents as to his whereabouts since they had a complete census of the region. The officer immediately begins to question him asking for his identification. His command of the German language is heavily blanketed with a thick Russian accent. Reinie hands him his card. The officer glances at it satisfied that he has his missing boy. With a brisk hand gesture to the soldiers, they respond quickly with one on each side of him, escorting him to a waiting truck.

There are several others already crammed into the full truck bed. Old, young, male, female, all clutching various possessions they had managed to grab before being escorted on their one-way trip to some obscure labor camp. It's a bleak scene but then when one understands that this generation has withstood two world wars on their soil and a world wide depression, the norm is a joyless existence. The Russians are managing to add "hopeless" along with "joyless." This ride is far from comfortable. No one says anything as there is really nothing to say. Reinie strains his eyes hoping to catch a glimpse of anyone that looks familiar. This group is made up of mainly farm families. These are farms that have been in these families for hundreds of years. It's land that has been carefully handed down from one generation to another. Now with authorities thousands of miles away and with a stroke of a pen, it is land soaked with the tears and often the blood of its inhabitants.

The Nazis had plundered these families earlier for able-bodied workers, either for labor camp workers or the army. Reinie's older brother, Stephen, had been one of these recruits. Only seventeen when he joined the Hitler Youth Corp and much to the chagrin of his family, he proudly wore the Brown Shirt. Reinie recalls one Sunday morning his brother arrived in church with his sleeves flamboyantly rolled just above his elbows in the Hitler Youth tradition. It was just in time for an old aunt to call him over and with a wicked little smile on her face, as he bent to kiss her, she raised her hand and slapped him ordering him to roll his sleeves down, *"Das sind wir nicht!"* ("This is not who we are!") Within the year Hitler's troops were all but decimated. These fledgling war machines, many of them hardly pubescent boys, were asked to sacrifice themselves to *Der Vaterland*. A week later Reinie's brother was dead.

Childhood is something this generation can't lose because it's a luxury they've never possessed. If necessity is the mother of invention, fear is the mother of survival. Being in the wrong place at the wrong time has little to do with weakness or fragility in life, it has more to do with inattention. Reinie's delusional sense of security in the root cellar put him into this situation, now he has to find a way to escape.

The truck finally lumbers its way into the rail yards to an indifferent steam powered behemoth belching black soot prepared to separate them from any sense of kinship to their ancestral roots. Its deadening hard blackness and foreboding hissing foreshadow dark pronouncements regarding any kind of future. Children, whose lives have not yet been tempered, are beginning to cry, maybe at nothing more than the mayhem and the loud bullying voices of rude soldiers.

People are systematically herded into waiting cattle cars. The soldiers have little regard for the hesitation they have to enter these dung-laden transports. These German evacuees are learning fast the backlash caused by the behavior of their Fuhrer's cruel S.S troops on those with whom they had clashed. Revenge is spewed from the lips of a Russian soldier as they berate those who believe they are too good to ride in a cattle car.

One last mournful whistle announces the train's departure as it jerks forward gradually picking up speed. One man is seen desperately running to catch the outstretched hand of one who appears to be his wife. Instead of flipping himself inside the boxcar, he falls under the wheels immediately severing both legs. All that can be seen is two Russian soldiers running to pull the top half of him from the still-moving train. The callousness of war has hardly caused a second glance except for a gasping wife whose sobs can only be heard by heaven over the chugging sound of the engine.

Like the train, Reinie's thoughts are running forward. Reinie had heard from his father of the German extermination camps for Jews and wonders to himself if the Soviets are following suit. Maybe this has been the fate of his parents.

He spends precious little time lamenting his bad luck. Looking around for a spot in the cattle car he can claim as his own he has to compete among families desperately endeavoring to build a little nest with their belongings, hoping it will give them some security. There are at least sixty live bodies jammed into this wagon. No one speaks. No one wants to give their fears a voice. Everyone had been told they'd be given housing and work in the factories but few believe it. Many of these persons are simple folks caught up in the turmoil created by their despotic leaders when all they've ever asked of them is for a safe place to raise their families. These leaders remain inaccessible for selfish reasons of their own leaving these simple people to become the scapegoats for the sins of their leadership.

It's approaching evening and beginning to cool. A man near the open door slides it shut hoping to avoid the cold draft. Then there is the distinct sound of chopping coming from the back corner of the car. Somebody has decided they are not going to use the slop pails left for them as toilets and have decided to chop a hole through the wooden floor. For the time being Reinie is satisfied to munch on one of his raw potatoes. Settling in, he finds some breathing room and soon falls asleep listening to the steady click of the rails.

Daylight arrives with no disturbances other than the closed box car has taken on the pungent smell of body odor and a bad toilet. A couple of the men slide the door open welcoming the fresh morning air. Marginal portions of food are being meagerly distributed among family members careful not to waste a bite. One beleaguered woman is frustrated over her inability to quiet her hungry child and tries to force an already dried up breast into the crying child's mouth.

Not willing to share what food he has, Reinie is satisfied not to un-cover his entire larder and continues to chew a raw potato. He feels quite confident that he will find a way off this train before it reaches its desti-nation and that he needs to conserve all his resources.

Before the hour is up, the train has begun to slow down. It soon be-comes apparent they are stopping to reload the coal tender and refill the boilers. Something else has caught his eye. The car directly behind them is being surrounded by soldiers. It soon becomes clear why as they begin to remove the body of an elderly man who was too frail to survive this dreadful ordeal. He had passed away during the night, having escaped more of the unkind rigors of this journey. The officer in charge is shouting orders in Russian to his underlings all scurrying to do his bidding, they soon return with a shovel. Along with the family, they dig a shallow grave in a field next to the tracks marked only by a cross of sticks held together by the old man's shoelaces. His shoes have become the property of the officer in charge.

All the soldiers are either involved with the funeral or watching what's going on. Surviving these impediments, as opposed to victimization, has less to do with age and more to do with attitude. A teen recognizes very few difficulties that can't be licked vs. someone at forty who has given in to defeat and found it to have taken possession of their life. The train is full of people whose lives have given way to defeat and are willing to surrender to whatever befalls them like so many sheep on their way to slaughter. Many of the younger people on the other hand are naturally rebellious regardless of who's in charge.

Reinie remains cautiously alert, keeping a watchful eye for any opportunity to make a run for it. This may prove to be the break he's been watching for. Keeping one eye on the soldiers, who are all turned away, he slips to the ground. In a flash he is under the boxcar, emerging on the opposite side to disappear into a thicket. Not quite willing to imagine himself out of danger he keeps moving until he hears the whistle and the subsequent chugging of the engine continuing its journey without him.

He's quite aware of the orphan problem, first under the Nazis and now the Soviets, the solution is often elimination. It's normally expected that when either of these governments begin to round up orphans, it's always with limited available resources that ultimately result in systematic starvation, neglect, or in the case of the Russians, a quick shot to the head. In the case of boys Reinie's age they are more likely forced into some kind of work camp. Reinie prefers to stay out of their reach for all of these reasons.

He has no idea where he is but knows he can't let his guard down as he did yesterday and chance a repeat today. "I can't be a dumbkoff like yesterday," Reinie scolds himself. With no one there to consult, he talks out loud to himself. He misses his brother Stephen. Stephen had been his hero and mentor. Sometimes when he's troubled he finds himself still talking to him anyway. *"What should I do Stephen?"* is oftentimes his mind-set when he's confused. Meanwhile he finds himself charging about in a thicket of scrub brush. Taking a moment to collect his thoughts and survey his situation he plops down on one of the many stumps that are left from the peoples' harvest of anything that can be burned for fuel. Now completely alone with his thoughts, he unfastens his rucksack with his food supply and changes of clothing. Settling on a can of fish, he recalls how he had helped his mother with that canning chore. It brings a homesick moment. It's a state of mind he feels he would rather not entertain. Some intuitive sense tells him that feeling sorry for himself places him in a vulnerable position, one that he can ill afford at this time.

Taking a sip of his precious water, he surveys his situation. *"Come on Stephen give me something,"* he says calling on his dead brother once again. His voice is full of a helpless confusion as he hopes to invoke some ethereal thought readjustment from his brother.

His ultimate decision turns out to be a simple one: merely stay put until dark and then follow the tracks back to the Baltic coast. It's the simplest idea and it makes sense. "From there I can make it to the sea and hop a freighter to Sweden," he calculates.

Reinie has had many unfortunate circumstances in his brief life but since there have been no failures the best thing he has going for himself is an unwritten notion that all things remain possible. It's a beautiful gift for the young and seldom squandered. He's boldly planning this next move with the assurance that with careful attention to details it will reward him with a favorable outcome.

The Russian army has proven to be a brutal, barbaric force for anyone to confront. The best advice from those who have had to deal with it is to avoid it. It has not been unusual for entire families to commit suicide rather than risk their lives to its cruel onslaught. All females are raped regardless of age. All males are brutalized in some form, from beatings to murder. Most children are systematically murdered, especially if they are orphaned and no longer under the supervision of a family.

It's soon dark. Reinie is happy he opted to wear the old navy bridge coat left hanging in the root cellar. (It's one his grandfather had worn in the previous war.) The nights are proving to be much cooler and rather than risk detection by lighting a fire, he finds wrapping in this all wool over-garment a comfortable substitution. Once back on the tracks, he feels the safety of darkness enveloping him as he begins what he imagines to be a fairly routine trek back to the Baltic coast.

CHAPTER 2

RHENA

The community is an obscure Polish village along the German border, not much different from other communities suffering from the German/Soviet struggle for dominance. About a third of the population is Jewish, a smaller number are ethnic Germans and the majority is Poles. On one hand there is a sense of community in that there is a dependence on each others' contributions to the community at large but on the other hand their lives revolve around traditions, language and religion. For the most part their primary allegiance is created through various connections with these three phenomena. This creates an insurmountable barrier between these communities that unfortunately precludes any semblance of a homogeneous social unit. Emotions almost always play a larger part in attitudes toward neighbors that are different than those stemming from pragmatic thought.

Thirteen-year-old Rhena Nowak is the youngest child of Abraham and Minnie Nowak, Jews living in the countryside around the village. Her father is a poultry farmer supplying the surrounding area with eggs and meat. He can also attribute much of his success to supplying poultry products to many Jewish wholesalers in the region. His prosperity creates a silent envy among the less-successful Poles competing for a share of the same markets.

The Nowak family also consists of three older sons, Herzl, 21, Solomon, 19 and Izak, 16. This is the Soviet-occupied part of Poland and consequently all religions are to be purged from the country. To facilitate this action they have declared that all boys must be sent to schools in Russia. The purpose of this is obvious: to re-educate the next generation. Izak has been sent off for schooling.

With Germany's invasion of the Soviet Union, the Nazis have regained control of this portion of Poland. First on their list is a calculated process of dispossessing Jews. To begin with they are all ordered to wear yellow armbands with a blue Star of David. It then leads to arresting all males between the ages of sixteen and sixty-five. Abe along with Herzl and Solomon are ordered to gather in the town square. From there, along with several dozen other Jewish men and boys, they are ordered to a near by wooded area. In the middle is a clearing. Some are handed a shovel, others are given a pick.

A German SS officer steps forward. He issues orders to dig a trench a hundred meters long, by three meters wide and one meter deep.

"We need you dogs to dig and not speak. If you find it difficult to follow this order, like all dogs you will be shot."

His Polish language skills are heavy with a German accent but there is no doubt in anyone's mind that he is a man of his word.

As the work progresses, it's hardly noticed that German soldiers are marching forward with another group of men. These are Polish men from the village. Abe recognizes many of them as neighbors he has given employment to and others that he has as poultry customers. Not yet sure what the Germans are expecting of them, they are ordered to turn and drop their shovels in front of the trench. Without warning a group of soldiers march in front of them and commence firing at those in the ditch. In ten seconds the only sound left is the echo of the rifles followed by the clicking sound of the bolt action on the Mauser rifles ejecting a spent round and pushing another load into the chamber.

The Polish men stand dumbfounded. They are immediately ordered to pick up the shovels and bury the dead Jews and they will be allowed to live.

The German SS officer continues to direct his cursing toward the Polish men. "You are Polacks and no better than the dogs you are burying. Soon we will be digging your graves."

When Abie and the boys don't return, Minnie determines that something bad has taken place. Rhena and her mother are terrified of the Germans as they have heard so many stories about internment camps and labor camps for Jews. With the resoluteness of a wife and mother, she orders Rhena to stay home while she harnesses a horse drawn wagon to drive to the village. It doesn't take long before she encounters a neighboring Jewish family, the Brokmans. They are heading in the opposite direction with a wagon load of belongings. She has never before seen the panicked looks from these elderly friends of a lifetime.

"What in God's name is going on?" she asks, stopping her cart.

Yaakov Brokman is driving the wagon while his wife, Ethel, sitting next to him and clinging to her shawl drawn tightly around her shoulders, hides her tears under her babushka.

"They've all gone mad," she says sobbing.

"Who's gone mad?" now demands a much more anxious Minnie.

"The Germans! They are shooting Jews in the streets!" sobs Ethel.

Minnie's fears are becoming a reality. "Did you hear anything of my Abe and the boys?" she asks more animated than ever.

"All the men and boys are dead and buried in a trench in the woods," adds a just as frantic Yaakov, "and the Poles are pointing us out."

"Oh my God!" says Minnie cupping her trembling hands around her nose and mouth, "What are we to do?" This unanswerable question carries a tone of defeat and desperation.

"We have family in Warsaw. We're going to stay with them until this insanity stops," says a slightly more confident Yaakov.

Minnie swings her wagon back around to the farm. Grief and fear overtake her return.

Rhena sees her mother coming up the lane. Running out to meet her she senses something is amiss immediately. "Where is Papa?" is her immediate concern. "Where are my brothers?"

Minnie looks intently at her daughter but can't answer. Silently and methodically she begins removing all the tack from the horse and wagon. Her thoughts are on how she is ever going to cope. Her fear and grief are quickly adding another component—anger. *"How can they do this?"*

No one in this part of the world has lived without hardship and that includes young children. Rhena has certainly had her share in her young life.

"Momma answer me! Where are Papa and my brothers?"

Looking up from her task, she shouts between her sobs, "THEY'RE DEAD RHENA. THEY'RE DEAD!"

The words strike Rhena with a force that stops the world. The wind stops blowing, the sun stops shining, all other sounds cease—leaving only the bluntness of the words her mother has just cried out. These words have a flatness about them. She feels helpless at their dullness and the seeming impenetrability into them. The wave of fear that overtakes her is new. She becomes quiet. Not because she doesn't want to speak, rather because she has no vocabulary skills to place into words her feelings of desolation.

Nowhere on God's earth are there thirteen-year-old children prepared to meet the intensity of this type of crisis—neither physically nor emotionally. Nonetheless the cruel intentions of those in power are purposely designed to bring this kind of despair to these families.

Seeing the bleakness in her daughter's eyes, her mother soon breaks the silence, pushing the lock of hair from Rhena's forehead, "We have to stay together, you and me Rhena. Thank God Izak's safe in Russia but you and me—we'll get through this. The Germans are going through their hate phase again. We just have to be strong."

Fear and anger prevent a time for mourning for these two. Work has to be done on the farm and they are the only ones left to care for things. By the end of the week this also radically changes. After returning from synagogue on Friday night, Rhena and her mother are met by a contingency of German soldiers at their home with an officer announcing to them that the German government is seizing their farm to support the German occupation. They are also told they can stay on as laborers as long as they prove to be an asset to the Third Reich. Otherwise they will be sent to an internment camp in the interior part of Germany.

They are no longer allowed to occupy their house but are relegated to a place in the barn. They are also promised food, provided the new German manager and his contingency have enough for themselves. On the other hand, they are told that if they work extra hard they could qualify for a few extra food rations.

After finding their rations to be inadequate, Minnie complains to the SS officer in charge. He strikes her hard enough to knock her to the ground, drawing blood from a split lip.

"We don't take the food out of German mouths and feed it to Jew-dogs!" he blurts.

What shocks her as much as the blow is the conviction with which this officer holds this statement to be true.

Rhena bolts from the sidelines, running to her mother's defense. "Please Sir, please don't hurt my mother!"

"Get these dogs out of my sight!" shouts the officer at an underling. "Make sure they wear the armbands."

The soldier takes another one of his many opportunities to mistreat what he has come to believe is a race of inferior sub-humans. He grabs Minnie by the hair and begins to drag her. With a scream, Rhena attacks the soldier who then lifts his boot and begins to stomp Rhena and her mother. Only when he fears he my cause an injury that will prevent either of them from working does he halt. Snatching them both to their feet he gives Rhena one more kick, ordering them both to get back to work.

Barely able to stumble back to the bleakness of their chores, they find they have been reassigned to a more demeaning task—carrying manure out to the fields. Both mother and daughter remain quiet, absorbed in their own fears. Knowing the Germans are looking for an opportunity to declare them unfit for work and then send them to an internment camp, they struggle to finish the day.

CHAPTER 3

IZAK

The days pass. Each one heralds yet one more repressive maneuver by the Germans toward the Jews. Hitler's war against Poland had lasted no more than sixteen days resulting in the annihilation of the Polish troops. They were no match against this German *Blitzkrieg*.

The Poles and Germans have never wasted love toward one another and neither of these peoples have ever wasted love on the Jews. Reasons vary: The Germans leadership is trying to rid the country of anyone other than true Germans in the attempt to build a mythical Aryan master race, or another reason may be that since Jews are not allowed to own property in many countries they have resorted to becoming bankers and control the economy, or that the Jews are guilty of killing Christ, or that Jewish people invite envy by being successful business managers where others are mediocre and on and on. But like all humans the only unvarying practice which all these fallen children are guilty of is to dehumanize the enemy to a point where it becomes easy to pattern such practices as ethnic cleansing into whatever way gleans the best results.

Rhena and her mother are no longer anything to the Germans or the Poles. They are regarded as disposable non-persons. Their future is provisional at best. On this particular morning mother and daughter have been separated. Minnie has been sent to the fields. Rhena has been sent on a dispatch by the German officer in command of the farm. She has set out on foot for the two-mile trek along with a right of passage to deliver papers to a command center posted in the village.

This trip used to frighten her, but now out from under the scrutinizing eye of the soldiers, it's the safest she's felt in weeks. There is no one else on the road. The grade is full of depressions left over from weeks of German tanks assailing its surface. Rhena finds herself singing a song as she straddles the rough ruts. The morning is new and the October sun is shining—impervious to the good or evil humans basking in its warmth. For this thirteen year old, it's the first time she's noticed anything lovely in a long time—it's a simple exhilaration.

This euphoria suddenly takes a turn as a lone figure emerges from a nearby wood lot at a spot where the trees turn to brush just before skirting the road. It startles Rhena and she turns to run. Suddenly a familiar voice calls out.

"Rhena don't be frightened. It's me Izak." A tall, slender young man wearing a bland gray wool school uniform of some sort with a bland dark winter overcoat begins to wave his arms.

Rhena stops, still clutching the dossier she is responsible for delivering. She looks back with a wary eye at this seeming interloper. She can't believe her eyes.

"Is it you Izak?" she shouts out. Her voice creaks with skepticism. It's been nearly a year since he went away to a Russian school in the Ukraine.

By this time he has made his way directly in front of her. "Yes it's me. Touch me if you don't believe me."

Rhena, playing the part of a detective, looks hard at this familiar but yet foreign brother. His eyes are darker giving his face a pale quality. He is taller but thinner. The familiar parts of him are hidden behind a military demeanor that was not a part of the boy who left. There is a coarseness about him that she is not acquainted with. The Russian schooling has definitely had an impact on his development along with his overall maturing.

Rhena is dazed. The suddenness of this circumstance has propelled her mind into a stalled mode. Her speech is halted as she struggles with any thought. Suddenly and involuntarily the tears begin to flow. Izak grabs his little sister in an embrace that has eluded him for this past year.

"How are Momma and Papa?" he asks. It would be hard to miss the excitement in his voice.

All the pent up grief that Rhena has been holding inside of herself suddenly comes streaming out in uncontrolled sobs.

"The Germans killed Papa and our brothers."

It's Izak's turn to be stunned. "Papa, Herzl and Solomon are dead? What about Momma?"

Still sobbing, Rhena says, "Momma and I are still alive but Momma says if it were not for me she would hang herself. The Germans took our farm and make us live in the barn and work for food. When Momma complained that we are not getting enough to eat, they beat us."

Izak cannot believe his ears. He could no longer endure the hard life of the Communist school system. He too had suffered the contempt of the Russians for no other reason than being a Jew. Their purpose is to wipe away all connections to his religion and to his family and rebuild him into a proletarian whose allegiance is to the State. When he showed signs of resistance they referred to him as a "dirty Jew" and beat him. When he saw an opportunity to escape he ran away. What kept him going for the several weeks to return home was the vision of the life he had enjoyed with his family. Now he has to digest the hard facts that this too is gone.

Rhena remains in a mode of silence as though she is awaiting orders from this ad hoc leader of her family.

Izak has taken on a faraway gaze. This is almost too much to stomach. But one thing he did learn from his experience with the Russians is if he is to survive he needs to adapt quickly to the circumstances of the day and persevere.

Quickly refocusing his attention, he clears a spot on the dirt road. Using a stick, he traces the position of the outbuildings of the farm as he remembers them. In the next moment he breaks the silence. Turning to Rhena, he asks her to point out where she and her mother are lodged. Rhena carefully studies the dirt map, satisfied she's done her best to identify the correct building, she hands the stick back to Izak.

"Tell Momma that I'll visit tonight after midnight. Now get along and do what you have to."

Rhena blinks a couple times, letting out a sigh that comes only from those who possess a sense of reassurance. Just seeing her brother gives her hope that things are going to get better. She gives her brother a quick hug. Now wary that this encounter may be observed by German or Polish eyes, she hurries on toward her destination.

Having completed her duty assignment, Rhena makes her way back home. As she passes by the spot where she had encountered Izak, she peers into the brushy area. Not seeing him, she begins to wonder if she had even seen him to begin with.

"Remember tonight around midnight," comes a voice from the thicket.

This reassuring pronouncement brings Rhena's lips into a miniscule smile. Her heart is lighter than any time she can remember. This emotion is unusual for anyone during this period.

When she returns to the farm, the first to notice is the commandant as he pats her on the head. "You are a pretty little girl," he says handing her two potatoes. Rhena doesn't know why but the leer of this *Lagerfuhrer* (camp commander) makes her uncomfortable.

Returning early in the evening to her barn habitation, she reports to her mother of meeting that morning with Izak. Her mother hardly shares the lightheartedness that Rhena is exhibiting.

"Oh Dear Lord what is he thinking? He was much safer with the Russians than he will be with these German savages. What will I do if they kill him, too?"

Minnie spends the rest of the evening fretting about Izak. She rehearses all the horrid scenarios that she can imagine that could happen to all of them if he's discovered. Their compartment had electricity but since the Germans have taken charge, they eliminated it. They are totally at the mercy of one incandescent light outside in the yard on a pole between the barn and the house. It's used for security, to shed enough light to prevent anyone from attempting to roam outside without being challenged. As an unintended consequence, it surreptitiously glows through their small window preventing them from tripping over things in the dark.

Izak has survived the Russians, not because he is smarter but because of a series of circumstances that allowed him to slip through their net. He traveled at night, raiding vegetable patches along the way. One time after pleading a case of a sick mother he needed to reach, he was able to catch a ride on the back of a farm wagon. Once he was challenged by a Russian guard and couldn't produce his papers, the guard let him go recognizing his attire as that of a student. Another time he was approached by some Polish police, he kept a rag over his mouth telling them he was suffering from typhoid, they immediately abandoned their interrogation.

This night is not to be an exception. Caution and patience prevail. The Germans are more of an enemy to him as a Jew than anyone so far and are certainly not going to deal with him lightly if he's discovered. The rumors of people disappearing and never returning are widely known among Jewish communities.

The night is one of a crescent moon validating its orderly pathway despite the disordered world it passes around. Along with only a small amount of cloud cover, Izak is able to slip across these well-known fields avoiding the patrol of German soldiers on the roads. Soon the long-familiar silhouette of a farm that has been a part of his life since birth materializes. It has the appearance of an old friend sitting innocently in the shadows. The moon's light seems to be innocuous to the beastliness that it's hosting.

Izak has only the memories of genial occasions as he pauses long enough to review his past. It's difficult for him to imagine that those innocent periods he longs for were merely intervals in a life that is now to be controlled purely by his ability to survive. It's a myriad of enemies he faces. Enemies that cause hunger for days on end, or that will hang him, shoot him, use up his strength in labor camps only to further their horrific causes and for no other reason than him being a Jew.

What's required of him to live for the next moment has little to do with hanging on to memories that distract him. Gathering his wits, he notices the military vehicle parked near the house where his father had parked the truck they used to deliver chickens. It's 7 p.m. and dark, normal for this time of year. He spends the next few hours lying in a field watching things wind down as farm personnel retire for the night. The soldiers are bivouacked in tents in front of the main house. They don't seem to have much of a security presence around the property. Cautiously he makes his way to the outbuilding Rhena described earlier. Encountering no signs of guards, he slips through what is still being used as a feed storage area and makes his way to a tack room that is now housing what is left of his family.

Tap, tap, tap. The sound is barely audible but to this mother it reverberates loudly across the tiny room. Minnie quickly exchanges glances with Rhena, already on her feet. The two of them unbolt the door. There stands before them a son and a brother who has taken on the expression of one who has lived lives beyond his young years.

For the moment neither mother nor son are given to say a word. For this moment there are no words. Izak steps through the door into the arms of this ready and waiting mother. Their embrace brings tears from eyes that feared they would never see this kind of moment again. In order to remain viable, sentimentality is a luxury that must be tempered with raw truth, no one understands this axiom better than this family.

"Mother we have to leave here and the sooner the better," said Izak. His tone has turned from cheerful to urgent.

Minnie turns her back to hide her sadness. She's torn. This is her home. She feels the need to stay and defend it. Nonetheless what her son is saying is also plaguing her thoughts.

"I know what you are saying Izak but I've been paralyzed with fear for your sister. After your father and brothers were killed, Rhena and I only had one another. I was afraid that if I tried to escape and was caught, they would take her away. If that happened, I would have killed myself if they didn't kill me first."

"I know what you are saying Mother, but from what I've heard many of our people are fleeing to Warsaw. They feel safer there in numbers rather than facing these Nazis bastards out here on their own."

Minnie turns and walks to the only window in the tiny room, looking out at the house she used to live in, she lets out a quiet sigh, voicing, "I wish I knew what to do Izak. I know what you're saying but at least for now I feel safer here."

Staring intently in the dimness, first at his mother then at his sister, Izak takes a deep breath, making a concession he says, "Okay Mother, only for now. But if you want to live, you are going to have to make the decision to leave sooner or later."

CHAPTER 4

RADINSKY

Unfurling his bedroll, Izak removes the small cache of potatoes and carrots that he's managed to pilfer along his travels. Handing each a carrot, nodding toward his sister, he says, "I'm going back to that spot where you saw me this morning. The last thing I want is for the Germans to find me here with you. We'd all be as good as dead. I'll come again tomorrow night. We can discuss this further." With that settled he hugs them both again and slips out the same way he had come in.

Morning arrives at 5 a.m. for this farm. There are hundreds of chickens that need feeding, eggs gathered, and others separated for market. As usual, all the workers line up for a roll call and are given their tasks for the day. The sergeant responsible for the division of labor dispatches Minnie by herself to the fields and sends Rhena to the house.

Minnie knows that to try to protest this decision will result in a beating that will in the end involve Rhena. All they have time for is a loving hug before they are ordered out to their assignments.

"Be careful, Rhena," warns her mother.

Rhena sees something in her mother's eyes that tells her there is something about this she doesn't trust. Rhena in turn cautiously reveals her fear of being separated.

The sergeant motions for her to follow him. He leads her to the house and through the back door to the small room containing a bath tub. She notices, by the steam hovering over the tub's surface, that it's hot water. This porcelain tub is one of the few luxuries her father had purchased for her mother. It strikes Rhena how something so familiar and normally inviting has turned into something so menacing. *"How can this be happening to us?"* is still her unbelieving and terrifying thought. The sergeant orders her to strip down, bathe, and put on the clothing lying on a chair beside the tub. She notices immediately that the outfit is one of her school uniforms. Climbing into the hot water she can't help but enjoy its warmth but it comes with an uncomfortable question, *"What is this all about?"*

With several unannounced intrusions made by the sergeant, she manages to finish. So far it's been an innocuous luxury to have her own wardrobe laid out for her.

With the precision that only comes in the German military, the sergeant delivers his quarry to his commandant, salutes, turns and leaves with Rhena quivering in front of a man old enough to be her father.

Commandant Koenig remains seated at his desk. His eyes have a seeming spark of kindness behind them but his smile reveals something more sinister.

"What's your name?" he asks with more than a bit of patronizing in his voice.

"Rhena Nowak," she struggles to articulate but instead it comes out insecure and shaky.

Wiping the corners of his mouth with his handkerchief, the commandant continues his questioning. It's more than obvious that he is pleased with what is standing before him.

"How old are you?" His leer continues as though he is waiting with great anticipation for her answer.

"Thur-thirteen sir," answers Rhena. She feels the nervous perspiration soaking her underarms.

The look on his face reveals how he regards this answer. It's exactly the kind of tidings he is hoping for.

"Come over here, little girl, I want to get a closer look at you," he says.

She in turn begins to tremble to the point of feeling that she may fall. The unmistakable dominance he knows he has over this young girl excites him. Her hesitation brings out a torrent of anger mixed with a perverse kind of excitement that only those sexually enfeebled seem to prefer.

"Do you not understand me? You will do as I tell you!" he shrieks as the spittle spews from his demented mouth.

Rhena tries as best she can to choke back the tears. At thirteen she is not worldly enough to be aware of what this man may want. Out of fear, she finds herself unwittingly moving forward despite her reservations.

Standing before her grinning tormenter, she can smell the strong odor of cognac on his breath. She whimpers and gasps between sobs as he takes the end of his swagger stick and lifts the front of her dress. She in turn tries to smooth it down triggering him to brutalize the back of her hand with a blow from his switch. A welt immediately swells causing her to cry out.

For the next hour her cries can be heard throughout the house. Everyone knows what is being done to her but none are bold enough to come to her rescue.

Finally the sergeant is summoned and ordered to return Rhena to her quarters in the tack room. Her face is swollen and bruised from the beating and blood is running down her legs.

Like many Germans of the day, the German staff in the house despises disorder. Rather than confront this atrocity, it becomes something where they shake their heads. It receives a "tsk, tsk" clucking of the tongue, they then quickly look to regain their *ordung* (order), turning their backs on the whole affair. German people have abandoned their principles and values toward other humans in favor of their obsessive need for this ever elusive *ordung*.

When Minnie returns at the end of the work day to find her daughter, whom she had left as a healthy thirteen year old, now crushed and traumatized, her heart is broken. The feelings go beyond humiliation. She is battling the belief that the German indignities thrown at her on a daily basis are wide spread and permanent; that they as Jews are considered to be sub-human and deserve to be treated as dogs.

The sense of powerlessness that has overcome this mother in her effort to protect her daughter is excruciating and harrowing. She fills a pan with water to wash her daughter's wounds and hopes she can in some way also wash a way the wounds cutting into this young soul. There is little spoken between them as there are no words adequate to express all the vile hurts.

Tap, tap, tap comes the soft knock at the door. As soft as this knocking is, it startles both mother and daughter. Fearful their tormentors have returned, Minnie guardedly opens the door. It's Izak. Even in the dimness of the room and before he is fully inside, he can sense things have changed. It shows in the quiet despair of death sucking the life out of his mother's face. Quickly glancing around for some apparent cause, he sees his young innocent sister hardly able to see out of her swollen eyes.

"Oh my God!" Without being told he comprehends immediately what has taken place. He has seen this same kind of human devastation left in the trail of his Russian captors. He has witnessed how these men, whose own mothers would rail at this behavior from these sons, have become so intoxicated with their power that they discard women as so much trash to empty.

Looking hard at his mother, Izak announces in no uncertain terms, "This permanently closes all those ideas that you can safely remain here."

Izak is waiting for a response from his mother. She can only sit with her head in her hands.

Speaking once again and trying to hold his voice down, he grabs his mother by her shoulders, "Mother, Rhena cannot endure this devastation again. We must leave tonight."

Minnie returns his pronounced gaze with one of her own. "How will we do that? The Germans will hunt us down."

Izak doesn't answer her question, rather he poses one of his own.

"Is there any of that syrup we used to mix in with the chicken feed when we wanted to fatten them up for market?" asks Izak.

Minnie looks at him with a resigned stare. This question seems stupid to her and a complete puzzlement especially at a time like this. With a disapproving look and a head gesture that suggests it's somewhere other than this room.

She finally answers, "It's out there in the feed room. Why are you asking such a stupid question when we have all of this risk we're trying to work through?"

Without a word of explanation, Izak retreats to the darkened feed room and soon discovers that the mixture his father had kept is still on the same shelf. Grabbing the jug, he makes a wordless sweep to the small window in his mother's room. Silently he looks at the yard between them and the house and the vehicles sitting in the yard and where there may be some security.

Still with no explanation, he barks an imperative, "Stay here and be ready to leave when I come back." With that he disappears out the same way he came in.

Minnie and Rhena suddenly realize that the reality as they have come to know it in the past few weeks, is about to change again. They abruptly begin to throw together what they believe they can carry.

Within a half hour Izak returns. He quickly surveys what his sister and mother have done to prepare themselves for this flight.

"Momma do you remember that fruit jar Papa used to keep out here with enough cash for odds and ends that would come up from time to time?" asks Izak.

Stopping dead in her tracks, she pauses for the moment as a light goes on in her head.

"Yes, I do and he used to keep more than that in that jar. Oftentimes he would trade gold or silver jewelry for chickens." With that she grabbed a stubby little candle she had been hoarding for some unknown emergency along with a few matches and headed out into the tool shed just outside the barn. In a matter of minutes she returns with a fruit jar full of gold jewelry, a number of American dollars and some gold and silver that has been melted into small nuggets.

"Papa kept this behind a loose rock in the tool shed foundation. He didn't know I knew about it but I always knew more than he was aware of," says Minnie satisfied that she at last is able to justify her nosiness.

Izak is visibly pleased. "This is going to get us to Warsaw," he says as he empties the jar's contents into his coat pockets.

Together they recite a Hebrew prayer for God to be with them. Within minutes they are on their way down a tree-lined fence row hoping to remain in its shadows until they can slip onto the road. Both Minnie and Rhena remove their armbands and dispose of them under a pile of field stones.

Rhena is excited enough by this new adventure that it has taken her mind off her traumas. As she is trying to keep up with her brother an un-answered question occurs to her.

"Izak what did you do with that syrup?"

Izak chuckles for the first time in his recent memory. "I poured it in their gas tanks. When they discover you're both gone, they'll be hellbent to find you. That syrup is going to slow the process down for awhile."

Minnie's thoughts pause as she trots along behind her teenage son astonished at how their roles have changed. It's only been a year or so since he left home. At that time he seemed totally dependent on his parents and now she finds herself trotting along behind, actually depending on him for their next move. War has a way of robbing the young of their youth.

"Where are we going for now, Izak?" is her question.

"We're going into town and find Joseph Radinsky. He has a truck. I'm going to offer him one American dollar to drive us the twenty-five miles into Warsaw," says Izak with an air of authority and confidence. (American money is sought after for its stability.)

Minnie can't help but wonder about this young son. "*Where has he learned this?*"

Radinsky is Polish and has no use for the Germans but he's not a great fan of the Jews either. He did business with Izak's father and always had respect for his fair business practices. Izak is hoping this good relationship with his family and the offer of American money will be all the enticement that's needed to seal the deal. Radinsky lives alone on the edge of the village and can be found without drawing any attention. He purposely keeps his truck disabled by hiding its carburetor and battery as the Germans will commandeer, for their own use, any usable piece of equipment.

The late October wind is sharp as they make their way along the road. The ruts are beginning to freeze making it necessary to be sure-footed or risk turning an ankle. Both mother and sister are carrying a feed sack with the few belongings that had been allotted them by their captors. They are impervious to the weather despite its chill. Nervousness keeps their eyes sharpened for any German patrols along the road and their minds alert.

Within the hour they find themselves just outside the village staring at the small compound of buildings belonging to one Joseph Radinsky. It's

9 p.m. The darkened house displays only one window with the dim flicker of a single candle still struggling to glow against the outdoor blackness.

To Minnie and especially Rhena, it is foreboding. It's a place they would not readily go. Radinsky lost his wife a number of years ago to pneumonia after the Germans took his fuel supply and he lost his two sons during the Blitzkrieg. The two females are quite content when Izak tells them to stay back in the shadows while he discusses things with the old man. As they watch from their concealment the mother and daughter are two persons together physically but much alone in their thoughts. It's as though neither wants to risk giving their dread a vocal pronouncement for fear that hearing it spoken will cause it to become insufferable.

Meanwhile, Izak has made his way to the door, announcing himself by pounding on its frame. It's not long before there's a response. He can see the candlelight moving across the curtainless window. The next moment produces a short grizzled, middle-aged man, heavily mustached and much less tidy than Izak remembers him. Peering up under the candlelight further gives him an outlandish appearance.

"Mr. Radinsky, my name is Izak Nowak. You used to haul chickens for my father Abie Nowak."

Izak pauses for a moment as Radinsky adjusts his candle. With suspicious and squinted eyes, Radinsky attempts to get a proper look at this late night buttinski. Satisfying himself sufficiently that Izak is not a German official of some kind, he breaks into a slightly more friendly face.

"Yah, I did a lot of work for your father," says Radinsky pausing for a moment and lowering his candle as though he is recalling a bygone more joyous period of life, then adds, "He was always fair to me. What can I do for you?"

Now that Izak notices his host's demeanor finally returning to a more neutral and less hostile expression, he does his best to employ a mature, business-like tone of voice as he continues, "I'd like to hire you and your truck to haul something else." Izak's expression quickly changes as the seriousness of his state of affairs creates a baleful demeanor. "Mr. Radinsky, my mother, sister and I need you to drive us to Warsaw tonight."

Radinsky recognizes the change in Izak's behavior going from a politeness to imploring. He studyies Izak as though he's trying to read the part he may not be saying. Not answering Izak's question directly, he asks one of his own.

"It's pretty well known the Germans have taken over your father's farm. Does this have something to do with that?"

Izak clears his throat to give himself the moment he needs in order to shove down the emotional hurt that is fighting its way to the surface.

"Yah, it does," he says clearing his throat once more, "the commandant raped my sister. She's only thirteen. I've got to get her and my mother out of here. I'm willing to pay you an American dollar if you agree."

Radinsky realizes full well the urgency of this request. It's a chancy asking. The Germans have little concern for either the Poles or the Jews. They regard them both as sub-human and are willing to cleanse the land of them all. Only if one can fulfill a needed role does one remain alive. Otherwise it's merely a matter of time before reasons are found for those unneeded persons to be eliminated.

Radinsky, as yet, has left Izak standing in the doorway. The idea that more thinking is required for further negotiations prompts Radinsky to look around as if to see who may be lurking in the shadows, possibly overhearing their conversation.

"Come in Izak and close the door behind you." Radinsky's demeanor has also changed as he realizes what it could cost him if he is found to be harboring a Jew.

The room has a darkness to it beyond its lack of good lighting. Radinsky has been dealing with the loss of his loved ones the same way too many of his fellow countrymen share the same family losses. They all have to come to grips in their own ways with this new German reality intruding into their lives. Radinsky has fallen into a depression, feeling that what the Germans are saying about them may be true, that they are a conquered people and are useless to the Nazi cause. In many ways he is ready to give up and join the rest of his family in death.

There is something, though, in the dilemma that this young man is facing that he remembers facing himself at one time. It's a similar enough predicament that this challenge is beginning to stir him. Whether it's an opportunity to fight back against what the Germans have taken from him or merely a sense of obligation to a fellow sufferer, he feels himself undergoing a stimulation of mind, body and soul that he has not felt in a long time.

"Where are your mother and sister right now?" he asks.

"They're hiding in the trees behind your shed," Izak responds.

"Go get them and bring them in here and let's talk about this," he says with a renewed sense of purpose.

Izak does not have to be told twice. He is out the door and immediately returns with his mother and sister. The dim light in the room is not enough to conceal the harried misfortunes their faces reveal. Minnie's look is one of a constrained reserve. Rhena's bruised and swollen face on the other hand, discloses the full intensity of their plight. The swelling in her body is turning to an ugly black and blue from the top of her head to the bottom of her ankles.

Looking at her wounds dispassionately is something normal persons cannot become accustomed to. It brings to the surface a disdain for the aberrant behavior of the one who is capable of doing such things to those who are weak. Radinsky is immediately taken aback by the distortion done to this young body and even more so by the tremendous sexual perversion in the person capable of bringing about this kind of degradation to a child. This kind of insanity is dangerous to all those who are perceived by these offenders to be weak enough to manipulate.

It's also been the experience of many Jews that there are other kinds of predators. Many of the Poles have been guilty of pointing out Jewish people to the Germans because they are envious of the Jews' wealth. Others may do it because they hope to gain special favors from the Germans for themselves. It's also typically found that humans can't control feelings much of the time anyway and in periods of danger are seldom capable of controlling most actions. The result is that humans will do things against their values to save their own skin.

Many of these Poles are slowly finding that they are only being used by the Germans for German ends. They are discovering that the Germans hold prejudices against any race other than their own no matter how much they (the Polish) seemingly cooperate.

Radinsky comes to an abrupt decision. He has had it with the Germans and is ready to make a different decision about the direction of his life. They have taken his character from him without physically killing him. Now he is able to do something noble that can help him find himself again.

"I've been a good God-fearing Catholic all my life. I've always believed that you Jews have been guilty of killing Christ but I do remember when I was a young boy an old priest reminded me that you are God's first children. If I don't help you in your struggle, I too will be guilty of killing Christ. Only this time it will be the Jewish Christ that lives in me."

Recognizing how rare this opinion is among Christians toward Jews brings on a smile of hope. "Oh, Mr. Radinsky I can't tell you how much we appreciate your help," agrees a surprised and grateful family.

"We are going to have to be careful. We will wait until tomorrow morning before we leave. Chances are the Germans will find you missing and send out orders to find and arrest you," says Radinsky with the confidence of a general.

Izak takes this opportunity to inform Radinsky what he has done to the fleet of German vehicles back at the farm. It brings a slight smirk to Radinsky's lips.

"Tonight we will get some sleep," he says. For the next half hour he opens small bedrooms that haven't been used since his sons went off to fight the Germans. The blankets have a musty smell to them. Rhena finds her first response to be that she doesn't want them near her face. Nonetheless within minutes she and the rest of the household are fast asleep. This is the safest she has felt in some time.

Radinsky is up at dawn, the rest soon follow. Some bread, tea and beets make a quick breakfast. He seems pleased to have people in his house once again as he plays the role of host making sure there's sugar for tea, jam for bread and knives for beets.

Izak is more than a little nervous. He has had a year with the Russians to learn how to bear up under these perverse conditions. He's done well since he's only had to be concerned with himself. Now he has to watch out for both his mother and sister and both of them need to change their mindset from that of victims to survivors if they wish to have the right attitude to move forward. The truth is, to survive in this kind of environment involves luck, savvy and a desire to live. There is little time to up their game.

Radinsky is rifling through dresser drawers pulling out warm clothing that had once belonged to his deceased sons and wife, letting this family pick out what they need.

"I've given this some thought as to how we should travel. Izak, you will be using some papers from my son, Alek. Rhena, you are going to become my other son, Bercik. Minnie will become Beatka, my wife," says Radinsky.

Rhena looks puzzled as to how she is going to become a boy in order to fulfill this deception.

"The way we are going to make this work Rhena, is you are going to be in the back of the truck with your head wrapped in these bandages," says Radinsky holding a spool of gauze staring at her bruised and swollen face, "because we are taking you to the hospital in Warsaw to treat the wounds you received from being trampled by a bull."

Turning to Minnie, he continues, "And you 'my dear wife' will be back there ministering to her. Izak, you will be riding in the cab with me."

Stepping out of his cottage Radinsky takes a deep breath of the cool air. He has not felt this alive since before the German invasion. Weather wise it's typical late October in Poland with a bit of crystalline frosting coating the morning. Making his way toward his small barn, he swings open the large barn doors revealing a 1930 Polski Fiat. The original black paint is now a dull, dusty grime. The truck bed is walled with wooden racks and topped by a tattered canvas covering along with equally tattered canvas side curtains for the cab. From the back wall, well hidden behind a pile of junk, he retrieves his battery and carburetor quickly reattaching them. He next rummages around under the seat until he produces a hand crank, carries it to the front of the vehicle, inserts it in a slot designed to receive it and gives it a quick spin. The roar of the old engine is immediate, shaking and sputtering its way to life until all the component parts warm up enough to agree to begin working together.

Minnie and Rhena move into the truck bed arranging the leftover hay into suitable layers to lay on while Radinsky and Izak pile their meager belongings in behind them. Satisfied there is nothing left to do, the time comes to leave.

The old truck willingly lunges forward as Radinsky skillfully maneuvers the decade old beast through the dirt streets of his village. If there ever was a muffler it's long gone, leaving a pronounced echo bouncing off each building as it passes by. It's early and men out tending to their animals give Radinsky a familiar glance. Soon they are cruising through the countryside enjoying the October sun rising just high enough to blaze through the turning leaves of a small wood lot. It seems that it may be The Creator's way of offering a small reprieve in the midst of turmoil.

The same sun has risen back at the chicken farm but it's not being enjoyed. The sergeant has gathered the workers only to discover that Minnie and Rhena are not present. He immediately checks their tack room quarters and does not find them. To say he is in a panic is an understatement.

"Gott fur dammin Shweinhund," (Goddamn pig dogs) is all he can think to say. He is well aware that the security of this compound is his responsibility and the commandant is going to be unhappy at losing a worker and even less happy at losing the object of his latest sexual attraction. Well aware that his duty comes well before his desire to go AWOL, he musters up enough courage to report the incident.

A torrent of cursing from Commandant Koenig follows the sergeant's confession. He's furious that anyone would dare disobey his orders and not remain where he has ordered them and even more furious that security was so sloppy that this incident even occurred.

"Sergeant you will mobilize the brigade, search the wood lot and the houses in and around the village. Keeping your rank is going to depend on your success. Now bring my car around and let's get started uncovering this *Gott fur dammin* rebellion."

The sergeant salutes followed by a Heil Hitler, happy that the dressing down is over for the present. He immediately orders all available troops to load the personnel carriers and begin the search. Within a mile the fuel has been depleted from the fuel lines and the syrup has entered the carburetor and completed its job. The motors are cooked, the search has come to an abrupt end. Koenig is last seen ranting alongside the road as the steam boils out from under the engine compartment of his command car. It hardly needs to be mentioned that a similar event is taking place from under his well-fitted hat.

CHAPTER 5

WARSAW

Radinsky is familiar with all of Warsaw but he's not always sure where the Germans are stationing checkpoints. He doesn't have to wait long before the traffic is stopped. His passengers are all pensive and for good reason. The SS has orders to arrest anyone without papers and send them to labor camps.

Each person is responsible for their answers. Their safe passage is going to be determined by their ability to all stay on the same page. The SS is in charge of this checkpoint and are being assisted by the Polish police who do much of the translating. Radinsky's face goes blank as the Polish police officer approaches the truck. He immediately recognizes him as a young man from his village. This officer is well-acquainted with Radinsky's family losses. All their lives are in the hands of this one young man. He carries through with his official function in beginning his interrogation.

"Where are you coming from?" is his first directive.

Radinsky informs him, finding it odd to answer a mutually known answer.

"What is your destination?" is the next directive.

Radinsky tries to cover his nervousness with the explanation that his son has been trampled by a bull and they need to get him to the hospital.

The young police officer gives his neighbor an anxious stare. He begins to blink as if this involuntary nervous twitch will allow him enough time to analyze this deception. For the sake of his own tenuous position he is trying to make a decision as to what is behind this deceit.

"Documents please," he continues. While he is looking them over and realizing the depth this lie is taking, one SS is behind the truck with a dog. Another is poking at Rhena with his stick. She lets out a sharp moan. Minnie throws herself between the soldier and her daughter. The dog lunges at Minnie as the soldier begins to loosen his grip on the leash.

Quickly reacting to this sudden state of affairs, the policeman makes a determination to quell what could turn into an ugly ending. Changing his speech to German he hastily explains the need to let them pass. A few more words are exchanged between the SS and the young policeman before they relent.

Radinsky exchanges a slight nod with the young man. That wordless expression pronounces a thousand thank yous.

Safely out of the sight of the SS, Radinsky pulls into a side street and stops. He sits for the moment making the sign of the cross and saying a little prayer of thanks. Soon they all have composed themselves and it's time to part.

Izak is the first to break the silence. "Mr. Radinsky, I really don't know how to thank you." With that Izak reaches into his pocket and produces the promised American dollar. Radinsky gives it a hard look. On the other hand he's well aware of the needs this family will be up against. For them survival is going to be a full-time endeavor

"I'm really tempted to take that and it has nothing to do with whether I need or don't need it. But I'm going to refuse it. You're getting yourself into something here where you're going to need all the assets you can lay your hands on if any of you expect to survive."

Minnie and Rhena are out of the rear of the truck and gathering their few possessions. Their world is changing once again. They are taking on a harried look that is becoming the norm for their lives.

Izak, in turn, realizes what Radinsky is saying has more than just a bit of merit but on the other hand, despite the extreme hardships everyone is finding themselves buried in, the fact he had given Radinsky his word also has merit.

"Please Mr. Radinsky, I would feel much better if you would honor my pledge to you and take the money, I know my father would have done the same."

Radinsky has had enough. He realizes that if he doesn't do something drastic he'll fall for this sales pitch. With a moment of thought he comes back with a counter offer of his own.

"Most of us are sadly weak humans. Since my family has died, I've been in a depression. Helping you with your struggle has given me back the dignity I needed to feel human again. The only way you'll be able to pay me is if you'll do a kind act for someone else today."

Izak is speechless for the moment. Radinsky has hit a nerve that has more depth than Izak's simple endeavoring to keep his word. Sometimes something good can be the worst enemy of the best.

Realizing the best he can offer Radinsky is a word of gratitude. "Thank you Mr. Radinsky. You're a good man."

"And I in turn thank you for the opportunity to serve my God by serving you," says Radinsky. "And by the way, you keep the documents of my wife and sons. I have no use for them and you may need them." He pauses for a moment with a bit of a twinkle in his eye and adds, "If they ever find them to be false, just do me the favor of saying you stole them."

"That's a deal," says a grateful Izak. With that he gives Radinsky a hearty handshake. Radinsky's truck turns back in the opposite direction as this mother and children start their journey down the street toward a future that is tenuous at best.

The first thing they are met by is a twelve-foot-high wall topped with barbed wire and what appears to be broken glass. This wall extends as far down the street as the eye can see. A gate suddenly opens and a group of men, women, and children lined in columns of three all wearing armbands emblazoned with a blue Star of David come out. A Gestapo guard is forcing the march.

Something inside of this small family tells them that if they are happy about nothing else, they should be happy they are not part of this brigade. As the columns march by, Izak asks a bystander, "What is this about?"

The bystander noticing they are asking a question that only a stranger would ask gives them a hard look before answering.

"They are Jews. The Germans say they are relocating them but rumor has it that nobody ever hears from them again." These words leave an ache in the hearts of this unsuspecting trio as to what is in store for them.

Rhena catches the glance of a girl about her age looking at her bandaged head. The girl's eyes have a barren look. It's the look one has when they've stopped fighting. Rhena tries to imagine what it would take for her to have the same expression.

This march brings to light the new dangers this move to Warsaw is presenting. Izak is determined to be undaunted in his role as guardian to his mother and sister causing him to react in a paternal way toward his sister. Bending close to her ear so only she hears, he says, "If we're going to stay ahead of these Nazi pigs we're going to have to be shrewd. It's going to be necessary for you to continue to be a boy until we get this risk of who we are behind us." Rhena looks at herself in the trousers she had put on at Mr. Radinsky's cottage, satisfied she has left the little girl she may have been a few weeks ago far behind.

Once again taking charge of the position in which they are finding themselves, he asks the bystander about the availability of some housing for his family.

The bystander gives them another hard stare before speaking, "How many zlotys can you pay?"

Izak is more than uncomfortable with the question. The last thing he wants to exhibit is that he has money. He manages to give it a quick thought before answering. "I don't have much money but I'm willing to work at anything."

The bystander is also assessing the situation. "How old are you?" he asks.

Remembering that his documents say he is Alek Radinsky he says, "I'm twenty years old." This lie gives him a three-year increase in his current age. He's hopeful this will make him more employable.

A further scrutinizing by the stranger produces yet another question. "What are you able to do?"

While he was in Russia they used him in a harness shop working with leather. "I've made harnesses for the Russian cavalry."

The stranger continues to look this young man over as though he's looking for some signs of character defects that may have eluded him. Finally satisfied that he's settled his assessment of this seemingly ambitious young man, he carefully crafts his words into a question.

"What brings you to Warsaw?"

Izak is just as careful to present a scenario that could easily be defended. He explains how he came home from Russia to discover his family had lost their property to the Germans, how his mother had become widowed by the sudden and unexpected death of his father, purposely leaving out the part about them being Jewish and being murdered by the Germans and now they believe that by coming to Warsaw they can start a new life. It's the same kind of story that's being told in countless settings throughout the country. In this case this story satisfies the scrutiny of this engaging stranger.

"So let me understand you, you are looking for a job and a place to live. I may be able to help you with both of these if we can work thing out. My name is Kaz Kaczka. I'm a cobbler. I make boots for the German army. Since you've already worked with leather, I believe you could catch on quickly. I'd be willing to take you on as an apprentice. For your wages, I'll give you and your family the upper floor over my shop. I'll provide you with food and coal as it becomes available."

Minnie doesn't wait for Izak to respond. "We'll take it!" she says. Women her age don't do well in indigent conditions. They generally like a safe place to nest with their family that they can use as their own. This is the answer to her prayers.

Before anyone can say anything more, Izak takes command before either his sister or mother blurts out their names.

"My name is Alek Radinsky. This is my mother, Beatka, and my younger brother, Bercik. He got trampled by a bull before we left." Izak glances around, a bit nervous as he questions himself as to how well he carried through with this deception. His mother and sister are not showing any sign of invalidating anything he has just said, being more than willing to say anything that will get them off these ominous streets.

Kaczka is also satisfied that he's heard an honest account of their lives and motions with his hand for them to follow him. He leads them down the street to the next corner. The sign over the store proclaims KACZKA THE COBBLER. He unlocks the door and leads them throughout the building. The smell of tanning leather brings back a memory that Izak would have sooner put behind him. The Russians had been cruel task masters and found young Jewish boys to be expendable. The promise made was they were learning a trade in exchange for their freedom. So they were encouraged by death threats to abide by whatever whims their tyrannical leaders compelled them to carry through.

The only thing that continues to encourage him in this case is that he will have a relatively safe place for his mother and sister and himself to live.

Kaczka leads them to a back door that empties into an alley. Continuing to conduct his tour, he motions them to a back stairs leading up to a landing and a door on the second floor.

"This is where I lived with my parents. My father also lived here with his parents. My grandfather started the business. All nine of my other brothers and sisters worked here at various times as we were all growing up. I'm the only one to stay."

The apartment is a large space traveling the whole length of the store. The first room is a kitchen with an old kerosene cooking stove, a pantry, a kitchen table and chairs, also an ice box. The floors are wood with a worn look. The dining area is also an unfinished wood floor but has a threadbare Persian rug covering its center beneath a long hand-made dining table with benches on both sides and a chair on each end. A large sideboard dominates almost an entire wall with a potbellied stove at one end. An arch leads into a parlor with an antiquated leather couch and matching chair. A large library table with a lower deck shares the center of the room along with a parlor stove. The only window is adorned with a dusty and faded maroon curtain as it over looks a side street below. Leading to the front of the building is a long hallway with various bedrooms on each side, each containing mismatched beds and dressers as well as forgotten stored possessions left by various family members as they moved on.

All in all, Minnie is satisfied. It certainly does not compare to her much more updated home that the Germans seized from her but considering their plight, she is more than grateful for the meager conveniences it's providing.

As soon as Mr. Kaczka leaves, Izak's thoughts return to his sister. "Rhena, I'm going to have to cut your hair boy-style if we hope to keep this impersonation believable."

With a resigned sigh, she begins to unwind the bandages circling her head. Her hair has taken on a twisted, matted texture. She caresses it for a moment as if to give it a final farewell.

"Okay Izak, do what has to be done."

CHAPTER 6

POTATOES

For the German family of Rudolph Koeler, their relief from the distress of the Allied bombs dropping on their home town and the resultant move this family made to the relative safety of the Baltic sea coast near Klaipeda, Lithuania, proved to be futile. The war is turning. Stalin has the Germans on the run. All of Eastern Europe is coming under the recriminating dominance of the Red Army. These soldiers are instructed to expel all ethnic Germans, confiscate all private properties and force the expellees into submission through the demoralizing tactics of murder, rape and beatings.

Neither the Soviets nor the Nazis concerned themselves with delivery food systems for any of these displaced peoples. Both, in turn, have only interests in gaining more land for the resources they hold and the strategic advantage their location presents. Both have policies to rid these lands of any opposition. The Jews pose a threat by controlling much of the wealth in Europe and have become the targets for those who in one way or another hold to the concept of limited goods: if they have more, we'll have less. Also with Germany suffering defeats under the Allied Powers, the German people, in turn, are suffering under the Soviet lust for recrimination. Stalin has no problem placing the war crimes of his hated enemy, Adolph Hitler, in the lap of ethnic Germans.

The end result of despotic leadership with its misplaced priorities is that food is more and more becoming the de facto source of wealth. Those who are able to gain a supply can use it to their advantage. If nothing more, it affords a temporary sense of self-confidence and well-being. This is the juncture in which Reinie finds himself as he has successfully escaped the Red Army. He still possesses a small but adequate supply of food and some water. Providing he has no reversals, it's enough to last him until he reaches the coast. Once there he hopes to catch a freighter out of the country.

Having spent the entire night trudging along the tracks, walking is beginning to take its toll on his legs and ankles. Nonetheless, his successful efforts thus far are leaving him quite grateful that this strategy is a workable solution. It has put to rest some of the doubts he's had about his safety. So far all he has had to be concerned with is getting out of the way of the trains coming down the track.

The light is just now beginning to reveal itself as morning approaches. It's time to find an adequate sleeping spot that will provide some shelter. Spotting a small wooded area just off the tracks, he ventures toward it for a closer look. The first thing he becomes aware of is that this area appears to have been used. Maybe not recently but definitely in the not too distant past. The ground is disturbed as though someone may have been searching for something. A half-dozen locations have the appearance of having had a shovel turn the ground. *"Maybe for some kind of small garden plots,"* he muses to himself. Out of curiosity, Reinie uses his booted foot to kick over a bit of loose dirt. The sudden appearance of a rotting human hand reveals the truth of what this clandestine grove has been used for. The impact is one of dismay. The truth of it saddens him. No matter how much one sees of these killing grounds there is no adequate way of training the mind for such atrocities. It is an unlovely world a person has to struggle with at times. For the sake of his own well-being, he can ill afford to let these sights vanquish him for long. Choosing to move to another area hopefully will create a diversion.

It's difficult for him to rid his thoughts of the possibilities that could connect this atrocious crime to the fate of his parents. His father was a high school mathematics teacher but since the war, the German education system has been in complete disarray putting all teachers in his district on leave. His mother has been a dutiful wife and mother. Neither of his parents supported the Nazi party in spite of his brother's involvement with the Hitler Youth. To imagine that his mother and father could be held accountable for any of the war atrocities is unthinkable.

Once he has moved on to the next wood lot, his mind is back to dealing with his own survival. This one proves to be a better choice as it appears to be a dumping ground for old railroad ties. It only takes him a moment to begin to arrange them into a makeshift shelter. Soon he is out of the wind and fairly comfortable. Sleep is another welcomed diversion. Tomorrow can be seen with the hope of it becoming just one day closer to having some order back in his life.

Before he drifts off, he removes the only book he has with him. It was left in his grandfather's coat pocket. It's a tattered old book and yellowed with age. It's his Opa's prayer book. Thumbing through the pages he stops at a prayer that thanks God for His gracious love. Trying as best he can, he puts that prayer into some kind of context considering where his life currently stands. With the book still open on his lap, he drifts into a much needed slumber.

Late that afternoon, Reinie is awakened by the chugging sound of a slowing steam locomotive. Peeking out of his hastily built fortress he notices something he had missed in the dim light of the early morning. Not more than a hundred yards down the track is a coal tender and a water tower for resupplying this huge behemoth. What catches his attention even more is the passengers debarking. *"They're Russian soldiers!"* With the reflexes of a cat, he ducks his head back into his hideaway. *"This is not something I need right now,"* is his immediate concern.

Watching the young soldiers roam around smoking, pissing, cajoling each other could give a less savvy person the impression of a common fellowship with such a group. But it would lead as quickly to the same bewildering mistake a person would make while watching a portrayal of innocence that young wolves exhibit romping around with one another and then imagine one could become part of their games. This group of young men is given its orders from superiors as to who is to be their enemy. The group's only concern is to follow orders as mindless automatons. The victims are too often the civilian population whose allegiances are suspect with no basis other than paranoia.

Reinie calculates this encounter to be brief. Generally speaking this procedure takes about fifteen minutes. One thing he notices is that along with the passenger cars carrying the troops there are a half dozen coal cars. What piques his interest is the absence of a covering on all of the cars with the exception of one. This one is covered with a huge canvas tarp. The ends are tied down with ropes save one that's come loose and it happens to be on the end closest to the ladder. He slowly works his way out of his bunker managing to use the thick brush as concealment. A closer inspection indicates there is something other than coal under that covering, something they want to keep concealed.

The train whistle gives a short burst. As if on cue the soldiers quickly load back into their assigned compartments. The crew on the tail end of the train have also re-entered the caboose. For Reinie it's time to make his move. With the swiftness of a cougar, he makes the thirty-yard dash to the ladder as the train begins to move. In no more than a few seconds he has scaled the ladder and tucked himself undetected under the loose end of the canvas. What he lands on is something that the one in need can readily believe to only occur but by Divine intervention. *"Mein Gott im Himmel, das ist POTATOES! DANKE, DANKE!* (My God in *Heaven*, it's potatoes! Thank you, thank you!) is all he can exclaim. *"It's no wonder they chose a troop train to carry coal and food!"* is a thought that springs forth.

Having quickly measured the worth of this cargo against his chances of starving, he fills every pocket his clothing permits. The miracle attached to potatoes is that eating them raw not only provides carbohydrates but also water, a good combination to have in this rough environment. This is the most uplifting thing that's happened to him since he had the job with the peat farmer.

Soon the locomotive picks up momentum and is traveling at a fairly high rate of speed. Periodically lifting the canvas and peeking out of his potato nest and as best he can, he undertakes the challenge to keep an eye on where this train may be taking him.

"The last thing I need is to end up in some Russian garrison." It's a dreadful realization but a real possibility.

In the meantime, the night is waiting for no one as the train speeds through the darkness. The miles click by. The risk of getting caught weighs heavy on his mind. His purpose is to get to the Baltic coast as quickly as possible with the minimal amount of risk. Reinie is torn. *"Do I stay in my relatively safe potato bin or do I risk being more visible?"* It's this kind of question that rushes through his mind when he gets to feeling too secure. *"After all, I'm out of sight and traveling but then when the time comes to get out of my snug potato bin safely, it could be out of my control. I have no idea where this thing is going or where it will slow down enough for me to get off,"* are other continuing thoughts. After much contemplation, he comes to the conclusion that at the next fuel and water stop he will look for an opportunity to make a getaway.

Several hours pass before he notices the engine beginning to slow. Peeking once again from beneath his hideaway, he pays close attention to the backdrop and the type of terrain they're entering. There is a lot more activity at this station than at the last. Bright headlights are piercing the darkness.

His anxiety begins to climb as he is becoming aware that it will be suicide to make a run for it. It appears the troops on the train are going to be transferred to the empty troop trucks that are beginning to line up along the track. There are no wooded areas that he can see, nor darkened areas allowing him a shot at getting away undetected. "*Get off now*," is one voice in his head. The other equally as loud says, "*Stay put.*" Paralyzed with indecision, Reinie finally settles on remaining where he is. That is, at least until he can develop a better plan.

The train slows to a stop. The hissing and belching noises of the engine along with all the commotion of transferring troops from the passenger cars to the waiting troop trucks causes Reinie to pull the canvas cover a little further down. But only to a point where his eyes are still able to see what is happening. The swirling smoke and steam are enough distraction to minimize any uncommon scrutiny in his direction.

As the disembarking of these troops is getting underway, it appears that the ruthlessness of the Russian military isn't restricted to the lowest foot soldier. The officers are screaming curses at anyone, civilian or military, to do their immediate bidding. The soldiers in turn are bullying any German civilians aside to accomplish their own ends. People are randomly being knocked to the ground. Every ethnic Russian citizen is infected with the notion that every ethnic German is responsible for the destruction of their homeland and therefore are to be treated as despicable enemies. They make no distinction between man, woman, or child as they are all equally brutalized.

The Russian military is accomplishing the same devastating impact on the Germans as the German military bore on the Jewish population. In both cases, in the beginning no one believes things can be as bad as reported. Next is the thought that *"it won't happen to me,"* and when it does, the shock isolates the person from the rest of their community. This then is usually followed by the realization that one is powerless, alone and beginning to fill with fear.

This is the juncture at which Reinie finds himself as he watches first hand how these soldiers demoralize German civilians. He discovers that his personal desire to survive prevents him from interfering with the misdirected debasement of his countrymen. For the moment at least, the only impact this behavior has on him is that he's happy it's not happening to him.

Within a short time the soldiers have cleared out leaving the train back in the hands of the German conductor. The next thing Reinie feels is the train beginning to move. His first sense is that it's moving in reverse. Peering out from under his canvas shelter he confirms this suspicion as he experiences his car being maneuvered to a siding. He finds himself completely at the mercy of these railroad undertakings. Reinie finds that he has no choice but to go along for the ride. Inside of fifteen minutes the brakeman has unhooked his potato car leaving him to sit alone as the rest of the train continues on to a new destination without him.

Sitting quietly for the next few minutes, he tries to digest what has just occurred and plan his next move. Decisions of this type are not always given the luxury of quiet contemplative thought and this occurrence is not going to be the exception. No sooner has the sound of the retreating locomotive disappeared, than it's replaced with the sound of advancing trucks. Headlights are flickering across a lane leading to the rail siding.

This is not the time for a curious observation. Within seconds Reinie is out from under his canvas, bolting down the ladder and bounding into a nearby ditch.

It's not a moment too soon as the first set of headlights illuminate the whole area. A command car from the German army materializes behind the first set of lights. It's one that's been commandeered from the Germans by the Russian army for its own use. From Reinie's vantage point, he recognizes the officer in charge as the same captain that was shouting orders back at the rail station. This time he's speaking in broken German rather than Russian. Another thing that becomes obvious is the people he's addressing are wearing prison clothes and appear to be Germans.

The captain steps out of his command car and waits until one of his underlings has formed the prisoners in two lines of six each. He begins his rhetoric in a degrading manner as he issues the work details. It's impossible to imagine that anything other than the potato car is at the center of his interest. Finally quieting for a moment, he then purposely begins to strut back and forth in front of his prison detail and deliberately makes his points with his pistol raised in his right hand.

"If any of you decide that a potato is worth your miserable life then feel free to steal one and I will feel free to put you out of your misery," he says making personal eye contact with the rows of prisoners while pointing his gun across their perimeter.

The Russians have placed the German forced laborers on less than half the calories needed to sustain a healthy body. The idea behind this is to keep their focus on survival rather than escape. If they aren't killed first, they generally fall victim to disease or a slow starvation. In this case they have been supplied with a stack of burlap bags and are expected to empty the potato car into the sacks and then pack the bags into the waiting trucks.

When examining how entitlements to food matters in these times, those on the bottom are always left short. Unfortunately the hungry are then forced to plunder and steal. The common penalty for stealing food is hanging as a testament to others to avoid the same treatment. At best they will be sent to a labor camp but not without a brutal beating first. Many don't survive.

From his hiding spot in the trench, Reinie feels a flash of fearful anxiety charge through his entire body as it seems his purloined potatoes are making a statement by pressing against him. The only thing that is preventing him from being noticed is the darkness and that's quickly diminishing. Some twenty yards beyond his location, he sees a stand of oak scrub with the leaves still hanging. Slowly he begins to crawl down the recess, praying he can reach them and be out of sight before dawn breaks. With much of his mind arguing against his body to move slowly, he soon reaches the brush.

It's not a moment to soon as he looks back at his path and observes the captain is urinating at the spot he had been laying only a few minutes before. The captain has a puzzled look as he reaches down to pick up a rogue potato. Rising back up with the varlet still in his hand, he takes a slow and methodical look up and down the ditch. It's a long moment for Reinie as he hunches lower hoping that he's sufficiently out of sight. For reasons of his own, the captain throws the potato to the ground and returns to the task at hand.

It's another hour of bagging and stacking before the work detail finishes, packs up, and finally leaves. Reinie didn't realize how much he had been holding his breath until at long last a huge sigh of relief comes pouring out.

CHAPTER 7

GULAG 18

Deciding to remain where he is now that full daylight is upon him, Reinie begins by assessing his premises. The ditch and the brush provide enough cover that he can conceal most of himself and yet enable him to keep a wary eye on any approaching danger.

He begins by taking stock of the potato horde he's built inside his clothing. By the time he's finished, he discovers he's accumulated fifteen beautiful potatoes. Feeling as though he can splurge a bit, he consumes the largest of the lot. With a full stomach sleepiness soon visits him. Wrapping himself in his grandfather's huge coat, he soon finds it's warm enough to put him into a sound sleep.

What he doesn't notice is that the Russian command car is back. Not only is it back, but it has brought along with it a troop truck with a dozen Russian soldiers. Without a sound being heard they have surrounded Reinie's camp and the captain stands over Reinie, smugly pelting him awake with his stolen potatoes.

Caught between deep sleep and consciousness, Reinie struggles to make sense of his situation. Before he can fully comprehend what is happening there are several soldiers jerking him to his feet. The first conscious thought running through his mind is, *"How in the hell am I to get out of this?"* As he's forced along with enough thrust that it causes him to stumble, his captor introduces himself.

"Get to your feet you filthy, despicable 'fashisty' dog," (a derogatory term referring to fascism by the Russians) resulting in yet another series of hard kicks from his hobnailed boot to help persuade him as to who is now in charge. "We have ways of dealing with you 'Gans' (another derogatory Russian language contraction from the word 'Hun') who steal food from the mouths of the Russian people."

"Should we hang the thievin' Gans bastard?" shouts a sergeant as he takes his turn giving Reinie a whacking by supplying a good solid slap to the side of his head. It is a hard enough blow to cause temporary deafness.

Reinie manages to stumble along to the troop truck where he's pushed and shoved until he boards. One Russian soldier takes particular pleasure in supplying a few more kicks and slaps to this already surrendered German teen. His added zeal comes from remembering his days as a prisoner of war in a German labor camp where he was nearly worked and starved to death.

"What do you think of this, you Aryan bastard? This shoe is on the foot of another for you. Now we do all the kicking. Let's see how well you do."

Hitler's Aryan minority had regarded the Russians as sub-humans along with Jews and Slavs. Now everyone who suffered under the Nazis is taking license to punish all Germans regardless of their individual sympathies. These soldiers are no exception as they continue to beat Reinie all the way to their destination. It can't come soon enough as he has lost consciousness.

The captain is furious with these men. "You have disabled a prisoner of the State. We need every worker we can get. Screwing German women is one thing but disabling a worker is not going to be accepted. The commandant is not going to take your actions lightly when he hears of this."

With this unsettling incident, Reinie is dumped into a barrack that once housed Russian POWs and is now housing an assembly of forced German laborers. Standing in the doorway overseeing this leg of Reinie's internment, the captain issues the order to the barracks leader, "Get this kid able to work as soon as possible!" The sternness accompanying this imperative strongly implies this obligation better happen soon or the barracks will suffer a consequence.

Reverend Otto Bretzke is the man in charge of this barracks. He's a thirty-five-year-old ethnic German expelled from Latvia. He is ordained as a pastor in the Lutheran tradition. He has no idea what became of his family after he made the near-fatal mistake of placing himself in the way of a Russian soldier to protect his young daughter from being raped.

Reinie's condition hardly draws an eye from the others. This kind of phenomena has become all too common. When humans are not provided with warm clothing, bed coverings, and adequate heat; when they are minimally nourished and overworked to the brink of exhaustion, the form of depression that turns into the norm is often exhibited as an indifference toward the sufferings of others. Personal survival becomes the primary concern; others contemplate suicide. Under this kind of pressure all ideologies and values become vulnerable.

Nonetheless there are yet a few humans who don't behave similarly in the interest of self-preservation. Much of this singular human phenomenon depends on how deeply their ideologies have become a part of them. Rev. Bretzke is one of these. He's a comely man not given to anger or victimization. When the question of his family surfaces, in an untroubled tone, he addresses the question by saying, "Wherever they may be, they are in God's hands." He gives the impression that he is a man of deep convictions. This is hardly a trait found with the average internee. Most arrive broken, discouraged and victimized. Many welcome death rather than deal with the harshness of the Russians. It's not surprising that many find him a beacon of hope in their seeming hopelessness. Others resent him for his unwillingness to join them in their resentments against their captors.

He's certainly not a man of noticeable characteristics. His head is shaved along with all the other detainees. The lack of nourishment has ravaged his body, giving him the appearance of a dead man walking. What draws attention to him is his uncompromising attitude. Despite the cruel conditions, Bretzke has kept his eye on those things that give him hope; a spark of kindness in the eyes of a guard or the easing of a single captor's hatred toward him.

Presently the condition of Reinie has taken precedence over the ennui of barrack life. Bretzke turns to the closest inmate and in a calm deliberate voice asks, "Can you get a rag and some water? We need to try and get some of the swelling out so this poor boy can see."

Without the presence of a man like Bretzke, Reinie more than likely would have been stripped of his warm coat and shoes by his fellow detainees. The lack of deep personal ideologies plays a role in how people react in harsh deprivation. The primordial need to survive can often set aside a lightly taken Biblical commitment to "lay down one's life for his brother."

Within minutes Bretzke is personally administering the healing balm of a kind hand as he attempts the useless effort to reduce Reinie's swelling. Nonetheless, it's love like this that warms an otherwise indifferent cold room.

Reinie is eventually brought around to a cloudy consciousness. The first thing he sees is a skinny man hovering over him. What strikes him as odd is a contrary demeanor of compassion dominating this otherwise hollow face.

"How you feeling, kid?" asks a smiling almost toothless Bretzke.

Immediately putting his hand on his face, Reinie attempts to make a quick assessment. "I don't know yet. Where am I?"

"You, my young friend, are in Gulag 18," returns the same smiling face as though he is denoting a five-star hotel.

As the mist in his brain begins to clear out, it becomes obvious that despite all his efforts to remain vigilant, he has failed. This alarming conclusion is rudely taking a negative toll on his spirit.

"Who are you guys?" asks Reinie still trying to piece the impact of this current episode into some meaning. He already has a pretty good idea that what he is about to hear is not going to be different than what he already suspects.

"We are ethnic Germans and have become prisoners of Russia," answers Bretzke with the same calm voice.

Under any other circumstances, Reinie would regard this manner of speaking reassuring but in this situation it lends itself more toward the level of a resignation than what he is hoping to hear. At least for the time being, the overwhelming pain from the kicks he took to his rib cage prevents him from commenting, but this doesn't prevent Bretzke from further explaining, "If you should wish and pray for anything at this moment, you should hope you are able to go to work in the morning. If you lag behind, you may not survive. Their next round of punishment is going to become much worse." By the time he has finished with this last comment, his whole demeanor has changed to one of earnestness.

Reinie catches Bretzke's sudden shift from calmness to apprehension prompting him to inquire further. "What kind of work do you do here?" he asks.

Bretzke continues to study Reinie's condition before he answers. "We cut timber into railroad ties," he says with an air of reluctance. This is a far cry from easy work. He knows that tomorrow is going to determine the fate of this young man.

The days are becoming shorter this time of year requiring things get done before darkness sets in. There are no lights in any of these barracks save a smuggled candle used only rarely. With no hesitation of mind or spirit, Bretzke shoots an order to the curious group of men gathering around waiting for some form of outcome to take shape.

"Help me get him into Lemke's bunk. He's not going to need it any longer."

Getting to his feet is a major accomplishment for Reinie. Even though every bone in his body feels as though it's been bruised or broken, he can't wait to crawl onto its filthy, lice-infested, wood-chip filled mattress and allow his poor aching body some relief.

"By the way my name is Bretzke," say this Good Samaritan as he places a supporting arm around Reinie's waist and leads him to his waiting bed.

"I'm Reinie," he says, doing all he can to speak and walk at the same time.

Morning arrives at daybreak with the clanging of a metal pot. Everyone, save Reinie, is up and out of their bunk holding a tin cup as two other prisoners scoop out a gruel of some type into their waiting container. The rule remains that only a prisoner holding his own cup can receive a portion. This prompts Bretzke to shake his sleeping pigeon awake.

"Wake up Reinie, wake up!" At the same time that he's pulling him to a sitting position, he unhooks Lemke's tin cup left hanging and jams it into Reinie's hand in time for the only nourishment he'll receive until the day's work is over. It consists of a thin barley soup mixed with sawdust to give it some thickness.

Being pulled on like this before he's awake causes Reinie to let out a half alert gasp. He isn't sufficiently aroused to completely process what is happening but is conscious enough to feel the plop of this strange mixture into his cup.

"Eat up Reinie. We only have a short time before we have to be outdoors for roll call," says Bretzke slurping down his last mouthful of gruel.

Many of the other men are lining up to use a toilet facility that consists of a trench with a plank. Most are suffering from diarrhea and barely able to work. If a man becomes disabled as a result of sickness, they often disappear, if they don't die on their own first. Those suffering from diseases such as typhus are often done away with before the disease wipes out a whole camp

Suddenly appearing in the dimness of dawn is the officer in charge of the day's work detail. It's Bretzke's responsibility to have things in order by the time he makes his way to their barrack and he's then expected to give a full report on the number of able men prepared to begin with the day's work schedule. The officer in turn gives the expected production quota for the day.

With this detail out of the way, the next assignment is to get the men loaded into the selected vehicles to take them to their work locations. Many of the prisoners are hobbling, barely able to walk much less work. The temperatures are tumbling down to near freezing causing those whose clothing is far from adequate for this kind of weather to shiver uncontrollably.

The Russian/Stalinist mindset behind all of this deprivation is specifically designed toward constantly reminding the German people of the terrible war crimes committed against the Slavic peoples by the German Army. A further advantage to keeping these prisoners in a constant state of survival prohibits them from plotting escapes.

The days grind on with little hope of things changing. Reinie's youth is the only strength he has that is sustaining him at this time. Within the first week he has already lost enough body weight to cause his clothing to hang on him as they would a scarecrow. Bretzke is beginning to notice a drop in Reinie's energy level during the work day and has some real concerns about his mental state also beginning to deteriorate.

"How are you doing?" says Bretzke one evening with a wary eye on the reaction of this young dependent. It's more than obvious that in spite of his physical healing rather quickly from the beating he sustained the previous week that some of the psychological circumstances may be more deleterious, injuring the deeper parts of him. He's become more withdrawn as the fuller realization of his situation is impacting his world.

"I'm not sure, Sir. I can feel my strength being sapped out of me," says the depressed young man.

Bretzke sits quietly for a moment before he makes a more penetrating inquiry, "Do you have any religious conviction?" He states this question rather hesitantly for fear he may be treading in a private area of this young man's life but nonetheless is willing to risk it for his well-being.

Reinie doesn't hesitate nor try to evade the question. "I do, sir. I'm confirmed Evangelical Lutheran." This, being the State Church of Germany and much akin to the Latvian Lutherans, is familiar to Bretzke since he has a similar religious background.

"Good," says Bretzke with a slightly more relaxed tone. "I'd like to pray with you, if you don't mind."

This request hits Reinie on his blind side. The last person who regularly did that was his grandmother Ida. It's not that he's opposed to Bretzke's asking. In fact, he finds it rather comforting in an odd sort of way.

As Bretzke begins, Reinie finds the words to be familiar old friends giving him an immediate sense of comfort. All in all the time it took didn't exceed more than a couple minutes and the rewards of being reminded that he is not alone in his struggle are more than worth the effort. Despite having to deal with the open Russian animosity toward all Germans, he's reminded that God still has one hand below him prepared to lift him above his vexations.

Bretzke had at one time been a pastor at a small Lutheran parish in the German region of Latvia. Germans found life in Latvia difficult after the war started with the Allied powers. Many were expelled when the government suspected they were Nazi sympathizers. When he arrived in Germany, Hitler had imprisoned him for refusing to vow allegiance to the Nazi Party. Now the Communists have him arrested for once again poisoning the minds of people with the opium of the Christian religion. Like so many Christian leaders before him, he is willing to sacrifice himself rather than turn on his faith. His wife and daughters have been deposed again and he hasn't heard from them in months. This type of separation of German families is typical under Stalin. The Communist protocol for recrimination against the war crimes of the Nazis is to wreak as much havoc on the ethnic German family as possible.

Morning follows night one more time. The routine remains the same with the exception of Reinie being pulled out of the roll call. He is immediately taken before the captain on the other side of the compound. Out of ignorance, Reinie fails to stand at attention before this superior officer. The sergeant in charge slaps him hard across the face. Quickly catching on to this neglect to protocol, he recovers fast enough to fulfill the obligation before something worse occurs.

The captain hasn't bothered to look up from his desk. He seems preoccupied with shuffling papers around. Still not bothering to look up at this young quarry, he begins his questioning.

"Your name?"

"Reinhardt Ludwig Koelher, Sir."

Still with his eyes only on the papers, he says, "Your papers report that you are seventeen years old."

Reinie is caught by surprise by this allegation as he has hardly been keeping track of the time. After giving it a moments thought, he says, "Yes, Sir, that's true."

"Have you ever served in the German military or in the Hitler Youth?"

"No, Sir. Not in either of them."

Finally looking up from his papers, the captain makes a quick glancing assessment of this hapless unfortunate.

"Good. Now I want you to sign these papers," says the captain pushing some documents across the desk.

Reinie glances at them. Noticing they're written in Russian he intuitively knows better than to make a fuss. He signs them, lays the pen on the desk, and steps back.

The captain glances at the signed document and without the slightest fanfare, he announces, "You are now in the Russian military." With the same motion, he hands the paperwork to the waiting sergeant. It's obvious the sergeant has performed this routine task many times before. With hardly a hesitation, he has Reinie by the arm and escorts him out of the building to a smaller compound. This proves to be a more secure environment with several military guards all displaying a reticent and a much more formalized behavior. None of these soldiers speak German and don't give a damn what becomes of any of these Aryan bourgeois. They go about their tasks the same as if they were herding cattle: a lot of pushing and shoving and little talk.

CHAPTER 8

WARSAW

Like so many people in Poland these days, one never knows what new governing twists one is going to have to adapt to in order to make it to the next day. At least for this day, Kaczka is more than happy to have three more laborers in his shop. He's created military boots, belts, holsters, hats and gloves for the Polish army, the Russian army and now the German army. These goods are all made of leather, tanned and sewn together in this shop the same as they have been for several generations.

Izak is also pleased to be reasonably triumphant in replacing some sense of security to his mother and sister after his father and older brothers had been murdered. He's quite attentive to supply them with what protection they may need in order to move along, especially in these uncompromising times. He's particularly concerned with how long Rhena will be able to pull off her boy disguise before she's found out. This will definitely be a game changer.

Rhena spends much of her spare time learning the city. She's only been to Warsaw once before when she was much younger. What she is discovering is that there is an open hostility to the Jewish population by both the Germans and some of the Poles. Consequently the Jewish population has been forcefully relegated into a walled ghetto and forbidden to leave. In order to insure that they realize they have been systematically banished from the general population and are not expected to return they have been placed under tight security. The German kommandant in charge has restricted them to 300 calories a day to insure that many will die before they are sent to extermination camps. Of course they are being told that they are being placed in areas that will provide jobs and housing.

On this particular day, Rhena is making her way into an area she has not been to before. She finds herself standing in front of a department store window looking at a particularly attractive dress and wondering if she'll ever see the days when something that pretty could be hers. A familiar sound catches her attention. It's two young boys speaking in hushed tones—and they're speaking in Yiddish. Since arriving at the cobbler shop, the family has been careful to speak only Polish. This phenomenon excites Rhena to the extent that she risks interrupting their patter by speaking to them in their common language. This causes them to stop abruptly. They both look at her and then at each other.

Rhena can readily read their body language and what she reads is that they are stunned by her discovery and both are ready to bolt. Quickly she appeals to them to stop and talk to her for a moment.

"Please, please don't run. I'm Jewish and need to talk to you," she begs running after them, waving her arms in a gesture of hopeful brotherhood. She is particularly curious about any news from their community and especially how these two have managed to avoid the ghetto.

Maybe because Rhena appears to be an older boy, they remain standing steadfast. At the same time, they continue to nervously look around hoping to avoid any curious onlookers. Whatever their concerns may be, they have decided to set them aside at least for the moment, allowing their curiosity to draw them in.

What grabs her eye is both are carrying a potato sack. Each bag appears to have something in it. The two boys continue to be nervous waiting to hear why this stranger wants to detain them.

Realizing she is going to have to make this convincing and to the point, she begins, "I'm new here and don't know anything that's going on with us. I'm hoping you can tell me."

"What is it you gotta know?" asks one of these children in a definite tone of apprehension maybe bordering on hostility.

Rhena in turn gives pause as to how much she should reveal. "My family has just this month moved here from the country. The Germans confiscated our farm forcing us to flee. So far we have been passing ourselves as Poles but I'm sure they will some day figure out that deceit. I want to know what we can do to avoid getting caught."

Her plea is full of an anxiousness that overwhelms these two youngsters. They can't be more than ten years old. They look at Rhena with a vanquished expression. Obviously she has mentally overpowered them with questions they aren't equipped to answer. Their response is to shrug their shoulders and run in the opposite direction.

Rhena is left standing alone with no more assurance about her family's welfare than she had before and now more perplexed than ever by the behavior of these two boys. It leaves her with no choice other than to return back to the apartment. After giving it some thought, she decides not to tell Izak or her mother about this encounter. She is sure her brother would disapprove of her exposing their identity to anyone for any reason.

The days turn into weeks and soon this new fictitious Radinsky family has settled in as best they know how becoming regular members of the neighborhood. Minnie has gone so far as to visit another neighbor lady. She has even grown accustomed to referring to herself as Beatka Radinsky.

The same cannot be said about Rhena who still is required to identify herself as Bercik Radinsky. She is longing for the day she can return to living her life as the young lady that she dropped off almost a year ago.

Izak, now as Alek Radinsky has also settled in with the routine of the cobbler trade. Kaczka has found him to be a reliable and valued employee, leaving him with more and more responsibility. On this particular day Kaczka announces to Izak that he attended a meeting. He and other shop owners in this section of Warsaw were ordered by the SS Commander to attend a meeting in a local gymnasium.

"What was it about this time?" asks Izak.

"They are dead set on putting every Jew behind that wall," says Kaczka pointing down the street.

Izak has purposely avoided that area. The sight of his people being marched by the hundreds every day to waiting railcars along with the terrified look on the faces of mothers with their children, is more than he can deal with. For the most part these families had at earlier times possessed the power to escape, but being law-abiding citizens, they were not inclined to break the law. Consequently times quickly changed. These same people have now become altogether powerless and have had any chance of escaping completely eliminated.

"Not only that, but they have told us that if we are caught hiring Jews we will be treated the same as though we are harboring. We will be shot along with the Jews," continues Kaczka.

This is disquieting to Izak. He realizes what kind of danger he can bring to the doorstep of this decent man. There always comes a time when humans discover they have not arrived to the safety of a home but are only resting temporally in a pleasant inn along the way. At best this has been a nice reprieve. Now is the time to begin to plan a new strategy.

All three members of Izak's family work at various stations throughout the shop doing various operations. He would like nothing better than to be able to pass this new information on to his sister and mother with a safer plan in place.

Minnie knows her son well enough to realize that something is awry. A new strain has overtaken his normally assured demeanor. At the evening meal he shares his concern with the other two. It goes without saying that Minnie finds this new change of events to be disconcerting.

"I know this past year has been one of pretense but I continue to hope the Germans will get past this hate phase. We've seen this happen before and they get over it in a short time," says Minnie wringing her hands around a small handkerchief.

"That may have been true in the past but this time they are much more organized and are intent on sorting out every Jew in the country," says Izak with the same strained expression. After pausing a moment for further thought, he continues, "Those papers Mr. Radinsky gave us have expired and it's going to be impossible for Rhena to continue to pass herself off as a boy."

All three sit silently with downcast eyes as their minds speculate on this frightening change of events. The evening turns to darkness and soon they fall into a restless slumber as this unresolved dilemma hangs over them. The next morning arrives with the same unsettled quandary. Silently they all go down the backstairs and into the shop to begin another day hoping some way of solving their predicament will flash before their eyes.

CHAPTER 9

MORT

Lunch break arrives and Rhena makes the decision to revisit the same part of town she had previously made contact with the two strange acting young Jewish boys. Not knowing what she hopes to accomplish, she nonetheless walks throughout the area with the hope of another encounter. Determined to carry through her mission, she takes a short cut through an area that had been destroyed by German bombers. Halfway through she notices some unusual movement in what appears to be an alley strewn with piles of debris from the burned-out buildings. Catching another glimpse, she realizes it's the two young boys she was hoping to find. This time she has a firm resolution to not let them run off. Staying safely back behind a pile of fallen bricks, she watches as they are met by an older man appearing from an opening in the lower level of this otherwise destroyed structure. He says a few words to them and then peers into the same sacks they had been carrying the last time she saw them. He gives them each what appears to be a coin and exchanges the full bags for two empty ones. They in turn begin to make their way back through the rubble toward the spot where Rhena is hidden. Making a split second decision, she grabs one of the startled boys before he can run off. While the other one runs back in the direction of the man, she wrestles this one and pins him to the ground. Speaking to him in Yiddish, she screams at him, "You tell what I want to know or I'll bloody you so bad your mother won't recognize you."

The boy can't be much older than nine. As he begins to fight her, he screams, "Go ahead and bloody me you dirty Polish pig. My mother's already dead."

This revelation stops Rhena for a moment. "I'm not a Polack. I'm Jewish like you. I want you to listen to me and not run away like the last time."

This disclosure does not stop his struggle forcing Rhena to slap him several times. This maneuver only serves to cause him to break out into screaming more epithets. Before she can administer another slapping she feels the stronger hands of someone yanking her away from her hapless victim. It turns out to be the older man she had witnessed making the bag exchange with the boys earlier.

"What the hell are you doing here?" he blurts out as he tosses Rhena to one side.

Rhena's mixture of fear, anxiousness and panic all flow out at one time as she bellows back at her attacker, "I've been trying to talk to these shithead boys and all they want to do is run away from me."

"That's what they've been instructed to do if a stranger comes on to them," says this older man, "and you sure as hell fit that description."

"I know but my family is in awful danger and I don't know where to turn. We're Jewish like you and we don't know where to turn for help."

The strange man's attention has suddenly switched from Rhena to the fact that all this commotion may alert the wrong ears. Grabbing Rhena by the arm he forces her down the path past all the scattered piles of ruins and through an opening into the basement of the wrecked building. He doesn't let go of her arm until he senses she isn't going to go on yelling or run back out side.

"What do you mean your family's Jewish and in grave danger?" asks the man.

Rhena spends the next ten minutes giving this stranger the rundown on her and her family's life over the past year. After concluding and having given all the information she can think of, she sits hoping that now this stranger is able to help her.

He sits listening respectfully as she recites the same story he has heard over and over from every other Jewish family who've encountered the Nazis.

"Let me introduce myself. My name is Mort Polanski. I'm not sure I can help you in the way you hope since every one of us is in the same damnable predicament. But I can offer you a way for your family to at least get involved in a resistance against those who would have Jews wiped off the face of the earth," he says.

Rhena listens to the words coming from this understanding man as she tries to evaluate what he may be offering her and her family.

"I've heard of the Jewish Resistance. My father always said it was illegal and full of Communists," submits Rhena.

"People say a lot of things. Right now we have no supporters or ideology other than trying to survive in a world that would have us all dead," says Mort in a rather flat matter of fact tone.

Watching Mort busy himself with a couple of other men and woman asking things of him, Rhena waits for a moment pondering what Mort just said to her before raising her next question. With a bit more than an ordinary amount of anxiety she asks, "Can I bring my mother and brother to meet with you?"

Looking quite intent as he quickly contemplates the possible outcomes of such an off the cuff meeting, he finally addresses her concern.

"You have to understand that you stumbled on us and if that's possible for a young girl like you, it's even more possible for the German secret police to do the same. We have to be extremely careful that things like this don't happen again. But to answer your worry, yes, I will meet with them."

Rhena's face takes a sudden relaxed expression. The tension created by her brother's proclamation of having to make a move has had a domineering effect on her whole being. At least now they can consider some options that weren't available before. "When? How?" is her only response.

With still a little more reflective hesitation Mort considers the *how* and the *when*. "Tomorrow at this same time," he says with a renewed assurance.

A large smile begins to spread across Rhena's face. "Oh thank you, thank you Mr. Polanski. We'll be here if I have to drag them. Oh and by the way, one more question, who are those two young kids with the gunny sack?"

Mort takes the next few minutes to explain that young boys like this are not required to wear the blue Star of David armbands and are secretly sent out of the Ghetto to buy food for others at great risk. If they are caught, the Germans tie them to the back of a wagon and drag them through the Ghetto until they are unrecognizable.

This information gives Rhena more to think about on her way back to the cobbler shop. The sobering aspect of all this is that she's coming to realize that there is not going to be a panacea for a better life any time soon and at best they may only be buying some time.

Izak meets her at the door. "Where in the name of God have you been, Mother and I have been scared to death the SS grabbed you." He's desperately trying to keep his voice down so as not to draw attention from some of the other Polish employees. Poles like to brag that they are capable of "smelling a Jew."

"I've got some news as to where we may find some protection," says Rhena, "I'll tell you more about it after work this evening."

Evening arrives and the remnant of the Nowak family gathers for the evening meal. Rhena lays out everything that she has experienced over the past few days. Izak remains a little more curious than interested but Minnie is apprehensive altogether. She states her reasons as clearly as she can. "These fascist Germans believe every Jew to be a Communist and Papa always said we should stay out of politics." (At this time there are right Zionists, left Zionists, middle Zionists, the Bund, the Communists and the Religious party.)

Izak remembers those words of his father but takes exception to them. "You're right, Mama. Papa did believe that but these damnable fascists have already made up their mind and pigeon-holed us all as Bolsheviks. So we have no defense against these opinions anyway."

Taking a few more bites of his supper Izak continues to contemplate their options. He finally concludes his thoughts.

"I'm going with you tomorrow and talk with this Mort guy and then we'll make a decision." With that settled for the moment, they retire for the night.

With the morning comes a new predicament. While getting started with the day's work agenda, Izak overhears a neighboring shop owner discussing with Kaczka the rumor that the SS are doing another hunt, business-by-business this time. They are looking particularly for Jews either hiding or being hidden. This news creates a new sense of urgency. It gives him pause as he considers how soon it will be before they need to be moving on to their next relocation. This decision doesn't take him long as he peers out the window only to see a German military truck with a huge red banner bearing a swastika making its way down the street. Forcing himself to remain calm, he slowly makes his way to the back of the building. Minnie and Rhena are just beginning to make their way down the back steps from the apartment to come in to work. They both catch the urgent look on Izak's face.

Rhena is the first to react. "What's going on Izak?"

He quickly informs them of this recent twist in German behavior with the added imperative that, "We must leave now!"

The three look at each other as they examine the other to understand what this is going to require. Izak catches a glimpse of the military truck making its way through the cross street. "I mean right now!" With his next motion he has both his mother and sister by the arm as he pushes them down the street. No words are being spoken but all their thoughts are firing at lightning speed. It's the time of the morning that many others are making their way to their work place making it easier to intermingle. Soon they have put several blocks between themselves and the cobbler shop.

"Okay Rhena, now it's up to you to get us out of here," says Izak having no idea where this "Mort" is located. Rhena, having caught the immediacy of this situation, takes the lead as she retraces her steps down through the remnants of former buildings. These cratered edifices hint of a former time when mankind was more interested in building than destroying.

Soon after rounding a pile of collapsed bricks, she recognizes the opening into the building where she met with Mort not yet twenty-four hours ago.

"There's the opening!" yells Rhena and heads forward as if on a crusade.

Before she can take a step, her brother once again grabs her arm preventing her from moving in a potentially dangerous direction. "Hold on a second little sister. Who you saw in there yesterday may not be the occupier today. Let's hang back here for a while and see who comes and goes."

Minnie has grown accustomed to this young son of hers taking control in these kinds of crises and has even come to depend on him. She continues to be amazed at how well he has marshaled them through the labyrinth of risks they've encountered this past year. For the present, they are content to stay back behind a pile of ruins. This measure allows them the seclusion they wish for as well as giving them a view of the doorway.

The morning ebbs away into the afternoon, thus far no signs of Mort. The weather is getting colder and Minnie digs around in her coat pocket for the work gloves she so conveniently stuffed there before she left the apartment. Her nose is dripping from the cold. This idle time leaves an opening for her mind to hark back to simpler times on the farm. It's a mixture of sadness and joy. She envies the joyous times she remembers as she was raising her children, almost wishing she had never had these times only to lose them in such a vile way.

As the day stretches into late afternoon, Rhena is becoming concerned that she is losing credibility with the no show of Mort. The amount of waning daylight is becoming a concern, not knowing what the night will bring. Izak has not taken his eyes away from any part of this building, continuing to scan it for any sign of movement. But now because of the encroaching darkness bringing with it a damp, some new decisions are going to have to be made.

"We are going to have to find some shelter soon. You two stay back here until I signal you to move forward." With that Izak begins to slowly move out. Trying to stay in the shadows, he inches along from one mountain of debris to another until he's worked his way to the opening. Once there, he quickly slips through the doorway, he again cautiously continues his slow, deliberate scrutiny of everything in view. Willing to take the chance on finding someone lurking inside, he slips through several rooms, bracing himself to meet the occasion. So far it remains a cold empty cavity marginally suggesting it may have held some human warmth at one time by the hint of pieces of leftover wallpaper stubbornly gripping to a wall.

As he moves from room to room, he remains struck by the lack of evidence that anyone ever occupied this building. Its silence echoes the crunching sound made by his boots sliding across the floor. Before long he's convinced that the existing rooms are empty and signals his mother and sister to join him. Happy to at least be out of the bitter wind, they are now more than willing to enter this gutted, darkened, ominous, bombed-out building.

This family has had their share of encumbrances and so far they have been able to overcome them. Cold is something many humans have to endure, but in truth, they never get used to. Nonetheless they decide to huddle up and make the best of it. It's also becoming obvious by their gnawing stomachs that they have spent a day without food and water.

Just as they are accustoming themselves to their quandary, they hear the instantly familiar sound of boots crunching on the floor and see two shadowy figures. Armed with nothing but loose bricks to defend themselves, they find they are totally at the mercy of these men. The light is adequate enough to make out that these two have also most definitely fallen on hard-times themselves. They're shabbily dressed and thin. Rhena recognizes Mort immediately. A smile of relief crosses her face as she reassures her brother and mother of her alliance with him. Izak and Minnie catch each other's harried glance as they gingerly wait for any sign of this brotherhood.

Rhena is on her feet grasping her mother and brother's hands eager to introduce her family. Mort studies them for a moment. He's taken by their seeming healthy demeanor, especially given these circumstances. They exchange a customary kiss and Mort gets down to business. "I want you to realize that what I'm proposing is not an easy avenue to a good life. But what I can offer you is an opportunity to let our enemies know that they cannot erase our civilization without a fight."

Minnie's face drops letting out a long sobbing sigh. Her hopes of living her life out in peace seem to be drifting into never ending tragedies.

This hopelessness is beginning to exhaust her spirit. She is finding her life changes more difficult to adjust to. "I can't fight anymore. I'm too tired. Things will never be the same and I'm too old to care anymore. I don't care to live like this. I've lost too much."

Her tears are understood by Mort. He's lost every single member of his family to the Nazi killing machine with the exception of one brother.

Mort has introduced his companion as his single surviving brother named Karol. He then addresses Minnie's sadness. "Mrs. Nowak, there isn't one family of our people who are either all gone or have suffered tremendous losses. We have the choice to either let these German barbarians mow us down like so many docile sheep or we can let them know that we think enough of our selves to fight them with nothing more than our spoons and forks."

Minnie is normally not of the fighting type. Her natural approach is to fall victim and surrender. "I realize that some of you are made to fight but I am too tired to care anymore," she laments.

Both Izak and Rhena rush to their mother's side trying to console her. It's as though all Minnie's tensions and losses over the past year are surfacing at once. Losing her husband, two of her sons, her home and fearing for the lives of herself and her two only surviving children has replaced any time to grieve her losses and now to find themselves on the run again is draining her will to live.

Izak is the first to speak. "Mother, these brutes would have us believe that we are sub-humans and not capable of feelings. Just by your sadness you are proving that this is far from the truth. We are all saddened by our losses but now is the time to let these savages know that we are willing to fight against their barbarous practices. There is no future for our generation if we let these thugs define and destroy us. We must resist their definitions of us."

Rhena has wrapped her arms around her mother in an effort to console her. "Izak is right Momma. They have bragged 'we have taken what we want from you.' I would rather die fighting than let another one of these animals violate me again. By demeaning us they hope to break us." Her mind has drifted back to the incident with the German kommandant at the farm. Remembrance of this happening used to make her feel depressed, now it makes her angry—and that may be true now within many other Jewish families.

Mort is processing what he is hearing from these latest volunteers. He is paying particularly close attention to Minnie. This is the kind of talk that the community can ill-afford to foster for long. Its deleterious effects can undermine even the strongest. He hopes that once Minnie gets involved with helping others, her center will be reconfigured away from herself to that of the needs of the community.

He has been involved with the Resistance since its inception. It's not unusual for him to hear these kinds of emotional swings within families or for that matter to have a variety of political expressions. This holds true throughout the whole community. He, in particular, views himself as a Zionist but has a realistic idea of other views. He is also in charge of smuggling food and other needed supplies into the Ghetto and can always use extra hands. As for these new volunteers, they are welcomed.

"Okay, boys and girls we have work to do. We have to get out of here while it's still daylight," says Mort motioning forward with a flick of his hand.

With that, he begins to lead them throughout a labyrinth of fallen ceilings and blown-out floors to a homemade ladder dropped from the first floor into the basement. Carefully making their way down its precarious footings the five of them arrive safely below onto a darkened and broken concrete floor. Mort is moving them about with the stubby end of a lighted candle. Karol quickly removes the ladder. For security reasons, he places it out of sight from the hole. The Germans periodically patrol throughout the ruins looking for hiding Jews. Consequently, it's necessary that they take extra precautions to conceal their traffic patterns.

With this simple candle as the only source of light, Mort leads them through to another small opening that leads through a broken brick wall into a small chamber with low ceilings. None of them are able to stand erect. It soon becomes apparent to the Nowaks that they are being lead through a sewer system. What seems like a never ending trek eventually comes to an end in another chamber that is much larger.

There are several more people in this section, both men and woman—maybe a dozen. They all seem to be busy. What's come about in this section is a makeshift warehouse with food stuffs, clothing, shoes, blankets, etc. All smuggled in from outside the Ghetto and in need of being sorted and blessed kosher by a Rabbi. This stash must be carefully kept secret from even the Jewish police, who are definitely in the pocket of the SS and it goes without saying that the Polish police sympathies are certainly not with the Jews nor with the SS Nevertheless in spite of the animosity the Poles feel for the Jews, they are more than ready to trade food for the gold and silver treasures these people have been able to withhold from the Germans.

Mort promptly introduces the Nowaks to everyone here and orders food and water for them. With everyone responding in Yiddish they quickly find a sense of belonging that has been absent from their lives for some time. Rhena gravitates to another girl around her age. Her name is Sara Leninbacher. They soon discover they have many things in common beyond their ethnicity. Both are happy just to have some things to share with another girl, as this same phenomenon seems to hold true with all young people and they soon find themselves forming a common alliance—seeming more to do with the commonality of their age rather than religious traditions or race.

Minnie too has found some other women who have welcomed her company. They are including her in helping to process all of these items that will eventually get distributed.

Izak is hanging on to the parts of this activity that involve Mort and his brother, Karol. They seem to be more concerned with a larger picture than simply sorting through things. He's also noticed that Mort is armed with what appears to be a small revolver that has managed to reveal its grip above his belt. It turns out that it's a Luger that once belonged to a German officer who had the misfortune of venturing into the wrong place alone. Without hesitation, Mort relieved him of its burden.

Approaching them, Izak makes his preferences known. "I want you to know that I've passed myself off as a Polack over this past year and believe I could be more effective on the outside than in the Ghetto."

Mort muses over this eager request as he continues to measure this new recruit.

CHAPTER 10

REINIE'S MILITARY CONSCRIPTION

An ethnic German seventeen-year-old being drafted into the Russian army can only be described as legal enslavement. Many of the international agreements between the Allies prohibit mistreatment of ethnic Germans. These are treated only as suggestions by the Russians. They have managed to circumvent most of these agreements by placing these prisoners into the military. The result is the atrocities against these people are never seen, much less reported by United States, British, or French inspections. It's obvious Stalin has his own agenda and is not concerned with any of those things that can hinder it.

Within minutes Reinie is escorted back to his barracks. Bretzke is the first to greet him and welcome him. He finds this greeting as welcome as one would if he were sent a rescue ship on a desolate island. There is something in this man's character that Reinie finds hopeful.

"I suppose they let you know that you are now part of the Russian military," chuckles Bretzke.

Reinie's head snaps up in surprise. "Yes! How did you know?"

By this time several more men begin to gather. "I'm a corporal and the Reverend here is a master sergeant," declares a smirking, tall skinny man named Albert. He's wearing a tattered coat he has recently relieved from a man who died a few days ago. His irony is in his smirk as they all fully realize the ridiculousness of these positions.

"When the International Red Cross is told this is a military camp, they can't inspect it," declares another inmate. His name is Gustave. He spent his career as an attorney until he legally challenged the Russian's misuse of the German people in direct defiance to the Potsdam Agreement. In light of this stance, his career became short-lived as he found himself arrested and "volunteering" for the Russian military.

"How do they get away with what they are doing?" questions Reinie. "Don't the Allies see what they're doing to us?"

"Of course they are aware but have obviously chosen to sacrifice us Germans rather than risk war with Stalin," says a disenchanted Gustave. His opinion of being held illegally continues to obsess his thoughts.

Bretzke listens patiently. He has been ordained in a confessional church. He has been raised to never see himself as a victim. In conscience, he could not give up his life for Hitler's concept of the Fatherland, especially Hitler's persecution of the Jews. To defend the Nazi perspective defied everything the Gospel has taught him. Now the communists are challenging his faith yet once again. He is being asked to set aside the Gospel in order to save his life. He has discovered what credos he is willing to martyr himself for and those he would refuse. This sort of allegiance to the Christian faith continues to defy the powerful, especially when their cruelest intimidations fail to break these kinds of people.

In all truth, Bretzke would be the first to admit that he misses his pastoral brotherhood but on the other hand he has discovered that wherever there are as few as two lonely Christians gathered in His name, Christ, as promised, is in their midst.

It frustrates Gustave that he can't get Bretzke to side with him in his hopelessness. It's true there is a part of Gustave that would prefer to simply surrender to his captors and just go mad but the storm within suggests that there is something dual about his morbidness. In spite of this inner encouragement to give up and go mad, there remains a remnant within him that doesn't believe in the mania. It's as though if he continually encourages himself to give up he can accept death as a quick remedy. Now he is hoping to find a friend in seventeen-year-old Reinie.

"This shit is never going to end, kid. A hundred years from now it'll still be the same. All we need to do is put a rope around our necks and it will all end."

Bretzke is still pondering Gustave. After all, Gustave too had been a theological student at one time but he mulled over doubt and inspiration and revelation until it all began to take shape in the wrong direction. That's when studying the law became a more logical career choice for him.

Bretzke also realizes that the "lower power" remains close to "The Higher Power" and is devoted to being patient in watching for a way in. He has been heard to say, "The worst can only enter when the best has vacated."

As a true man of God, Reverend Bretzke is not present to judge any of God's children, only to encourage each of them to include the simple message of Jesus in picking up the pieces of their broken lives. Here in this obscure gulag he deals with the simplest aspects of reality: fear, doubt, depression. There is little or no room for long discussions on the theological debate between "state church" and "free church." He tends toward being a compassionate shepherd rather than a legalistic overseer. With him there is no exaggeration or complicated language when confronted by a man who is struggling to find the words to share his innermost thoughts. He rather has a ready ear and the simple message of God's love for those finding themselves either at death's door, or struggling to stay away from it.

Bretzke continues to let Gustave vent his frustrations without any interference. He readily recognizes that the rigors of the expulsion and the anxiety of unfair and illegal prison life are causing him to be "beside himself." Gustave does not do well when his "German order" is disrupted in such a volatile manner.

During his career, Bretzke has done much introspection. By being so much in touch with his own human imperfections, it provides him with a keener awareness of the shortcomings in others. Gustave is no exception. Bretzke recognizes the abandonment of his faith and the darkness that has replaced it. With such a man, reminding him of his hopelessness with the expectation that such an action will jolt him out of his discontentment is a lesson in futility. Instead the good reverend has given Gustave simple tasks that will provide order in his life as well as those in the barracks. It may not be enough to save his soul but at least it's a start in a more positive direction.

The work load expected to be completed every day by these men is never reduced to match their failing strength due to malnutrition. Those who can't continue are often found dead in their bed. When it becomes obvious that a man is not earning even the miserably small ration of calories the Russians provide him, he is taken away and never seen again.

As men die they are stripped of anything that's deemed useful in furthering the life of the pilferer. Bretzke has appointed Gustave the distributor of these articles as it fulfills his need to have even the most ghastly projects done in a fair and orderly manner. More prisoners are sworn in as soldiers and are replacing those that have given way to starvation or disease. The life span of a man in these conditions can range from a week to months depending on his resourcefulness and the strength of his determination to survive.

Reinie has been here now for several months. He has survived cutting timber through the bitter cold of the winter and has never in his young life appreciated the first warm day bringing on a thaw like he has this year. These elegant rays of warmth freely rendered by God's sun are a luxury that would equal any opulence provided for royalty. It's giving birth to a renewed sense of hope, one that is bringing with it a strong desire to have this place be a part of his past rather than hovering into his future.

On one of these days, he finds himself working alongside Bretzke stacking brush into piles to be burned. They are out of the direct sight and earshot of any guards. It supplies an occasion to bring up a question, "Reverend have you ever had an opportunity to escape from here?"

This query catches Bretzke by surprise. It gives him pause for a moment as he appears to be bringing something forgotten back to mind.

"I've never given escape a thought but I have had the opportunity to leave here on one occasion," says Bretzke. This admission brings to Reinie a facial expression that can only be interpreted as stunned.

"You had the chance to get out of this hellhole and you let it slip by?"

Again Bretzke pauses long enough to look into Reinie eyes which really are the portal into his soul. He's trusting his pending answer will be understood by this young man.

"I was asked to deny my Christian faith, first by Hitler and now by Stalin." He makes this statement using the same tone of absurdity as one would if being asked to deny the truth of the world being round. "I lost my ministry with the Latvians, the Germans and the Russians but I have regained a ministry here in this hellhole, as you have correctly called it. But now it's with people whose religious vitality desperately needs to be recovered."

Reinie is young but old enough to be impressed by the immeasurable conviction this man holds to be of comfort to these lost, baffled, weakened, often confused and sometimes, forgotten souls. It causes him a great contentment to discover such a man still exists in this perverted world and even more so that he is still able to hold ever so firm to his Christian convictions. He envies him in a strange sort of way in spite of the guilt caused by this man showing him how far short that he is from this type of selflessness.

Nonetheless for now, he will remain diligent in finding a way out of here. While working in the woods he has managed to find a few of last fall's herbs poking through the snow to add to his diet. These have not significantly strengthened him physically but the clinging to life demonstrated by this ancient life form has invigorated his young mind to seek a freedom that his whole being longs for.

Through the winter there has been a Russian sergeant named Boris who has been kind to Reinie. When he could, he would slip extra bread or a potato to him. He never asked for anything in return. On this particular winter day Reinie has received his work orders for the day. It takes him to a remote work area that had been cleared some time ago. He thought it odd that he was left there alone. Soon he discovered that he was not alone. Sergeant Boris appeared from behind a pile of cut wood. He has a half bottle of vodka in his hand and from his appearance he probably had already consumed the other half.

He's not a particularly large man by any means. The vodka has left his countenance a ruby red making several moles on the side of his face to appear as bubbles erupting in a beet stew. The look on his face can only described as a pathetic leer. His uniform is disheveled and despite the coolness of the morning his entire tunic is unbuttoned. Sitting on a fallen log, he pats a spot next to him motioning for Reinie to come sit down next to him.

"Come over here my young German proletarian and have a drink with me," he says swinging the bottle by its neck. "You've been a good boy all winter and deserve a little reward."

Reinie has learned enough Russian to communicate on a low level. In this case he suspects what may be beginning to take place with this event. Cautiously he makes his way to his appointed seat. Catching the tossed bottle he tips it up, feigning taking a long draw and hands it back.

Boris is drunk enough that he makes no bones of what he expects of Reinie as he begins to caress his thigh. "You ever get horny in that miserable barrack?" he laughs as he becomes bolder, grabbing Reinie's crotch.

Reinie flinches. He's suddenly aware of the full impact of what is going to be expected of him. He has hardly had time to analyze this turn of events. Not sure what it's going to take to get out of this weird scenario, he does the only thing that comes normal to him. He jumps up and backs away.

This action enrages this former "Good Samaritan" as he lashes out with curses toward every ethnic German in the world. "I'll have your ass one way or another you pig dog of a German. Either here where it can be pleasant or back at camp where you will find things not to your liking. Now take your damn pants off and bend over."

Reinie is trying to think as fast as he can. "Okay, Okay let's have another drink first."

Boris grabs him by the back of his coat and pulls him into his face and slobbers a kiss on Reinie's unsuspecting mouth. "Oh you blond haired German boys always taste so good," he slurs as he tips the bottle up and empties its contents down his gullet.

Reinie's thoughts are racing. *"I can't run. He'll catch me for sure and I sure as hell can't let him have his way."* In a moment of panic a plan develops. He quickly complies with Boris' demand. Watching Reinie slip his trousers down around his ankles excites Boris all the more.

In his drunken arousal, Boris struggles with getting his own pants down. Finally satisfied that having them resting on his boot tops is good enough and still staggering around with his penis in his hand, he stumbles toward his seemingly compliant dupe who has remained in his bent over position. As he feels the first contact of Boris' skin against his own and with the speed of a mongoose Reinie raises up and strikes Boris with a cast off eighteen-inch limb laying at his feet. The blow from the makeshift club catches Boris unawares and sends him reeling to the ground. Before Boris can recover, Reinie's pants are back up and around his waist allowing him his next move. With Boris yet struggling to get to his feet and his pants tripping up his every attempt, Reinie renders him unconscious with yet another well-positioned blow to his already alcohol-soaked brain.

With his fight or flight modality quickly shifting from his fight mode to a flight response, he glances around. Seeing nothing, he begins, starting with Boris' boots, to pull off every stitch of clothing this man has on his body leaving him naked. Quickly replacing his boots with Boris' and using the belt, Reinie quickly rolls Boris' clothes into a tight bundle. He then carefully leaves a ragged shirt of his own as though carelessly cast off and begins to drag Boris' clothing by the unfastened end of the belt behind him. Hopefully on discovering his cast off shirt, they will use it as a scent for the soon-to-be, pursuing dogs. By dragging this bundle of clothing behind him and wearing Boris' boots, he prays that it may be enough to confuse the dogs allowing him an escape through the forest.

Checking his newly-acquired watch, it is 8:30 a.m. With a bit of luck he could have until evening before they return to pick him up. Remembering that this camp is east of the railroad tracks, he opts to head north in order to stay parallel with the rail line. His plan is to eventually continue his trek to the Baltic Sea by rail but only when it becomes safe to do so. With all his newly captured gear he is ready to roll. He is especially grateful that this drunken soldier had enough presence of mind to include a lunch and a canteen of water.

CHAPTER 11

1943 WARSAW GHETTO

The Judenrat is a council of Jews in the Ghetto picked by the Germans to see to it that the Nazi High Command's orders are properly carried out. Even though this council is leading a doomed community, they still attempt to relieve the needs of its people. Under threat of severe retribution this committee is expected to deliver a list of all Jewish names in the Ghetto. They in turn have developed a Jewish police force to enforce the rules. The people in this group are usually brought in from somewhere else, usually places like the Ukraine. This action is designed by the Gestapo to reduce the chances of them having a sentimental connection to the community. As capable enforcers of the Reich's General Government for this area, they feel these foreigners are more dependable than hiring neighbors.

As yet, Mort and his resistance group are still quartered in the supply bunker. Mort contemplates Izak's wish to be assigned outside the Ghetto. "Does the name Jewish Combat Organization mean anything to you Izak?" asks Mort.

From Mort's tone of voice, Izak concludes that this must be an important question. He has heard of it, in a manner of speaking, from the Polish workers at Kaczka's cobbler shop but only in a critical sense. They described it as a group of Jewish communist misfits who think they're smarter than everybody else and just want to cause an uprising.

Not wanting to give this unflattering description as an answer, Izak decides to deny any awareness of this outlaw league, "No, I don't believe so."

Mort catches a bit of nervous hesitation that usually accompanys a lie. "Izak, you said that you worked at Kaczka's Cobbler Shop. Am I correct in that?"

"Yes, sir. That's right," he answers while nervously trying to clear his throat and not real sure where this line of questioning is going to take him.

"I know exactly where that is Izak. Do you recall those Jewish families wearing those armbands displaying the Star of David as they were marched down your street?" he asks. His voice is taking on a more defiant tone as he continues his interrogation.

"Yes, we saw them every day," Izak answers, still not sure on which side of Mort he is going to land in this seeming inquisition.

"Where do you suppose they were on their way to?" Mort's questions are now carrying a rather sarcastic pronouncement.

"We were told they were taking them to Treblinka to await a resettlement location where they needed workers," says Izak a bit more confident in his response.

Mort is near a controlled rage as he considers this deceptive piece of propaganda the Germans are disseminating and the broad orbit it has reached.

"Those lying bastards have taken more than 200,000 of our people so far and have sent them to Treblinka. But not for relocation unless they mean to the pit they bury them in after they've gassed them all to death." Mort is beginning to quiver, "We can't let these deaths go unanswered. The Torah clearly calls for 'an eye for an eye'."

His brother, Karol, quickly intervenes at this point. "Our whole family was taken a month ago. We received word back through reliable source that the Germans were shipping in excessive amounts of diesel fuel. The source stated that they were taking it to Treblinka to run huge diesel engines and that they are using the exhaust to gas our people. We haven't heard from our family since the day they were supposedly 'relocated,' nor has anyone ever heard from their people again."

Mort takes a deep breath and regains his composure enough to continue. "So you want to be placed on the outside? The Resistance needs people on the outside but until I get to know you better, I'd prefer you where I can evaluate you closer. For now I want you to work with Karol. He'll give you work that needs to be done."

Compared to Mort's more verbose personality, Karol is more reserved. It might be said that he is the eyes and ears of the Ghetto. He makes it his business to keep abreast of the facts and rumors throughout the community. All this must be done undercover. He has been able to penetrate the Judenrat and the Jewish police through a high-ranking member. This is extremely dangerous as oftentimes suspicion of treason alone is enough to get one killed.

An assortment of Jewish thought and actions hold dear any means through which they can defy the Germans and maintain their cultural heritage. They illegally continue to educate their children when even the most severe dehumanizing policies are brought against them. They treasure their dignity enough to defy the German efforts aimed at destroying what they value as an intricate portion of Jewish culture. Anyone who classified these efforts as passive was soon disappointed. On the other hand it's unfortunately true that in any community there is a cross section of people where hardships will cause many to give in to despair. Suicides run rampant in these days. It's not unusual for any family to have had this experience with their loved ones.

The Gestapo also prides itself in its ability to keep abreast of the various resistance groups arising across the community. Suspicion of alignment with one of these groups will automatically have you moving up on their list for relocation or hanging. They use the Jewish police to keep them informed. Most Ghetto people do not trust this agency and consider them as turncoats. They have been known to be much more brutal than even the Germans. Karol knows for a fact that these same teams of Ukrainian Jews are also used as guards at Treblinka.

"What they don't know is that when they are told they'll be rotated at the end of a year of duty, they'll end up just as dead as those they've been guarding," says Karol with a justifiable smirk. "These guys are all about the money, prestige and power they are given. They actually believe the Germans are going to make exceptions and forget they are Jews."

Izak remains quiet as he mulls Karol's words over in his mind. With a forward thought that has suddenly made its way to his mouth, he finds he is forming the words every Jew has wondered, "Karol, why do you think the world hates us and wants us dead?"

Karol has heard this question asked many times. As a matter of fact this conundrum has been discussed by every Jew in every country where they have found themselves in exile. He still struggles on many levels over this question as he politely attempts to satisfy Izak's probe.

"I believe it starts with our culture being the oldest in the world and not having a country of our own." He says this with an eye drifting off toward some inward longing.

"Life itself is not so much a test for us. We know what works and doesn't work in our communities, whether it be in business, education, religion or social norms. Consequently, we are able to move up much faster along the roads to a successful life than our host countrymen. This creates a lot of envy and frustrations with those who feel that we are foreigners trying to dominate or replace their way of life. In other words they find it much easier to eliminate us rather than finding themselves more often than not, incapable of competing with us."

Izak listens to Karol with a spirit of agreement as he remembers his father's struggle with Gentile neighbors. His good business traditions displayed themselves in success after success while his Polish neighbors were more often than not failing.

Rhena is also paying close attention to what's being said. Without much thought she blurts out, "Rabbi Koleshki said that God likes Jews better and that we're his favorites."

Both Karol and Izak mentally step away from this analysis for the moment. Karol finally breaks out in a snarky grin, "Well nowadays, He sure as hell has an odd way of showing it." Rhena takes a step back as her face turns a red. She quickly realizes the absurdity of what she has just said in contrast to the conditions she presently finds herself experiencing. Karol spends the rest of the evening getting them settled in for the night.

This bunker is also vaulted and appears to be an underground grotto carved out under a larger upper construct. There are people sleeping in every available space. Some have fashioned sleeping quarters out of any available materials such as straw, paper, or any discarded rag that will help hold body heat. Most of them are young, oftentimes being the only one left alive in their family.

Morning arrives with no particular fanfare. People are milling around waiting to use makeshift toilets. This bunker has not had to worry about a water system as there is a well with a ready made supply of fresh water.

Minnie has been invited to join a group of older women to fix a kind of potato pancake for the dozen or so people stirring around preparing for the day's tasks. She is particularly drawn to an older woman named Eva.

Eva, she discovers, is the grandmother to the two youngsters Rhena had run into on her initial visit and an aunt to Mort and Karol. She is also the "head hen" for any food or clothing distribution. Minnie immediately feels comfortable enough with her to ask a few questions.

"How long have you been here, Eva?"

"Close to a year now," she says. "My husband was called in by the Germans for some kind of meeting. He never returned. When I went to the council to inquire about his whereabouts I was told he had been taken to the eastern front to do bookkeeping. Mort insists that he's been murdered. But sometimes I think Mort's thoughts are too destructive."

"Do you feel safe here?" asks Minnie further.

"When I first arrived here, I thought there would be some safety, but now I'm not so certain. These young people keep stirring the Germans up." Eva pauses for a moment then continues with another thought, "My husband always maintained that the war would be over soon and all this would come to an end."

Rhena has also aligned herself with Sara, the girl she had met the night before. They are presently engaged in putting their hair in braids. Sara lost her parents to Treblinka. Like so many of these other survivors, she was hiding when the Germans came with their so called "transfer papers" and took all the family members they could find.

Rhena begins to trade some similar experiences with her new friend when she asks, "How did you manage to hide?"

"My father and his brothers built a false wall where some of us would hide. The SS never did find that one, until they heard my baby sister crying. They tore it down. My sister wouldn't stop crying so they put a pistol in her mouth and shot her. I was in the attic hiding, rolled up in old carpet. They never bothered to unroll it. They arrested my family and left my dead baby sister. Some people from the synagogue came and took her and gave her a funeral. That was last fall and I haven't seen or heard from any of them since."

What Rhena notices particularly is the lack of emotion in Sara's voice as she tells her story. But then when she in turn is asked to tell Sara her own narrative, she finds it to be so surreal that she too has shut down emotionally. There has never been a time since their individual deprivation that their personal survival didn't trump the time needed to properly mourn their losses. Nonetheless, at this period of time it's much too risky to let one's guard down for the sake of bereavement.

Karol picks through the collection of waking bodies until he finds Izak who has barely slept a wink all night. He's been kept awake by the firm awareness of how much this holocaust is steadily powering the full brunt of its realness into his world. It becomes even more of an actuality as Karol rousts him out of his nest.

"Wake up. We've got work to take care of and a short time to get it done," says Karol as he gives him a slight kick.

Izak startles out of his drowse, not sure of his whereabouts. He shoots up as though he's been spring loaded. It takes him a moment to ascertain his new environment. Rubbing his eyes, he gathers his wits. The potato pancake aroma is overwhelming. It doesn't take him long to find its source. Giving his mother a peck on the cheek along with a couple of slurps of tea to wash down the breakfast, he's ready to launch. Clicking his heels in a bogus impersonation of an SS soldier along with an imitation salute, he reports for duty.

Karol is not impressed with his hi-jinx giving him a deadpan reaction. It's not that he's a humorless man. It really has more to do with the urgency of his mission. Within the hour they are to meet with a member of the Judenrat along with a member of the Jewish police. Karol finds that he has no time for the nonsense of this attempt at humor.

Minus a signal to begin their trek and without even a glance to see if his young charge is astute enough to recognize a non-verbal command, Karol ducks out of the bunker and back into the sewer. *"We'll see quickly what this wanna-be Resistance fighter is made of,"* is his private thought.

In spite of their oftentimes varying political attitudes, the success of the activities these young combatants have laid out is much dependent on all of them being of one mind. In simple language, their survival is all based on their ability to set aside political differences and embrace a common goal. This special bonding among them requires a cohesiveness that cannot be learned outside of the fraternity. Their common cause is to inflict as much pain on the enemy as possible and come out as survivors.

Izak is quickly catching on as to what is going to be required of him, particularly if he plans on proving himself to Mort. It's going to require a maturity that goes beyond his seventeen years but is still capable of preserving his youthful spirit. With an invigorated sense of purpose, Izak unquestioningly falls in step behind Karol, trusting that his leadership is reliable enough for him to reach this end.

Hunched over a lighted candle, Karol leads them unerringly through the maze of turns and twists of Warsaw's sewers. At some points there is ankle deep water and other places it dry. From time to they are met with other candle holders also scurrying along with a sense of purpose. Like so many worker ants, they are responding to the specificity of their individual missions. Most of these have to do with getting food and medical supplies into the Ghetto but a few are carrying bags of coal scavenged from the basements of bombed out buildings. Some is bought on a regular basis from "righteous" Poles also referred to as "Aryans."

Soon they emerge out of the subterranean cavity into what appears to have been a factory. There are still the remnants of what had been a productive enterprise, possibly providing several hundred workers a livelihood.

Now it's in ruins for the sake of some enigmatically challenged ideology supported only by a group of misfits bent on a path of ethnic cleansing.

Karol, still in the lead as a man with a clear destination in view, continues to weave his way through fallen glass, bricks, vent ducts, broken machinery and other unidentifiable rubble. Soon they are ascending a precarious set of stairs onto the roofless second floor. With the sure-footedness of a goat, Karol leaps across a piece of missing floor big enough to drop a car through. Without a second thought, Izak successfully makes the same move, landing only a yard behind. Without a word having been spoken by either of them since they began on this jaunt, Karol breaks the silence.

Stopping just as abruptly as he started, he turns toward his accomplice. "You stay here and keep watch. I'll be right there in that room," he says pointing to a room twenty feet away with a couple of well-dressed male figures monitoring their every move. "If you see anything suspicious, warn me immediately," he adds.

Izak is left with the feeling that he is going to be held more than a little responsible for the outcome of this liaison Karol has arranged. The look on Karol's face strongly suggests that he expects him not to not screw anything up. Izak gives his best attempt at appearing to be confident but a small insecure nod is all he can muster. With that, Karol continues on his way to meet with these clandestine collaborators.

Izak has a mixture of nervousness and excitement as he prepares himself to carry through with his first assignment. In spite of the cold temperatures, he can feel the nervous sweat streaming down his sides. Glancing in the direction of his just exiting commander gives him the sudden realization that from this point on the outcome of his decisions is going to determine his trustworthiness. The thought of this being his responsibility and his alone, gives him a new sense of worth.

He can see Karol along with the two other men engaged in a discussion. Their tones are serious and too low for him to hear what is being said. What strikes him odd is to observe the contrast these two other men are presenting as they are dressed in their business attire standing among the ruins of a building where this wardrobe was once common place.

The meeting is quickly over and Karol returns. His face has the same stoic appearance it did before the parley. He says nothing and in his now usual manner of expecting Izak to unquestioningly trot along behind him, begins to retrace his steps.

Arriving back at the bunker, Karol immediately seeks out Mort. Within a couple of minutes both Mort and Karol are calling a general conference among all the people. About a dozen are still hanging around and eager to hear what they have to report. With a more serious than usual tone to his voice, Mort begins. "We've gotten some inside information substantiating the Germans yet unwavering determination to empty this Ghetto into the Treblinka gas chambers. From the reports of those close to this operation, they want this finished as soon as possible."

After a moment of silent reflection on these words, Mort continues, "We have the option to either go quietly as sheep led to slaughter, or we can fight back."

An older man in the back wearing a worn suit coat and a soiled shirt speaks up. "That's insane to imagine we can win against the Germans with their tanks and guns."

Mort's resolve remains steadfast. "That depends on what you mean by win. We may not win an arms battle but we can win the battle to keep our dignity. What I'm saying is that we can go down fighting and not as sniveling cowards whimpering all the way to our death. We must show these vile mongrels that we are not who they say we are."

Mort allows a moment for any more opposing comments. Satisfied, at least for the moment, that he has everyone on the same page, he continues, "Karol has met with people who can make this happen for us. We have access to a cache of weapons and ammunition if we move swiftly."

Interest quickly picks up. Rhena and Sara move closer along with everyone else to hear more of what Mort is saying. It's obvious he has something important to express as he slowly paces back and forth, staring intently at everyone in his view.

"I need a group of you to join me in going out into the community to help raise enough money to buy these weapons and the ammunition we're going to need. However, we have little time so we must move swiftly. What I need to know now is how many of you can I count on to help with this project?"

With this said, the bunker nearly empties as they fall in behind him. Within an hour enough money is raised to buy what is available along with many more people, men and woman alike, willing to join The Resistance. Mort is overwhelmed with the new vigor his people are suddenly presenting. The smiles covering faces that have not smiled in such a long time brings a new joy to an otherwise joyless outcome. By mid-morning word has spread among the community of a renewed effort to stop the flow of deportations. Rhena and Sara are determined not to be left out of the turning point of this new effort.

Nervously approaching Mort, they wait until they see a break when he's not issuing orders. Gaining the courage they need, they confront him, "Mr. Polanski, we want to be part of the Resistance along with the men so if there is any place you can use us we're ready to go."

Mort stops dead in his tracks as these young ladies stand directly in front of him forcing him to take on their request. His eyes dart back and forth as he reviews not only their petition but also measuring their resolve. Looking them over for a moment, his face suddenly lights up like something just occurred to him. With only that moment of hesitation, he makes a decision.

"You girls go with me this morning. I believe I have some work for both of you and maybe a few more." With that decision, Mort looks over the rest of the teens among those still occupying the bunker. In a short time he has gathered up all the young volunteers he needs including Izak. This choice pleases Izak no end.

None of this is sitting well with Minnie as she sees her only remaining children ready to sacrifice their safety for what she is thinking are, *"Foolhardy escapades."* Calling them over to where she's standing in the background, she implores them to not be so ready to jump into the path of danger, "Please think this over. We have come this far. If we stay out of trouble and do what the authorities require of us, we can escape all this turmoil." Both Rhena and Izak look at one another incredulously. They can't believe their mother's naiveté. Both also realize that regardless of what they may say to dissuade her, her sense of a false security with the authorities prevents her from seeing the truth. Besides both know that nothing short of their non-involvement with the Resistance is going to comfort her.

"Don't worry Momma. We'll be alright," says Izak as his mother continues to grip both their hands.

"Oh how I wish we could go back to the farm. I knew who we were there. Here I know nothing," says Minnie through her tears.

Mort is beginning to organize his squad of half-grown teens. "We have to move quickly so stay with the group and keep up." With that said, he moves out.

Izak and Rhena both pull loose of their mother's grip, kissing her on the cheek and run to catch the rest of the group. Mort is leading them back into the sewers. What had been dry the day before now has ankle deep water. The only sound is the sloshing water echoing off the sides of these underground canals. No one is saying anything. Each person is alone with his or her thoughts. Soon Mort has led them through to another street and into another underground cavern. He leads them into an abandoned bombed-out building on the other side of the Ghetto.

Stopping for just a moment to check his bearings, Mort motions them on up a flight of stairs to an upper floor. Once there, he motions them all into a group. He's standing in front of an opening that appears to be an air vent. In a low tone he begins to speak.

"On the other end of this vent is a man with several rifles, pistols and ammunition for both. What I need is a volunteer to crawl through here to the other building with the money and begin the physical process of delivering the weapons back through the vent."

With the words hardly leaving Mort's lips, Izak is front and center. At this moment he can feel his own pulse pounding against his temples.

"I can do that, sir," he says without trying to sound eager.

Mort looks him over. What he is hoping for is that these young people will be skinny enough to fit through the vent. Izak looks to be a bit too large. Mort passes him by for the moment looking over some of the smaller girls. Spotting Rhena and without a word to Izak, he motions her come forward. "You, little Rhena. You'll do." He then chooses four more of the smallest girls.

With this task in place Mort approaches the opening and knocks four times. The sound reverberates across the metal duct. The agreed two knocks echo back. The next step is to make clear to this group that they are to follow Rhena into the vent.

"Okay skinny little girl, you are to hand this package to the people on the other side," he says handing her the money-filled envelope, "When they give you the guns and ammunition, you are then to hand each item to the first person behind you in the vent, that person will hand it to the next person like a fire bucket brigade until we pass everything from that building to this building."

As soon as each of these girls confirms they understand their instructions, Mort helps them into the vent. This pipe is approximately twenty-feet long bridging the two buildings with at least a sixty-foot drop between them. When the question of the human safety of this maneuver is weighed against the human cost of not performing it, it always falls on the side affecting the most people. In this case it's clearly on the side of taking the risk in the hopes that more than these few will be saved.

Fifteen minutes later with a sagging and groaning vent shaft and no major catastrophes the girls have been able to pass a half dozen rifles and two pistols along with a few hundred rounds of ammunition back through the perilous passage.

Mort is visibly pleased with this turn of events. As the weapons have passed without a hitch from these persuadable nonpartisans safely into the hands of the Resistance, he feels a touch of an emboldening joy. It's the kind of happiness that precedes the possibility of this becoming a game changer. It doesn't even have to be a game winner just as long as they as a people can demonstrate a meaningful resistance. This is an opportunity the whole Jewish Fighting Organization has been waiting for. The sentiment for defiance has been in place for some time. What's been missing is anything close to an even-playing field. What these weapons guarantee is they can at least now resist in some cases with deadly force.

Too much of a celebration is a luxury that can't sustain itself long without risking detection. After all, the marauding German patrols are ever present and obsessively determined to root out every Jew on the planet. With a renewed sense of purpose, it's time to get back to the bunker and plan the next maneuver.

Izak finds himself nearly carrying his weight in a bag full of ammunition. He's struggling with it but knows he can't let Mort detect his weakness lest he see it as a sign of incompetence. The weapons are useless without the bullets. The girls in turn are also responsible for the rifles and smaller arms. Marching back in single file, their undernourished bodies give the appearance of belonging to a ragtag army of scarecrows.

Mort is quietly reflective on the way back to the bunker. His first thoughts are beginning to mix with a new reality. Employing these arms is inevitably going to produce a change in the near future. *"There is no question that firing on the German army is going to hasten our demise but we can at least die courageously,"* is his recurring thought. Choosing how one is not going to die can be a freeing thought. With this new development a trip to Treblinka may be avoided.

Managing to dodge the German patrols and the Jewish Police (let alone the sycophantic Jews who would panic at the sight of armed resisters and likely turn them in) they arrive undetected back to the safety of their bunker.

The sight of these weapons is creating a renewed excitement. Many of these men have served in the Polish army and have a fond respect for these instruments. Mort allows these Partisans a few minutes of reflective memories before he gathers them around to begin a discussion of ideas.

"We need a method of operation. We can't just start shooting Germans without getting the most for our efforts. We have a limited supply of ammunition, every bullet has to count. In other words, we have to have a kill for every shot taken," says Mort.

A man by the name of David Wahlstetter is the first to react to Mort's game plan. He has been with Mort since the beginning of the deportations. Having lost both parents and an aunt, he's well aware of how persuasive the Germans have been in getting the Ghetto people to fall for their deceptive promise of a better life after they are resettled in the east.

"Give me a rifle and ten cartridges, place me on the third floor of any building and I'll guarantee you ten dead Germans, one for each bullet," says David with the confidence of one who is able to deliver. There is no room for bluster. It turns out that he had been a sniper in the Russian army and a well-decorated one at that. Mort has all the confidence in the world that David is capable of delivering on this seeming boast.

"Okay David, you have an assignment. We have inside information that the Jewish Police accompanied by German soldiers are going to start another wave of deportations day after tomorrow. We know what sector that will start in. You are going to be there along with your rifle to greet them."

Word is sent out among the various resistance fighters that events are beginning to come to a head and to be ready for what ever outcomes are going to begin to unfold. This means that over the next couple of days the rallying point is going to be around defending underground bunkers, putting Molotov cocktails together and being prepared to make sure our small-scale resources aren't wasted.

Mort and his fighters have all come to an agreement. "Our plan is to hit the Germans hard enough that they won't be so inclined to under-estimate our strength. The end result is the hopes of delaying some de-portations long enough that many more of our people may be smuggled out." This quickly becomes the focal point behind their courage to move forward with this plan.

Most Jewish life in all of Europe has met head on with their host country wanting them out. The result is that despite the Jewish protests coming out of these communities concerning their horrific mistreatment, the rest of the world has turned a deaf ear and regards it as a local issue. The Jewish Fighting Organization sprang out of this disregard.

"We must refuse to let the rest of the world decide our value. If we are going to survive as a people, we must fight for our lives and let our detractors know that our lives are going to become more expensive." These are words Mort and many others have come to live by and are also willing to die by.

A cloak of secrecy is stressed and re-stressed. Many in the Jewish community are still of the opinion that these resistance fighters are just making the Germans mad and the reprisals that are being taken against them is the fault of this band of lawless fighters.

The rest of this day is spent preparing for the Tuesday when the authorities will be making their way into the Ghetto to select the people for the next forced "resettlement." Meetings between the couple dozen Resistance organizations are keeping many of the younger generation busy while the older people are either too old or sick or even too complacent to get involved. Many more than what one would hope for have given up, deciding to choose suicide rather than let the Germans kill them.

While Mort is busy with the armed effort of the Resistance, Karol is determined to get more of their people out into the wooded areas where another group of the Resistance has sunk deep into the forests beyond the German's effort and determination to root them out. In order to accomplish this endeavor, it requires the cooperation of Polish nationals to either aid in the rescue attempts or at the least turn a forgetful eye at what they see.

Izak is working with Karol to gather more information from Aryans who are friendly toward the Jewish cause. Many of these are Catholic clergy who have acted independent of their Bishops to help smuggle orphaned Jewish children to Polish families who are willing to take the risks to conceal them.

On this day Karol is leading Izak through a new maze of tunnels that lead to a different part of Warsaw. This underground network has been marked with various materials, from paint to chalk, intended to acquaint the traveler with their location. After an hour of making their way through this maze, Karol stops. In front of them is a ladder leading upwards to a manhole cover. It's the permanent kind that has their ends embedded in their concrete wall. The luxury of rungs is not always available as the Germans have cut many of these steps off in the hopes of discouraging the use of these tunnels. In this case the steps lead upward to an opening in an obscure alley behind a Catholic church on the outskirts of the city.

With Izak close behind, Karol carefully slides the cover to one side and slowly raises his head above the opening. All he sees is the typical alley debris of abandoned and broken household materials that suggest they may have belonged to some previous era living a different life style. As soon as they extract themselves, Karol motions for Izak to slide the cover back in place and to follow him. Within seconds they slip through a set of folding doors that lead to a chamber beneath the church.

The first thing that comes to sight is a slightly illuminated room ahead of them. They're soon greeted by a rather tall, thin man. He's bearded and dressed in typical Polish farm clothing. He and Karol immediately embrace and exchange greetings.

"Moshe, I hope I am finding you well," says a rarely smiling Karol to this esteemed compatriot. He can't help but notice the humble dress this famous partisan is wearing.

Moshe Malinowski is by far the most celebrated rural legend and savior to so many escaping Jews. He has been responsible for creating a network where thousands of his people have found ways into Sweden, Denmark, Palestine and some even as faraway as Canada and Shanghai.

"Karol, my old friend. Yes, I'm still a day late and a dollar short but then for dying we always have time," replies Moshe with a wry grin.

Karol turns to Izak and pulling him by the arm presents him to Moshe. "Izak I want you to meet my friend. He has without a doubt done more to help our people than anyone. You can ask anyone. They'll tell you the same."

"Karol, Karol, what you don't see with your own eyes don't invent with your mouth," says this noticeably embarrassed Freedom Fighter. Turning to Izak he says, "This old friend is better than two new ones but he exaggerates. In truth, alone I'm not that important. It's only when we all work together that we are able to do good things."

Izak is impressed by the humility this man exhibits. He wonders if he could do the same.

CHAPTER 12

WOLFSKINDER

Reinie has managed to stick to the forested areas. From time to time throughout the morning hours he has heard the distant wail of a locomotive. This sound gives him confidence that he is still on the right track. What disturbs him is that the common ordinary sights and sounds of his native land are recomposing themselves as events which now must bear a suspicious eye and ear. Things can no longer be taken as they seem.

His destination remains the Baltic Sea region where he hopes to get a boat to Sweden, which by some miracle has managed to remain a neutral state throughout the war. Around noon, he encounters an unexpected impediment. It's a stream about twenty meters in width. Surveying this misadventure for a moment, he decides to view it as a possible game changer.

"I haven't had a bath in months," Reinie says. "What's more, I need to throw off any of my lingering scent in the event they try to hunt me with their dogs."

Within minutes, still wearing his prison clothing and holding Boris' stolen pack of clothing, boots, and lunch high over his head, he's soon up to his neck in cold water. In less than a second, he experiences the numbing chill rushing over his bare skin. As invigorating as it feels, he nonetheless determines after a five-minute stroll downstream that any scent will hopefully be done with. Dragging himself bone-chilled to the shore, he strips himself naked, tears off his ragged prison garb, and tosses it into the current. It occurs to him how nice it would be if all his present concerns could float away as easily as these disappearing symbols of his imprisonment.

Untying the dry bundle of Boris' clothing, he can't help but wonder how Boris must feel now about his contribution to this escape effort. Taking a moment to chuckle to himself about how difficult it's going to be for Boris to explain all this, he begins to make a more thorough search of this donation. To his surprise he discovers a bundle of German and Russian currency neatly folded in an inside pocket along with a couple gold coins. It is much more than a sergeant in the Russian army should have at any one time. This more or less confirms the suspicions that Boris could be bribed for special favors.

The cloudy sky seems to be flying apart trying to let the sun warm his emaciated body. Not willing to wait for that miracle, Reinie slips into Boris' dry Russian uniform. Another surprise "gift" from Boris is a military identification card. The picture is worn enough that unless one looks closely he may be able to pass. He folds the gold coins into the currency and slips it all into the side of his sock for safe keeping, then splurges on what's left of the confiscated lunch. He's flabbergasted to find how much his stomach has shrunk and how full he feels with such a small amount of food.

Upon checking his new timepiece again, he's amazed at how accurate his estimation has been as it's shortly after noon. Reinie is becoming more aware of this luxury of being free and finding such pleasure in something as mundane as a pocket watch. Entertaining himself with its ticking sound for a few minutes, he winds it a few twists and places it back in his pocket. He makes a new resolve to be much more alert to those things that could take this freedom away once again.

With this new resoluteness, Reinie tries to come up with a plan to put as much distance between himself and his captors in the shortest period of time. His mind continues to hark back to the railroad. *"I've got to figure a way of getting on one of those north bound freights."* Hearing the alluring sound once again of a nearby train, he estimates it must be less than a mile away. This new found purpose excites him as he hastens his step toward the distant sound. The forest is thick with fallen limbs and branches causing him to trip. Stumbling several times gives him the rational motive to slow down and measure his steps—after all isn't this the German way? *"Think Reinie, think!"* is becoming his mantra.

Forty-five minutes later, sweating and exhausted, Reinie stands before a bare railroad track. There is nothing about this particular topographic point that remotely suggests he could hop on a speeding boxcar: it's flat and straight. What does come into sight is a series of hills in the distance, maybe five or six miles up the tracks. With no other choices but to keep moving, he begins his self-ordered program. The sides of the rail bed are made up of loose stones with no assurance of a good foothold forcing him to walk between the rails. The rail ties are spaced just close enough together that it doesn't allow his usual stride. All in all, this trek is proving to be much more laborious than first thought. His focus is entirely determined by where his next step is going to land. Four boring hours later he arrives at the foothills of the ascent. It is definitely more challenging than it looked. His water is nearly depleted and he doesn't see any immediate way of replacing it.

He retreats back into the forest and conceals himself as best he can to regroup his thoughts. Finding a reasonably hidden berth, he lies down for a quick nap. A cool breeze wafts the fresh scent of pine across his face, soothing his spirit in a beguiling way. He soon drifts off into a peaceful sleep.

His next conscious moment is a startling pain in his side. Reinie snaps his eyes open only to find himself pinned to the ground by a heavy foot on his neck.

"Wake up you dirty *schweinehund*," growls a voice from above and still firmly keeping his foot on his throat. His first panicked thought is that the Russian guards have been able to track him down. With clearer eyes, he isn't looking at a Russian guard but rather a raggedy unkempt young man about his own age. Unable to speak with his vocal cords compressed, he makes an effort to rise up. This endeavor finds an even more crushing retaliation as his attacker puts his whole weight behind his effort to keep him debilitated. Despite his inability to move upward, Reinie is still able to shift his eyes around in that direction.

This raggedy stranger is shouting orders at what appears to be about a half dozen young people ranging in age from maybe ten years old to seventeen years old. Some are carrying carbines.

"Check his sorry ass for weapons," he barks speaking German at several of the younger ones as he continues to keep a firm foot on Reinie's neck. The youngsters scurry around, rifling through his pockets. Meanwhile another boy is placing a rope around Reinie's neck. As the boot is being released, he can feel the grip of the noose beginning to shut off the blood to his head.

The raggedy young man barks another insistent order. "Throw the end of that rope over that tree limb and hang this Roosky."

Reinie has been dragged to his feet in this interval and is desperately gasping and coughing for a breath. *"Please God help me to speak."* He feels as though he's about to pass out. He realizes that this German group of vigilante youth are about to hang who they believe to be a Russian soldier. All he can feel is the rope tightening and his neck stretching as his full weight is dangling off the ground. With all that he can muster with what air he has left in his lungs, he manages with a gasping voice to utter, "I am a German!"

Raggedy Guy snaps his head in Reinie's direction. His demeanor is a puzzled frown. "Where's his identification?" he bellows at a younger sycophant. The younger boy produces it immediately. He scrutinizes Reinie as his feet are jerking and his eyes begin to bulge. "This guy isn't the same guy in this picture," says Raggedy Guy as he concludes his scrutiny.

With a hand gesture, he orders Reinie to be lowered. With the same frown he takes a closer look at his intended sacrifice. Raggedy Guy is looking at the identification and then at this writhing uniformed soldier at his feet struggling to loosen the noose enough to get a breath. More than just puzzled, he orders the rope removed.

Still in full control and relaxing on a stump, with Reinie remaining at his feet, he gives him time to recover. After a few minutes and still with intermittent coughing, Reinie manages to begin to breathe easier.

"Okay Mr. German let's hear your story and it better be good because I don't mind hanging you twice."

Reinie spends the next half hour filling in the details of his life over the past six months. The part about the possibility of the Russians pursuing him with dogs has struck a chord.

"I don't like the idea of any Russians showing up," says Raggedy Guy, now looking provoked once again. "We've got to get out of here."

He signals to another young man with a nod. That young man begins to spread what appears to be pepper throughout the area as they begin a retreat taking them deeper into the forest.

"If those dogs get this far along, it'll be as far as they'll be willing to go with snoot full of pepper," says Raggedy Guy as he begins his withdrawal.

Reinie is recovered enough to be on his feet ready to tag along without an invitation. Nobody objects. The terrain is the same rough terrain that encouraged Reinie to take a nap a short time ago. The strain of his escape, a near-death situation and the challenge to keep up with this wolf pack of survivors is bringing him to near exhaustion. Within an hour and a half and after plodding through deep ravines of overgrowth and small creeks they emerge into a canopied area of matured hardwoods. There are a series of military tents with maybe fifty young people milling around. None of these people appear to be older than himself. What catches his attention is the number of emptied fifty-gallon steel drums being used for various kinds of meat smokers. He also notices a partial carcass that appears to be the butchered remains of a horse. One of the boys who was part of the group action involving his capture tosses a bag he had been carrying to the ground. It is full of turnips and potatoes gathered after a night's worth of raiding various abandoned root cellars.

The war-torn countryside yields little in new planting as the advancing Russian army has decimated everything in its path. The German farms have been confiscated by these same Soviets, forcing the previous owners into labor camps to face a future of starvation, disease, or to be worked to death. What they couldn't carry off, they left behind. Oftentimes these kids are pillaging around still rotting bodies left in the wake of a Russian scourge. The Russians in turn don't always find everything, thereby providing these young German pillagers a small bounty.

Raggedy Guy seems to be much more settled down in this more secure atmosphere. Offering Reinie a dipper of water, he extends his hand. "Sorry I had to rough you up the way I did but we can't be too careful. These damn Russians are getting thicker than flies around here. My name is Richard Hasse." Having already explained to Richard who he is, Reinie shakes his extended hand. Feeling a little more emboldened he takes a chance on asking Richard a few questions.

"What exactly is this place?"

Richard rolls a cigarette as he contemplates the question. Pausing long enough to light it, he studies the exhaling smoke. It's evident he's uncomfortable with the question.

"Look around you Reinie and tell me what you see," answers Richard with a request of his own.

Reinie searches the background, "All I see is a bunch of kids."

"That's what I see also. A bunch of kids with no parents and no one who gives a damn whether they live or die. Most of them are orphaned. Coming from families left with mothers who have died of typhus or mothers having been raped and brutalized to death for having resisted their Soviet assailants. Every girl above the age of ten has been molested by Russian soldiers. This, of course, is after their fathers had been either murdered trying to protect them or sent to labor camps. Others are kids whose parents died on the way to gulags and they managed to escape. If there's a tragic story, one of these kids owns it," says Richard, taking another drag on his cigarette. Some of these kids are Polish, some are German and many are Jewish.

Giving a moment's thought to what Richard has just said, Reinie is silent as a fuller impact of what this new Soviet domination means to them as Germans hits. The only question he feels compelled to ask is, "What's going to happen to them?"

Taking the last drag on his cigarette, Richard butts it with a dramatic sigh, "I honestly don't know. But then none of us know our future. We only know today."

Looking back again over this sea of children as young as eight years old, he sees a deliberate effort on each of their parts to portray a sense of belonging. Many of them are siblings from the same family. Others are single children with no relatives, now left totally on their own but lately finding a new meaning to life as they struggle with their loss. Each is hoping to adopt this camp as a makeshift place to keep their identity.

"If we can get to the Baltic coast, we have a chance to get into Sweden or Denmark or even into western Germany," says a confident Reinie.

"*You* may get to the Baltic but for me that's not a possibility. I'm a hunted man," says Richard in his pragmatic tone of voice.

Reinie is taken aback at Richard's statement of finality. "Why do you say that Richard?" he asks as though he is sure he can provide a solution by simply adding, "After all we're *all* hunted."

Without a word Richard has removed his shirt exposing his bare torso. Reinie remains mystified. So far this demonstration tells him nothing. Still without a word spoken, Reinie lifts his left arm. There remains the statement brainwashed into him since his father, a Waffen-SS officer, placed his son in a training camp for promising Hitler Youth. It's a black-inked letter "A" tattooed permanently giving a medic the information of blood type but more than this it forever connects him to Hitler's SS.

"This mark insures me that my future is limited. Unlike you only worrying about avoiding the Russians, I have the whole world after me," confesses Richard.

This takes Reinie back to the day his older brother rolled up the sleeves of his brown shirt to proudly show off his tattooed AB blood group type. This "blood group" was much more than simple information to a medic. It also aligned the bearer to a special distinction from ordinary soldiers. He has sworn a special allegiance to *Der Fuehrer*. But now the only distinction it gains its owner is a prompt execution.

For today the immediate necessity to provide this growing camp with food and fresh water remains its primary concern but always with a watchful eye for the enemy. Richard has become its de facto leader in spite of no official election. Maybe it's because of his background. If his military training has done nothing else, it emphasized leadership. Every aspect of life here is predicated on not being discovered. Making it through another day is the only reward offered for this kind of life. Because of the adolescent makeup of this camp and Richard's ability to make decisions, they look to him for security.

Again, in all likelihood because of his leadership background, Richard has, in fact, become the adult all these children look to to insure another day of life. He finds himself unable to turn his back on the suffering of these defenseless kids. In turn he has been pulled into a role he hardly asked for. There are nearly as many girls here as boys. However, in the end most will likely perish because of bad luck not because they lack of skills or smarts. The Russians continue to tighten the noose around any rogue Germans who are not willing to do their bidding and are especially ruthless with orphans since they have no apparent advocate. They more often than not regard these children as dispensable.

Richard himself carries the scars of a brutal confrontation he had in combat. The Russians were in the process of overrunning the town he and a group of teens were ordered to defend to the death. He had been minimally injured by shrapnel and managed to continue to fire a MG 08 machine gun long enough to cause the enemy to retreat. This allowed a day to evacuate the town. Those that remained alive fled with whatever possessions they were capable of carrying. Orphans were left to fend for themselves.

The young lieutenant who had been their commander was killed along with an equally inexperienced sergeant. This left a ragtag group of teens to make decisions separate from any command center. As in any uncoordinated war effort, mayhem takes mastery. Each soldier is left to be his own tactician. During this period of suspended combat, the young German soldiers who were left had a moment to decide their fate. The question of whether their cause remains worthy of their life or if they need to place their thoughts and actions against certain odds that insure they will die. What is left of the town by the time the Russians resume their shelling, besides the torn bodies of the dead, is Richard, several of his fellow Hitler Youth lads, and a couple dozen terrified orphans. Things are not looking good for them. Richard's natural inclination is to take things in hand.

A nearby forest is the only apparent option for a retreat but their window of opportunity is limited and must be swiftly coordinated. Richard has already made his decision.

"Anyone wanting to go with me is welcome. I find our position here indefensible and am ready to abandon it. What I'm going to suggest is that each of you gather all the food and drinking water you can carry and meet back here at dusk."

By dusk his little band of compliant cavaliers is gathered like so many lemmings waiting to be marshaled. Each had followed instructions to the tee. They came with water and food. Richard along with the remaining Brown Shirt compatriots still with him, gathered up all the weaponry and ammunition they could salvage, loaded it into a hand cart and began their flight into the forest at the edge of town.

No sooner had they than the Russians began to bomb the town. It continued all through the night until dawn. When they felt this seeming stronghold had been tenderized enough to risk a ground siege, they moved forward once again only to find no resistance.

This small consort of half-grown children unquestioningly followed Richard. Uncomplaining they trudged on. Fear drove their journey through the night even though the terrain was rough and unforgiving. The smaller children were supported by the older as they had a tendency to stumble in the dark and fall behind. By morning they had put considerable distance between themselves and their enemy.

This was the beginning of this marauding band of thieves. As time elapsed, the immediate need for flight gave over to other needs such as shelter. Fortunately Richard was aware of a hidden and abandoned military supply encampment nearby where they were able to commandeer tents. Never certain where they stood on the priority list of their conquerors, they nonetheless formed a network of sentinels ready to sound the alarm in the event of an enemy breech.

The onerous leadership of both Germany and Russia has been willing to sacrifice any number of lives as a justifiable end to their own personal ambitions. This account brings them to their present situation. It's only when adult leaders fail their constituents by disregarding the well-being of their communities and treat them as pawns in a chess match does it result in this horrific chaos. The end result of this policy has created unendurable chaos among their own people. Without a doubt women, children, and the elderly are always the tragic victims. People who have no dog in this hunt. Many children are made orphans before their civility is completed. They've had their innocence torn away leaving a raw underside. In many situations Richard has found himself acting as the surrogate parent to these orphans. It always results in battling their childish self-centered natural tendencies in favor of working as a team for the well-being of everyone. A daily dose of fear is the only human emotion that consistently places them on the same page.

In this circumstance things have been going well enough to have some squabbles begin among a couple of the girls. It escalates to a level of hair-pulling and name calling.

"You lying Polack-Jew bitch. You stole my lipstick," says a blond-haired fourteen year old.

"I didn't steal anything from you, you little Nazi witch," says an equally impudent dark-haired girl maybe a few years older speaking in broken German. No one has stepped in to attempt any sort of settlement. They rather seem to be enjoying the interruption in what has become an unremarkable routine. Realizing the danger of what actions like this can lead to, especially when it threatens the safety of the entire group, Richard steps in. He begins by physically separating the two girls. There is no question in anyone's mind who has spent any time with either of these young women that they are tough as nails and have survived because of their tenacity.

Richard makes quick work of the disputed lipstick by grabbing the tube and crushing it under his foot. In another quick maneuver, he places the younger, more aggressive girl on a seat that had been commandeered from a deserted disabled truck.

In spite of their common predicament, these girls hate each other. This small tempest has been brewing for some time and is finally coming to ahead. Both have taken to a man's world rather readily nonetheless both have a strong feminine disposition. The intense overwhelming tendency to still be female has caused one of these young ladies to be willing to risk the wrath of the other by filching her tube of lipstick.

Richard recognizes in a second who the true owner of the now flattened lipstick tube is. The fourteen year old's lips begin to quiver as she realizes the full thrust of her loss. It remained the only girly connection to her previous life.

CHAPTER 13

MOSHE

Moshe Malinowski, Karol and Izak are waiting in the caverns beneath Saint Stanislaus Catholic Church on the outskirts of Warsaw for one more person. Father Stephen Wesak has also been a relentless supporter of underground railroad that moves these ghetto orphans from certain death to a chance at life. The German chief of police has signed an order indicating that Poles discovered harboring Jews of any kind will be dealt with without a trial. Despite the surety of severe retribution many other of these righteous Poles continue operating in the face of the Nazi counter efforts.

Father Wesak is the last to arrive. Izak is introduced and once again is surprised at the cohesion of thought among portions of the Aryan population. It's always been those professing something from their Christian faith that has condemned him as a "dirty Jew." Now this priest is introduced to him as one who has remained sympathetic to the plight of his Jewish neighbors despite the risk.

"We have found room for four more. Unfortunately, two of these families request children young enough where they haven't learned a language. They fear the dialects of older children could arouse suspicions," reports Father Wesak.

The Church's official stand is that any children hidden in churches or monasteries have to be converted. Father Wesak makes little of this for the time being. First and foremost he wants as many of these children kept alive as possible.

This challenge is discussed and found to be manageable. It soon gives way to Moshe asserting his need for a person with a special skill set. He addresses this demand to Karol.

"We have need of someone who looks Aryan enough to pass as a Pole and possesses good Polish language skills. One who can easily blend in without drawing attention to themself."

Izak can hardly contain himself. This is the thing he has been longing to do. Not wanting to come across as overbold, he makes the decision to hold his tongue for the time being.

"What exactly would you expect from this person?" Karol asks.

Moshe measures the question. He gives a glancing thought at the good Father. The last thing he wants to do is reduce his credibility in the sight of the people who are willing to take risks for his Jewish people. But now he finds he can't measure his words in a way that will allow him to be seen as a man willing to turn the other cheek.

"We need someone who can deal with gun dealers in a way that doesn't arouse any suspicion. The last people they want to deal with are Jews. But they're greedy enough to deal with a fellow Pole as long as they believe the risk of getting caught is low."

Glancing once again at Father Wesak, he doesn't see any indication of disapproval. Instead the Father recognizes the uneasiness of the moment and takes a second to arrange this awkward state of affairs into an opinion.

"First, I want you all to know that many times we priests have to make pastoral decisions that may conflict with our Bishop's official opinion. My own private opinion driven by my conscience is that you may have to go to extraordinary means to protect yourselves against this evil. My continual prayer is that these children are protected in whatever way allows that end to be accomplished."

Izak continues to be amazed. This is a part of Aryan humanity that he has had little or no contact with. Except for a few recent occasions, his entire life has been one that has had to deal, in a negative way, with being a Jew.

The time soon arrives when all that can be discussed has been said. With time frames agreed on for the transport of the children and comradely embraces shared, Karol and Izak begin the trek back through the maze of damp tunnels.

The day is late on their arrival back to the safety of their bunker. Izak is greeted by his harried mother. Her mouth is smiling at his safe return but her eyes continue to show worry.

"Oh Izak, must you worry me so? There are so many other things you can do that are less dangerous," says Minnie holding his face in both her hands. He can smell the pungent odor of onions and garlic clinging to her skin. For a moment it takes him back to a gentler time when he was young boy and his mother would contest his behavior in the same way. He finds a familiar consolation in this mother-son exchange.

Izak would have to admit that what he is doing definitely keeps him at a high level of anxiety. Nonetheless, for him to do otherwise would be a worse death.

"Momma, you worry too much," is his only reply. What else can he say?

Meanwhile Karol has found Mort. The two of them are off to themselves in a far corner of the bunker. The miasma left from the cooking stoves and the cigarette smoke of those lucky enough to find them leaves these two in a haze. The conversation appears to be quietly intense. Both seem to be talking over the top of the other at times.

The many people who have met their obligations of food gathering as well as those responsible for gathering currency for more arms are beginning to funnel in. The women in charge of the food detail have their undertakings set up cafeteria-style allowing each person, as they filter in, to grab a bowl and eat at their leisure.

In the past the extraordinariness of these vaulted ceilings holding up this basement hideout have done nothing more than house supplies for the various enterprises carried on above them. They are at last receiving their due as a great structure as each brick echoes the appreciation for the role they've been assigned to provide safety to a beleaguered community of God's children.

The camaraderie runs high among the participants involved in the various resistance movements. It's no wonder the Germans have taken note of the exuberance of these young ghetto Jews. The type being more likely to form these troublesome groups have of late become the prime targets for "relocation." In many instances a quick bullet to the head serves the same end and leaves room on the trains for the more compliant and trusting victims.

Soon Mort and Karol emerge into a larger more central portion of the bunker. It's obvious they have something important to say. There is no longer any hope for survival to those who remain law-abiding citizens. At best life will be limited to the few who decide to take their destinies into their own hands. Mort begins once again to reiterate the pronouncements for an end of their own choosing. His voice is taking on a stronger intonation as he is sparing no restraints.

"In the coming days we are going to be met by unrelenting deterrents. As we have sounded the alarm that the Germans are planning a much larger and more thorough removal of our Ghetto, in turn our resistance groups have joined forces with the Polish resistance to supply us with more arms. As a people worthy of the dignity God has given us, we are determined not to go to our death as so many fish caught in a barrel. We can die with the dignity that comes with defying our accusers and their hellish propaganda."

Pausing for a moment to draw on a cigarette, he continues. "Karol is in charge of getting more children out of here and I'm dedicating my life to killing as many of these Nazi bastards as I can. Those of you who wish to stand with either cause gather behind us."

Izak is drawn to the action inaugurated by Mort but as he begins in that direction, Minnie with a no nonsense distinctiveness pushes him into Karol's line. Looking at his mother with surprise at her tenacity, he knows better than try and defy her. Her look is the same direct look he saw as a youngster when he would try to overpower her decision.

Karol, noticing the commotion turns to Izak and with a wink says, "Good choice. You'll live longer."

Rhena and Sara also line up behind Karol. Minnie's expression has returned to the strained look of a worried mother. She realizes the probable result of all of their fates but doesn't wish to be left alive one moment after the death of either of her last two children. She hugs them both as she turns to join the other women. They have been assigned to make Molotov cocktails.

Mort takes his crew to the cache of weapons. Each arms himself with a rifle or pistol and as much ammunition as he can carry. Another group carries boxes of Molotov cocktails. They are given water and food and assigned to their positions.

The underground intelligence indicates the enemy will be making a surprise visit early next morning. The word is out for those who have been contacted for deportation to not report and to stay off the streets. As the young Ghetto militia members make their way to their assigned posts, they are greeted by emblematic street scenes that have become common place for ghetto life. There are workers with hand carts picking up corpses with hardly enough flesh left to bury. Children dressed in rags with sick and dying parents are begging for food. Other already orphaned children are trying their best to stay alive only to find themselves already marked for death. Frozen pipes and raw sewage are left to find their own ends. Nonetheless in spite of all this misery there are still people clinging to the hope that it's only a matter of time and the Nazi insanity will stop.

On another front, Karol and his brigade are making their way to a hidden location housing a group of orphans. The effort at this point is to keep these children healthy long enough to make a perilous journey that can last several days. They range in age from newborns to a couple years.

Helpless children continue to be the victims regardless of who makes the decisions. The Nazis determine at what rate the Jewish children will die slowed only by the limitations of their killing apparatus. On the other hand, these benevolent rescuers are choosing who can live deterred only because of a lack benefactors. However, they are of one mind: to get as many children out as possible

The woman in charge of this orphanage (disguised as a hospital or risk the Nazis emptying it of the undesired children) is not given any special consideration by the Jewish council nor given any special treatment for these orphans. It seems that all those in power roles find meeting the needs of these innocents too high a maintenance problem to deal with. Considering their limited resources, it's easier to let them die.

All the people committed to this effort no longer have an intact family. They have all suffered the loss of parents, spouses, brothers, sisters, neighbors, friends and many have had to endure the loss of their own defenseless children. Unfortunately some find themselves here out of shame and guilt over their inability to protect their loved ones. Many others remain dedicated for all kinds of benevolent reasons. In doing so, they have committed their lives to finding havens for these who cannot survive but for the selfless efforts of themselves.

There is the usual sense of urgency here this evening as the caregivers pack all the needed supplies these babies are going to need plus providing two wet nurses and giving endless details to the specific needs of each of them. Rhena and Sara as well as the others involved in this risky venture are taking time to listen to the instructions being measured out by these nannies.

Karol also has a sense of urgency to make use of the limited time they have left to bring a good result to this undertaking. He's becoming visibly agitated as the process to move this program forward is being stalled with all this verbiage.

"Please ladies we have to move forward. We have a deadline to meet and a closing window of opportunity to get it done," pleads Karol attempting to be as patient as the mission allows.

Giving a quick head count of the number of children being prepared for this evacuation, Karol notices several more than he had placements for. Rather than argue with these ladies whose habit it is to count on someone on the other end of this project to find arrangements for the extras, he knows Father Wesak will find room somewhere in various willing convents and monasteries.

Izak and several of the other males are at a complete loss as to what their role in all this is to be. All of them are supplied with forged documents identifying them as Poles. They have put on different clothing. For the SS to discover a Jew on the Aryan side of the wall means immediate hanging.

Much to the satisfaction of Karol, the troupe is soon under way. They have gained the use of kerosene lamps to help guide them through the darkness of the sewers. These are proving to be much more convenient than candles. The babies are presently content and well fed. They have all been placed in a bag to be carried on the back of their chaperone and then suspended by a support strap across the carrier's forehead. This allows each caretaker to carry needed supplies.

Izak and a few of the other boys have discovered what their role is. It's not exactly what they had envisioned. They would have preferred a spot on top of a building armed with a rifle, picking off Germans. Instead they have been assigned the task of carrying the two year olds. The way is as arduous as anyone can reckon. There are places where the water has risen and the smell of raw sewage permeates the air. Some sections are so low they demand crawling on one's hands and knees, others allow a six footer to stand up straight.

The hours can't go by fast enough. The contentment of these children never seems to be on the schedule. The wet nurses are exhausted from a hard day at the orphanage as is everyone else. What keeps these programs moving forward is an altruistic urgency mixed with a healthy dose of adrenalin.

After nearly an all-night journey, the familiar ladder leading up to the alley behind St. Stanislaus comes into sight. By this time the children are stressed, making a cacophonous sound that can't be hidden. The church staff is ready to make this transfer as quickly as possible. They have the back doors open and are ready to guide this bad-smelling, motley crew into the safety of its fortress walls. The babies soon disappear into another section of the church leaving this heroic team to eat a prepared breakfast of kielbasa and cheese.

Their attention shortly shifts from breakfast to a figure dominating a narrow corridor leading into their chamber. It's Moshe. He and Karol embrace as is their custom.

"I can't express in words the importance of your work, Karol," says a visibly impressed Moshe.

In an attempt to take Moshe's attention from himself, Karol introduces the entire team to this legendary figure.

After a short respite, Moshe calls Karol aside. "I'm wondering if you have given any thought to coming up with someone who can work with me and the Polish resistance. We are still in negotiations with them to bring in more arms."

Karol signals Izak to come into their circle. He says, "I believe I have your man."

Moshe remembers Izak from their previous get together. Looking him over, he proceeds to ask him a few questions, "What makes you think you're the guy I need?"

Izak's mind is running at the speed of light as he quickly processes Moshe's question. "Because I spent a year successfully passing myself off as a Polack. I know how they think and talk."

Continuing to look him over, Moshe returns with another question, "Why should I believe that you're not going to cut and run if things get a little dicey?"

This last question leaves Izak stunned for a moment. It takes him a minute to review his life over the past few years. "Because, Sir, I have never run from anything."

Moshe can't help but be taken by the tenaciousness this young man is attempting to put across.

"How old are you son?" is his next question.

Izak clears his throat. He's quite self-conscious of his young age.

"Eighteen, soon to be nineteen," he admits.

Still watching for a crack in the behavior of this young blood, he poses yet another question. "Can you follow orders?"

Of all the questions Moshe has asked, this is the one both of them realize is the most important.

Without a moment's hesitation or evasion of mind, he shoots back, "Yes, Sir!"

A small, wry grin makes its way to Moshe's face.

"Okay kid we'll give you a try," he says embracing Izak, kissing him enthusiastically on both cheeks.

Rhena is watching and listening as best she can the goings on between her brother and Moshe. The reality of what she is watching is that her brother is going off in another direction alone. What is even more evident is that she and her mother are going to be left alone without his strength. This gives her a tinge of panic along with an awareness that things are changing yet once again. He hugs his sister goodbye.

"Tell Momma I'll be in touch," he says as he heads off with Moshe.

Satisfied his job is finished, Karol gathers up his entourage and makes ready to return but not until he asks Father Wesak about a chance of other placements.

"Let me take care of these first, my friend, and then we'll see about others."

With enough said for the time being and everything finished for now, Karol's group is anxious to be on its way. Measuring each step, they gingerly head back down the ladder, disappearing once more into the sewer and leaving Izak behind with Moshe.

CHAPTER 14

THE REBELLION

Karol's team finds the journey back to the Ghetto not nearly as exhausting. Nonetheless, by the time they reach the bunker they're all ready for some sleep. These operations are as emotionally draining as they are physically.

Minnie's face takes a more relaxed look as she spots Rhena. She gives her a hug and kiss. She then begins looking around for her other progeny.

"Where's your brother?" she asks. Her countenance immediately returns to a harried look.

Rhena has stressed about this encounter all the way back from the church. She is well aware that this moment with her mother will remain front and center until Izak's fate is determined. Trying her best to play Izak's absence down, she struggles for the right words hoping she can pull it off. She manages to begin slowly with a relaxed tone.

"He decided to stay back and help with placing the children," lies Rhena.

Her mother places her hand to her mouth with a gasp.

"You are telling me he's not coming back aren't you. He's dead isn't he?" Minnie begins to sob.

Karol, overhearing the conversation, puts a comforting hand on Minnie's shoulder at the same time giving Rhena a glance that says, *"Let me do what I can."*

"Mrs. Nowak, what Rhena is trying to tell you is that Izak's skills are needed with Moshe and no, he isn't dead. Our resistance efforts are taking on many different facets and we must use all our tools in the best way we know how," says Karol.

Minnie will have no part of this and is almost inconsolable. Her friend, Eva, eventually intervenes long enough to let her get her cry out of the way. Karol, certainly not wanting to spend time with matters he considers to be beyond his power to resolve, wastes no time moving on to other pressing tasks. This leaves the women to do for Minnie what he considers to be more within their purview anyway.

In a short time Mort enters the bunker. With an abrupt hand signal, he motions for Karol to join him. Karol knows without being told something is about to take place. The tension on Mort's face tells the whole story. Information is making its way through the underground that the Germans are planning a full assault on the Ghetto. Making their way to a remote corner, Mort begins to question Karol about Moshe's ability to deliver some weapons.

Before Karol can respond the resonating sound of a number of explosions rip through the air of the bunker. There is no mistaking this for an accident.

"OH MY GOD. THEY'VE COME!" shouts Mort. The look on his face reflects that of a man who is shaken to his core. In the next motion, with rifle in hand, he is on the move. His adrenalin shoots throughout his entire body placing every facet of his being on high alert. Within minutes he has placed himself in a position to have a clear view of the whole street. Directly in front of him are two SS soldiers laying dead in the street. Their normally intimidating black uniforms are helplessly bloodstained.

His brain spins in high gear as he realizes for the first time that they have killed two Germans and the rest of the brigade is beginning to retreat with shots still continuing to hit their mark. Three more downed enemy soldiers lay dying alone in the streets as their comrades pick up their pace into a full retreat. Looking up, he catches the form of David Wahlstetter in his assigned sniper tower.

There is no cover for these surprised SS soldiers. Their normal punctilious sense of order has quickly crumbled. Now, out of fear, they abandon their dead leaving them laying where they fall, making a full retreat out of the Ghetto. The best laid plans have a way of changing when one takes a hard hit to the gut.

After the last shot is fired there is a silence. It's a silence that marks an unprecedented event in the lives of all Jewish people. What has just happened is that a handful of resisters armed with nothing more than a few rifles, pistols and homemade grenades have staved off one of the most powerful armies in the world. Granted, they all realize that at best this victory will be short-lived but for this precious moment, they can celebrate a victory.

Within minutes of this triumph a fuller appreciation of this success erupts into spontaneous cheers. Mort is ecstatic. He runs from fighter to fighter hugging each and kissing cheeks. As the news spreads of this unprecedented shutout win, people by the hundreds are beginning to emerge from underground bunkers. A stranger to this whole scenario would have believed they had won much more than a mere street fight. Winning this skirmish is as noble to this ragtag army of resisters as if they had won a war. For to this handful of fighters this victory lacks nothing. It is indeed as sweet a reprisal as could be asked for. At least for this day they have succeeded in successfully tormenting their tormentors.

The celebration can't be stemmed. People are in the streets playing music and dancing. They're relishing every minute of this victory. The by-product of defeating this group of trained German soldiers is a renewed belief in themselves as a people. Many more young men and woman are exhibiting a willingness to fight and showing more than a casual interest in joining the resistance. A small victory such as this is enough to rejuvenate these younger people's willingness as individuals to fight not just for themselves but for their whole culture.

The words of a smiling old Rabbi are overheard as he puts his hands and eyes up to the heavens. "They may kill us all but we must show them the value in what is being put to death. It will be the world's loss. But for now we drink wine and dance."

As these things go, the good feelings begin to diminish as new information comes to light. The word on the street is that the Nazi forces are regrouping and will seek reprisals in their own way and in their own time. They know they had been broadsided this time and are more than determined to make these Jews pay dearly for every German who dies in the streets.

Mort is busy with a fresh sense of purpose. He is busy coordinating the twenty-two or more resistance groups left to try and defend the mere 50,000 left of the 400,000 Ghetto Jews who lived here. He is well aware that the Judenrat is a council made up of Jews who can never be trusted because they are coerced by the SS and the same is true of the Jewish police. Part of the responsibilities of both these organizations is assisting the Nazis in selecting the next group to be sent to the Treblinka gas chambers. The only reward these agencies receive is a reprieve for themselves for turning on the rest of the community.

"The self-serving black guards actually believe they will be spared if they cooperate," says Mort with a contemptuous grin. Pausing for a moment, he adds, "When their usefulness is finished, they'll be finished." He is obviously taking more than a little delight with this second thought.

Now more than ever, Mort can use Moshe's connections to the Polish resistance. He needs every weapon they can lay their hands on. Recently they were fortunate that in the rush to retreat a Nazi soldier dropped a large caliber machine gun along with a box of ammunition. This piece of luck gives them an extraordinary advantage they wouldn't have without it but they need much more. In just the last day they have had more than 400 young male and female resisters want to become part of the Ghetto resistance. Along with that, they are relying on the skills of saboteurs to improve their use of the Molotov cocktails. It's possible to wipe out a tank when one of these devices is in the right hands.

Mort is obsessed with killing as many Nazis as possible and his primary emphasis is on getting the weaponry to accomplish this goal. "We need to get word to Moshe as to how badly we need these weapons. He needs to understand the urgency of this operation," says Mort to Karol.

Karol agrees and promises his brother that he'll do all he can to make this happen. Since they've demonstrated significantly enough that they don't have to lie down like cowards, they have emboldened the community enough to raise more funds for arms. By the next day Karol has sent a dispatch to Moshe along with the funds.

Unexpectedly, within hours Izak makes an appearance. He first runs into Karol. "What the hell you doing here?" blurts Karol.

"I've got a surprise for you," says Izak motioning Karol to follow him.

He leads him back into the sewer where they encounter four other compatriots. They are standing around a push cart loaded with at least a couple dozen rifles along with several crates of ammunition.

"Mazel Tov." It's all that Karol can come up with at the moment but then it's all that needs to be said. Within moments his Mazel Tov has drawn enough attention back in the bunker to bring all the help they need to get things unloaded.

All this hoopla has brought Minnie to the forefront. She is looking straight at her son. Izak makes eye contact at the same time. Approaching his mother, he manages a stupid grin.

"Hello Momma," is all he can muster.

With one swift swat, she smacks squarely across his face, leaving him startled.

"What do you mean to worry your momma like this?" With that she embraces him covering him with kisses.

"Momma stop! Stop! Stop!" Noticeably embarrassed, Izak tries to pull away from his mother's near death grip.

Finally letting loose of him, she grabs him by his ear.

"Promise your momma, you will never do this again."

Not able to move without tearing his ear from the side of his head, Izak exclaims, "Okay Momma, okay, I won't."

Rhena is also happy to see her brother. The two of them drift off to a part of the room where they can talk for a few minutes alone.

"Tell me, brother what you did to get these rifles," implores his sister.

Izak begins his tale by telling her how Moshe has a hidden compound in the forest and how well organized and dedicated his resistance group is.

"Together with a small number of the Polish resistance we assisted them in attacking a Nazi supply truck bogged down trying to get through a muddy road. We split the loot up and this is part of it," offers Izak.

Rhena listens intently with a tinge of envy for the part her brother is playing in the resistance. He in turn is curious about what happened with their encounter with the SS in the previous days. Rhena gladly shares how shocked the Nazi troops were. "When our guys opened up on them, they ran like baby girls," she reports with a good portion of glee in her voice. "The street was littered with their dead guys. They were so scared they left them there," she continues.

Izak listens with interest. It's obvious that he has yet some unanswered questions to ask his sister.

"Were you part of that attack?" His concern cannot be hidden. His voice tells it all.

Rhena knows her big brother well enough to know when to downplay her part in anything dangerous.

"Well yes," she says with a clear amount of hesitation, "I was well hidden with Sara and we threw some grenades."

Izak is wrought with concern for his little sister's role in this dangerous undertaking. But unlike his mother, he only says, "Be careful little girl. You know I love you."

The tears well up in both their eyes as the realization of how tenuous both their lives have become.

"I love you, too, big brother."

They take a moment to hug one another and go their separate ways.

In the meantime, word has reached Mort and within minutes he arrives on the scene. The sight of the rifles gives him a revived sense of accomplishment. Their Polish benefactors aren't particularly "Jew lovers" but they have been inspired by the tenacity of these otherwise peaceful people and their never-ending supply of gold. They have come to realize that both are fighting a common enemy and are happy to have an ally.

Several members of the other resistance groups have been notified. They in turn are given a share of rifles and ammunition. These weapons may seem insignificant against the seeming inexhaustible supply of arms provided to Hitler's SS guard but it is significant for this community to have the ability to bring forward such unrest among their adversary. The underground news of this has reached the death camps and is inspiring even those Jewish resistance groups that have managed to invade these places to dig yet deeper roots.

What remains disheartening is the lack of concern the rest of the world is taking toward offering any support. This kind of wide-spread reinforcement would significantly improve their chance of survival. At this point moral victories are all they can hope for and then try to envisage these to be enough to sustain them through another barrage of Nazi attacks.

Despite the overwhelming odds, Mort's small band of partisans stay committed. They know what they need to do and are willing to place themselves in harm's way to simply have their efforts undermine Nazi ambitions.

Despite Minnie's protests, Izak returns to his commitment with Moshe. Rhena and Sara also find themselves choosing assignments that most certainly will draw them into a deeper engagement with risk.

Regrettably Minnie has withdrawn more and more into despair as the daily events in her life seem to be quickly spiraling downward. She daily reviews her unremitting circumstances and how they continue to plague her. She finds them to be unrelenting and much too intrusive. The growing disconnect between her past life and the reality of the present continues to cause her great distress. Consequently, as her days move forward her temperament deteriorates even more and she finds her life impossible. Recently she is spending more and more of her day wishing for death. Unfortunately the sun can't shine through a window whose owner has pulled the blind.

Rhena, like so many of the young, tends to trust the moment. *"I'm alive now. I'll worry about death later."* The young can hardly imagine not having life and usually live it this way right to the end. It's truly a gift they've been granted and have naturally embraced.

She has become more involved with the community militia along with Sara. They have volunteered to make Molotov cocktails along with many more of the young. It's an arduous chore, increasing the likelihood that those involved will leave this world smelling like gasoline.

Sentinels with radios and ram's horns are set throughout the Ghetto ready to sound the alarm. On the fifth day following their first encounter, those on the walkie-talkies begin to radio the alert at one of the gates leading into the Ghetto. The Nazis have launched another offensive. There is a mad rush for each person to cannonball toward their assigned post. The adrenalin is pumping in every man, woman, and child as the sight of a tank becomes more than a distant prospect.

This extremely prodigious monster lumbers its way into the Ghetto with its diesel engine echoing off the walls of the buildings. This only tends to magnify its already imposing presence. Behind it is a column of soldiers fully armed with fixed bayonets ready to engage in hand-to-hand combat. Without warning, the tank suddenly discharges a round announcing its mightiness. With the accompanying compression, the huge giant squats down on its haunches forcing the ground around its track to blow out a cloud of street dust. Simultaneously, a hundred yards down the street, another explosion rocks a building as the shell finds its target. The brick and mortar debris from the structure bounces off the street like so many marbles in a playground.

With this unprecedented change of events, there is not an immediate response by the Jewish partisans. They are, at least for the moment, trying to assess this new development. Rhena and Sara have been placed on top of a three-story building along the narrow street. The tank is lumbering its way slowly and purposely, swinging its cannon-fitted turret from side to side implying its readiness to fire at will. Without warning another shell is fired, drilling its way through an apartment building. Its chosen path has now brought this deadly machine directly below Rhena.

She is barely peeking over the top of the wall in the hopes that she won't be discovered. In doing so she notices something that catches her attention. THE HATCH IS OPEN! She can feel her heart pounding and her palms are sweating. In a flash she grabs a grenade, pulls the pin, stands up still peering over the retaining wall and in one toss she lands the grenade into the tank's open turret. A moment later there is an explosion with the tank simultaneously coming to a halt.

As if on cue, shooting begins from every corner of the street. Once again the SS soldiers retreat leaving their dead lying in the street. Once again they draw back through the gate that holds in these newly-enlivened avengers. If this were not enough, the Polish resistance has placed snipers on the outside of the wall and is selectively picking off SS officers.

There isn't the same jubilation among these wary partisans as the last time. A greater realization that the Germans intend to increase the stakes until they win is causing this apprehension. Not to say these Jewish fighters aren't in awe of this teenage girl's performance as they readily lionize her but a somberness has replaced their inclination to celebrate.

There can be no question as to the bravura shown by Rhena on this fateful morning. Disregarding overwhelming odds, she managed to miraculously save the day, which had begun with the Nazi's full expectations of wiping them out. From here on Mort stops dismissing her youthfulness and her gender as a liability and begins to include her in his strategic planning.

She works tirelessly to prove herself worthy of the new responsibilities that have been placed on her. Sara remains her closest confident and shares her vigor for risk. The younger men in particular are willing to view her as a competent comrade in arms. Notwithstanding the risks, she is accepted on an equal footing with the male partisans and now insists on joining with partisan missions.

"We are all part of the same destiny. We all need to live or die together as one," she is heard to say as she encourages a group of younger people to join the Resistance and to take up arms. A rift has developed between the younger and older people in the Ghetto where the older people remain convinced that if they obey the Nazi directives they'll remain safe. They can't believe the German leadership could be so remiss as to destroy a talented Jewish work force. They are determined in their belief that the irresponsible youth are jeopardizing the Ghetto. But with a constant stream of communication and connectedness between the different factions of the Resistance, the younger people are much more aware of the truth in the devastating rumors that are coming out of these so called "work camps."

At this juncture, Karol is determined to smuggle as many people out of the Ghetto as possible. Rhena has become one of his most trusted envoys as she serves as a guide for those underground groups who need to move quickly through the sewers. She particularly finds this satisfying because many of these groups wish to be taken to Moshe's forest enclave where she can then see her brother.

On this particular mission she, along with Sara, has brought a group of bomb makers to Moshe's encampment. It's an enclave deep in the forest area outside Warsaw. These partisans know these forests like the back of their hand. The Germans are reluctant to search them out for fear of getting lost or surrounded.

This compound is made up of 120 combatants, both men and women. They live in various crude huts made of logs and thatch that have been hastily thrown together and made to look like the terrain. Most dwell in underground dugouts called *zemilyankas*, all well-camouflaged. Some have made haystacks in abandoned farms their abode.

There are also many non-combatants. Some who are too old to fight nonetheless do various tasks like gathering fire wood, baking bread, or repairing weapons, even making or repairing boots. There is no skill that can't be utilized.

As is true of every person in these war-torn countries, food is a constant concern. Feeding this many people every day is no easy task and requires diligent effort. In some cases the Germans have abandoned military compounds with huge stores of food but in turn have left the area heavily mined before retreating. All of these have to be carefully compromised at great risk. During these life threatening times, most Jews have set aside dietary restrictions in favor of survival and will eat anything that will move their survival forward. The local population of farmers is expected to supply the Nazis with a quota of cows, pigs, chickens and potatoes each month but if the partisans get there first and take them at gun point, the poor farmer has nothing to give the Germans.

Smoke from fires is always a risk so fires are kept small and inside. Smoke inhalation is a reality that can't be avoided and causes many to have lung problems. If this were not enough, bathing is practically nonexistent. Consequently, they're for the most part covered with smoke soot.

Typhus spread by lice is an ongoing concern. The close quarters and inability to regularly boil clothing exacerbates the problem. Some are willing to risk sleeping outdoors all winter rather than risk the disease. The medical demands are unending, putting a strain on their sparse supplies. Bullet wounds are numerous. The bullet is either left in to fester or someone with limited expertise removes it using only various knives. Infection is common and so is death.

Right away Rhena asks the whereabouts of her brother. She's informed that he's on sentinel duty and seeks him out. After finding him in a tree stand near the edge of a village, they exchange embraces and begin to quiz one another for the latest goings on in each other's life. Izak is particularly concerned for their mother.

Rhena tries to be positive in dealing with their mother's depression alone but is happy to re-establish her relationship with her brother considering that he's the only other family confidant she has.

"I don't think that Momma wants to live anymore," reports a despondent sister. "She's beginning to look so old."

"Things have been hard on all of us and I see people like momma all the time but I'm afraid you're right. She's rightfully tormented by the way her life has fallen apart," says Izak regretfully.

With Izak's sentinel duty over, the two of them make their way back to the main camp. It's just in time to have Moshe call Izak into a conference along with several others. Moshe has been involved with the resistance movement in various ways for twenty of his thirty years. The strain this kind of life exacts shows on his face. His parents were among the earliest of Hitler's victims taken to Auschwitz and gassed. His father was a machinist and had been promised work in a war plant. Along with a younger sister they barely walked through the gate when they were led to their death. His mind is never far from these tragedies. They serve to fuel his resolve to prevent this from happening to others.

Moshe informs them of a new development. They have received an intelligence report stating that a supply train with munitions and rations is making its way to Warsaw for the purpose of resupplying the SS brigade stationed there. The unrelenting concern Moshe has for this project is how they can overcome the increasingly difficult odds and successfully commandeer this train.

"We desperately need those supplies for ourselves. The only problem is they will have superior manpower and weapons to our few carbines. We need to come up with a plan that will make an even playing field," says Moshe. "That's why I have called this meeting. I believe we have to make this work or we aren't going to make it here."

All eyes and minds are paying close attention to everything he has to say. Everyone is quietly racking their thoughts for a workable solution.

One man suggests, "Let's commandeer the engine and stop the train."

This plan is immediately eliminated due to the impossibility of getting enough men on a train without being shot.

Another suggests they wait until the train stops for water and coal. This too is full of conditions and circumstances that can't be overcome when facing the superior force that's reported to be on board.

Rhena and Sara are on the outside edge of this discussion as neither of them have been invited to share their opinions. They can hear clearly all that's being suggested. Rhena is looking at the group of people she just brought to the compound. Among them she sees the answer to their dilemma. Coyly walking in on the discussion, she has her arm shyly half raised in an attempt to be asked to speak. The men all turn their attention toward Moshe to see how he handles this interloper. He stands quietly for a moment deciding how he's going to handle this uninvited interruption.

Rhena doesn't wait for Moshe's okay before she begins to speak. "You have your answer in these men I brought today. They are bomb makers and have served us well with our battles in the Ghetto. I suggest you use them to make enough bombs to blow up the entire train. That will either kill or stun enough of their troops to allow our men the upper hand."

Moshe along with everyone in the meeting is silenced by the forthright solution to their problem. Izak in particular stands astounded at his sister's quick resolution. They were all aware of Rhena's heroic action against the Nazi tank. Now they are experiencing first hand how this precocious teen's mind works.

A grin from ear to ear accompanies an embrace and kiss from this war-worn warrior as he readily accepts her plan. He finally finds the words to address her. "Young lady you are brilliant. I heard of your boldness in the Ghetto. Now I'm beginning to see it for myself. I'd like to invite you to help us put your idea into action."

Rhena is taken aback yet again by what she may be getting herself into. Glancing at her brother, she can see the pride he has in her as he nods an okay.

The rest of the day is spent in scheming how and where will make the best time and place to act. By the end of the day, they have visited several places along the tracks to determine the best place to carry through with their initiatives.

Moshe would like to have this maneuver take place in such a way that the Jewish resistance doesn't receive the blame. There are plenty of Polish resisters about that could also be held responsible as well. He's hoping they can pull it off without leaving any kind of silent signs.

By late in the afternoon they have found what they consider to be an ideal location. It's far enough away from the area the Germans know is active with Jewish resistance, yet close enough to make a decent getaway. It's also decided that none of their dead or wounded can be left behind because an easy identification can be quickly made due to each man being circumcised.

All that is left to do now is to place sentinels around a perimeter to keep watch for anyone nosy enough to disrupt their work. With this done, they begin the arduous task of discretely placing the bombs under the middle of the tracks. A half dozen are placed strategically along a 500-meter stretch. Each is wired individually to a plunger detonator.

This train is expected to come through at 2:30 a.m. The decision is made to stay on site until the train arrives, which by this time is only six hours a way. The weather is beginning to change as it's now the end of March and the days and nights stay above freezing temperatures. They are in a remote enough area that they feel they can risk a few small fires to at least take the chill off.

Sentinels are repeatedly changed as they continue with a hard-nosed concern for security. Izak is taking his turn at midnight so he will be available when the train comes through. The Germans pride themselves on how efficiently they continue to remain on schedule despite being at war, so 2:30 a.m. means they had better be fully prepared at 2:30 a.m.

Rhena and Sara have both been given detonators. The plan is when Moshe first blows off his the rest are to simultaneously detonate theirs. This will hopefully have a devastating effect on everybody who will be riding on the train. They calculate the train will be ready to plunder as soon as things quit moving which could take at least twenty seconds considering the speed the train will be traveling.

Everyone they engage has to die. There can be no witnesses left alive. If not dead already, they need one bullet to the head and all handguns, rifles and cartridges must be removed along with any valuables that can be used to barter for food later.

The night is quiet save for a forlorn wolf howling in the distance. There are some parallels that can be drawn between the wolf and this little band of partisans. Each has their own agenda and both hope that their struggle to remain at the top of the food chain will concede to them a good outcome. There is no moon and the sky is clear. It could be a good night to live. Or die.

The first sound to attract their attention is a faint rustling of the wind. Moshe is barely seen as he bends down on his knees with his head turned in such a way that his right ear is on the track. With the distant train pounding on the rails reverberating in his ear, he hurriedly rises to his feet. Making his way back to his station, he announces, "It's on its way. Be ready!"

The faint wind sound is becoming a rumbling as the big steam-driven Goliath comes closer. Rhena's hands are beginning to tremble slightly as she places them on the handles of her detonator. Her breathing and heart rate have increased. She realizes the importance of this mission and in less than a minute all hell is going to break loose. The big headlight on the engine is oscillating from side to side searching its way closer and closer. Moshe has the detonator that will blow the track out from under the locomotive. Rhena and Sara and several others will dislodge the railcars. Izak and fifty or so additional partisans will attack the derailed train. The locomotive is close enough now that denoting the headlight's slight vibrating movement is visible and the thundering sensation shaking the ground is felt by everyone.

In a split second Moshe has plunged his detonator handle to the bottom followed by a huge explosion. BOOM! Fire and steam are bursting into the sky abruptly lighted up by the explosion. The engine's momentum is still pushing it forward but now on its side digging up dirt, rock, trees and every other unfortunate obstacle in its path. In another split second Rhena and her group have followed Moshe's lead. BOOM! BOOM! BOOM! What follows are railcars being tossed in the air like so many cardboard boxes. The sound of the explosions has quickly passed leaving only the screeching sound of twisting metal ripping through the thawing ground as boxcars tumble one over the other.

Barely has this carnage stopped when Moshe and the rest are swarming the wreckage like wasps. They fire on anything moving. In short order, satisfied they have controlled the situation, their attention quickly turns to searching out the cars carrying rations and weapons. Within minutes a hoot is heard indicating a successful discovery. The doors have been ripped open spilling their contents throughout the landscape amid broken bodies of SS guards. Their entire attention abruptly turns to looting these disabled boxcars. Within an hour this ragtag militia has stripped everything that can be useful. Moving back into the concealment of the forest, they make a hasty retreat knowing that by now the enemy will be aware that this train is way off schedule and will begin an immediate search.

Several hours later Moshe and his compatriots are back in camp. A celebration accompanies their sense of success and well-being by breaking open a portion of the rations and passing them throughout the camp.

Attention soon turns to the cache of rifles. They have retrieved sixty rifles, twenty pistols, crates of ammunition, six boxes of the "potato masher" type of German hand grenades, and several boxes of dynamite, along with dozens of boots, coats and hats. German uniforms are prized because they afford a Jewish partisan access to areas where they normally would be looked at with suspicion. On the other hand, to be caught wearing one will bring the most severe retribution.

Izak has been proving himself to be a valuable asset. He has pretty much assumed the responsibility of getting extra weapons to the Ghetto. With this raid Moshe has agreed to send forty rifles and all twenty pistols along with ammunition and several boxes of hand grenades. Mort will be grateful for any little bit that filters his way.

Moshe is not interested in battling the Nazis on the battlefield as he has chosen to fight them through sabotage.

"Disrupting their transportation and communications with dynamite shakes the confidence of the Germans. It lets them know that we are not merely going to go as passively as they had expected," he has said on more than one occasion.

Mort, on the other hand is confined inside of the Ghetto walls. His battle is one of defense whereas Moshe's is admittedly much more offensive. Nonetheless, Mort has proven that armed Jews willing to kill are capable of striking fear into a Nazi soldier.

Karol appreciates the efforts of both these men, one being his blood brother, the other a brother Jewish partisan. As for his crusade, it's devoted to getting as many Jews as possible out of the Ghetto before they fall victim to the fatal Nazi propaganda informing them they will only be relocated. Many have figured out the Nazi lies and have already agreed that if there is a way out of here, despite the danger, they would be willing to go. Moshe also is in sympathy with Karol in getting as many of these intact families out as possible, allowing them to join up with his partisans until other arrangements can be made.

Meanwhile Izak, Rhena and Sara spend several days with Moshe planning a strategy to get the munitions into Mort's hands as well as how to work more Ghetto refugees into his camp. With a plan to include both, Moshe sends as many partisans as it takes to help implement a strategy of action. Within twenty-four hours they are back in the Ghetto with the much needed munitions and a workable plan.

The Nazis have not been heard from in some time but that does not mean they have given in to this Jewish Fighting Organization. There's reliable information working its way through the many Jewish underground networks that the Nazi commander in charge of this region has been recalled to Berlin and replaced by another who has vowed to bring the Ghetto to its knees. The information is that his name is Jurgan Stroop. He is 100 percent dedicated to his career. Whether he dislikes Jews is secondary to his dedication to orders and his willingness and ability to carry out an undertaking. The only immorality he envisions in this entire slaughter of Jews is their resistance. The "good" he commends is the camaraderie and tireless effort of his soldiers to continue to hunt down Jews and be prepared to exterminate them in any manner orders demand.

Mort has also brought about some positive changes of his own. He has been successful in waking the younger people out of a passive mindset prevalent among their parents' generation and shown them how they can either die as cowards or as fighters for a life they value. It has brought about 700 new recruits since those early SS encounters. They have busied themselves in manufacturing bombs and making bunkers in every conceivable basement and learning how to navigate the sewer systems. Many of these bunkers are family projects to include even their elderly.

Karol has also been busy organizing an escape for those who are considered as desperate. He is aware that the entire Ghetto is full of informers who hope to gain safe passage for themselves if they report the resistance forces. Mendacious promises made by the Nazi information ministers claim they should be on the look out for Ghetto ruffians out of a loyal sense of duty. They are told these people are no better than any other criminal and to turn them in to the Jewish police for the well-being of their community. These lies lend a bogus sense of respectability to the collaborators as well as to the underlying motive of the SS. Still he labors tirelessly for those he finds are ready to take a different route that is nevertheless, far from risk free.

There are Ghetto families who continue to tirelessly work in their family businesses. Many do this because they want a sense of normalcy despite their world caving in all around them. They still dress as business people going through the motions of normal life. They generally consider the resistance groups as upstarts and oppose them as a group, almost always refusing them financial aid.

Then there are those educated, professional Jews who desperately try to hang on to a culture that is being systematically dismantled by the Nazi insistence to rid the world of all Jewry. To them this intention is so inconceivable that they don't seem to have the will to do anything to fight against such unthinkable tyranny. They are much like the frog placed in heating water that remains in place until he's boiled to death.

Karol finds himself sorting through the different mind-sets forming the denials of his people. Understandably it's not a perfect system, so caution is always of utmost importance. He has had to deal with misguided

Nazi collaborators since the beginning of their oppression. It still amazes him how many of these Jews, even when selected for deportation, put on their finest clothing for the trip, acting as if they are on their way to a seaside resort. To them the idea of a death camp is unimaginable. Despite these difficulties, he feels it his responsibility not to allow those who are undeniably going to their own death like lemmings, to lull others to sleep along the same paths. Certain that he has a pulse on his community, he's careful how and with whom he recruits.

Thinking back, Karol remembers when Izak and his mother and sister first arrived in the Ghetto and how much Izak wanted to find something he could do using his Polish language skills. Reviewing this recollection, Karol calls Izak aside.

"Are you ready to put your Polish hat on once again?" asks Karol rather pointedly. Izak also has a much more Aryan look about him than Semitic.

Not sure where Karol may be going with this, his first reaction is a puzzled look. His second thought is that to remain looking puzzled too long does not match the confidence he's built with Karol. Quickly recovering, he responds, "Sounds interesting. What's the plan?"

With a pensive expression on his drawn face, Karol begins, "Sometime soon the Germans are going to bring the wrath of Satan to us. I have a number of people, maybe a few dozen that are still willing to try and get out. The Germans have discovered our passageway behind the church and sealed the cover. That is no longer an option for us. What I need you to do is go to the Aryan side and organize an alternative way back here to get these people out."

The mental strain in Karol's voice acts on Izak's solid determination to get started with this assignment. Arranging for Polish workman's clothing, a pistol, money, and false papers, he makes his way over a portion of the wall at daybreak when it's least guarded. Slipping unnoticed into the street as a Polish workman on his way to his job, Izak, committed to succeeding with this mission, makes his way toward his old neighborhood where he recalls a group of sewer workers used to hang around a bar after their workday. He knows many of the habits of these laborers revolve around heavy drinking and the limited income they have to do it with. Willing to take his time he begins to re-acquaint himself with some of these men.

After a few drinks a man named Joseph remembers Izak as Alek Radinsky.

"Hey Radinsky, where'd you disappear to? I thought you was working for old man Kaczka in the cobbler shop."

"I used to. I went into different work," says Izak, making himself sound rather business like.

Piquing his interest the man pursues his questioning.

"Oh yah, what kind of business you get into?"

Giving him a little knowing smirk, Izak continues his pretense.

"You know those Jews on the other side of the wall got a taste for vodka, too," says Izak, ordering another drink for his old acquaintance. "I figured out a way of getting it to them, or at least that was the case until the German criminals closed their passage to me. Now I have to figure a different way to continue doing business with them."

Izak lets his words work their way into Joseph's mind all the while continuing to make small talk and supplying him with yet another drink. A bit later and still chatting, Izak begins to push for a little more information on Joseph's work.

"So you still working in the sewers, Joe?"

"Oh yah, I'll be working there till I'm dead," says Joe with a bit of resentment. He adds, "I've worked for Polish, Russians and now I'm working for Germans. All the same to me as long as I get paid. They all take a shit and they all gotta have somebody make sure it's goin' somewhere."

"How well you know these sewers going into the Ghetto?" asks Izak apprehensively.

The alcohol has made its way into Joe's thoughts.

"Hell yah! I know every inch of those sewers. Just like the back of my hand," say Joe with a slight slur.

Willing to patronize Joe a bit longer he orders more drinks.

Stepping up his strategy another notch, Izak says, "I'll bet for the right price you could show me a short cut into that Ghetto."

"For the right price I could show you where Hitler's turds are hiding."

Izak manages a hardy laugh at Joe's attempt at witticism.

Giving Joe another moment, he presses on, "What kind of price would you be asking?"

Catching Joe in the middle of a gulp and stopping him for a second, Joe has a look of puzzlement, then with a smirk of his own says, "For what? To show you Hitler's turd?" With that statement, Joe is holding his sides in laughter at his put-on.

"If you wish. All I need is to find a short way in there," adds Izak.

Settling down at the seriousness of Izak's request, Joe says, "How about a bottle of vodka?"

"You got a deal," says Izak shaking Joe's hand to seal the deal.

In the next few minutes Izak has purchased a bottle and he and Joe are walking down a side street that makes its way to the avenue one block short of the wall. Joe, still dressed in his work clothes, holds his hand up pushing Izak into the shadows. Satisfied they're alone, he motions for Izak to follow him. In another moment he leads him to a manhole cover only one block from the wall. With the skill of a man who has spent his working career managing these passages, he lifts the manhole cover and even in his drunken state demonstrates deftness. In another step, he secures his lamp on his hat and is motioning Izak to go down the ladder. In his next move, he is behind him re-securing the cover.

Leading him in a direction that seems to be running parallel to the wall, Joe suddenly takes a branch that gives Izak the sense that they are now heading directly toward the wall. With Joe in the lead, after another twenty steps, they find themselves standing in front of a ladder.

"Take 'er to the top, open it up, and you'll be standing behind the Jewish Council Building," says Joe.

At the top of the ladder, Izak lifts the cover just enough to catch a view of the Council building. Satisfied, he makes his way back with Joe to their starting point. Handing him his long-awaited prize, Izak shakes his hand and thanks him once again.

With Joe well on his way in the other direction, Izak quickly disappears back down the manhole. Lighting his candle, he retraces his steps back to the Jewish Council Building. Once more lifting the lid, he emerges and makes his way back to Karol's bunker.

Karol is surprised to find Izak back so soon but is greatly relieved to see him. After giving Karol the rundown of his undertaking, Karol makes a surprising statement.

"I want you to go get some rest. Tomorrow morning at dawn I have two dozen men, women, and children that will be depending on you to lead them back to that side street."

Izak, relieved to get some rest after his bout in the bar with Joe, is soon fast asleep. Meantime, if he is to rescue anymore of his people, Karol is aware that with the Nazi determination to empty the Ghetto, he must move quickly. He is also aware with the latest information that something big is about to develop within the Ghetto.

Mort is sensitive to this same intelligence. No one expects that 700 Jewish ghetto fighters are going to defeat the most dangerous army in the world. But all 700 are determined to let the rest of the world know the

Nazi description of them as a people is a lie. They are determined to make the Germans pay with as many German lives as they are able to take in payment for the Jewish lives that have been stolen from them.

Rhena and Sara and other young women have willingly taken up arms to defend themselves as well as all those who have not been misguided by Nazi lies. These courageous young women are bravely joining the fight alongside the men, sharing the same concerns and hardships. Rhena and Sara are placed side by side in a bunker. The two of them have settled on two pistols apiece and a couple grenades. This allows them to hit and run without a lot of extra baggage. Some others are armed with rifles, fuel bombs, and Polish pineapple-style grenades.

Over the past few years each of these fighters have become much more knowledgeable of the Ghetto scene than any of them could possibly imagine. Each of them are familiar with places where the Nazis can be bottlenecked into dead end streets. They have also become acquainted with several tactical ways to hit a threatening German military with a harmful enough strike to give them pause. This leaves them with a degree of confidence that they may live to continue the fight yet another day.

Rhena, Sara, and the other young fighters have taken on much more responsibility than would normally be expected of teenagers. In waiving their opportunities to leave, they have already committed their lives to this cause.

Mort is fully aware that it is ludicrous to imagine they can continue to embarrass the German army by forcing them to retreat in the face of such a ragtag offense. With the April night waning in favor of dawn despite the lack of approval from those forced to ride in on its coattails, they are met with an unprecedented report of a German reaction this morning. It's not as though they didn't know it was coming, it's just that they always hoped it would be "tomorrow." Nonetheless, Mort remains diligent to his compulsion to defend the Jewish people in spite of their seeming passivity. There is not a building in the Ghetto that he is not in some way involved in defending.

With the information that the Germans are building a militia outside several of the fifteen gates surrounding the Ghetto, Mort has every fighter on full alert this morning.

At the same moment, Izak is awake and preparing to fulfill his commitment to the two dozen people awaiting him to oversee their long awaited escape. These poor people have little or nothing left of possessions. They have been urged to carry only absolute necessities, such as food, water, and warm clothing. Each of them live in the hope of a life free of repression. Meeting them for the first time reminds him how valuable each Jewish life is. The older children are seemingly aware of the danger of this mission as they try desperately to keep their younger siblings quiet.

Karol is delivering some last minute instructions as they have been worked out overnight.

"This is Izak. He has risked his life many times in these sewers advancing the resistance. He is to be listened to with total authority as he has become an expert on maneuvering throughout these passages. If some of you don't make it, it will be because you didn't listen to what he has told you."

Turning to Izak in particular but yet for all to hear, Karol continues his directives.

"When you arrive on the other side slightly lift the manhole cover. This will signal a waiting van. That driver will drive over the top of this manhole. There is an opening cut in the bottom of the van allowing all of you to quickly climb aboard in secrecy. Quickly is the word here. There is a German checkpoint less than 500 hundred yards from this point. Hopefully they will be preoccupied with what seems to be building in the Ghetto this morning. Also we all know that these moving vans have become quite common as they are continuously busy carrying off confiscated Jewish possessions and aren't given much notice."

Motioning for Izak to begin, Izak has a few instructions of his own.

"It's important that you do not make any noise. These passages echo any conversation increasing the chances it will reach the ears of those who willingly cause us trouble." He says this with the conviction of one who knows the ropes.

The fear generated by this operation without a doubt is placing these ordinary people far outside their comfort zone. It's obvious the nervous tension is beginning to build as they, in single file, begin their hurried trek toward the small insignificant canal leading to their dream of freedom.

Izak is boldly out front leading this desperate pack of pioneers ready to abandon a failed way of life for the promise of a chance to rise above their fate. Rather than promoting his own standing in this important venture, he looks around at the preparation going on in the Ghetto this morning. It's obvious something big is brewing in the air. A loud whistle suddenly catches his attention. Turning toward its origin, he is confronted by his little sister all decked out in battle clothing. Running out to greet him, she gives him a brief hug with that moment left open for his approval. Giving her a wry grin and a nod is enough to secure her a place with him.

"Tell Momma I'll be back later today," he says, still moving forward and letting her fingers slip through his.

Arriving at the rear of the Jewish Council, Izak skillfully leads his small group down into the bowels of their city. Several small lanterns are distributed among them. These are lit as the group lines up in a serpentine formation to begin the next leg of their quest.

It soon becomes apparent that parents are struggling with frightened children. Some of them are resisting to the point of having to be pulled. Another mother is struggling with a crying baby. She is left with no option than to cup her palm across the baby's face. With all the conflicts facing each individual in these seeming surreal conditions, Izak is able within a short time to bring them to the next leg of their journey.

Cautiously lifting the lid, he spots the guard building down the street. Turning the other way, he spots a van slowly but purposefully making its way toward them. After what seems like a long time, the lid is finally lifted again. There facing them is a man above them lying prone in a darkened van sliding the cover aside. With a hand motion the long line snakes its way upward through the opening in the van floor. Several of the lights the group is carrying quickly light up the interior of the windowless truck revealing only its empty readiness to move them on the next leg of their escape. There are more than a few relieved faces as they are safely helped out of the sewers.

The last person in this party is the young sobbing mother as she makes her way through the opening clutching her dead baby. This was the crying child whose mother cupped her hand across its face to stifle the noise and in the process inadvertently smothered the child. She is rightfully warranted her broken heart as many try to console her. The death of a loved one, regardless of its frequency, will agonize those left behind and remains as something impossible to rehearse.

Izak is satisfied that he has finished his role and slips back into the sewer trusting his little band of escapees to find their way to Moshe's forest encampment. Standing alone on the ladder as he watches the van sluggishly pass unnoticed by the guard shack, he makes a decision to climb back out. Sliding the cover back in place, he makes his way back around to his old neighborhood. Standing across the alley, he watches the traffic going in and out the cobbler shop. A soft spot remains in his heart for all those who aided him and his family. While allowing himself this unsanctioned moment to reminisce, he doesn't notice a Polish policeman looking him over. Not recognizing him as belonging in the neighborhood, he approaches him.

"Let me see your identification," he roars with authority as though he is a bandit.

This confrontation is a total disruption to his mind flow. It's caught him on his blind side causing him to fumble with his papers. They fall from his hand. His reaction is one he cannot retract. He cusses but not in Polish. HIS CURSE IS IN YIDDISH!

The policeman stands, glaring at Izak as though he had personally watched him kill Christ. In less time than it takes to say "dirty Jew" he has him on the ground and manacled.

CHAPTER 15

FRIEDA

Mort is busy checking his short-wave operations for any breaking information as to what the Germans' next move may be. The Ghetto has caught the tension that comes with waiting for the jailer to come take his prisoner to the gallows. They are visibly shaken as more severe retributions are expected. The consensus is that what is about to come will be much harsher than anything experienced so far. Many people who have found working on creating the bunkers an elixir, are now finding waiting in them a form of self-imprisonment.

Rhena and Sara have been tireless in working for the resistance. This morning has been typical of a day for them. They post themselves everyday along with the 700 others committed to this endeavor. What sets them apart is the same thing all soldiers have in common: a determination to remain committed to their cause.

On this particular morning the Germans have sent through each of the gates a series of bodies dragged by ropes behind a donkey. They are well acquainted with the uncivilized and brutal tactics of their tormentors. It's done with the expectations the Jews will be thrown into a state of discouragement and become more compliant. One of the gate openings is near Rhena's post. What she sees is not something she has not seen demonstrated by the Nazis in the past. It's a young man swaying by the neck on a makeshift gallows placed on a farm cart drawn by a sickly cow. But something familiar about this newest victim catches her attention. The shock of blondish red hair catches her eye. There is no one else in her world who possesses this feature. She finds herself drawn out to the corpse in an unmistakeable familiarization. Her hand immediately covers her mouth in a shocked gasp.

"OH MY GOD! PLEASE TELL ME IT'S NOT IZAK!!"

Instead, as his head swings around his misshapen face stares at Rhena in a entreating expression of regret. It's almost as though he's apologizing for his death.

As hardened as Rhena has become to death this event has caught her as nothing ever has. The first thought that crosses her mind is how she will keep this from her mother.

Seeing how Rhena is reacting has caught the attention of her fellow partisans. Rushing to her side, several are already removing the rope from his neck. Others have provided a stretcher. They have all suffered the loss of loved ones and have shared with one another the pain of these losses. With hands wet with her tears, Rhena closes the eyes of her brother.

Jewish burial law is simple but specific. The body must be guarded by a fellow Jew, washed, dressed in clean linens and buried in a Jewish cemetery before sundown. Thankfully there are caring volunteers who willingly take over in times like these. Izak's body is carried to a place that has been set aside for these events. Rhena sits with him for a while.

Sitting alone with her brother for the last time, her mind reaches back to earlier years, to their childhood days on the farm. She can't help but look at herself in comparison this morning sitting here with yet another dead family member. Her hate and desire for revenge grow as she recalls the events that have driven them all away. She recalls a simple joyous reality of times together with her father and brothers and how all of these have been torn one by one from her life. Even the difficult times seem simple compared to this. Unfortunately in days like these, even tears must be short lived. Sara rushes in to warn her that they need to get back to their post as the SS have begun to move into the Ghetto. There is a change coming about and it appears to be a big one.

Touching her brother one more time with a prayer on her mind, she answers Sara's call. The overwhelming advance of soldiers entering through several gates at one time outweighs every other consideration. An immediate response must be taken to continue meeting these new challenges. Without the luxury of battlefield experience, each of these refinements the Germans bring to the forefront has to be met by these partisans as it unfolds. Once again the SS are bringing heavy tanks to the front to attempt to intimidate with an overwhelming show of fire power.

Mort gets the sense they are measuring his strength and resolve to stay in the fight. The first blast is directed into a four-story residential building. A hundred or so chaotic residents, old men and woman and children come pouring out. They are immediately caught up by Nazi infantrymen and herded into a line and pushed to a point outside the gate. Another contingency of soldiers meet them at this point and begin to herd them toward the rail yards for deportation. This number is hardly enough to meet their hunger for Jewish blood. Another blast into another building provides about half the amount provided from the first effort.

In the chaos, a partisan manages to lob two gasoline bombs onto the tank setting it ablaze. The tank driver struggles to escape through the cockpit cover only to be set afire. His screams are welcomed as an expression that his weapon has been compromised. The residents are scattering in every direction. This slow chewing away at an enemy may satisfy the military objectives of other armies but it's only the sureness of efficient results the Germans seek as satisfactory. It's considered a waste of a good mortar to glean such a small harvest.

The soldiers are even less efficient. Rhena and Sara have worked out a dangerous ploy from a ground-level abandoned storefront. Sara will pretend a leg wound in clear sight of a couple of stragglers. After disobeying a command to stop she ducks into the building. As if on cue they imagine a helpless teen girl and boldly pursue her. Once inside and at the girls' choosing, they ambush the dawdlers with a blaze of pistol fire, one held in each hand. Escaping through a well-traveled route to another location and do it all over again.

Playing peek-a-boo diversion from various positions, Rhena and Sara have positioned themselves deeper into the Ghetto while continuing to draw a half dozen soldiers behind themselves.

"Sara I think it's now or never," says Rhena. Sara can hear the tension in Rhena's voice as she gives her the little nod assuring her that they're both on the same page with their next maneuverings. In the next second, Sara steps into the street not more than ten yards from their pursuers. Just long enough to challenge their collective mind-set to give chase. As cautious as they were trained to be, the sight of a more or less defenseless young woman puts their training into intermission. Immediately after entering the building they are met with a pineapple grenade rolling across the floor. The blast hits the six of them with such force that it is doubtful any of them would wish to survive.

Rhena and Sara already know the outcome of this ploy but nonetheless re-enter the room to view the devastating impact. Both stand for just a moment before looting the bodies of anything that can be utilized toward their defense such as guns, bullets, knives and medicine.

Rhena is quiet while quickly finishing. Her thoughts can't help but hark back to the sight of her brother's lifeless body. The thought that continues to bounce around inside her head as she rifles through the belongings of these dead soldiers is, *"I wish I could kill you bastards again and again."* They can clearly see a group of soldiers intent on positioning themselves to do some damage to their building. Within seconds they are out through the back of the building making their way out of the area.

By afternoon, the frustration of Commander Stroop is reaching an unacceptable level. He is managing to log more Jewish casualties as he successfully smokes many out of their bunkers with various kinds of gasses. But only a few here and there with 50,000 still left is a far cry from the quick solution he had originally envisioned.

The afternoon wears on with cacophonous sounds of shooting and explosions spent by both sides. The day has been played out with Commander Stroop reviewing alternative approaches. One of his advisers recommends using bombers to carpet bomb the whole city and eliminate the Polish resistance along with the Jews. The use of bombs and air power on "subhumans" is regarded by Stroop to be a waste when a cheaper, more efficient method is readily available.

At 5 p.m. Stroop pulls his dead and wounded from the fighting zones. Mort and the resistance fighters do the same. The higher count of casualties is definitely in Mort's court. Nonetheless he spends much of the rest of the evening congratulating his ragtag volunteers on their earnest defense of the Ghetto for one more day.

Rhena makes her way back to her bunker. Her mother is beyond consolation in the face of all the bombing and shooting all day. Rhena can't imagine what would happen if she were to discover Izak's fate. There is no way she can bring herself to unwrap that happening to an already emotionally fragile mother.

Minnie has contemplated suicide many times but for reasons known only to herself has not followed through. Perhaps it's because she still continues to possess an urgent need to nurture her remaining children. The loss of everything that has brought her happiness except for her two remaining children has devastated her world. The changeless threat of more loss assails any fragment of remaining hope. Her life takes a narrower and narrower path of purpose as it continues on its downward spiral.

Rhena has unconsciously reversed roles with her mother. She finds herself cradling her exhausted parent as though she were a child in need of comfort. Both have aged in the past few years. Looking at her mother's haggard, careworn features alerts Rhena of the mental strain this misfortune has placed on so many of the older generation. Both consumed with fatigue, mother and daughter, fall into an exhausted slumber.

Human casualties are taking their toll daily in the Ghetto. The streets are littered with those suffering from starvation, aggravated with epidemic proportions of typhus. Several dozen dead bodies are picked up every day. It's not unusual to have a report of several of these bodies hanging from ropes by their own hand.

Men like Stroop are counting on these alternate exterminations to occur, thus lessening the need to waste railcar space. His only quarrel with these methods is they are way too slow. His intentions to empty this Ghetto remain on course. Overnight he has decided his plan. The next morning without warning he begins his own "final solution." Several tanks begin to fire at specific residential targets creating the usual general mayhem. It appears a new strategy is quickly being put in place. Dozens of soldiers rush in with flame throwers setting fire to first one building then another. The full force of his intentions is quickly brought to everyone's attention. Stroop plans to burn everything to the ground that prevents him from reaching his objectives. Many people empty into the streets, fleeing the flames. Others, frozen in disbelief, hang from balconies, windows and roof tops in the expectation of rescue.

Sentries have sounded the alarm. Rhena and the other fighter's attentions are immediately brought to adjust to these changing and unrelenting circumstances. Torn between staying back with her mother in the safety of their bunker or commandeering a position against this new assault, Rhena is quickly caught up in the urgency of the battle. Assuring her mother she would be back, she grabs her weapons and along with the others makes her way to the streets. Minnie has a forlorn and pale empty expression as she watches her daughter tuck pistols and grenades into her pockets, then turn her back and leave. Even the imminent danger is underrated against the extreme desolation this poor mother is undergoing.

The black smoke at the street level is shocking. If the Germans can be credited with nothing else in this horrific assault against mostly unarmed people it is that they are masters at bringing order to chaos. People are being rounded up by an overwhelming number of SS guards.

Concerning the Jewish attempt at defense against this outrage, what can be agreed on is that it is a far cry from the military precision demonstrated by their Nazi nemesis. Nonetheless the resoluteness of these fighters day after day leaves the Germans realizing these battles are costing men and resources that could be used in other areas of the war.

Rhena is placed in a bunker that allows them to ambush the advancing SS forces. Her thoughts remain focused on the task at hand. They have successfully repelled the flame throwers for the morning hours but the advancement of what appears to be a major build up of armored cars and troops places a dampening effect on their ability to hold this horde at bay.

The sound of machine gun fire suddenly breaks the standoff. Mort and another fighter have placed themselves on opposite sides of the street armed with two machine guns. These are the only heavy weapons the resistance was able to recover from a previous German retreat. They have allowed the soldiers to advance until they have removed all the frantic citizens in columns and marched them out. Just as they are advancing on the next building to be burned, Mort and his fellow partisan open fire on what the Germans had come to expect as a routine operation. Dozens of them drop before they can organize a retreat.

Having done as much damage as they can expect before the Germans reorganize, these two Jewish warriors make an escape. These small victories never go unnoticed by either side. These small victories always initiate a yelp of joy from the outnumbered Jewish fighters.

Stroop is stopped once again. He can't help but face another frustration. He struggles with the stubborn resistance these normally passive people are mustering. After all, isn't it he who is bringing the overwhelming power of the German army to bear upon them? Yet in light of this, he is still somehow managing to maintain his passive aggressive persona, while continuing to suffer through yet another unacceptable halt to his project. Calm on the outside but on the inside he remains in constant agitation. It's an unspeakable admission that he has such a formidable foe despite their few numbers, especially when found capable of bringing him to a standstill.

Taking advantage of the cease fire, Rhena's concern for her mother has entered her thoughts. Without a word to anyone, she slips out of her fortification and cautiously makes her way back to her mother's bunker. What she sees takes the breath right out of her. The SS has found their subterranean bastion and are marching them out one by one with hands held over their heads. There is her mother pale and sickly hardly able to stand with her tormentors pushing her. Seeing her trying to struggle to her feet initiates an act of filial affection. Slipping in among those frightened and confused people forced together by this sudden development, she makes her way to her fallen mother and manages to get her to her feet in time to avert a probable bullet to her head.

The temperament of these SS guards over the assistance Rhena is providing only angers them as they abruptly push her aside. Their script for those who can't make it on their own is to be whisked off and shot immediately. Her mother falters and falls yet again. Her weakened condition guaranteeing she won't be making any railcar trips. Rhena is still being pushed and cajoled along. Looking over her shoulder, she has one last glance as her mother is being dragged to the side. In less than thirty seconds she hears a single shot. Hearing that shot is a sound of finality that never leaves a person. It can't be removed with any human help and the Divinity only seems to be concerned with what a person does with this experience. Either way it's hers forever.

Even though Rhena is being ushered along on the graveyard road with little to deter it, long ago she made the decision as to how she is *not* going to die. Clutching the two pistols in her coat pocket reaffirms her resolve that she will not end her life in a gas chamber. There is little or no time to create a plan as in minutes she is on the loading platform along with other deportees being packed into these waiting cattle cars. The sounds of frightened weeping children, the prayers of old men and woman, the spiritless atmosphere of despair are all Rhena is left with. Abruptly the huge door is slid shut and darkness overtakes the cabin of this seeming hearse. She can make out the sounds of her fellow Jews being mercilessly loaded into neighboring boxcars while they too are the final outcome of the same time proven success the Germans have demonstrated over and over again with this process.

She finds herself pushed back into a crowded corner. What immediately catches her eye is a tiny glimmer of daylight peeking through a hastily boarded up opening that may have served as a window in some earlier use. The smell of smoke from their burning homes clings to the bodies of everyone, permeating the air of this already stuffy transport. A feeling of claustrophobia begins to envelop a few already hammering their fists on the doors. After what seems like hours, but with German efficiency, has in reality only been fifteen minutes, the train begins its eager jerking motions. With the same predicable efficiency the engine is soon propelling its cargo zealously forward on a well beaten path.

Millions of Jews have already been moved through this process with little to no resistance, holding true to their centuries old compliance to their weakness toward fatalism. The clicking of wheel on track has mesmerized the frail, lifeless spirits of those who have found it even too late to cry as they watch their world being left behind.

Young Jewish women like Rhena are not cut out to become willing participants in this collapse of strength within their heritage. True to her God given gift to choose life, she is already preparing for an escape. The daylight coming through the nailed slats is beginning to fade. With a knife previously removed from a dead German soldier, she begins to pry the wooden strips. Slowly they loosen with a creaking sound hardly audible above the din of the pounding railcars. The fresh air is a welcome relief in spite of its coolness. Her undertaking has caught the attention of others as she continues to widen the opening. Soon she has a gap in the side of their railcar large enough to allow a person to wiggle their way through. She stands on her tip-toes as she peeks out at the speeding terrain whipping by.

Dusk is upon them. Even with this escape hatch wide open, leaping out would amount to suicide.

"There has to be an opportunity where this train will slow enough to let me get a jump. Don't wait until it's so dark you can't see."

Rhena continues to talk to herself as her adrenalin begins to affect every succeeding idea. Realizing the time is running out for any reasonable maneuver, her eye catches what appears to be a steep bank dropping into a gully. It looks as though if she were fortunate enough to jump onto where the slope of it would put her momentum into a downhill slide and reduce her impact, she could survive without a lot of injuries. After managing to pull her body into a sitting backward position, she twists her body around and hangs outside the opening with her feet just reaching the bottom of the boxcar.

Turning her head to look down the track, spots her drop point directly below her. With one thought only, she releases herself. While she is yet in the air she looks up in time to see a German soldier positioned on top of the car with a rifle pointing directly at her. She hears the crack of the shot and the whizzing sound it makes as it barely misses her head. Her next sensation is a jolt as she begins a less than masterful tumble down what has turned out to be sand and loose gravel. As landings go this couldn't have gone any better. Laying still for a few moments the first strange sensation she becomes aware of is how quiet it has become at the bottom of this ravine. Her next realization is that she is still in one piece.

She spends the next few minutes spitting dirt. Sand and gravel have covered her body. Her clothing has also taken a beating. She has been jounced around enough to notice her pistols are missing. Since she began carrying them they have given her a sense of security she found she doesn't possess without them. Looking back up the incline, she spots both these elusive weapons lying in the sand. She makes the short run back to the top, retrieving her pistols on the way.

On the other hand, to remain alert to every sound and sight in her orbit, coupled with her resourcefulness, courage and strong nerves rather than pistols, are the weapons she's going to need to weave her way back to Warsaw. She has come a long way from the fearful adolescent she left behind on the farm.

No longer able to hear the sound of the train, her thoughts hark back to a time when she was a child and her family would take the train on a holiday. She is able to picture her last dress she wore and how her brothers teased her about wearing it to attract the boys. Even under these circumstances it's an exciting and wonderful memory. How the same train could take them to so many wondrous places and now be no more than a funeral procession directed to carry them to their destruction. How sanity has taken such a dreadful turn is beyond her comprehension.

The night is coming fast. The last reddish rays of light in the western sky are fading into a purplish black as the sun continues its nightly journey. Her thoughts are speeding from one side of her head to the other. "Okay Rhena organize, organize!" she shouts out loud. "Follow the tracks back." Getting back to the Ghetto has more to do with reestablishing herself in an environment that is predicable rather than imagining it will be safer. This outside environment is totally foreign to her. It occurs to her that she is in strange waters and has no familiarization with how the Germans are dealing with Jews on this front.

Staying off the roads where the Germans have regular patrols makes sense. She has no identification and would run all kinds of unknown risks by unnecessarily exposing herself to these dangers. Sticking to darkened areas such as the rail tracks seems the practical solution. And not having a warm place to get into for the night, the walk will keep her warm. The darkness continues to remain uneventful, unless random reflections of where life is taking her are considered eventful.

This is first time in several years that she has had the luxury of being totally alone with her thoughts. In the quiet of the night her mind suddenly and unexpectedly goes to thoughts she has not visited since each of them happened. All the losses she has experienced are catching up to her. At once an overwhelming feeling of loneliness washes over her mind, body, and soul.

The tears begin to flow for everything she has not had even a moment to mourn. She finds that she is experiencing a broken heart for the loss of her entire family, calling to mind her relationship with each of them. Allowing herself this private occasion to scream as loud as her feelings are demanding, she unashamedly lets her emotions have their way. After several hours of walking, reflecting, and weeping for the world that she had looked on as near and dear to her heart, the realization makes its way into her reckonings that she is not going to ever bring these things back.

"I guess I'm going to have to change my life plans once again. I have to let the past go if I'm going to survive, at least let it go long enough so it doesn't dominate me. Please God help me." Her head begins to fill with the realization that her survival is no longer part of a group effort and is entirely in her own hands. This is a new perception. Times have changed yet again.

There is a gradual lightening of the horizon. The eastern sky holds the promise of a beautiful day. The urgency of making herself disappear before daylight is taking precedence over any remaining reminiscences. The bit of dawn beginning to have its way over the darkness reveals a field with a group of last season's corn stalks still standing in an otherwise empty field. On one end is an outbuilding that has the appearance of housing a few cows. Manure piles on the side of the building are a dead giveaway. What catches Rhena's eye is the pile of hay under a rickety old lean-to. It's just the kind of concealment she needs to bury herself under for a day's worth of sleep.

There is also what appears to be a small concrete reservoir full of water. It's obvious that this is water for livestock but for the present it's what she needs after a night of walking. Drinking her fill, she next takes notice of a pail of feed. It's full of oats. Pushing a handful into her mouth she heads for her haystack only to be met by a middle-aged woman coming out of the barn carrying a lantern in one hand and a pail of milk in the other. They equally startle one another.

They stand for the moment looking at each other, both hoping the other isn't dangerous. Rhena is the first to speak. "I don't mean to frighten you. I've been traveling all night and saw your water trough."

Remaining motionless the other woman continues staring at this begrimed interloper.

Disturbed by the silence, Rhena is compelled to speak again. "I hope you aren't offended by my trespassing, but I was so thirsty I was willing to take the chance of not being discovered. Now I'll just be on my way."

The woman on the other hand stands gazing at this dirty forlorn looking teen not having a clue what she is being confronted with. Finally speaking she demands Rhena's full attention. "Wait just a minute young...," she stops short, squinting at her. "Are you a boy or a girl?" the woman questions her in Polish.

"My name is Rhena...Rhena Radinsky. I'm a girl," answers Rhena with a half truth, using the Radinsky name.

By this time the farm lady has her lantern held up over Rhena's face scrutinizing everything from how she answers to how she appears. "Are you running from something young lady?" she continues, moving the lantern from side to side.

"Maybe," says Rhena ready to bolt away if this interrogation is pressed to where she will be forced to incriminate herself.

"Are you a bandit?" she asks further as she makes her way to a nearby pitchfork against the hay lean-to.

"No, I'm not a bandit," she says measuring her words, not certain where this lady is taking all this information and certainly not wanting to shoot her even though she has convinced herself that if she needs to she will.

"Okay Missy you've told me that you've been traveling all night. Now you show up ready to hide in my haystack. I'm not sure I'm ready to trust you. I have no idea what you're about. You may want to rob me."

Rhena is beginning to lower her defenses as she considers these seemingly legitimate questions now thrown in her direction.

"Oh no ma'am, I would never do anything like that," says Rhena in her most assuring voice.

"Well you're sneaking around my farm stealing my water and oats. So if you're not a thief then tell me what you're about. You can start with where you're coming from and where you're on your way to," says the farm lady using an even more exacting tone of voice.

Rhena gets the idea this woman is reprimanding her but finds she hasn't had time to develop an adequate defense against her brazen and more than magisterial personality. In light of this, Rhena has already made up her mind that she is going to hide her Jewishness by using that Polish name her family borrowed from Joseph Radinsky back in what seems like a lifetime ago. Being a country Jew and attending a Polish school her Polish language skills are perfect without a hint of a Yiddish accent. Her next step is to begin to tell the truth even if she has to lie to do it.

"My family is all dead. Hitler killed my father and two of my brothers several years ago when the Nazis took Poland. My mother and other brother are also dead. They were part of the Polish resistance. I was picked up by the SS with several other resistance fighters and was on my way to the Treblinka gas chambers when I managed to squeeze through the boxcar window and escape the train."

The farm lady is quiet as she listens to Rhena. Nonetheless her body language is speaking volumes as though this account is striking some confidential, cloistered recollection.

Rhena is paying close attention to each reaction her words bring about with this curious woman. She can tell they are having some kind of an emotional impression but that's all she is able to pick out. Whether it's favorable or unfavorable is left sheltered behind her featureless expression.

Quickly regaining her upper hand and with the same controlling tone this unusual woman, now for no apparent reason, suddenly extends a rather unexpected invitation.

"You look like you could use more than a handful of oats for breakfast. You come with me to the house for something with more nourishment. Besides, all these oats will do for you is make you shit."

Rhena, still on the defensive, is bowled over with this sudden change in this capricious lady.

"Thank you so much for such a kind invitation Mrs. ...," she pauses not knowing the woman's name.

"My name is Frieda Goldberg. You can call me Frieda."

Rhena recognizes the name "Goldberg" as a Jewish surname but chooses to leave well enough alone for the time being.

Although Rhena feels that she is intruding, the invitation stirs her deep inside in an unfamiliar way. She nonetheless manages a congenial acknowledgment, "Thank you very much Frieda that sounds wonderful."

Dawn is becoming daylight. With her usual abruptness Frieda hands Rhena her pail of milk to carry. She then fusses with extinguishing the light in her lantern as they make their way along a well worn path toward an equally well worn farm house.

Her home is made of field stone, typical for this part of Poland. It's a rather large structure with two distinct floors. Entering through a heavy wooden plank door gives way to Frieda's kitchen. The first thing Rhena notices is the large kitchen cook range dominating the room. It's exactly like the one her family had back on their farm. The sight of it delights her as this simple memory sweeps over her.

Frieda courses her way from one of her kitchen stations to another with the deftness of a domestic engineer. On one of her passes, she brings two large pails and hands them to Rhena.

"See that pump outside the door? Go fill these pails with water."

No sooner had she finished with this task when Frieda comes across the room carrying a pot full of hot water, setting in front of Rhena. Then pointing to a tub in another room off the kitchen she announces. "You're not sitting at my table smelling like you do. Take all this water and get in there and get yourself cleaned up."

Sheepishly Rhena surrenders to Frieda's imperative. It's a luxury she hasn't had in recent memory and one she gladly adheres to. Laying in this tub forces a memory of the last tub bath she had a few years previously when she found herself in the hands of a sexual predator. This memory is thankfully interrupted by Frieda entering the room with an arm load of clothing.

"Take your pick from these clothes, Missy. They're all clean."

In an unannounced move, Frieda grabs Rhena's dirty clothing expecting to put them in a pile for a good washing. In so doing, two guns and a sheathed military knife drop to the floor. At this point Rhena has no other choice than to let the chips fall where they may. Sitting naked and with no other options, she remains rooted in her tub watching Frieda scoop them together and set them on a small table next to her bath.

"You may need these again," is the only remark she pays to this unprecedented event. Returning to her simple task of gathering dirty clothing she says "I'm going to get these washed up," as she continues to make her way back out the door with Rhena's filthy clothing.

Not sure what to expect next, Rhena complies with Frieda's bid that she put on the clean clothing and goes back out to the kitchen for what she expects to be some form of inspection. Instead she is greeted with a stack of pancakes, some fried potatoes, a bowl of butter and a cruet of hot tea.

"Sit down and eat, Missy," Frieda motions toward an empty bench around a full table that could have satisfied a queen.

Rhena takes a deep breath as the aroma of this alluring feast penetrates her senses in a homey way. She finds herself sitting down in front of more food than she has seen in ages.

With a close eye Frieda continues her surveillance of this young waif. "So you say you're a member of the Polish resistance. That must explain why you are armed the way you are."

Torn between eating and remembering the importance to keep her Jewish secret from this prying woman, Rhena acknowledges Frieda's questioning with a simple nod as her attention is on the food. *"This meal would be a lot better if I could just eat without having to be on my toes,"* remains her prevailing thought. Up to now she's been able to keep her story straight. In trying to stay ahead of Frieda's questions, she attempts to throw her onto another course.

"Being a female in times like these, one never knows who one's enemy is going to be. It pays to have protection."

"Are you familiar with the resistance, Frieda?" she asks between bites.

"Not too much," she replies and then adds, "can you fill me in?"

Rhena feels the squeeze. Looking down at the smoothness of the table planks, trying to remain cool, she lets out a little sigh as she continues to try and measure her words. "The Germans are putting a lot of pressure on Warsaw. When they caught me the Polish resistance was on the outside of the Ghetto wall and the Jews were on the inside. The last I saw was the Germans burning the Ghetto building by building."

Frieda is looking at her guest with a bit of suspicion. "Tell me child how you managed to still be carrying two pistols and a field knife after the Germans arrested you?"

The noose Rhena is creating for herself is tightening as Frieda gives her a look that indicates she has a lot more questions where these came from. Rhena realizes she is going to have to change strategy with this inquisitor.

Frieda crosses her arms as if she knows exactly what she is doing to this street urchin. She lets her squirm for a few seconds before she relents.

"Okay you don't have to answer me right now. It's just a question," Frieda says with a slight grin putting her hand under her chin, "You can tell me later."

Rhena contemplates Frieda's words for a moment. She is surprised as well as confused by how easily Frieda has been able to maneuver her. Still not sure how she is going to respond, she tries a little grin herself which when competing with her deception only made her lips twitch.

Changing the subject, Frieda interrupts Rhena with another invitation, "Why don't you stay here with me today and get some rest? I have a spare room you can use."

For a moment Rhena doesn't respond. She is really unsure what to do. This stranger is penetrating all of her defenses. Frieda doesn't wait. She takes both Rhena's hands in hers, pulling her to her feet, "Come on, Missy. Follow me before you fall asleep at the table."

Rhena realizes that as tired as she has become, she has no defense against this benefactress. She is aware that there are many things she is absolutely unsure of but for some unspoken reason this does not seem to be one of those things. There is something about this woman that is trustworthy. Willingly rising to her feet she follows Frieda to the second floor. Opening a door to what is an obvious bedroom, Frieda motions for Rhena to enter. The room has a musty, old comfortable smell to it. It's a plain room with a hand-built dresser, a quilted bed, a small chair, an antiquated Persian rug and a porcelain chamber pot. With the deftness of one who has performed this operation many times, Frieda throws open an inside shutter. The path of the sun penetrates through the window exciting the tiny particles of dust. It strikes Rhena as plain but a charming and inviting room nevertheless.

"Okay Missy you get some rest and we'll talk later," says Frieda as she abruptly backs out through the door closing it behind her.

Left alone, Rhena takes off her shoes and lays down on the bed exhausted. It's the first real bed that she's slept on in a long time. She is feeling an odd bittersweet mixture of peace and anxiousness. As she begins to drift off to sleep her anxiousness evaporates giving way to a calm that has eluded her for years. For the next eight hours, Rhena doesn't make a conscious move.

That is not to say that her unconscious being remains satisfied with this kind of inactivity. A short time before awakening, a strange phenomenon takes place. She astonishingly, has developed a real awareness that with a small amount of effort she can fly. Probing into this perception a bit more, she concludes that all it will take is to run down a small hill until gaining the proper speed, make a well-intentioned hop in the air and take off. To her surprise it works. The exhilaration of actually flying envelops every cell in her body. At first staying below tree-top level is satisfaction enough. It gives her a sense of well-being to merely be flying above all the turmoil below. She soon discovers she has risen above tree tops and power lines. At first it scares her, nonetheless the promise of yet even more exhilaration draws her to still higher levels. She suddenly becomes aware she has risen so high that there is nothing left above her and now she is up so far that she can't control her descent. Terrified she is going to crash, she startles herself awake with a scream. Fully awake and sitting up in bed, she is relieved to have not experienced the finality of her screwball illusion.

This scream also brings Frieda on a full run. Throwing open the door, she stands to see Rhena safe after such a terrifying scream. Quickly realizing it resulted only from a dream and not some intruder, both are greatly relieved.

"Well Missy do you think you got enough sleep?" asks Frieda with her hands firmly planted on her hips.

Before Rhena can evaluate Frieda's interest concerning her sleep, she is dealing with more than just a tinge of embarrassment over this situation. She's battling a feeling to just jump up and run.

"Frieda, I am so sorry I made such a fuss. I sure didn't mean to. I truly apologize," says Rhena taking a deep breath still sitting in bed.

"Missy, you certainly needn't apologize for anything. I'm just happy to see you without your throat slit," laughs Frieda.

There are times one chooses friends, then there are times friends find the other. This budding relationship between these two seems to be resulting from that latter path.

Rhena has fully recovered and is back downstairs sitting at the table warming her hands around a cup of tea. Taking a quiet sip, her mind contemplates her next move. While more than aware of this young woman's uneasiness, Frieda hopes to put a more cordial dimension to this kinship.

"Rhena, you may have noticed I'm alone here. My husband and daughter were taken by the Gestapo some days ago. If you haven't already figured it out from my last name, my husband is Jewish. My daughter is considered an 'Aryan Jew' and was subject along with my husband for deportation. They were to contact me to join them when they discovered where they were to be placed. I have not heard from them since. On the other hand I'm not Jewish, I'm German. My family has been here for several generations and as a result I'm not eligible to be deported with them, so you see, I'm still here."

Rhena sits listening for a moment. This is not starting off well. She hesitates giving any adverse reaction to what Frieda is telling her. Frieda is isolated out here in the country, cut off from any information other than what the Germans choose to propagandize.

"You haven't heard anything from them at all?" questions Rhena. There's an awkwardness in her asking. It's not that she didn't hear Frieda say that she hadn't heard from them, it's just that she is feigning the fact that she already knows the answer. Honesty can many times be unbelievably troubling.

"No I haven't. Then again I'm not so naive as to believe these Nazis about anything," says Frieda with an air of pragmatism.

This admission gives Rhena the release she has been hoping for from the beginning of this uneasy exchange. The idea that Frieda would still be expecting her husband and daughter to waltz through the door at any moment is incredibly naive even for the most gullible. The German propaganda machine was overwhelmingly effective in the beginning, but as time passes they are losing all credibility as their lies become more and more apparent.

Continuing on with her thought, Frieda has another appeal, "Rhena, I know you say you are on your way back to Warsaw to rejoin the resistance. I would like you to consider staying here with me for a while. You know maybe take a break. I can't pay you a lot but I can pay you something and I can certainly use the help this time of year."

This is an unexpected entreaty. A hush descends. Rhena is holding back a somewhat restrained politeness. She's not certain what her reaction is going to be. She certainly does not want to offend her host but this offer has caught her on her blindside. With her entire family dead, she feels more than a little adrift. She drops her eyes in thought as to what this could mean. Looking up she begins to form some words.

"Frieda you have been more than kind to me but I have not been entirely honest. My name is not Rhena Radinsky and I'm not Polish. My name is Rhena Nowak and I'm Jewish. What is true is that I am a fighter with the Jewish resistance. Not the Polish."

Thinking she has dropped a bombshell, Rhena sits back anticipating the fallout from Frieda. Instead she waves her hand in a dismissive motion, saying, "Missy, I'm a step a head of you." Picking up Rhena's freshly washed laundry, Frieda pulls out her coat and displays the front left breast. Rhena looks on perplexed.

"This is what gave you away," says Frieda as she continues to smooth out the material, running her hand back and forth across the rough edges.

"This is the outline of a Star of David that you obviously tore off right here," she says pointing to the stitch marks with a knowing little smirk.

Rhena takes on a sheepish look as she examines this same piece of evidence. Still not sure what she is going to do, she seems to be dawdling or thinking—or maybe a little of each.

Frieda takes this opportunity to repeat her offer.

"Missy, I'm asking you again to consider staying here for awhile. I believe we both can benefit."

Rhena finally breaks her silence, "I have no papers. If the Germans come they will kill you as fast as they will me."

Smiling, Frieda boldly declares, "We'll cross that bridge when we come to it."

Sitting for a moment in a quandary, Rhena recalls her dream and how helpless and powerless she felt she had become. Perception and facts often become muddled. Unable to clearly sort through her tired confusion the thought follows, *"Maybe I am tired and really do need a break."*

Inwardly comfortable with this insight and with no obvious explicable reason given, Rhena agrees to set her independence aside and take Frieda up on her offer. Maybe she longs for the mother she's lost and seeks it vicariously in this relationship. For whatever reason each may have, they give each other a hug as if to seal the agreement.

CHAPTER 16

ANOTHER BUNKER

Over the next several months this alliance flourishes as each has found a reason to have the other in their life. They have shared much and helped each other heal much through that mutual sharing. Rhena has fondly discovered that a girl can be taken *from* the farm but the farm can't be taken *out* of the girl. She has quickly become an asset. They have planted a large garden and have even managed to get an early cutting of hay in the barn's loft. In not having to tell Rhena everything that needs tending, Frieda has found time in the day to instruct this young homeless girl in some of the finer details of domestic engineering, as well as teaching her the German language.

The summer has come on bringing with it warm evenings. The war continues to rage. One man's insanity battling with another man's insanity gives soldiers the assurance of full employment. Despite the lunacy of the times many of these evenings are spent laying on their backs looking up a the stars. Rhena especially finds this exercise therapeutic. It allows her that flying experience with out the fear of falling. It also restores her hope in the One who created it all and the belief that, The One is still larger than man's wars.

Rhena has heard about the Ghetto. How the SS completely burned every building, eventually leveling the entire community. She and Frieda have spent many evenings discussing the travesties of this action.

"I knew many, many of those families, I helped protect them," says Rhena. Pausing for a moment as she reflected back, "I helped get children out of there to the safety of some righteous Polish families who were brave enough to risk the possibility of their own death for these children to have life."

Frieda also has her own cross to bear. Her family deserted her when she married a Jew. "My relatives tried hard to kidnap me when they discovered Bernie and I were going to get married. My father even sent the police to apprehend us. Of course all this failed. We were much in love. Even after we had our daughter Celia, they still continued to shun us."

"How did you manage to keep the farm after they came for your husband and daughter?" asks Rhena thinking back to how the Nazis confiscated her family's property.

Frieda develops a little smile over this question. "Bernie saw what was happening to Jewish properties so he sold the farm to me. When this ploy was discovered, I want to tell you that peeved the SS commander more than anything else. He personally shot our bull just for meanness."

As if this conversation awakened an old fear, Frieda's tone suddenly changes.

"There is yet something you need to know Rhena. I want you to come with me."

With that said, she begins to lead Rhena to the barn. Making her way to a manger in front of a stanchion covered with hay, she picks up a pitchfork and begins to clear the floor. Rhena stands idly by watching Frieda pushing hay off to the side. What quickly takes shape is that this feeding trough is bolted to a trap door. Rhena knows exactly what this is as she helped construct many of these secret bunkers in the Ghetto.

Satisfied that enough debris is cleared to give Rhena a clear look at this ingenious contraption, Frieda motions Rhena over.

"Come here and give me a hand with this,"

Rhena readily complies. Together they fold the big hinged door up and back leaving it resting against the inside wall of the barn. This maneuver exposes a cavity with a ladder leading down.

Frieda leads the way with Rhena close behind. The light from the hatch lends enough light for her to grasp several stored candles. She lights them and reaches up to close the hatch. The scent of damp earth permeates their noses as their eyes adjust to the candle light.

What is illuminated is a three-by-three meter room with three single cots, canned goods, several small stools and a table, a chamber pot, home canned water and a shotgun placed there for reasons other than for hunting. The ceiling is composed of the concrete slab used to floor the stanchions. It's obvious that this bunker is built for concealment.

Looking around as one does when revisiting a familiar chamber, Frieda explains, "We built this to protect ourselves from the Russians. We never imagined that we would need it against the Germans, too."

Scrutinizing an environment that has become all too familiar in this part of the world, Rhena also feels a sense of familiarity, even more so than Frieda since these compartments had become a large part of her life in the recent past.

Frieda begins to speak again with an even more seriousness tone. "Rhena I want you to pay close attention to what I'm going to tell you. The Nazis are going to be coming by here in the next few days to collect a quota of food they have demanded from me. I don't think I have to explain why you don't want to be discovered. That's why I believe you need to become familiar with this shelter. You may find that you have to quickly retreat down here on a moment's notice."

Frieda has no way of knowing just how broad this young woman's survival experiences have already spanned in the course of her short life.

"I do know the reprisals the Nazis will take not only against me but also you. At the least you will forfeit the farm and probably your life. Why don't you save yourself the trouble and just let me leave?" asks Rhena, as one who has resolved a dilemma.

In an unexpectedly swift move, Frieda is on her. She cocks her arm back and slaps Rhena across her face.

Rhena reacts by leaping to her feet, grabbing both Frieda's arms and forcing her to the dirt floor. Frieda shows no will to fight back instead she lays on the floor both shaking and weeping uncontrollably. Rhena realizes immediately that Frieda is undergoing a breakdown of sorts. Her reaction promptly switches from one of self-defense to compassion. Without a thought, she picks Frieda up and cradles her. While gently rocking her, she recognizes this lashing out on Frieda's part has little to do with her and a whole lot to do with Frieda losing her husband and daughter. Holding this woman and allowing her to grieve is the most Rhena can do. There are no words that can replace the human touch in times such as this.

In time Rhena releases her friend. They both rise to their feet. Still wiping the tears from her saddened eyes Frieda embraces her young friend.

"I'm so sorry Rhena. Please forgive me, I couldn't stand the thought of failing another person I care about," says Frieda as she examines the red finger marks left on Rhena's face. Still sobbing she reminisces, "I can't believe they're gone. I watched them going further and further down the road in that damned truck until I couldn't see them any more. Even with that, I expected to turn around and see them standing behind me. You can't believe how helpless I felt standing there watching the last of the road dust settle."

Rhena is content with comforting Frieda. As long as she is needed to give consolation to someone else she can put off facing her own loses.

"At this point I haven't grieved for anyone, not even my mother. I know I should but everything has happened so fast and at least for the present I have a full-time job keeping myself alive. I suppose it's coming but for now, I just don't have time to think to much about it." These are Rhena's thought as she reexamines herself to see where she stands with this. She does this somewhat hesitantly never wanting to kiss the devil good morning until she meets him. A small glimpse of Izak's distorted face twisting on the end of that rope flashes by and not to hesitate here too long, her mind then races back to replay the shot that killed her mother. She isn't ready to face what she sees with Frieda.

These two females, one a teenager the other in her early forties, have found that much of their experiences have a commonality despite their age difference. This, along with a mutual need for support, is creating a bond that is stronger than many mother-daughter pairings.

The last thing she wishes to do is to alarm Frieda but she also knows it's ultimately her responsibility to protect both of them as best she knows how. The next day and without telling Frieda, Rhena reacquires her old Ghetto habit of arming herself. Keeping her weapons concealed beneath her baggy clothing, she goes about her daily routine of caring for the garden and the animals. It's a process she's grown accustomed to. Over time she has developed quite a relationship with the different animals around the farm, spending time talking with them.

"I want you boys and girls to realize things are dangerous out here for all of us. We are going to do the best we can to make sure that you are all taken care of but there may come a time when you're all going to be on your own. If that time comes, I wish you all the best."

These critters listen respectfully but they in turn are blessed with the innate gift of not worrying about the future. That's not the case with God's higher creatures. Even when they are assured by their Creator that He has everything under His control, they still try to work out a better plan. But then that's just the nature of the beast.

As Rhena is coming up the path from the barn toward the house, she spots Frieda surrounded by what appears to be a half dozen armed men. Ducking back behind some of the overgrowth, she can see them but they cannot see her. They don't appear to be German soldiers as they are dressed in ordinary peasant clothing. Not able to hear what's being said, she continues with pistols drawn and firmly gripped to sneak through the underbrush, soon getting within three meters of these men. She is now able to decipher that they are speaking in Polish. What she is beginning to pick up from their conversation is that they are demanding food. Frieda is arguing back the fact that she has no food except what the German military have imposed on her to supply for them.

When the man doing the talking pushes Frieda aside and begins to make his way toward the door of the house, Rhena, remaining concealed fires one shot over his head with the firm warning, "If you or any of your men make one single move the next shot will be through your head and not over it."

This turn of events has quickly gotten their attention. For the moment they stand stunned not aware of where this danger may be lurking. One man in this group armed with a rifle drops to his knee, aims in Rhena's direction and returns fire. Rhena fires back hitting this man in the arm. Meanwhile Frieda has moved out of reach of the men.

Still hidden, she shouts back one more ultimatum. "One more dumb move like that and I'll kill you all! Now all of you drop your weapons and lay face down on the ground!"

Some begin to drop their rifles immediately; others turn and look at their spokesman. He stands stupefied watching his wounded compatriot grabbing at his arm and howling in pain. Not able to discern what may be happening, he now throws his weapon to the ground with the others quickly following. They all comply and are soon laying face down.

Not willing to expose herself yet, Rhena shouts at Frieda to pick up their weapons and move them out of reach. This done, she emerges still carrying a pistol in each hand. Approaching the seeming leader, she places the pistol to his head.

"Who the hell do you think you are storming in here like this demanding our food?" Without waiting for an answer she cocks her pistol in his ear. "I got a half a notion to blow your stupid Polack brains out just because you're so damned stupid."

Frieda, frightened at what is about to happen, quickly intervenes.

"Rhena wait! Don't do anything! I know who these men are!"

Not sure she's ready to remove her handgun from this seeming adversary's ear, she nonetheless glances in Frieda's direction, giving her at least an indication she'll wait to hear what she has to say.

"They're partisans! They belong to the Polish Resistance! They're on our side!" Frozen in place and scared to death that Rhena will pull the trigger, Frieda shouts this out so fast it almost becomes one sentence.

Rhena still has enough adrenalin flowing to alert this man that with even this advocate he is not out of danger. Looking down at the man at her feet, with her mind racing, she shouts out just one question. "Who is Mort Polanski?"

Without hesitation the man, still face down, quickly shouts back, "He was the head of the Jewish Resistance in the Warsaw Ghetto."

This reply abruptly gives Rhena a pause.

"What do you mean he 'was'?" she shoots back.

"Haven't you heard, when the Nazis burned the Ghetto, Mort and what was left of the Resistance, found themselves trapped. Rather than let the Germans have the satisfaction of killing them, they blew themselves up."

Rhena realizes what she is hearing is exactly what she had always heard Mort declare they would do when they found themselves in this predicament. Nevertheless, it is still shocking to hear all this and to actually process it as reality.

At last satisfied that she is no longer dealing with an enemy, she lets them all up. Still somewhat wary of their food demands, she is yet concerned, the same as Frieda, that the Germans will seek reprisals against them if they aren't able to deliver their quota of food stuffs.

The leader introduces himself as Stosh Lavitski. Fully aware of how close he and his fellow partisans came to death at the hands of this seeming weak, innocent teenage girl, they are readily giving this situation a new dimension.

"I'll tell you what we are able to do if you'll agree to it," says Stosh.

With the attention of both Frieda and Rhena, he continues, "We'll be willing to pay you under the table and sign a receipt for you to give to the Germans thanking them for having allowed us to hold you at gunpoint and take their provision."

Both Rhena and Frieda look at one another. Both agree that as dangerous as it may be, cheating the Nazis out of provisions is too enticing to pass up. "Okay, you got a deal."

With this matter settled, they turn their attention to the poor guy who took Rhena's well-aimed bullet to the arm. It's apparent the bullet went clean through without hitting the bone and bandaging him is relatively simple. Stosh makes out their receipt, turns the payment over to Frieda for the food, and soon this band of volunteers is making their way back into the forest.

The women sit quietly for a while to digest the events that over the last hours came in bringing pandemonium and have now gone out like a breeze. Frieda is the first one to break the silence.

"Where in God's name did you ever learn to fight like that Rhena?"

Rhena remains quiet for a moment as she ponders Frieda's question.

"I honestly don't know." Hesitating once more, she adds, "And that's the truth."

The day ends on a good note.

The SS squad responsible for collecting provisions from the local farmers usually shows up before noon to make their collections. They decide Rhena will sleep in the bunker for the few days until they come. It would not go well to be caught harboring someone without identification papers who is also a Jewish suspect.

As if these two possess special powers of premonition, the SS arrives the next morning on cue. If nothing good can be said about this team, one would have to agree they're predicable. Even when they aspire to do an evil deed, they're always punctual.

Frieda is left to face the ire of these Teutons on her own. Thankfully she's German and by feigning the proper disgust for what the "Polack dogs" had done in taking advantage of a single female, she is able to convince the captain of this squad that she had truly been violated by these villains and only at the threat of death stepped aside and gave them what they wished.

It seems as though this squad is never going to leave. What makes it doubly trying for Frieda is, as she busies herself with the captain, the rest of his crew is nosing around every nook and cranny of her property including the barn with the bunker.

Rhena suspects what is going on as she can hear the muffled tones of men above her. Not wanting to risk being detected or emerging before they have abandoned their search, she sits quietly with the shotgun in hand and forgoes the urge to lift the lid and peek out. She is certain it would take more than this bunch to uncover her underground Kasbah.

Showing him the receipt with the signature of Stosh Levitski is the final insult this Nordic elite can bear. A soulless Slav has outflanked him. This last ploy of Frieda's has abruptly transferred the anger of this enraged Aryan captain from her to this sub-human Polack. His last words before leaving are, "This pig will pay," as he crumples the receipt in his fist.

Frieda sits looking out her kitchen window at the disappearing fleet of military vehicles. She lets out a sigh of relief as the last truck melts into the horizon. After giving them time to get some distance away and still with a wary eye toward the road, she makes her way to the barn. Using the bolted on feeding trough as a pry handle, she forces the lid to Rhena's safe haven forward. Without needing a second invitation, Rhena optimistically pokes her head above her ceiling. She hardly requires assistance as she happily scoots up the ladder to greet the sunshiny morning.

This little community of two have managed to integrate into their lives each small victory over these overwhelming negative forces—all of them hell-bent on destroying them. Lately they've come to realize this often enough so that with the completion of each day. It's a celebration.

Like many German families, Frieda's has raised her as a follower of the great German protestant reformer Martin Luther. She has taught Rhena the "Our Father" in German. Reciting this ancient prayer together celebrates they're being "delivered from evil" just for today.

And celebrate they do. Frieda brings out a bottle of wine she has been preserving for just the right occasion. It's a bottle her husband Bernie had made. She had been saving it for a celebration with him and her daughter Celia upon their safe return. During these past few months with Rhena, she is beginning to accept that the likelihood of them returning is zero. In turn, valuing each day as though it were her last is much more prodigious. For the evening meal, they butcher a chicken, pull some early onions from their garden and drink wine. A lifetime of living has already been jammed into their lives.

The resilience of these day-to-day survivors of this war is aligned with a special cognition and a lot of luck to sidestep the full weight of the factories, machines and armies with all their armaments, and above all, the enemy's firm determination to destroy anyone standing in their way. Those who are lucky enough to ride ahead of the tidal wave of these events will live to celebrate their victory.

CHAPTER 17

TREBLINKA

From the farm, the death camp of Treblinka is less than twenty-five kilometers in a north-easterly direction. Nearly every day since Rhena arrived at Frieda's home, a train pulling cattle cars has passed by the farm. There is a somber reality with each click of the wheels. She knows where it is bound and what cargo they contain. In deference to Frieda, she says nothing, knowing that unbeknownst to her friend this is the train that carried her husband and daughter to a dreadful final stage of their lives.

The Nazis have gone to great lengths to continue the illusion of an ordinary depot at the Treblinka arrival platform. It's complete with a large clock and what appears to be a reception area. With such a familiar surrounding, the people arriving here are expected to disembark without resistance.

Several months earlier a father and his eighteen-year-old daughter found themselves arriving on this platform. Their names are Bernard "Bernie" Goldberg and Celia Goldberg. Bernard's father had been an American Jew who gave his son the American nickname, Bernie. Soon after arrival the confusion began. No one knows where they are or what's going on. The Germans soldiers are screaming orders at everyone.

Everyone is trying to make decisions as quickly as possible. At first they continue under the impression that they are in a processing line for relocation. But they are separated. It soon becomes apparent that how one answers the questions determines what line they will find themselves in. No one knows what answer will give them an advantage. The stress levels climb as families are separated: fathers from wives and children and many times children are left without either parent. Bernie is confronted by an impatient SS officer asking what type of work he does.

"I'm a farmer, sir," he answers.

The SS officer stares hard at him for a moment then grabs one of his hands, rolling it over he appears to be examining its rough surface. Satisfied with what he sees, he orders Bernie down what appears to be a ramp leading to a large building.

On entering, Bernie along with a few other able-bodied men are met by a Ukrainian guard who begins to push them ordering them to strip naked. They are immediately filed into what appears to be a makeshift barbershop. There are several Jewish men in striped prisoners' uniforms equipped with scissors and hand clippers in preparation to shave the heads of these newcomers.

More confused than ever, Bernie tries to initiate a conversation with his assigned barber.

"Brother tell me, what is happening to me?"

The man, who has probably been asked this same question by countless other confused arrivals and ordered under penalty of a beating not to talk with anyone, in an almost inaudible voice makes only one statement.

"Pray brother."

Even more confused, they are next led into another area where they are given the same striped uniforms worn by their barbers. It's quickly becoming apparent that this is not a holiday trip to be relocated. He begins to feel an overwhelmingly sinking feeling. It's a commonality experienced among all those who discover they have been duped. He begins to experience a weak and hopeless feeling as this new reality begins to take root. Trembling, he follows a guard who has just shoved his rifle butt into his back ordering him to "move!"

The guard next leads them to a barracks where they are turned over to a thin sickly looking man who identifies himself as Louis Simon.

"I'm to show you what you're supposed to do here," says Louis.

With a weak gesture, he motions this new crew to follow him. They are next led to a collection of carts and wheel barrows. Each man is ordered to get hold of one. With this conveyance in hand, they head back out to the rail track. The cars they rode in on are empty of the human cargo they held just an hour ago except for what appears to be a few older people who were unable to survive the rough rigors of the uncivil train trip and died.

Still accompanied by a guard, he orders them to begin to clean out the dead and other trash left in the cars. They pile bodies and discarded clothing along with human waste left by those unable to hold their bowels all into the same cart, all to be treated as equal debris. Bernie is devastated. It's just beginning to sink that whatever this camp may turn out to be, it definitely is not a relocation camp.

During all of this activity, Louis's weakened condition causes him to fall. Not yet having an understanding of the mind-set of their jailers, Bernie jumps to the man's assistance only to be met with a rifle butt to the back of his head. The blow drops him to his knees.

In Yiddish, Louis weakly attempts to yell at Bernie, "Get up or they'll kill you!" At the same moment Louis falls once again. This time the same guard that has just administered the rifle butt grabs Louis by the collar. He drags him over by one of the wheeled carts and forces him to lie on top of another body already there. With that he shoots Louis Simon in the neck leaving him to be disposed of along with the other dead.

Realizing how rapidly life has changed and how quickly he is going to have to adapt if he wishes to survive, Bernie jumps to his feet.

In the next few hours Bernie comes to realize that the only reason he is still alive is because the Nazis need workers and he is strong enough for the time being. His next assignment more than confirms this thought. He finds himself standing before a large building with a hermetically sealed door waiting for the guard to give the order to open it. As the big door swings open what unfolds before him is a scene that no civilized human ever imagines he is going to have to deal with. *"My God, all the rumors that we've heard about these camps are true."* Crammed into the cubicles of this giant shower room are hundreds and hundreds of naked dead bodies of men, woman and children. Led to their deaths under the impression they were being deloused and bathed. Instead the shower heads spewed hydrogen cyanide gas instead of the expected water. This process was driven by two large diesel engines designed for tanks and now redesigned for the murder of fellow humans.

It's easy to pick out the mothers. They died still clutching their children. Older couples are also found dead in each other's arms still attempting to comfort the other. Others are found crumpled in front of the door with bloodied hands that fought unsuccessfully to get the door back open.

Once the doors are open, the guards have no patience with these *sonderkommando* (Jewish unit workers). Bernie feels the sting of a whip on his back as a Ukrainian guard pushes and curses him to work faster to clear the bodies out so when the next train comes in they will be able to "process" the next group. The Nazis have proven to be competent in finding just the right amount of depravity in their Ukrainian guards to assign them to a unit that fits them. After all, a man works much more efficiently if he enjoys his work.

The first body he is compelled to drag out is a man he recognizes from the train. He had talked with the man about their eventual destination. His heart races as he comes to the realization that he may find his own daughter within this desolation of human lives. Not wanting to risk another beating, Bernie is torn between the anxiety of finding his daughter in this dead room and how he may react if, God forbid, he does. Bernie yearns for something, someone to comfort his grieving spirit. The words of the Shema come to his lips, "The Lord is our God. The Lord is One."

Body after body is pulled out to a nearby pit and dumped. The smell is overwhelming. There is already a layer of bloating bodies from the day before or possibly even longer. As each body is extricated, it becomes obvious that all are not dead. One young boy, maybe three years old is found alive and moaning. The guard summarily grabs the child by a leg and tosses him into the pit alive. In this community vicious and unseemly behavior among the guards toward prisoners guarantees a promotion. The more killed at the hands of these guards, who enjoy killing, the less the Third Reich has to deal with bringing the "Final Solution" to its conclusion.

As the last body is hauled to the pit, Bernie is exceedingly relieved that he did not have to see his daughter if she were indeed to be found in this killing room.

The exertion of this overwhelming physical task, even for this farmer accustomed to hard labor, has left him hungry and thirsty. There is obviously no relief in sight as the guards kick these prisoners off to their next grim task. Transition to this macabre way of life is indeed a disorienting experience and shakes one to the core of what it means to be a human. Everything one ever held as a civilized value has to be renegotiated. Failure to adapt results in immediate execution.

Meanwhile, Celia has also been selected out along with a few other girls to become a slave to the Third Reich. She was chosen because of her farm background and the fact she is only half Jewish made little or no difference. If she had been full German and gotten this far and was now a witness to this clandestine pogrom, she would have died along with the Jews anyway. On the other hand, young Jews that show promise as manual laborers generally are singled out and then summarily worked to death. After going through the humiliation of having to strip naked in front of a group of leering guards, she also has her head shaved and is given a prison uniform. They are totally at a loss as to what is happening to them. The Nazis have once again successfully accomplished the secrecy and deception of the true destiny of these transports.

In the typical German way of wasting no time, within minutes she is assigned to a Jewish woman named Sylvia. She in turn is ordered to show Celia and several other young women the next step in this bizarre unfolding of events. Sylvia is in charge of the women who are to be the clothing sorters. She is a young woman, maybe in her early thirties, who was a seamstress in her previous life. She is still alive because of her skills at making tailor fit officers' uniforms.

Not one of this new group have a clue as to what they are sorting. Unbeknownst to them it is the clothing of their fellow passengers that arrived with them only an hour ago and have since been gassed.

Celia is paired with a woman who has already been there for some time to learn the process.

A few days later a new group of women is brought in. Pointing to Celia and a girl about her age from the new group, Sylvia barks out an order.

"You two will sort through all male clothing. Anything left in the pockets will be dropped in buckets that you will be provided. When you fill two buckets, carry them to the sorters over there," she says pointing to another group of woman busy with the task of sorting through the buckets for valuables. Wanting to stress one more point before sending them off, Sylvia lowers her voice.

"Do not allow gold or silver to be seen by the Ukrainian guards. They'll steal it."

It's apparent that the Germans in their need for the wealth of the Jews considered the Jews possessions more valuable than the Jews themselves. To ensure that these transferees bring only their best, they are encouraged to travel with only those things that they consider their most valuable.

As the old hand, Celia is the first to introduce herself. Her new partner's name is Sara Leninbacher. She was captured by the Nazis along with some Poles outside the Warsaw Ghetto.

After a long day, Celia shows Sara to their barracks where she meets other women who are also part of the Nazi work force. The quarters are Spartan by design but livable and fairly comfortable. These barracks have planks for flooring as opposed to barracks for those who are working in the quarry and have only a dirt floor. The food is also plain but edible. What these neophytes are quickly learning is that they are the exceptions to the rule in this camp. They have been spared because they—at least for the present—are useful to the Nazi machine. They also are learning that the majority of the workers here labor at back-breaking projects either in the stone quarry or in the forest supplying wood to keep the fires going to burn the bodies that can no longer be buried.

These quarry and forest workers usually have a turnover rate of just a few months due to the harshness of the work combined with no medical attention to disease and extremely limited caloric intake.

These women are soon pulled into union with the other women by the initiatives of Sylvia. Sylvia owes much of her longevity to her ability to organize and keep her workforce performing with a high level of efficiency. After Celia and Sara are assigned an area for sleep, they spend some time learning about one another.

"My parents have already made their visit here. That was over a year ago. I received a postcard from them when they first arrived but then I never heard from them again. My suspicions are pretty well confirmed that they never left this camp," says Sara.

"My father and I were packed in the same cattle car along with as many as it would hold. As soon as we were on the loading platform, they separated us. I fear the same for him that you fear happened to your parents," says Celia in a heavy tone. The two of them are soon fast asleep.

In another part of this camp, well hidden from this area, her father is housed in a similar barrack. His is also designed noticeably different than the barracks housing the majority of the apparently disposable workforce. He is concerned about the fate of his daughter. This soon proves to be an exercise in futility as there is never time for anything other than an all consuming concern for the minute-to-minute fate of oneself.

The morning begins with revelry from a boisterous guard ordering everyone to be out of their bunks, get their toilet needs taken care of, eat whatever is presented and be glad you got something in spite of its quality or taste. Then, despite the weather conditions, be prepared to immediately line up outside of their barrack and be accounted for. This exercise will last as long as it takes for the officer in charge to make his rounds.

In the short time Bernie has been here, he has noticed how each man more or less avoids the others. It appears that each prisoner has a full-time job merely staying alive. Also the Nazis in their developed sense toward their own security have been able to seek out those prisoners who for an extra piece of bread will inform on the activities of others. The Nazis, in their proficiency, have purposely created this atmosphere of distrust in order to prevent the kind of fraternization that could foster a rebellion.

The first assignment of the morning given Bernie along with another man is to make a visit to each barrack and pick up those that have died duing the night. Today he is paired with a German Jew named Leo Gantz. Leo has been here for nearly a month and has done nearly every task the camp has thrown at him.

"Before I arrived here, I was employed as a civil engineer in Berlin. I am sure the only reason I'm still alive today is because they are planning on building another gas chamber and need an on-site engineer," he acknowledges to Bernie.

"I don't understand what they want from me. I'm a farmer," says Bernie.

"That may be the thing that makes you an asset. Being a farmer says your resourcefulness is just what they need day to day," expresses Leo with an air of certainty.

With all the prisoners who are physically able to work out on the various job locations, it leaves only the sick and dead confined in the barracks. As the two make their way into the first site they are confronted with the smell of total and absolute degradation. Bernie has never in his life seen such squalor. Dysentery runs rampant throughout the camps. It's caused primarily from putrid water. Some bunks are crusted and stained with fecal matter. There are a half dozen emaciated men lying in their bunks too sick to get up.

The mattresses are nothing more than straw or rags. Either way the lice can be seen crawling throughout them as though they are being kenneled and waiting in great anticipation for their donors to return.

Two of these men have already died. The Ukrainian guard who has accompanied Bernie and Leo is already rifling through these dead men's belongings looking for anything of value. These guards are not just cruel but they are also thieves. They'll steal anything they think they can get away with as long as it will buy at least a bottle of vodka.

"Oh my God!" gasps Bernie. He's standing looking up at something that he ignored as they came in. At first it appears to be nothing more than a coat hanging from a rafter. With the coat making a twist around it becomes apparent that there is a man inside it with a piece of rope around his neck. The man is so emaciated that there is hardly anything other than a skeleton with some skin.

"Oh my God, Leo. He's hung himself," exclaims Bernie dismayed.

The Ukrainian guard bursts into uproarious laughter at the shocked attitude Bernie is exhibiting. It's the same guard he had the day before who shot the faltering prisoner trying to clean the railcar. Now his laughter has switched to a growl as he grabs one of the poor sick wretches out of his bunk. The man, nearly comatose, releases diarrhea that splatters across the guard's boots. Slamming the man to the floor he begins to curse him as he kicks him over and over until the man's small amount of remaining blood begins to trickle from his ears and nose.

Bernie's blood shoots from his feet to his head as his anger explodes. Before Leo can stop him, he has leaped on the guard from behind and with his unrestrained strength he has both arms wrapped around this cretin's neck and slowly squeezes the life out of him despite the efforts of Leo to stop him.

Bernie is gasping for air, looking stunned as this guard now lays dead at his feet along with the poor wretch who he had just minutes before kicked to death. Leo is frantically running to the window to see who may be privy to this mayhem, terrified at what could lay ahead for himself.

"Oy Gevalt! You stupid meshugence! Look what you have done now!" screams Leo. "We're as good as dead!"

Bernie is beginning to recover. His mind is churning out a response he hopes they can pull off. These "special units" that pick up the dead around the camp are often left alone by the guards because of a fear of contracting disease. Bernie had heard this earlier from some of the *sondorkommandos* back at the barracks.

"Quick help me get his uniform off," says Bernie beginning to tear at the dead man's clothing. Leo is at a complete loss. He hardly knows which way to turn. For the lack of any thought of his own, he begins to follow Bernie's lead.

Within minutes they have the guard naked. Bernie's mind is traveling at a high rate of speed at this point. Till now Leo has been in an absolute panic mode. Suddenly the light is coming on and he is catching on to Bernie's plan. Without words they haul the body of this dead tormentor to the barrack door, check for any other guards. The coast is clear. In one swift move they throw his body on the empty cart brought along to haul the dead away. With this task soon finished without a hitch, they quickly place the other dead over the top of their victim along with his uniform thereby concealing their felony.

Bernie returns to the barrack for one more adjustment. The guard's weapons need to be hidden. Leo takes the lead this time. There is a seldom-used stove in this barrack. His eye is on the stove pipe. Quickly he has it dismantled and reassembled with a rifle, a pistol and their ammunition packed inside the tube.

They then proceed to another barrack hoping to get a couple more bodies to insure covering their deception. Soon they have a cart load and begin their journey to the pit. Knowing they will confront a few guards along the way they conspire on another leg of this illusion. Each time they see a guard they begin to yell "typhus, typhus, typhus."

The guards can't get out of the way fast enough. They consider it bad enough that they have to work with this "vermin" without catching their diseases. The cart is slowly making its way straight to the pit. Neither Leo nor Bernie have said a word to the other. Both are able to discern their next move without words.

Finding themselves at the rim of this huge open grave, they systematically begin to unload their cargo. This procedure is so routine that little attention is paid by the guards. Careful to place a few bodies over the top of their dead tormentor, they routinely return to their assignment.

CHAPTER 18

TREBLINKA—THE SUMMER OF 1943

On the eastern front deep in the heart of Russia, for the first time the Germans begin to feel the bite of defeat. It's changing things on the home front as well. The mood of the keepers in the death camps is no longer that of a relaxed methodical one-sided killing zone.

The recent reaction to this growing phenomenon is to speed things along in their murderous pogrom so as to leave no witnesses. Prisoners are being transferred to more western camps and plans are in place to increase the number of gas chambers and crematoriums to facilitate the objectives of the "Final Solution." One member of the inner circle of the German military was overheard to say as he pondered the "Final Solution" in the shadow of a possible defeat, "We will either be hailed as heroes or as the most murderous people in the world."

The mood of the Treblinka command is in a severe flux. The camp commander decides to dig up all the mass graves of the gassed victims over the years and burn them so as to leave no evidence of Nazi misdoings. This is to hedge against the possibility that the tide of world opinion could go against them and the true purpose of these camps be discovered.

The task is hurried along with extra crews delegated to cut more timber as fuel for the fires that are now glowing in the night sky as if the gates of hell have opened. The work of exhuming the decomposing corpses is made quicker with the aid of a machine capable of digging thousands of bodies in a short time and piling them as workers throw them one at a time on a flaming pyre built from a grid of railroad rails. The decaying corpses are soaked in kerosene, gasoline, or diesel fuel, anything they can garner to ensure these corpses burn down enough to leave no evidence of a human being.

The disappearance of the Ukrainian guard is taken in stride by the command center. It would be completely out of the scope of German thought to imagine that these drunken Slavic guards are much more dependable than any other subhuman. Many of these men were recruited from the ranks of Russian POWs. Others are strictly mercenaries. The common denominator with all of them is that they possess an unusual propensity to inflict pain on other living creatures. It's been a matter of observation that the Nazis are easily able to sort out the perverse types from among these defeated nations and then to utilize these depraved POWs for their own nefarious ends.

What the Nazis have not given much thought to is that within their own ranks there could be a Jewish sympathizer. They are sure that once anyone has had dealings with Jews they will join them in their quest to rid the world of such vermin. While there is scrutiny toward guards that have a nose for stealing Jewish gold, there is no close scrutiny for this fraternizing kind of behavior among the guards. Nonetheless, risking danger to himself, there is a POW Ukrainian guard named Mikhail who has befriended the *sondorkommandos*. He has on occasion surreptitiously supplied these unfortunate victims forced to turn on their own people with extra food and he keeps them aware of the snitches as well as he can. He isn't a man of many words with the inmates for fear of other guards taking notice and dealing out some sort of retribution. The sympathy in his eyes for the wretchedness ordered against all of these families with children, parents and other loved ones is apparent.

The danger of snitches is a constant concern among the prisoners. There is always an opportunist who will turn on their fellow sufferers if promised their own suffering will be abated, even if only temporary. Consequently, the heroic actions of these two new combatants are not a camp news story. But nonetheless it has managed to be a point of discussion among a select few that Leo knows to be trustworthy.

One evening shortly after this incident and after a grueling day of digging up bodies for burning, another *sondorkcommando* named Barak visits Bernie. He's a man in his early forties who has been kept out of the gas chambers because of his carpentry skills.

"I want you to know that we all will do what we can to keep your heroic deed alive among our people. Some of us may live to tell the story that at least a portion of us were willing to risk death for justice."

Bernie is somewhat taken aback and more than a little nervous over the attention he's drawing from people that were nowhere near the incident. Looking over at Leo, as Leo is the only other link between himself and their secret, Bernie's demeanor silently displays his dismay over Leo breaking the trust he imagined they shared.

Catching Bernie's fear over his betrayal of trust, Leo attempts to explain. "Bernie there are things happening in this camp that you aren't aware of. Not everyone is willingly going to the gas chambers without an effort to get out of here. There is an underground movement to form a brigade to escape from this hell hole. Your effort is the kind of act that lends encouragement to all of us involved.

"I also don't want you to be concerned about our little episode with that guard getting to the wrong people. We know who the snitches are, thanks to a righteous guard who keeps us informed."

Bernie's facial expression shows a bit of relief but it's still apparent that he's not comfortable with this episode reaching the ears of people he doesn't know.

Listening carefully to Leo, Barak picks up the conversation once again.

"We've formed a committee for our liberation, either as escapees or for an epic death in the attempt. We need men like you who are willing to go up against these wolves."

Bernie settles down a lot after hearing what Barak says. His face takes on a more sober expression. Every day he discovers to a greater extent just what the full dimension of their situation as Jews fully means.

"How long do we have before they get to us?" Bernie asks.

Barak is somewhat taken aback by the seeming naiveté of this possible recruit.

"Today, tomorrow, who knows? But one thing you can be sure of is that it will happen. There will be none of us left to tell the world what has gone on here unless we make it happen. These monsters are hell-bent on gassing every Jew in the world. If we don't make the effort to escape, it will remain their chapter in history to write claiming it a mystery what happened to all of us."

Everyone has had an opportunity to speak their piece. There is a silence in the room as all eyes are on Bernie awaiting his decision.

Bernie is uncomfortable with this kind of attention. After all he's just a simple farmer caught up in the insane ambitions of demented despots, whether German or Russian. Wiping both his hands across his stubby beard, he lets out a sigh.

"Okay I'm in. What do I do now?"

Barak has a look of satisfaction with Bernie's decision.

"First let me thank you for deciding to join us. You are now a member of a secret organization whose end is to escape this place. We must succeed to tell the world of the crimes committed here."

There has been a gradual progression of younger men drifting in as this conversation has continued.

A young man by the name of Zev is the first to speak, interrupting Barak.

"You can help us dig. We've started a tunnel."

Barak raises his voice against this young man.

"You boys should forget that. There's enough snitches around here that these Nazi mamzers will let you dig the whole thing and then when you think you've put something over on them, they'll surprise you with a trip to the gas chamber and the rest of us will have to carry your dead asses out to be burned."

Not wanting to have their project undermined by more thoughtful minds, Zev and a half dozen other young men throw their hands up in disgust and bolt out the door like men on a mission.

Barak turns to Bernie and Leo. "I don't want those boys to know of our plans. They're way too dangerous and flamboyant with their schemes."

Bernie has returned to a pensiveness. Meantime he has sat down in a chair with his hands folded between his legs and his head hanging. In a moment it becomes obvious, as he wipes his big rough hands across his eyes, that he is crying.

Leo is the first to notice.

"What's come over you Bernie?"

"It's my daughter, Leo. I don't know where she is. I haven't seen her since they separated us on that damnable platform. I really fear the worst."

Barak speaks up with an intensity and a genuine concern in his voice.

"That's simple enough. I'll get our Ukrainian guard, Mikhail, to run an inquest."

"Can you really do that for me?" questions a still weeping Bernie but now they're tears of relief.

"I'm certain it can be done. If she's working anywhere in the camp, Mikhail will find her."

"Her name is Celia Goldberg," volunteers Bernie almost laughing with relief that this is going to be taken care of. He pauses for a moment as the reality of what this inquest may also reveal hits him. "I'll want to know either way," he adds with his voice returning to a somberness.

CHAPTER 19

SURVIVAL AT ANY COST

Celia and Sara have become fairly proficient at what they do. The macabre aspect of sorting through the valuables of people who have not yet cooled from the cruelty of their execution is never completely absent but then one soon gets lost in the performance of doing a repetitive task. Even the Germans have given up on trying to keep these women from talking. The only thing they demand is that all items be cataloged by value and purpose. Women's natural deftness with household items, keeps this work open for those who show a diligence to follow the Nazi obsession for order.

A Ukrainian guard who may be trying to cut one of these women out of the group for his own pleasure may find a resistance from several of them that he hadn't counted on. Early on these women formed sisterly bonds with one another for the sole purpose of protecting each other from the misogynous tendencies of all these men—Germans, Ukrainians and even Jewish male prisoners. The easiest prey for these drunken perverted guards is to grab a naked woman running for her life from the gas chamber, force her into a nearby barrack and rape her, and then send her back to be gassed.

Sara is a seasoned Jewish Resistance Fighter from inside the Warsaw Ghetto. She was arrested along with a group of Polish fighters just outside the Ghetto. The Germans have no more use for the Polish Resistance than they do the Jews. Because she had false identification identifying her as Polish and since she was a female no alternate identification could be decided as with a man's circumcision.

It may be her captors are treating her as Polish rather than Jewish and thus have given her a reprieve, or it may be just the fact that she's a healthy young woman and able to be worked. Either way she doesn't seem to pose a threat. The majority of the security concerns are with the men.

One woman in Celia and Sara's barrack is a Jewish woman named Ruchla. She is particularly agitated. She has been in the camp for nearly two weeks. When she arrived they took her feeble-minded son to the infirmary, telling her he would be evaluated by a doctor and returned to her. After a brief interview they then took her out of the line to the gas chamber and put her in the work line.

"I don't know what they could be evaluating this long on Aron. He's a good boy, he's never hurt anyone," says Ruchla.

The other women in the barracks have tried to comfort her without telling her the truth.

"Maybe they've found some tasks for him to do," one woman offers.

Another says, "Maybe they found some treatment for him and are keeping him in the hospital."

The next day Ruchla is agitated beyond reason. Her breakfast is left untouched. The blank stare in her eyes tells the whole story. "I will not be put off any longer. I'm going to demand they let me see my son. They can't do this to a mother, can they?"

Celia is the first to try and bring reality to this grieving mother.

"That probably is not the best thing for you to do right now, Ruchla," says Celia sitting next to her. Putting her arm around her, she tries to give as much support as she can.

Ruchla has dropped her head into her hands as she rocks back and forth and begins to weep. "They've killed him haven't they," she wails.

Her words strike her hard as this is the first time she's been able to speak the unspeakable out loud. It's as though to speak them gives them truth. Ruchla is inconsolable. No one is able to say anything because there is really nothing to say. Everyone knows what this place is, including Ruchla. It's just that the pain of confronting that unspeakable truth is an impossible torment for everyone who has lost their loved ones. Especially when it's to the insane whims of these maniacal and ruthless leaders.

In a few minutes the roll call assembles the women and they soon begin their monotonous day of sorting. Ruchla is particularly despondent. She stays much to herself all morning. The others give her space but are also ready to do whatever they can to help her through this adversity.

By noon their attention has relaxed. The women are taking a lunch break and are depositing their scissors in a tool container under the watchful eye of a guard. Ruchla slowly makes her way along with the other women, her expression is woeful and dark. Suddenly without a hint of warning she springs like an unleashed cat with scissors in hand aimed directly at the neck of the unsuspecting guard. In a split second the blood is squirting from a severed carotid artery.

The guard lets out a blood curdling shriek as he pulls the buried scissor blades from the deep gash in his neck. In the next second Ruchla has grabbed the guard's fallen rifle. Aiming it directly at his head, she fires a shot leaving only a small portion of his skull intact.

While the unscheduled gunshot catches the attention of every guard in the yard, they nonetheless are caught unprepared. Before they can respond and in the confusion Ruchla runs toward the electrified fence surrounding the compound. She throws her entire body into the mesh of wires sending the full force of the current through her.

By this time the confused guards are rifle butting everyone in sight. The remaining women are herded into a bunch and commanded to lie face down on the ground. They are then kicked and stomped mercilessly by the guards until the camp commander arrives.

He looks fresh and crisp in his SS uniform with all its bold red insignias flashing out against their black background. What sets this man apart from the other officers is not his size or looks but rather his companions. It's a large Rottweiler dog in one hand and a Luger in the other. He orders the women to their feet in spite of the beating they have just endured. Those who can't respond to his command are immediately and systematically shot with the pistol. Convinced he now has the attention of the remaining women, he orders them into a single line and begins a diatribe against all of them.

"Count out in blocks of four," he shouts.

The women begin a cadence, "One, two, three, four, one, two, three,…"

After the remaining sixteen women finish, he orders all the number fours to step out.

"As an object lesson to all you ones, twos, and threes, you will now watch as these fours are hanged in honor of your obstinacy."

With that said and a wave of his hand a number of guards surround the condemned women and begin their march toward the gallows kept in clear sight of everyone. In less than five minutes the deed is done. The bodies are left hanging there for the next three days including a Sabbath.

Celia and Sara are among those spared. But spared is a relative term. They along with the others have been spared a hanging, but not from being forced to strip naked and undergo being raped by their Ukrainian guards.

It is the way all things go in these camps designed for only one thing—the quick or slow death of those finding themselves here. Oftentimes it is not enough that the tormenters demand their death, but many times prefer to degrade, subjugate and mentally dominate them before they murder them.

So this event ends only to have some other form of human degradation assigned to them. For most of these women they would agree to become obsequious and servile to these "pigs" in order to live another day. Survival at any cost is the mantra among the young. The threat of death and false rumors of staying alive prevail in every corner of these camps.

Prostitutes are provided for the German personnel working in the camps. These come from German, Polish and Russian women finding themselves incarcerated for so called anti-social reasons or as political prisoners. False rumors abound that after six months as prostitutes they will be set free. Jewish women are considered hygienically impure and therefore are not provided for German personnel, but are regularly raped by the Ukrainian guards and secretly raped by German personnel.

With stressful circumstances changing every hour, Sylvia is doing all she can to keep herself and her adopted family intact. She considers many of these subordinate women as younger sisters.

"There are some good reports coming in that tell us the Germans are being beat back significantly in Russia. If we watch ourselves and stay healthy enough to work, we may live long enough to see freedom," says Sylvia with an encouraging report.

Celia and Sara listen to this message with skepticism. For all that Sylvia talks of with the hopes that it will calm her work crew, it only serves to provoke these two to imagine they could wrest out their own freedom sooner.

"I appreciate Sylvia and how she tries to look out for us but I know from all I've experienced with these Nazis that as soon as we become expendable they will either have a bullet in our head or we'll be making soot clouds over Poland," says Sara with her chutzpa.

"I agree with you," says Celia. "But what can we do to get ourselves out of this hell hole any sooner?"

Sara remains quiet for the moment as she appears to be plotting something. She looks around to make sure no idle ears overhear what she is going to say. Satisfied they're alone Sara, begins to unfold her plot.

"You know that pig of a guard that took me to rape me last week, well I pretended I enjoyed it. I flattered him by telling him I had noticed him around the camp and how I hoped it would be him that got me. Now he thinks I'm his girlfriend."

"Well I'm glad you enjoyed it, I sure didn't. That pig that took me stunk so bad I thought I would throw up," says Celia with disgust remembering what an animal the man was with all his grunting.

"I didn't say I enjoyed it. I said I pretended I enjoyed it. That pretense may be the thing that's going to help get us out of here," reiterates Sara with more of her impertinence.

"How can you even imagine that somebody like him could help us get out of here?" asks Celia with more than a bit of skepticism.

They both return to their sorting as they notice one of the guards seems to have more than the usual nonchalant attitude for what they are doing. He is conferring with another guard as that guard points in their direction. Now he is making his way to their location.

The girls attempt to appear too busy to notice. Nonetheless this kind of attention can only be regarded as disturbing. Both can feel their stomachs rising up into their throats as the guard stops directly in front of them.

"Which of you is Celia Goldberg?" he asks.

Celia feels her body go numb with fear. She is all but paralyzed as she steps forward unable to speak, with the expectation that her time has come.

The guard looks her over for just a moment. He has a different look about him than the others. There is something different in his eyes. What surfaces is an unusual look of compassion. Just as quickly as the fear had grasped her, a sense of well-being replaces it.

"Is your father Bernie Goldberg?" he further questions.

Now some apprehension again replaces what a moment ago was calmness. Celia's voice takes on a bleak tone.

"Ye-Yes, he's my father. What's happened to him?" she replies with a quivering voice.

He continues to speak with a calmness uncharacteristic of these Ukrainian guards. "Your father is working in a different part of the camp and doing well. He's been concerned about you. I'll be happy to report to him that you are in good health."

Celia can't help but look perplexed at this seeming oxymoron of a man. Not quite sure how she can be having a civilized conversation with a nemesis such as this. It remains awkward as she tries to find a proper way of thanking this seemingly kindly guard.

"I can't tell you what this news has done for me. I thank you from the bottom of my heart for taking the time to do this for us."

"My name is Mikhail. I truly wish there was more I could do for you but unfortunately there is nothing else," he adds with a tone mired in regret.

The rest of the day goes along much easier than normal for Celia after receiving this bit of unsolicited good news.

The next day is sunny and warm. Summer is announcing itself for these people in an uninvited way. The days are longer which means the workday ranges from sunup till sundown. Disease and starvation remain the constant companions of these hapless captives despite the season. The morning roll call is interrupted with an announcement that there are going to be more hangings this morning as a dozen young men from camp #1 have been apprehended emerging from a tunnel they had dug to the outside. All the camp are required to watch.

Celia is particularly attentive as they drag the miserable beaten bodies of these boys forcing them to their feet as they place the nooses around their neck. She hopes she will not see her father in this exhibit. She is sorry for these young men who merely wanted to live but relieved that her father is not among them.

The method of hanging these escapees is to leave their toes touching the ground, thus preventing them from strangling as long as their toes don't give out. It's a slow, cruel strangulation taking as long as fifteen minutes to complete. The Ukrainians find it particularly amusing and take wagers as to who will last the longest. The camp is also obliged to stand watching for the corpses to be cut down and ultimately pitched onto the pyre.

There is so much death every day in this camp that the Germans don't realize that those who have not committed suicide are people who have adjusted themselves to these daily horrors with a degree of callousness. It's certainly not because they've accepted its repulsion as a way of life but nevertheless have adapted themselves to its dreadfulness in order to survive. The prayer on the lips of even the most irreligious is "God, if there is a God, save me."

CHAPTER 20

LIBERATION AND REUNIFICATION

The name tag on his uniform says Brutka. He's a stout man who had been in the Russian army. During the long German siege into Russia, the Germans took many prisoners. Brutka is one of these. Rather than waste the military training of these POWs, they place them as guards in the concentration camps. Usually they are chosen for their beastly behavior toward Jews, Gypsies, the retarded and homosexuals.

Since Sara's forced pairing with Brutka, he has become especially enamored with her. She has been leading him on for weeks. She now has him believing that at their first chance she will have another sexual liaison with him. As part of their job, it's her and Celia's responsibility to bring the sorted clothing to the rail head for packing. Since he is in charge of packing all the classified clothing into the railcars that will be shipped back to Germany for some type of military use, she sees him every day.

On this particular day Sara and Celia have lagged back in order to be the last to bring their bin of wares. Brutka is pleased with this arrangement as when they are finished there will be no one else behind them to interfere with his long awaited tryst with Sara.

"Hello," she says demurely.

It takes no more than that to have this fool rush in like the sex-crazed lout he is. In a matter of seconds, he is pulling Sara into the railcar pawing at her as he throws her onto a bundle of clothing.

In an attempt to slow him down, she says with her best effort to smile, "Wait, wait I have something special I want to do for you."

Brutka stops abruptly with Sara's dress lifted in mid-air. His eyes are wide open with anticipation. He doesn't say a word, he merely responds with his whole body going limp. She turns him around, pushing him down on the soft bale of cloth.

Now standing over him with a provocative stare she begins to disrobe. His eyes are as big as they can get. He can hardly believe this is actually happening to him.

Next she begins to undress him, starting with the only thing he cares that he is free of—his pants. She has his pants down around his boots. He, by this time is so full of anticipation that he is putty in her hands. She rolls him over on his stomach and with his own belt binds his hands behind him, all the time giggling as though this is the prelude to something that's going to be fun.

In another swift move, she removes his service knife and sinks the blade deep into his unsuspecting neck. The only sound he makes as his legs kick is a gurgle.

Celia is on the outside of the car, both as a lookout and an accomplice. Sara, still naked, shouts, "Quick get in here and slide the door shut."

This train is on a schedule—a German schedule, which means that only in the event of the second coming of Christ will it be off its docket.

Celia leaps aboard and together they slide the door closed. The only light that makes its way into their car is from a small window in each end of the car. Both are breathing hard, not sure what is going to happen next. It's expected that within a short time the train will be making its way south toward Warsaw and then to Germany. For now it's imperative they both keep their wits about them.

The first urgency is to stay still long enough not to be heard scraping about and to stay out of sight of any rail personnel who may be nearby laboring to finish their tasks and get this train moving. Since these cars are not believed to be carrying a human cargo the doors are seldom checked to be latched shut. The three of them were the last to be lingering in this area and are as far as railroad personnel responsibility, they see no one unaccounted for.

The engine sounds its departure whistle, the car jerks as the locomotive pulls all the slack from the couplings of each boxcar. These two near escapees hold their breath as the car moves uninterrupted through the gate. Twenty minutes later they look at one another for a moment and both burst into tears. They hold each other while laughing and crying at the same time.

After an hour they feel the dread of this dead body riding with them. They agree they need to get rid of the extra passenger. Stripping every trace of identification from him leaves him naked. Climbing atop a bundle of clothing, they watch out the small window for a convenient place to dump the body.

"Look there," points Celia as a truss bridge appears down the track. It crosses over a tributary river feeding into a much larger waterway. She continues her thought, "Let's dump our dear Brutka right there."

It's a decision that does not require a vote. Both are in total agreement. The massive car door is slid open enough to allow a body to be pushed out. Together they drag the naked body to the door's edge and just as their car is beginning to cross the trestle they give it one last heave. Poor old Brutka's dead body bounces off the side of the bridge once before going airborne then hits the water.

Celia is looking over the landscape. Her heart pounds as she makes a surprising discovery. "I know this area. Our farm is along this track. We're only about twenty kilometers away," she exclaims.

They had originally planned on getting off the train somewhere along the way and sticking to the forest. This new development is worthy of some additional thought.

"I think we need to get off this train soon. We don't know where it stops and what kind of security there's going to be around it," says Sara in her usual matter of fact tone. Celia has found that she relies on Sara's sharp perception, allowing her a leadership position.

"Okay," Celia agrees unenthusiastically, for her eye has turned to something else. She has her eye on a dress poking out of a bundle. Many times while sorting through these victims' clothing her mind would wander as she secretly desired that she would at some point be able to once again wear a dress like many of these.

Pulling it out she holds it up to herself. A smile is beginning to make its way across her face. It appears that it's her size. Sara looks a bit surprised at the enthusiasm Celia is displaying over rummaging through these belongings. She, in her typical pragmatic manner, disparages Celia's choice.

"That will look damn good in the woods. It may not keep the bugs from biting or keep you warm at night but it will look damn good," says Sara. Her voice is full of sarcasm as she also begins to rummage through these castoffs. She has found a pair of man's pants and a lady's coat that fit. After setting these aside, she is overcome with Celia's exuberance and she too slips into scavenging. Finding a flowery print she slips into it.

It's as though they are trying to make up for all the days they missed growing up. They laugh and giggle as would any other young women their age trying on clothes with each other. Unfortunately all of the young women who previously wore these clothes can no longer share in this innocent past time.

The days are longer but not long enough for this duo to dawdle. It's imperative they develop a plan and it's best they do it while they continue to have an advantage.

Celia is paying particular attention for any landmarks that look familiar. She's beginning to spot farms that she remembers from the days her family would take the train into Warsaw.

"Oh look there," she says pointing to a farm, "there used to be a big Jewish family that would get on here. They had at least a dozen kids. I remember because they all smelled like garlic."

Her thoughts begin to wander. *"I wonder if any of them are still alive."*

Both are quiet as they reflect back on the past hour. The anticipation is building for their next step of getting off the train.

Celia finally has something to say. "I know my mother can hide us but I hate to put that burden on her. We're only a couple miles from the farm now. This train is traveling too fast to get off here."

Celia's mind returns to a time she and the neighbor boys would hop on the train and ride up the big hill. "About a kilometer on the other side of our farm is a steep grade that will slow the train enough for us to leap out."

Celia's heart is in her throat as she leaps to the window on the other side of the car. They are passing her home. There in the dimness of the evening sun, she spots her mother working in the garden. It's a scene that she feared would remain only as a silent, distant memory. She lets out an involuntary scream which her mother doesn't hear over the rumbling noise of the train. She also wonders about the young woman working alongside her that she doesn't remember seeing before.

Within seconds the train has sped on with the potential to leave this scene as only a memory stored with the others. Celia is beside herself to get off this train. The sight of her mother has reignited the pain of all that has been taken from her. The recent daily concern with her own survival has overridden her link with a normal life. A hate and resentment is building within her. There remains a fear that something may yet prevent her from a chance to recapture her past.

In a couple of minutes, the engine begins its climb. Celia has the door open as far as it will go in the anticipation of leaping to freedom. It's almost as though this contrivance that has played such an active role in carrying so many to their death is now attempting to purge itself of its dastardly image in releasing this duo.

Celia has only one thing on her mind and that is to get home. Sara is well aware of this obsessive change in her friend and is ready to be there with her. The darkness of their Treblinka experience is suddenly overridden with the great anticipation of a new life. Even though this new life may still have its dimness it remains brighter than any death camp.

Both are sitting with their feet dangling over the edge of the opening. They are more than prepared to leave behind those moment-to-moment death threats that constantly hung over their heads. The locomotive slows to a crawl in its attempt to conquer the big hill.

At the same time they both yell, "Jump."

Both land on their feet as the boxcar haven has done all it can for them and continues down the track without them. They both hustle into the forest refuge before they are seen by the wrong person. Anticipating the possibility of someone over analyzing the crime scene, they carry all of the bloody clothing as well as Brutka's uniform, planning to hide it in the woods. Sara has his rifle slung over her shoulder along with a belt of extra cartridges and his field knife. She feels a strong sense of well-being with this extra protection.

Celia knows exactly where they are. This portion of the forest has been her playground since she was a young child. Within fifteen minutes they are at the edge of their hay field. It looks as though it has just been cut. Her mind returns to how many times she fought with her father about cutting hay and what she would give to have those days back again.

Sara remains an observer. She has an idea that Celia's quietness probably bears an emotional component. Willing to let Celia have her time, she remains silent also. After standing at the edge of this field staring down at the farm for a period of time, Sara says, "I know what I'm going to say may not set well with you but I think we need to stay out of sight for a couple days. We have no idea what may be going on around here. I think we should just watch from the woods."

"I know you're probably right," admits Celia with a sigh, "but we are going to need food and water tonight. Let's wait until dark, I know where there're both."

They content themselves to remain out of sight and watch. Everything is so familiar to Celia. Her eyes well up with tears as she recalls the day the Germans came and took her and her father. How she watched her home disappear behind her with her mother left behind. How naive they were about the relocation propaganda the SS officials had assured them was going to reunite them again.

As her mind continues to wander over how her reappearance will put her mother at risk, there is also the question of who the young woman seen with her mother is.

Soon the lamps in the house go out. It's time to make a move. The night is warm and quiet with a full moon rising in the east. Trembling a bit from anticipation, Celia says, "Okay Sara, stay close behind me."

Attempting to move as quietly as possible, with Celia taking the lead, they begin to make their way across the darkened field. She leads Sara stealthily around in back to the barn and to the same water trough Rhena drank from a few months previous.

After taking on all the water they can hold, hunger continues to plague them.

"Stay here Sara, I'll be right back," says Celia as she makes her way near the house to a root cellar. She uses the front of her skirt as a pouch and within minutes returns bearing potatoes and turnips.

Chomping as they go, they return to the forest's edge. With thirst quenched and hunger diminished, fallen leaves form a soft bed. The smell of the crumbling leaves mixed with the aroma of damp earth is perfume compared to the odor of burning human bodies. Before falling asleep both have similar thoughts and individually thank God for rescuing them and pray that He continue His protection and care.

Neither of them awoke until late in the morning. The July sun is warm and inviting. They are amazed at how comfortable they are. No guards, no sorting, even the simple joy of having potatoes and turnips to eat at will is a luxury. They have a friendly forest on one side and an inviting home on the other. There is a sense of safety and security in this quiet domestic setting that neither of them thought they would ever enjoy again.

Celia is content with their decision to wait and watch. It is affording her the chance to observe her mother in a different way. Before was taken away, she led a fairly normal life. She was many times at odds with her mother as most young people are with their parents. But today she can't help but gaze across this fresh mowed hay field with a different set of values. A few months ago this task would have been thought of as drudge work. Today she happily embraces a sense of community with everything this home stands for knowing she would gladly complete even the worst task this farm demands rather than ever return to the slavery of the past few months.

They are positioned approximately three hundred meters from the house and barns. This provides a distance to observe but not be observed.

Celia watches with a longing heart as her mother goes about her duties. This new and different vantage point allows her to see what had nearly disappeared from her life forever.

The enigma remains as to who this mystery girl is. It's obvious that she is lodging with her mother. Whoever she is, she seems to have a deft familiarity with the work that needs to be done as they observe her masterfully moving from one task to another. It's too far away to see her face clearly, but there is something about her that is familiar to Sara.

"There is something about that girl—maybe the way she moves—that I'm sure I've seen before," says Sara with a feeling of puzzlement.

It's a little past noon when Celia decides that she's been an observer as long as she can stand it. A little reluctantly Sara relents.

"Okay, but has it occurred to you that back at the camp they have done a roll call and we're the missing team? We have no idea how they are going to handle that. I mean, we don't know if they will send someone here to check if we came this way. We don't know who is coming and going out of here."

Celia is no longer listening but is already making her way across the field. She is on a run. Her eyes are fixed on the chicken coop. Her mother has only a moment ago disappeared inside. Her heart is pounding so hard she feels she may faint. She stops in front of the door as her mother is just backing her way through the opening with a basket of eggs. When she turns she is startled to find someone standing in front of her and even more startled when she realizes who that someone is. Dropping the basket full of eggs, both her hands slap her cheeks as she shrieks, "Oh my God! Oh my God! Oh my God!" It's all she can say as she moves forward toward this daughter who has returned from the dead. Taking her hands from her own face she begins to stroke Celia's face as if to prove to herself that this is not a cruel illusion.

Both stand speechless in front of the other with eyes filling with tears. In a moment this mother has spontaneously thrown her arms around her daughter and this daughter is returning with a hug of her own.

"It's really, really you! Oh my God I can't believe it's really you!" says Frieda with tears streaking down her face.

Now half crying and laughing, Celia bursts out, "It's really, really me!"

In the mean time, Rhena is coming down the path, only becoming aware of some kind of commotion moments before. Sara swings around with rifle in hand facing this seeming stranger. Both stand dead in their tracks as each stares at the other.

Rhena speaks first.

"Sara?"

Sara can't believe what she is seeing standing not even five meters in front of her.

"Rhena?" Both their voices have an element of uncertainty. The last time they were together was when the Nazi soldiers grabbed Rhena and her mother to be deported.

"What are you doing here?" they both say in unison. This can only be described as an unhoped for and surely an unexpected reunion. Both break into huge smiles as they grab hands and spin in a circle like a couple of long lost school girls.

They all spend the next few minutes talking over the top of one another trying as best they can to make sense as to how all this is taking place. Still giddy over the liberation and reunification, Frieda, returning to her basket half-filled with broken eggs, proffers the next suggestion.

"Let's all go to the house and have lunch."

CHAPTER 21

UPRISING IN TREBLINKA

It's early July in the Treblinka death camp. The temperatures are crushing. Those who are in charge of manning the fires are near heat exhaustion. They can't burn the bodies fast enough by hand so the Germans have brought in an excavator. Nevertheless, the Germans remain in a frenzy fearing the advancing Russians will discover their malicious crimes.

The Jewish workers know that as long as they are useful they remain alive. As soon as they fall ill or become starved to the point of weakness they will be shot or gassed and replaced with new transports coming in every day.

The secret committee Bernie joined is well aware of the need to move swiftly. Not only are they concerned with escaping but also dream of avenging the deaths of the millions of Jews who have died here. They've considered setting the entire camp on fire before their planned escape and assassinating the cruelest of their tormentors.

"I'd be willing to do this even if it meant I'd lose my own life in the process," one of the conspirators is heard to say.

A similar coup had been planned back in April. Unfortunately the leader of that group failed to salute the camp commander correctly and suffered a blow across the face with a swagger stick. The man had been an officer in the Polish army and reacted by drawing a knife on the commander. The result was the commander leaped out of a window leaving his assailant alone long enough to poison himself rather than be tortured for his unseemly reaction.

More recently a new capable leader has emerged. He also had spent time as an officer in the Polish army and has been trained as a physician. His name is Lech. He's a methodical man. He's been asked to assume the leadership of this ragtag group of partisans. He is familiar with the kind of weaponry the Germans are using and their tactics.

"I will take command of this opposition under one condition." He pauses long enough to look Barak and a few others in the eye and then continues. "That there is only one commander. I understand that many of you have been involved with planning this operation for some time but I'm going to ask all of you to set your notions aside and work off one plan and one plan only. If you can all agree, I'll take command."

It only requires a moment to contemplate this offer. They surround this new leader promising their allegiance and their willingness to die for this greater cause.

It takes him the better part of July to assess the situation and devise a strategy. He takes special notice of the men assigned to walk around spraying disinfectant. From this observation he orders another group to abscond with as much gasoline they can find. Several men work in the garage and are able to steal several gallons of fuel. He also is paying close attention to the arsenal. From this he takes a special interest in the guard who is assigned to the room adjacent to the dispensary. For starters, he's a German guard with a fondness for cognac, gold and women.

After realizing that their time may be running short, Lech poses a question. "Barak, when are you and your men supposed to start building that new brick building by the arsenal?"

"It's scheduled for this week. We're waiting for some more materials," answers Barak.

Giving this a moment of thought, Lech asks, "Are you still on good terms with that guard quartered in the arsenal?"

"I am as long as I supply him with gold, booze and the newest young prostitutes."

"Let me know the minute you get started on that building project. In the meantime I'd like you to form a committee of a couple dozen of our best men, preferably those who have had some firearm experience. I want you to place them in the gravel ditch and on your work detail the day you get started."

Word begins to spread to the various units to be ready to take their assigned positions in the next few days. The idea of anything other than the drudgery of camp life excites these partisans to a new and refreshing measure of lightheartedness.

Within the next couple days all of Barak's materials have arrived. It's a Monday morning. He has been able to select the work crew he wants and has placed them in their predetermined positions. In the meantime Lech is keeping an eye on the arsenal. The slightest disturbance inside the arsenal could bring the wrath of the whole guard unit down on them. He's waiting for the guard to leave his quarters. It's been half the afternoon with no luck. Not willing to wait any longer, he delegates Barak to make up a pretense to get the guard out of his adjoining room.

Barak knows of only one ruse that will surely compel this soldier to leave the coolness of his quarters. Rapping gently on the door with hat in hand, he appears servile as this military man answers the knock noticeably agitated.

"Sir, I hate to bother you but you asked me to keep my eyes and ears open for any train that's carrying in a new group of prostitutes. I heard there's one coming in this afternoon and I know how much you enjoy getting first pick."

The demeanor of the man takes a sudden change for the better.

"Well aren't you just the best Jew? What time is that train supposed to be here?" he asks with a growing degree of intensity.

"I'm not sure. I heard a couple of officers discussing it and couldn't ask any questions, sir," Barak says bowing his head in an even more obsequious manner.

From the look on his face, it's obvious this guard feels fortunate in having this information passed on to him.

"Well let me reward you for this fine piece of info," he says smiling, handing Barak a large piece of bread and a cigarette.

"Oh thank you sir," says Barak shoving the bread in one pocket and the cigarette in another as he backs away leaving this predicable situation to work. Within a couple minutes the guard leaves his quarters and heads toward the train station.

With no time to lose, Lech goes into action. The first thing that has to be done is for a man to get into the arsenal. It's imperative this be done promptly and with precision. Lech chose this assignment for himself. The door is quickly compromised with a forged key.

Meantime in back of the building beneath a window is a pile of discarded building materials. A group of partisans has been assigned to be there with a cart. In a matter of moments, Lech has popped out a window pane and is handing rifles, grenades, pistols and cartridges through the opening. The men are piling the arms on the bottom of the cart and placing all the debris over the top. The next step is to head for the rock pit. Once there they begin to distribute to the combat unit the twenty rifles, boxes of grenades and an assortment of pistols all loaded and ready to fire.

Another group in charge of disinfecting the camp has replaced their disinfectant with the stolen gasoline and has been busy all morning and afternoon spraying anything and everything in the camp that will burn.

With everything in place at 3:45 Monday afternoon on August the 3rd, 1943, a lone shot near the Jewish barracks serves as the signal. Simultaneously all over the camp people hear the explosions of grenades as they begin to ignite the gasoline-soaked buildings. The only buildings that couldn't be reached by those doing the disinfecting are the bath houses where guards are stationed.

In the typical German manner the troops are organized and begin to put down the resistance. Their emphasis is on preventing any prisoners from escaping. On the other hand that is exactly what Bernie's unit is delegated to do. In the chaos, the Germans have been prevented from reaching the power house that supplies the electricity to the fences. The electrical poles with the large transformers feeding the electrical power to the camp are up in flames causing huge electrical explosions

Bernie is in command of a unit to cut the fences allowing the prisoners to stream out as they are able. The towers are manned by Ukrainian guards in charge of protecting these fences from any attempt to use them as escape routes. But on that designated single shot fired into the air announcing the start of the escape, these guards were individually lured down by Jews offering gold. Each was killed and his weapons taken. Each encounter of these armed partisans with guards resulted in dead Ukrainians.

As fast as the towers were vacated, the Germans filled the vacancy with soldiers with automatic weapons that are continuously spraying the entire compound with strafing rounds. The collateral damage to their own troops is as much as the resistance are causing.

Unfortunately the Jewish partisans are all trying to escape through the small holes in the fences allowing the Germans to concentrate their offensive attack on this single perimeter. Bernie and his unit are the first to escape. There are 700 more behind him who are being systematically mowed down as the try to escape throughout the entire camp. Within fifteen minutes the Germans have called in reserves from a neighboring penal camp. They are pouring in with weapons blazing into the chaos of prisoners running in every direction, mowing them down by the dozens. Lech and Barak have already been killed.

As hot as it is this day, all the prisoners are required to wear striped pants. They have put other clothing on under these uniforms in preparation to shed the outer layer to blend in with the citizens around the countryside as quickly as possible.

Right away, Bernie strips off this outer layer of Treblinka prison clothing for what he hopes to be the last time, without delay he is on a full run across fields, swamps and ditches toward a distant forest. The Germans are coming in from all directions firing on anyone not wearing a military uniform. He knows they will be reluctant to follow anyone into the wooded areas for fear of being ambushed.

A shot rings out just as he is about to enter the vegetation on the edge of the timberland. He feels a slight sting in his arm. Dropping to the ground, he has no idea how severely he may be wounded. Placing his hand on the spot that stings produces no blood. He quickly begins to crawl away from this spot as he spies a lone guard advancing toward him. He has manages to crawl further into a stand of grasses.

From this vantage point he can hear the rustling of the grasses coming toward him. With no further warning the guard has spotted him and without hesitation aims his pistol to fire only to have it jam. Bernie expecting to be executed on the spot springs into action. The only weapon that Bernie has hung on to is the wire cutters. As the guard struggles to free the jammed cartridge, Bernie has the wire cutters stuck deep onto the man's temple.

The man goes down hard. Not sure how much damage he's done, Bernie grabs the jammed pistol from his hand, rustles through his pockets for anything of value and runs deeper into the forest leaving the guard to fate. He continues to hear the faint sounds of gunshots for a full hour after his escape into the woods. Not sure what lies before him he just knows that as long as he continues running, he is putting more distance between himself and the perimeter of the German army, and the better his chances of escaping.

Finally willing to slow his tempo, Bernie begins to pay attention to the landscape. Nothing looks familiar. Nonetheless, he begins to search out a resting spot. At this point he is far from being fussy. After the many horrific months in Treblinka, he could fall asleep on a fence and still find it comfortable. He finds himself in a cedar grove with a nice clearing. This is the most freedom he's enjoyed since way last spring. Not quite ready to trust a prolonged rest, he soon talks himself into pushing on until dark. The only thing he is aware of is that he's heading south. For now it's good enough. He's been dreaming of this moment where he would find a place deep in the woods. A place where he could find a safe spot to sleep until he had all the sleep he wants. Any place is good enough for this vagabond as long as it's a long way from Treblinka. Taking a few minutes to unjam his confiscated Luger, he resigns himself to sleep.

Bernie awakes the next morning hungry and thirsty. Since this is not a new phenomena, he simply pushes it away for the time being as he continues to revel in simply being free. The woodland birds are joining his celebration with an early morning serenade. Searching the forest carpet for a few minutes, he discovers an ample amount of onion-like plants referred to as "leeks." Gathering as many of these as he can eat for the moment, Bernie decides to forge on south but use discretion from here on.

"The last thing I want is to do something stupid to return me to that hell-hole," is Bernie's immediate thought as he much more carefully reviews his options.

Shortly he hears a familiar sound. It takes him by surprise because it's so close. Snapping his head around, he discovers that he's no more than twenty meters from a road. Instinctively he ducks down. A farmer on a wagon is coaxing his pair of mules to pull a load of hay down the road. Waiting till the farmer passes by, hoping to remain unnoticed, Bernie darts out of the brush and hops unseen onto the back of the wagon.

The smell of the hay is a magnificent scent. It awakens the realization that he may still have a farm. It also pulls him into the awareness that he has lost his daughter. The latest report from Mikhail was that Celia was missing. That's the only information he had. In a death camp that can only mean one thing. The reality of this comes home to him on the back of this hay wagon on this lonely road, he weeps for her.

There is never a safe time for one to mourn the loss of loved ones as events change so quickly. To stay alive, one must have survival as the top priority. This time is no exception. Bernie spots a German military vehicle approaching from behind. The silhouette emerges of an officer's car with a machine gun mounted on the rear. It's too late to try and hide in the hay. Soon they are upon them. He's hoping for the best but expecting the worst. In another second they are not more than a few meters away. What is readily apparent is that the passengers of this vehicle are not wearing uniforms. It's obvious these men are not German soldiers rather they appear to be partisans who have somehow commandeered this enemy vehicle. They are content to speed on by but not nearly as content as Bernie is to see them keep going.

"Thank God!" is the only thought that Bernie can bring to mind. So far not even his driver is aware of his clandestine passenger. Bernie's only

wish for the moment is to be invisible. "*The last thing I need right now is for anyone to know anything about me.*"

What happens next is unanticipated. Bernie finds he is riding through a village. His first thought is to get off the wagon but his second thought is to stay put until the driver passes through. A stranger is a problem in any small village. They are looked upon with great suspicion. Not willing to take the chance, he digs into the hay and hides.

Not recognizing any landmarks, he decides to remain hidden in his nest for a while longer. What he hasn't noticed is that his driver has guided his wagon off the main road onto a farm lane. When he finally becomes conscious of this change in directions and having no idea of his whereabouts, he feels he has no option but to ride out this dilemma.

The ride is rough. The only sound he can hear clearly is the driver giving commands to his mules. A while later, maybe a half hour, the wagon comes to a halt and the number of voices increases. The caliber of his anxiousness is reaching a new level. He doesn't have to wait long for things to take a turn.

"AHHHAAGG!" Comes a yelp from deep under the pile of hay. A sharp stab to the leg initiates this reaction. A pitch fork is the culprit but even before Bernie can process what is happening, he is being pulled out by what seems to be a hundred pairs of hands. He finds himself on the ground with a boot pressing on his throat.

Bernie is on his back looking up through the trees from a vantage point that readily appears to be dark and formidable.

"Tell me quick why I should not break your neck," comes a voice much higher above the boot pressing against his larynx.

With a hand on the man's boot, he tries to rearrange its position to reply. Finding himself in this compromising position and barely able to utter a sound. With a raspy gasp he comes back with a knee-jerk Yiddish response.

Immediately, he feels the boot relax. The man stares at him surprised at his outburst. The man above is now bending over extending his hand in a friendly gesture. Without a thought, Bernie grasps it and finds himself being pulled to his feet.

With a perplexed look the man responds in Yiddish, "What the hell are you doing here?"

Finally getting his wits back, Bernie makes a hasty profession with no idea what he may have gotten himself into, "I've been in Treblinka and managed to escape a day ago. I hopped on this wagon hoping to avoid any German patrols."

The man making the interrogation pauses for a moment, staring intently at Bernie. All he sees is an extremely thin man with baggy clothing and a shaved head. With a curious tone, he soon poses another question. "You've been in Treblinka?"

"Yes," is his simple reply.

"What in the hell is going on over there? All we have seen since yesterday is black smoke," further questions the perplexed man.

Still not sure of his status with this group, he throws caution to the wind. Nervously he explains the conditions of the camp, how they had initiated a revolt, and that there were probably more who died than escaped.

"They are gassing thousands. The only thing that kept me alive was that I was able to do hard labor. They had me as part of a unit that carried the bodies from the gas chamber to the pyres for burning. If any of us showed any problem with that task we'd be tortured, shot or hung and thrown along with the others on the fire.

"The Nazis came and took me from my farm. My daughter was taken along with me. The last I heard is that she is most likely dead. My worst fear was that I would find her in that pile of bodies we had to burn."

By the time Bernie has finished answering all the questions posed, he finds himself surrounded by several dozen armed men. While talking he notices a couple of familiar faces. They belong to that group that passed him earlier in the German military car.

It seems at this juncture there is nothing left to do but make some introductions. The man who initially had Bernie pinned to the ground extends his hand again. "My name is Moshe Malinowski. We're part of the Jewish resistance. Fortunately for you."

"I've heard of you. But never knew for certain that you existed," says Bernie with a sigh of relief.

"It sounds as though you've had the kind of experience that we can use. If you're interested, we have a spot here for you," says Moshe with an inviting smile.

"Right now I could use some water and I feel a little faint, I haven't eaten much in the past few months," acknowledges Bernie as he searches for something to sit on for a moment.

Instantly someone produces a chair. Bernie willingly accepts it. Another person offers him bread.

Over the next few days he begins to get some strength back. It also allows him to give some thought to his plight. It saddens him beyond words to have to imagine his life going on without his family, especially his daughter. Even if his wife is still at the farm, how could he go home and face her without Celia?

He realizes this camp is like a Sherwood Forest with Moshe being Robin Hood. There are many other Jewish people who are finding a safe harbor here as refugees. They have been rescued from the German hangman by Moshe and his group of partisans. Orphaned Jewish children who have not been placed with other families are there and many families that are still intact. All together there are probably more than a thousand people taking refuge in this compound.

They have set up a forest community complete with a bakery, a cobbler, a barbershop and a physician who is able to get his hands on stolen drugs that have come from raiding a train loaded with supplies meant for Germans on the eastern front. But even with all this they are far from being safe. Recently the Germans have begun to put pressure on these forest partisans by sending as many as 20,000 troops to stamp these groups out. Many of the Jewish partisans have joined forces with some of the Polish partisan fighters to add to their number of resisters to stave off this determined German offensive.

After a week of rest in this oasis, Bernie is gaining strength. He has no hard commitment to stay, although Moshe has made it clear several times that he could certainly use another person willing to help defend their operation.

Like so much in times like these, things have a way of changing rapidly and usually without warning. This is one of those days. Reliable information has reported an unusual number of German troops gathering near the edge of the forest. The partisans depend on the local peasants to supply them with food and depending on the circumstances most keep quiet. Others, for various reasons, give in and divulge their location. The Germans are oftentimes confronted with a blended Polish/Jewish resistance.

The Germans send planes every day to locate these camps. From time to time the Russians also detect their locations and drop supplies by parachute. The partisans use the white parachute material for making winter clothing that blends in with the snow.

On this particular day, the partisans have draped the parachutes from a recent Russian drop over an area a quarter kilometer from the real camp to lure in the Germans. As they begin to fire on the bogus camp, the partisans are picking off the German planes with machine gun fire.

The next day the alarm rushes through the camp to be ready to pack up and move to another location. Their method of operation is to avoid any confrontation with the superior fire power of the German army in favor of staying out of their way and continuing to clandestinely assault their trains, power lines, communication systems and storage depots.

Within an hour the first unit is already moving out. They must stay under the canopy of the forest to avoid detection from the German airplanes. The Germans on the other hand have suffered many casualties from the hit and run tactics of the partisans who are well-acquainted with these woodlands. These ragtag resistance fighters have successfully ambushed many a superior fighting unit.

An unlikely ally has been the Russians. From time to time they have air-dropped supplies including carbines and ammunition. It has little to do with any particular concern the Russians have for the welfare of the Jews but more that they share a common enemy. They are willing to let the partisans soften up the enemy before they become involved. On the other hand the British and Americans Allied Powers have given little support to these brave partisans for any reason.

The prideful arrogance of these Nazi tormenters can stand no defeat, especially at the hands of these "sub-humans." Every licking they take only serves to step-up their resolve to wipe every Jew from the face of the earth.

Deciding to stay with the group rather than risk detection out on his own, Bernie asks for a rifle.

"I think you made a good decision," says Moshe giving him a hug and a kiss on the cheek. Arming himself with a Russian carbine and a handful of ammunition, he falls in with a group. His never considered any fear of being killed. All he wants to do is kill as many of those Germans who have been responsible for destroying his life as he is able.

Speaking to Moshe in response to the invitation to stay on and become a partisan, Bernie expresses his sentiments. "I doubt I have any family left. These yutz know nothing except death and destruction. I just want to kill them all."

It's difficult for Bernie to describe his feelings. After being held a prisoner and helpless so much of the time the ability to fight back is an all new experience. He finds that he is learning quickly how to digest it. Revenge is a human emotion that takes little or no effort to embrace.

Moshe gathers his unit for a parley. He is well aware of the defeats the Germans are suffering in Russia and plans on re-energizing his partisans with that information. "As you all are aware we are on our way to re-establish a camp up near Bialystok. We have to move quickly. The bridge crossing the Narew River has to be destroyed as soon as we cross it to prevent the Germans from pursuing us. It's going to take a concerted effort on all our parts to get this done before we have to contend with their harassment.

"Here is another phase of the German dilemma. We are well aware of the German defeat in Stalingrad. There is a reported group of retreating German soldiers making their way through Belorussia. This group is depending on a rail shipment of supplies coming out of Germany headed in the same direction we are. We need those supplies much worse than they do. They are planning on transporting these materials to the front by truck convoy at the rail head."

Moshe spends the next few minutes dividing the units. Some are to remain as an escort for all the unarmed men, women, and children, others are assigned to take out the bridge. All partisans understand that if they are caught they are provided with a pill to kill themselves rather than risk being compromised under torture. As for Bernie, he is to continue on with Moshe's unit to commandeer the truck convoy.

Moshe re-emphasizes a point he alluded to earlier, "We have to be just as vigilant with this retreating group. They're still dangerous and under orders to kill any resistance that gets in their way. Just beware that we are deep in enemy territory and have them both in front of us as well as behind us."

Within a single morning the camp is deserted. Bernie and enough men to crowd into the commandeered German military car, make their way north in hopes of looting Nazi supply trucks. They have an ample fuel supply along with an auxiliary fuel tank to get them to their destination. The roads are rough dirt. Nevertheless they plan to be at their destination by night.

Making their way through some of the villages on their route they observe the Nazi strategy to intimidate and punish partisan sympathizers. In retribution for supplying partisans with food or refuge many of these righteous Poles have been killed and their homes have been burnt to the ground.

Moshe and the rest of his crew, save Bernie, appear to have little or no reaction to these atrocities. They seem not to notice as they speed through to the next barbarity, acting as though this is just another pleasure drive in the country.

Bernie is noticeably agitated at their seeming lack of care until he remembers how he had to harden himself to the part he played in the daily elimination of thousands of his fellow Jews. Hauling body after body to a fire just to survive and satisfy an unquenchable Nazi appetite for burnt Jews. This unwelcome holocaust devastation thrown at him seems to feed his own quenchless thirst for revenge.

The more thought he gives it, the more he hopes that in this collective act of resistance he can rid himself of the remorse he has for the role he played in that inhuman action against his own people in order to survive.

"*I hate these Nazi bastards*" is more and more dominating Bernie's thoughts. Killing those who have hurt him and those he loves is more than a passing mental preoccupation. His mind harks back to the two guards he has already killed only to discover that he has a rage within him that has an affinity for its own kind of retribution.

The chosen spot for an ambush is in an extremely remote and wooded area. If it weren't for the rigors of war lapping at their every activity this would be a perfect retreat for one seeking a quiet solace through nature.

Unfortunately there is no room for the luxury of solitude when it pertains to war. Moshe is already pulling out an SS commander's uniform from the car trunk. It's evident that its rightful owner at one time sat in this conveyance and it is even more evident that he is no longer among the living as there appears to be a bullet hole in the chest.

Moshe strips his own clothing off yielding to the necessity to redress and appear as the enemy. Along with his own sergeant's uniform, he tosses the officer's uniform in the direction of Bernie and a couple of enlisted men's uniforms to two others. The other two men are to remain out of sight armed and ready to respond.

The plan is simple. As the German convoy makes its way toward its objective these imposters will have the road blocked using their bogus military vehicle. Bernie is to do the talking since after his stay at Treblinka, he is familiar with the German military attitude and furthermore his German language skills are excellent. Moshe will remain posturing as a non-commissioned officer demanding the paperwork of each of the drivers. On a given signal the drivers will be compromised in whatever manner secures a victory for the partisans.

At daybreak the sentinel sounds a short blast on a whistle sounding the alarm. All involved quickly scramble to their assigned stations. Having shaved the night before, Bernie looks properly arrogant in his uniform. With feet spread, swagger stick properly positioned behind his back, he holds his other hand positioned in such a way to be understood as a gesture to halt.

There appear to be four military trucks in this convoy. The lead truck is occupied by a driver and a sergeant. The sergeant exits the truck and immediately clicks his heels and thrusts his right arm forward voicing the familiar "Heil Hitler" salute.

In his best German, Bernie begins to demand an accounting of all drivers. Within a minute all five of these soldiers are standing at attention directly in front of him. As the agreed upon signal to shoot, Bernie drops his swagger stick. When he bends over to pick it up, a barrage of bullets flies over him and into these Nazi soldiers leaving them in a crumpled heap dead at his feet.

Bernie stands for a moment looking at these hapless enemies. He comes to an immediate conclusion, *"I'll never be afraid to die as long as I can take you bastards with me. I'll die on my feet, not my knees."* The next impression running through his whole body is a disappointment that they can only be killed once. His hate for this enemy is enduring.

In another few minutes the partisans have dragged the bodies off the road and stripped them of everything useful, leaving them naked and un-identifiable. Their attention turns to their booty. The back of the trucks are loaded with food supplies, medical supplies, arms and ammunition and some radio equipment along with boots. Without a lot of fanfare this band of hijackers still masquerading in their enemy uniforms, makes the decision to stay this way until they feel safe enough to discard them. The most dangerous part of this mission now is returning back to the forest hideout. There are two reasons for this fear. One, because someone may follow. Second, is getting past their own guards who may not be aware of their mission.

The trucks are turned around with a new partisan driver in each with Bernie in his command car and uniform leaving Moshe to drive and lead the way. The authoritative nature of these uniforms and this official-appearing military brigade eliminates a lot of nosiness. When it comes to the German military, most people find it much safer to keep a low profile and not get involved. This attitude prevails in the villages as well as around the countryside.

CHAPTER 22

REVENGE

Winding their way back on rough roads they make their way into a village. Since their new retreat is only about ten kilometers from here and they don't want to arrive with the German trucks before dark for fear of being seen, Moshe makes a decision to stop at a village market and feel the atmosphere for the amount of Jewish sympathy. It's a region in which he's acquainted.

As usual, these Polish people are respectful to their Nazi intruders—at least as much as concern for their well-being dictates. They condescend when necessary, at the same time avoiding any direct contact if not obligatory.

As Jews and as a foreign culture they have grown used to people disliking them for no other reason than merely being Jews. Now they are masquerading as Nazis feeling a similar estrangement from these same people but this alienation stems from their strength rather than their Jewish weakness. This is a whole new dimension for them. It's becoming more and more apparent that as armed partisans they are also gaining the respect of the local villagers. It's certainly not a new fondness the Poles are developing for Jews. Rather it stems from respecting a man with a rifle.

Moshe relates an incident from early in his partisan participation when he had been without food for some time. He entered a Polish country store asking for food and water. The proprietor, along with several other people chased him out beating him with shovels and rakes. He returned the next day with a rifle slung over his shoulder. The proprietor along with the same group still hanging around gathered up all he needed for several days, gladly handing it over to him.

This experience has colored his method how to handle local people when it comes to a partisan need. "You only ask once. If they tell you they have nothing to give you, you then push them aside and take what is needed."

His disguise as a member of the German military is drawing the expected reaction. Most try to have no eye contact and stay out of the way—that is except for one vendor selling chickens. He steps out in front of his display.

"Could I interest you gentleman in a young capon?" he asks obsequiously.

Bernie is the one he is speaking to. His Polish is spoken with a German accent. Staring coldly at this seeming impertinence, Bernie uses the end of his swagger stick to examine the carcass. He asks in German why this capon is superior.

With a slight smirk the man declares using German words tainted with disgust, "Because no Jew has touched his greasy fingers to this chicken." His eyes turn to a dead look of hatred as he is sure this man in uniform shares the same sentiments toward Jews.

Bernie is taken aback. This loathing is felt every day by Jewish people that are being hosted in their countries but it is something he's never gotten used to. Before he reacts badly with this bigot he catches a restraining look in the eye of Moshe.

Moshe steps forward with a question of his own but in Polish. "Are you hiding some of these 'greasy finger' Jews?"

"Hell no!" says the man returning to speaking Polish. "But I got a Jew chicken farm taken from one of these Jew bastards when you guys took over the country."

Moshe is beginning to become more interested in this guy and begins to follow through with some more questioning.

"You ever hear of any Jew partisans around here?"

"No. The only ones I've heard of up here are the Poles. The Jews are supposedly more south of us down by Warsaw."

Moshe continues to dominate the questioning.

"May I ask you good man what is your name?"

"Richard Meir, sir."

"You sound like a good man, Mr. Meir. Where can we reach you if we should need some information concerning any rumors of Jewish partisan movements in this region?"

He gladly gives him his address and along with it a present of the capon.

Moshe and Bernie shake his hand and commend him for his willingness to fight against the lawlessness of these illegal partisan groups.

The two of them are satisfied that their move north has so far remained undetected. They return to their convoy and begin the arduous task of locating their fellow combatants.

"I don't like anything about this guy. I think he could be dangerous to us if he ever finds out our whereabouts," says Bernie.

Moshe listens carefully but has no remark for the moment as he fiddles with the radio. Shortly, they make contact with the main group to discover that the crew sent to slow the Germans has successfully blown up the bridge and that they are all reassembled in a former camp.

Hearing this is good news to Moshe and his troupe. As soon as it's dark they pull off into the forest to hide the trucks and request a gang to come help unload their bootlegged supplies.

Over the next few days the camp is refitted. Moshe has called a meeting among the squad leaders. Anytime a move like this is made a reevaluation of purpose and targets must be quickly made. Another concern is the whereabouts of the enemy. The sentinels are radio equipped and able to make immediate contact. Part of the duties of these sentinels is to get close to the enemy but remain undetected. They often stay out for days at a time reporting on the enemy's whereabouts, probable intentions, number of troops, tanks and types of munitions. There is seldom time for leisure and today is not going to be an exception.

Interrupting this meeting is a radio attendant. He makes a point of talking in hushed tones directly into Moshe's ear. Moshe has a sudden shift in posture that anyone who has fought with him knows when they see it. His back becomes erect and all his nerves begin to feed his movements while pumping his body fluids directly into his brain.

Changing his previous agenda, he raises his voice so all can hear.

"The Germans have found a way around the bridge we blew up. It slowed them but obviously has not deterred their resolve to have a confrontation. I'm sure they have somehow gotten word about the success we had in pirating their supply convoy and want retribution despite their disadvantage of entering into our forest.

"We will give them what they want but I'm sure they probably won't care for the outcome."

According to the sentinel report, an enemy squad of a couple dozen men is in the lead and no more than a half day's march behind. They could be arriving in this vicinity before dark. This forest is speckled with farms that have cleared large sections for tillage leaving many acres bare. The Germans will make use of the roads as much as possible, always cognizant of an ambush.

Expecting this to happen, Moshe devises a plan to suck the Germans in. Needing a half dozen men to be the bait, he asks for volunteers. Bernie is the first to step forward. His thirst for German blood is growing as the constantly nagging awareness of the losses he's suffered at their tactics allows him no relief. Five others soon joined him.

The plan is to meet the leading patrol and engage them, gradually retreating as the main body catches up. They will draw the enemy through a field toward a place where the open field narrows with forest on both sides. There they will be caught in a cross fire, killing them before they can retreat.

Moshe continues to instruct his lieutenants, "I want to place a hundred men on both sides of this clearing but I want you in trees shooting down toward the enemy. This will place you high enough to insure that none off you get caught in your own crossfire. But do not fire until I give the order. As soon as I call retreat, you will pull back and disappear into the forest. Our idea is not to defeat them since that is impossible. This is to let them know the cost it will take to defeat us."

The plan is initiated within the hour. Bernie and his crew are placed on the road to await this enemy lead patrol. In the distance they can make out a couple dozen or so German soldiers cautiously making their way toward them. Giving them a fairly safe distance just within shooting range, Bernie and his compatriots begin to fire on the patrol. They are not causing any damage but then neither can the enemy inflict damage on them. The idea is to hold them in this position until the main body catches up and to gradually begin their retreat.

Realizing they are being fired on, the German patrol digs in to assess their situation. In the mean time they have radioed back to the main company for support. With in the next forty minutes that support reaches their position and begins to push forward when they see they're only dealing with a handful of partisans.

Phfft, phfft, phfft is the sound of enemy bullets reaching Bernie and his partners as the bullets whiz overhead or hit the soil around them. Bernie is amazed at how cool and collected he is. He has no fear. His total focus is on drawing the enemy into the trap. So far his group is achieving their goal as the Germans draw closer and closer.

For the time being this small band is returning enough fire to make the Germans believe this impertinent crew needs to be taught a hard lesson and are pressing hard toward them. At present, these few partisans are fortified in a fence row returning only enough fire to appear to be dangerous. Shortly it becomes apparent that they need to make a move.

The Germans are sure this is going to be an easy victory to hand to their Fuhrer as they boldly chase their retreating saboteurs. The contest continues as Bernie and his fighters retreat even further into the field, still luring the Germans forward. There are now dozens of German fighters filling in behind the retreating partisans with even more catching up wanting to be part of this easy victory, obviously oblivious to what is awaiting them.

Moshe is paying close attention to the number of enemy soldiers pouring into this vacant area between forests. Giving it a minute of silence as the shooting from both sides has momentarily ceased, he blows his whistle with the result of hundreds of bullets reigning down on these haplessly duped Nazis.

The German commander remains helplessly on the road with tanks that cannot maneuver through wooded terrain. He has no other choice than to watch his adversaries massacre his troops and then blend unseen and unscathed back into the landscape. To further dishearten him and the few remaining defeated soldiers, he's left with the responsibility of recovering his dead and wounded.

For the partisans, this mission came off without a single casualty. It's hardly a time for celebration but rather a time for thankfulness to God for delivering them one more time. Immediately on returning to camp

Moshe, along with his command group, wearing prayer shawls set an example and do just this.

This has been a bitter sweet victory for Bernie. His bitterness toward the culture that he believes has caused him to suffer irreversible losses keeps him from any kind of gratitude. He has gone off by himself. He is obviously not in the mood for any kind of satisfaction for the number of killed Nazi soldiers. For him it's still too few to fulfill his religious conviction of an "eye for an eye."

Realizing that he's trapped in his hatred, he's helpless to do anything to alleviate it. His desire to kill all those that are even culturally responsible for the destruction of his family is unquenchable.

A few days pass without any major eruptions. Bernie's brooding has taken him to approach Moshe about a possible problem they are both aware of.

"Moshe, it's been bearing hard on me as I think about that German-Polack back in the village who offered himself as a Nazi collaborator. I believe he should be dealt with before he becomes a danger to all of us."

Moshe listens as he always does leaving any action toward this man to a bit more thought and discussion. As the days go by Bernie continues to push the issue even harder. It's as though he's become obsessed with this man's bigotry.

Moshe has listened to Bernie's concerns but makes a decision not to address any of them for the moment. "Bernie there are all sorts of bigoted people but we sure as hell can't kill them all. Some are bigoted in thought but never put it into action. I don't like this guy any more than you do but he hasn't done anything other than run his mouth."

For Bernie this is hardly the decision he was hoping to hear. He returns to his dugout less than ready to let this decision stand.

The next few days prove to be uneventful as the camp falls into a routine. The villager who bragged about getting the Jew's chicken farm continues to plague Bernie's thinking. That night he decides to leave the partisans and try his luck on his own, maybe even making his way back to his old farm.

He also decides that before he leaves the region, he is going to pay the chicken farmer a visit. Of course he has no intention of relaying this decision to Moshe. He feels that it's his duty to stamp out these Philistines with their Jew-hating attitudes. *"The world will be a better place without this man and his hatred for people he knows nothing about,"* is his prevalent thought.

The next morning Bernie faces Moshe, turning in his rifle along with his decision to be on his way.

"I hope you understand there isn't going to be much we can do for you once you've stepped out on your own," states Moshe with no hesitation or evasion of mind as he lays the rifle aside for the moment.

It becomes clear that Bernie's mind is set. He's hell bent on doing things his own way in his own time. They part as friends and Moshe gives him a canteen of water and some bread with the option to return anytime.

Once Bernie reaches the road, instead of turning south in the direction of his farm, he chooses to turn north in the direction of the village farmer. He recalls how the farmer laid out the details as to where he lived. Making his way toward that address, he is cautious to stay off the edge of the road near the forest should he have need to hide.

By the afternoon he has arrived at the Richard Meir chicken farm. It's nicely laid out with a number of long buildings obviously built to accommodate several thousand chickens. He spots a man coming out of one of the building. On a closer, he recognizes him from their previous meeting. By now he has caught the attention of his suspect.

Meir begins to walk towards Bernie with a perplexed look as though there is something he should remember about him but can't quite put his finger on it.

"Something I can help you with?" asks Meir.

"I doubt there is anything you can help anyone with," says Bernie, his voice dripping with sarcasm.

This response gives Meir a moment of pause. It's apparent he's at a loss as to what this stranger wants.

Bernie continues, only this time he speaks German. "I'm a man of many faces. The last time you saw me I was in a German uniform."

This affirmation brings that same little sneer to Meir's mouth that had not set well with Bernie the first time.

"Oh yes, you were the crew out looking for Jews. I sure as hell wish I could help you. The last Jew I had anything to do with was the slimy bastard who had this farm before we shot him along with a bunch of his kind. We pretty much cleaned this area out." He chuckles at his accomplishment.

Bernie listens. The reason why he felt compelled to look this man up has come more than alive. "Well Mr. Meir, like I told you, I'm a man of many faces and today I'm the avenging angel of every Jew you've ever murdered."

With that said, Meir is more confused than ever at this strange meeting.

In the next second Bernie has his pistol directly in the center of Meir's forehead and pulls the trigger. He drops like a pole-axed steer in a crumpled mass at his feet. With the pistol still in his hand he swings around in time to see a pitch fork come right at his abdomen. With no time to move he feels its tines sink into his gut.

It's bearer is a young boy no more than fourteen-years-old. "You KILLED MY FATHER! YOU DIRTY BASTARD. I HATE YOU!" He's sobbing uncontrollably as he falls to the ground lifting his dead father's head.

Bernie drops his pistol, grabbing the pitch fork with both hands and with all the strength he has, he jerks it out of his gut. He is now functioning on adrenalin alone. His thinking is gone. It's become fight or flight.

He finds himself completely controlled in the flight mode as he runs stumbling out toward the road. His next sensation is that of something penetrating his back. He stumbles and falls to the ground. Struggling to get to his feet, he is met with the distorted face of this teen screaming the same words once again.

"I HATE YOU! YOU KILLED MY FATHER!"

The boy had picked up the dropped pistol and fired a shot into the back of this saboteur who has just changed his whole world.

The last conscious thought Bernie has on this side of eternity hits him hard as he realizes that, "I have become my enemy." With that he breathes his last earthly breath.

CHAPTER 23

A MOMENT OF FRESH AIR

Like so many families who have found themselves torn apart by this horrific intrusion of maniacal governments, Frieda Goldberg is more than elated to have her daughter back home safe. What's more she has welcomed Rhena and Sara into her home. Between these four able women, they have succeeded in keeping the farm going as a viable source of food and security.

It's approaching fall and from all accounts the war seems to be turning in favor of the Allies. The Russians have had the Germans retreating all year. But the German retreat doesn't mean they've capitulated. From time-to-time they continue to flex their muscles, weakened as they may be, especially when it involves their obsession to destroy everything Jewish.

On the other hand rumors persist that the Russians are seeking retribution from all people bearing a German name. The fact that these ethnic Germans live in eastern bloc countries and have never been a citizen of Germany makes no difference. Joseph Stalin has been heard to say, "Kill them all and let the devil sort them out."

Frieda and her small makeshift family have done well so far in sidestepping any fatal assaults from any of these male-dominated foreign armies. What has taken their place for special attention is the local Polish Resistance. These well-meaning partisans come quite often looking for food. Sometimes they offer a small amount of money and other times they give nothing.

Reliable information has come into the region that the Treblinka camp has been evacuated but not before any remaining Jews had been killed. The fate of husband and father Bernie Goldberg remains a mystery. The only thing that is more or less a given is he would have made it home by this time if he were alive.

Meantime, the harvest season is in full swing on the Goldberg farm. Stosh Levitski, the local leader of the Polish partisans in this area has agreed to bring in a crew to help with much of the work in exchange for a portion of its bounty. He didn't have much trouble getting workers when they discovered it to be a farm with only young women.

These young Polish boys are tripping over each other and themselves to be of any service that gains even the slightest attention from these young women. When it comes to Frieda, though he won't admit it, Stosh has a soft spot in his heart for her. Some have noticed a glint in his eye whenever her name comes up.

"Our relationship is strictly platonic," he states over and over with his mouth saying one thing and his eyes telling a more hopeful story.

In spite of the strife that accompanies a war-weary country, the God-given human biological demand for a mate is only on the back burner for so long. They take the biblical imperative that states in no uncertain terms that "It is not good for man to be alone" literally.

Frieda does not discourage the personal attention Stosh pours on her but because of the unsettled circumstances surrounding her husband's disappearance, she plays a fine line of appreciating it without encouraging it.

Stosh also remembers the first introduction he had to these women, when he was forced to lay on the ground, and further recalls how impressed he has become with the strength they possess without his or any other male help.

"Frieda, I won't make any bones about it, you are one damn good looking woman. Without pushing myself on you, I'd like to get to know you better," he says as forthrightly as he can.

Stosh is taller and more handsome than the shorter, stockier men this region usually produces. Frieda can't deny that he has a certain attractive charm about him despite his less than romantic forthright character. Within this attraction, he also possesses an honest transparency that Frieda finds homey.

"Stosh, that's sweet of you to say but I know that you know that I'm a married woman."

"I realize you regard yourself as a married woman and I certainly honor that. But I also deal in realities and if I even imagined that your husband was going to return, I never would be talking to you the way I am. You see Frieda, I don't believe your husband is going to be returning."

There is an unmistakable compassionate tone with his honesty and she finds it difficult to be angry with this kind of candor.

She remains silent but touches his hand affectionately before turning to finish a chore. Stosh watches her with longing eyes as she retreats. He is forty years old and has never been married. It's not that he hasn't wanted to, rather it's because circumstances in his life have never allowed it to happen.

Being an ethnic Ukrainian he had entered the military as a minority in 1923. Setting this fact aside as incidental, he dreamed of having a military career. Because of his zeal and dedication he hoped for a place in Poland's new experiment with democracy. Within a few short years the country was upside down with that failed experience giving way to a strongman dictator who managed to throw himself along with the rest of the country into turmoil as he went in and out of power for the next dozen years.

Stosh managed to move forward despite the chaos to reach the level of Major. Being a minority and always aware they were not receiving their due, he defected and began a partisan military that favored an alliance with the Soviets. This is what brought him to be fighting against the Germans. His basic core is that of a good man who seeks fairness for a broad range of problems. His weakness is that he fights to live the impossible dream of human equality in a country that will not tolerate it. As a result Stosh has allied himself with the Soviets in the hopes the minorities in Poland will receive a stronger voice under Communism.

Stosh's partisan group has accepted Jewish fighters, although reluctantly, and at his insistence all partisans are to try to overlook their prejudices. Nonetheless this kind of forced kinship becomes a high-maintenance endeavor.

It's December 1944. The war on the eastern front of the homeland has turned in favor of the Allies. What's left of the German army is made up of a ragtag number of aged home guard soldiers with limited arms trying to hold positions with no support from the regular army. They quickly fall to defeat.

The Soviet army is systematically filling the vacuum created by the retreating Germans with a repression of their own. The wrath of the Russian army is to ignore any semblance of compassion. Any lingering human in their path is shot if it's a male and raped if it's a female . . . and then shot.

As the year is beginning to come to a close, the flavor of victory is on the taste buds of the Russian leadership. They are putting pressure on the partisans friendly to their endeavors to lay the groundwork for an easier victory. This has called for the resistance fighters to make a larger footprint.

Stosh's fighters have been called on to ensure that abandoned German military installations are trustworthy and free of landmines and booby traps. The silent understanding is that he, along with similar minority compatriots, will be given positions in the new government.

After having basically withdrawn from the war and simply helped maintain the farm for a year, Rhena and Sara are drawn more and more into Stosh's enthusiasm over the dawning of a new day for Poland.

He's willing to overlook the shortcomings of the Soviet soldier in lieu of the high praises of the Communist toleration for what he refers to as the "proletariat" and in opposition to a repressive "bourgeoisie." These young women have never been political and are struck particularly by the passion Stosh demonstrates toward his views.

On this particular cold day in December, Stosh has received a request for assistance from a Soviet commander. He's being asked to secure a military ammunition depot the Germans are attempting to move by train back to Germany. The Nazis have sent a squad made up of Hitler Youth lead by an aging veteran of the Great War to carry out the assignment.

Stosh has gradually made his presence a part of Frieda's life. It's finally been accepted by all, and especially by Frieda, that Bernie will not return. On this particular day he is paying a visit to inform Frieda of this new assignment along with assuring her he'll return soon.

She listens as one does when they have been told something they didn't care to hear. She has always been aware of Stosh's commitment to the cause but this may be the reason she is reluctant to give herself to him. Trying to force a smile in support of what he does, she breaks into tears instead.

"Oh Stosh in all honesty, I wish that I could support you one hundred percent but I can't. I've already lost too much in this damnable war.

Please don't come back until you're sure you can stay." Her heart is about to beat out of her chest as she attempts to suppress the tears welling up.

He knows exactly what she is trying to say to him. He steps into her life one step further as his long arms reach out to her, drawing her into a firm embrace. He can feel her warmth and longs for it to be something he can share.

Not successful in turning away, she falls into his arms. She feels a strength in his human touch and its power to comfort her this way. She in turn cleaves to him in a way she has never done before.

"*Cherish the moment. Cherish the moment,*" her brain shouts to her over and over as she continues to let the moment dictate their next move.

Stosh finds himself continuing to kiss her as he moves her into her bedroom kicking the door closed behind them. They spend the rest of the hour exploring each other as they never have allowed themselves before.

Later that afternoon, Celia, Rhena, and Sara, already growing weary of the sedentary life of a winter farmer, are returning from visiting with a group of Stosh's young partisans. The recent changes in the events of the war have encouraged Rhena and Sara to want to become involved again. To their satisfaction they have brought both the hands of God and their hands together in helping this beleaguered farm lady but now they feel compelled to demonstrate this same union in re-entering the fight for Jewish survival against the Germans.

When they enter the house, they find Stosh and Frieda sharing a pot of tea. All three girls notice something about the two of them sitting there together, maybe it's a particular look of contentment.

Rhena is the first to express a change in her frame of mind. "Stosh we have spent the afternoon in your camp. I understand you may be about to start a new chapter in fighting in more of an alliance with the Soviets."

She pauses for a moment measuring Stosh's reaction and what words she is going to say next.

"Yes and I'll bet that you and Sara want to be part of it," says Stosh.

Both girls are on their feet, quickly forgetting the words they had so carefully selected for their argument to convince Stosh for admittance.

"Yes. How did you guess?"

"I've never known anyone to retire from this way of life with as little compunction as you two have. It's something personal within us that needs to be worked out to some kind of conclusion and we live and die doing it," says Stosh in his pragmatic tone.

With a smile from ear to ear, Sara is the next to express her quieter contentment, "When do we start?"

CHAPTER 24

THE ROAD TO DANZIG

It's the winter of 1944-1945. The Germans are retreating on all fronts but like any wounded beast their bite remains dangerous. What is driving them out on the eastern front is the tenacity of the Russian army. They have ramped up their hatred for anything that is even remotely German thereby capturing a sense for revenge. As Stalin drives the Germans westward, he unilaterally takes control of the eastern bloc countries and begins a cruel retribution against all ethnic Germans by confiscating their properties and expelling them into slave labor camps. The partisans in these countries struggle to land on the right side of those in power and will assist in expelling these ethnic German families, if they are rewarded with positions in the new communist government.

Hitler, on the other hand, has on his watch created circumstances that have put his country in great peril and resulted in irreversible damage to his people. Furthermore these fourteen million ethnic Germans outside of Germany with no homes or homeland to go to is a direct result of his failed maniacal lust for power. These are the forgotten families destroyed for no other crime than being German. Resentments are being stoked to seek retribution all across Poland, Lithuania, Albania, Latvia, Bulgaria, Czechoslovakia, Hungry and even into Yugoslavia at the hands of Marshall Tito.

With this new backdrop in place, the Polish partisans are also happy to play a role in co-operating with the new power brokers. In exchange each group is hoping for an opportunity to compete for attention regarding their own causes.

Stosh is among those willing to do his part in ridding the country of its Nazi taskmasters. These brave men and woman have time after time spilled their own blood in preparing the ground for their Allied partners to have successful campaigns.

Today Stosh is being called on by the advancing Soviet army to do some reconnaissance. There is an ammunition depot twenty-five miles away. The Russians have information that the Germans plan on sneaking this cache out at night. The question they want answered is how many soldiers are left to guard this compound.

Because women are not perceived as an enemy they are often able to move about without suspicion. Younger men who are not in the military are looked at with great suspicion. This creates an opportunity to penetrate the German compound using women. Separating Rhena and Sara from the rest of the group, Stosh unfolds his idea.

"I have a plan to get the information we need for this mission. We have been successful in preventing much of the needed supplies from reaching this outpost. That includes any medical supplies. One of the things these Nazis are terrified of is contracting typhus. They are accustomed to regular delousing and among the materials we've been able to prevent from reaching them is their supply of DDT."

Rhena and Sara are listening intently but not quite sure where this is going.

Seeing that he has captured their interest, Stosh proceeds with his plan.

"We have enough stuff from these abandoned facilities to make false documents to get us in to visit with the Pope," he says with a chuckle.

"We've made up all the official documents to get into their compound. Our cover is to fumigate that facility and I need you two girls to become the fumigators."

Stosh pauses momentarily to let this small measure of the objective of this mission sink in before carrying on with the rest.

"Once you are inside, we need to know how many men are there and the layout of the inside of these buildings." Pausing again he carefully assesses their demeanor. He's not sure exactly what he can expect from either of them but he's certain from his observation over the past few months they will be trustworthy.

"Do you think this is something you can handle?" he continues his questioning.

Both Rhena and Sara look at each other speculatively. They can never be sure of the success of any mission. The question here is whether they are confident enough in Stosh to take on this project.

Within this look they give back and forth is the confidence and support each is hoping to gain from the other. In unison both say, "Yes, we can do it."

"This is going to be like the old days back in Warsaw," says Sara with a bit of nostalgia in her voice.

"I don't know how you can refer to that time as 'good old days,'" rebukes Rhena with more than a little disgust. The next few days are given to arranging for this espionage operation. The timing, the presentation, all the way down to the type of clothing they will be wearing—all have to be taken into consideration before actually implementing it. Failure is not an option.

It's a Wednesday morning in January. All the paper work has been forged and ready for the scrutinizing eyes of the guard at the guard shack. The two arrive in a stolen state vehicle bearing wording indicating it is a vehicle from the health department. Since Rhena has learned to speak German during her stay with Frieda, she is expected to do the talking.

The guards go over all the documentation in a typical German fashion with a close eye to detail. They also go through the work van inch by inch until they're satisfied these two possess all the necessary security clearances. They radio ahead and are given the okay to allow them to enter.

The facility is located at the end of a long road that's been strung with double fencing and then interlaced with barbed wire. Reaching the main gate, they are directed toward a service entrance. Arriving there they are greeted by an officer and assigned to a corporal whose duty is to escort them around the facility.

He's not any older than these two. Trying hard to impress them with his importance, he takes them to a dorm room that appears to be the main housing for the enlisted men. From what they can gather it's capable of sleeping around a hundred enlistees but there only a handful of the bunks seem to be occupied. They go about their business without raising any suspicions.

As soon as they finish, the young corporal methodically leads them to another room. From all indications it's a storage room for uniforms and different seasonal clothing. This room also indicates that this facility is capable of supplying many more men than are currently here.

Finishing, they are led to another location down a hallway. This turns out to be the laundry. Again they have a strong sense that this facility is operating nowhere near full capacity. Next is the dining area, then a conference room, followed by a series of vacated offices.

Not having done anything to raise suspicions so far and wishing to keep it that way, they continue to go about their business in a professional manner. Soon they finish with as much as this young corporal is willing to allow them access to.

They notice a pair of double steel doors that are closed. They are definitely ominous and of interest. Wondering where they might lead to, Rhena uses her German language skills a bit more.

"Are you going to allow us through here so we can finish?" She asks, pointing in the direction of these steel barriers a bit more demurely than she has thus far.

Part of her curiosity is met when the doors unexpectedly open from the inside. A quick glance confirms an earlier suspicion of a lower floor. The first thing that's noticed is a stairway leading to a lower region. The person exiting is taken aback for a moment having been discovered by strangers.

The corporal meets the disapproving look from the man exiting the stairwell but in answer to Rhena's questioning, he quickly takes her and Sara by the arm and turns them around adding, "No. You won't be allowed down there." This confirms their speculation that there is a bunker below.

It doesn't take more than a few minutes for the girls to finish up and complete their work. Soon they exit the compound and make their way back to the rendezvous. What greets them is more of a surprise than what they were expecting. Stosh is accompanied by a middle-aged man in a Russian officer's uniform. Stosh has a rather official look about him as he introduces Captain Leonid Abakumov.

After the introductions are behind them, Captain Abakumov wants to get down to the business of debriefing. For Rhena and Sara to be doing espionage duty as volunteers doesn't seem to bring anything but intimidation and rudeness from this beggar. They've risked their lives for the common cause of defeating the Germans only to discover their captain is a distinct misogynist and in particular against Jewish women. Nonetheless he takes their information and over the next few days uses it to decimate the German armory.

Their camp has a number of Russian soldiers that have accompanied this captain even though their platoon is bivouacked less than a hundred meters from the partisans' camp. The girls finished their debriefing days before and returned to their bunker. They have decided they are not going to put up with this new turn of events involving these Bolsheviks. Late one night, they are awakened by one of the Russian soldiers demanding they accompany him to the captain's quarters to answer a few more questions.

Pulling themselves together, they accompany this soldier across a grassy knoll to the Russian camp. A military tent with a dim lantern lighting it is their destination. The captain is accompanied by another man. It's not possible to tell what rank this man is as both men are half-clad and obviously drunk.

"Welcome ladies," is the greeting issued from the vodka wet lips of their interrogating captain. He has a three quarter empty bottle grasped firmly around its neck. Waving the bottle in the direction of a military cot, he says, "Have a seat, ladies."

Looking at one another with that look that can only be deciphered as *"What the hell is this coming to?"*

Slurring his words with a seamy grin Abakumov adds, "Don't be afraid. We just want to invite you to have a few drinks with us."

Realizing how fast this can escalate beyond their ability to escape, they both start inching toward the tent flap when Abakumov jumps up with a pistol, hammer pulled back and its barrel pressed against Sara's temple.

"Like I said ladies, relax. You're good looking for a couple of Jew girls." His grin has been quickly replaced by a hateful sneer. "You look way over dressed. I think maybe you'd feel more at home if you begin by getting out of all those uncomfortable clothes."

Meanwhile the other man has joined in with growing anticipation. He's on his feet and just as drunk choosing to aim his amorous intentions in Rhena's direction. He also has a cocked pistol pointed at her.

Rhena has both hands in her coat pockets when suddenly there is the unmistakable report of two gunshots. BAM, BAM! She has surreptitiously discharged a slug from each pistol into the guts of this hapless drunken Russian. He is blown back on a cot grasping his midsection. The blood is gushing out between his fingers.

Sara reacts as best she can against the startled captain. As drunk as he may be, the reflexes of a lifetime of military training cause him to swing Sara around with his arm across her neck and the pistol still pressed firmly against her temple. Shouting at Rhena, he orders her to place her hands above her head or watch her friend's brains fly out of her skull.

At the same moment, Sara's head flies back smashing Abakumov directly in the nose causing him for a split second to relax his grip as the blood rushes from both his nostrils. Sara drops to the tent floor out of reach. In the next second Rhena has discharged another round into the heart of this would be rapist.

Wasting not a moment, they slit a hole in the back of the tent and are out and running for all they are worth back in the direction of the partisan camp. It's dark enough to make the journey unseen. Behind them they hear the shouting caused by the discovery of the two bodies. They both are well aware that it's just a matter of time before the Russians will be storming into their camp seeking retribution for the killings.

As they race back, they encounter a partisan guard alerted by the gunshots. Both the girls recognize him and him them.

"You see nothing," says Rhena as they race by leaving him with a bewilderment he can only express as, "What the hell..." and then leaves him totally speechless.

Arriving at their little bunker safe at least for the moment, they embrace each other in a hug of relief. They have survived another close call together. Realizing this is at best, a temporary reprieve, they grab up a few of their belongings, nervously watching for any movement in the direction of the Russian camp. Without a goodbye to anyone, they make a quick retreat into the surrounding forest.

Their breakout is followed by the sounds of Russians cursing the Polish partisans and the partisans wasting no words back on their attackers. The two of them find themselves roving forward in the dark until they can no longer hear the tumult. With no idea where they are or where they are heading, they continue to wander until daybreak. The cold winter has given them a break as a thaw has melted the snow but is quickly replacing it with a layer of thin mud surfacing the top of the frozen ground.

With all the security of the past few months stripped from them once again, the two find a new sense of danger and adventure and a reinvigorated love of life as they stop and survey their options.

They sit calmly. As short-lived as it may be, a quiet reprieve from the weariness of their lives is a welcome respite—it's a small bite of freedom. Even though they have found themselves to be vagabonds yet once again, it's as though life remains theirs. There is a calm exuberance about them. Maybe it stems from being young and a part of creation, or maybe because good luck continues to fall abundantly. Either way they both feel a closeness to God as though He is theirs alone.

Both of them are accustomed to the Spartan conditions of cold, hunger and psychological stresses. Some women, like some men, do not adapt well to adverse conditions but then some women do better than many men. These two seasoned survivors are among the females that do. They concentrate better than men and tend to want things perfect. This at times has prevented them from responding as fast as one needs to in an adverse field situation but these two are living proof that they have successfully overcome this basic female demand.

Across Poland's vast terrain of forests and farmland, hills and mountains is the port city of Danzig. Word has it that across the Baltic the Swedish are willing to take Jews trapped in the tyranny of both Hitler and Stalin.

"If you and I are going to survive, we're going to have to escape the insanity of this region. There are rumors that the Russians are running roughshod over anyone in their way," says Sara.

"I think that may be an understatement, Sara. We've already had a taste of their bullshit. These people aren't going to be anymore civilized than what we've had to put up with the Nazis," says Rhena. For many centuries, Jews have experienced State-sanctioned repression. It has always unleashed unimaginable cruelties regardless of which State is in charge.

"What do you think about this Danzig rumor. Do you believe it?" asks Sara.

"I don't know what to believe anymore. But there is only one way to find out—we have to go there and see for ourselves."

The departing darkness is giving way to a gray winter day. It's the kind that isn't freezing cold enough to take the moisture out of the air, thus leaving a damp chill on everything. The natural way to survive these times is to sleep during day out of sight and to travel at night under a cloak of darkness.

At least for the present their immediate concern is to find a temporary place to get out of the weather and get some rest. Having grabbed what little food they had stored in their dugout, they are happy to find it includes a couple cans of Spam obtained from some American food distribution somewhere.

They have found themselves in rough terrain with limestone outcroppings popping out everywhere. Taking solace in the quiet of the moment, Sara's eye catches an inviting looking rock formation. Upon closer examination it proves to be a small cave.

"This is going to be perfect," says Rhena examining some of the usable litter left by some previous sojourners. Among the discarded items are various pieces of Polish military uniforms probably hurriedly abandoned during some previous skirmish. After making beds out of this debris, they doze off for a well needed rest.

CHAPTER 25

TO DANZIG

They are awakened later in the afternoon by the sound of voices. Quickly becoming alert to any impending danger, they are both to their knees as they peer out of their cave on what appears to be a merry band of children ranging from the ages of eight to twelve years. They are accompanied by nearly as many young teens ranging in various ages to maybe early twenties. The oldest appearing is a tall blond young man. Some of them are armed with rifles. It also becomes obvious to Sara and Rhena that they are speaking German.

Suddenly both girls are face to face with a dirty-faced boy about ten-years-old who had been crawling around on the rocks and has managed to surprise them. He stands, visibly surprised at his discovery. Without warning, he bolts off the rocks toward the young blond-haired man.

Sara and Rhena remain dumbstruck as they, without warning, have their hideout so quickly compromised.

The blond-haired man is not hesitant to get his brood protected behind some rocks. As soon as this maneuver is accomplished, he shouts in the girls' direction ordering them to identify themselves or be shot.

Silently and individually both girls come to a similar conclusion. Rhena is the first to articulate.

"I don't see where a young guy with a bunch of kids is anywhere near as dangerous as the situations we've encountered so far."

With this shift of thought, Sara in turn makes a similar observation. "I'm with you. They don't look too tough."

Rhena emboldened by this group's lack of intimidation hollers back, "Who the hell are you to be asking me?"

"You'll find out soon enough if you don't show yourselves," is the return shout.

Knowing that being armed with nothing more than a couple of pistols is not the best position to be in when facing rifles—even if they are only being wielded by a bunch of kids—they make a decision to acquiesce somewhat. "We're lost trying to make our way to the sea," shouts out Rhena.

"How many of you are there?" comes a return call.

"Only two."

"Show yourselves and don't do anything stupid where we're going to have to shoot you," says the young man with an air of authority.

Cautiously and slowly and short of being docile, they stand up with their hands in their pockets grasping a pair of pistol grips, indicating they still aren't overly anxious to please.

Equally as cautious, the blond man commands them to move closer.

As the girls move forward, they keep a keen eye on the developing state of affairs. Suddenly they are aware that an armed group has circled around behind them. It's obvious that this is no backwoods, hayseed kid they're dealing with.

"The way you have your hands in your pockets suggests that you may have some plans. I'd advise you take them out empty," says Blondy.

"You may advise that but from my position if there's any chance you'll decide to start shooting I'm personally going to shoot you first," says Rhena with an equally committed voice.

Recognizing the commitment each has in protecting their own behalf, they slowly and cautiously begin to respond to each other as weapons begin to be lowered yet remaining suspicious of the other. With the girls continuing to move forward, they attempt to make some simple introductions.

"You say you're on your way to the coast. What for?" asks Blondy, still trying to keep the upper hand.

"Basically it's to get away from all you assholes wielding guns," says a defiant Sara. Despite his seeming arrogance she nonetheless finds him attractive in a strange sort of way.

He too, now that they have somewhat cleared the air, finds himself curious as to what these two young attractive women are doing out here in this godforsaken tundra.

"Do either of you have names?" he asks.

Hesitating for a moment, the two girls glance at one another. They're hoping it comes out right. Speaking at the same time and somewhat over each other, "My name is Rhena." "My name is Sara."

Again both speaking together one says, "We're sisters." The other declares, "We're cousins." Hearing their faux pas they reverse themselves, making it no better.

With a wry grin on his face, Blondy asks the obvious question, "Well which is it sisters or cousins?"

Realizing how stupid they have just sounded, Rhena tries to lessen its impact, "Oh pick which ever one you prefer."

This makes Blondy chuckle for a moment.

"Now I suppose you would like to know who I am?" he questions disarmingly.

"I'm sure you have that down pretty good," says Rhena sarcastically, still not ready to acquiesce her independence to anyone.

"My name is Richard Hasse," he says much more humbly than Rhena was expecting.

"Let me ask you the same question Richard Hasse, why are you out here in this godforsaken tundra?" says Rhena with a clearly prying tone.

Not quite sure how he wants to respond, he hesitates as his mind meanders around attempting to measure his answer.

"Do you see all these kids?" Not waiting for a response, he continues, "They're all orphans. Their parents were either Jews sent to concentration camps or German parents sent off to Stalin's Gulags or Polish kids whose parents were killed in bombing attacks. Their parents died from suicide after being raped or died protecting their families."

This is not the answer either of these young women expected. It leaves them speechless as they survey the ragtag army of children, many of them bearing arms with belts of live ammunition draped across their chests.

Sara finally forms a response. "What are you planning to do with these children?" she asks. From the intensity in her voice it's apparent that it's heartfelt but at the same time unnerving.

Listening to her, Richard is aware that he has touched something in her akin to fellow feelings about his dilemma. He's also aware of the dark curl of hair draped across her forehead that he longs to brush back. His words come haltingly. His plan has been determined for some time but now because of the deteriorating political and social structure of the region, he's found it imperative to go into action quickly.

"We are going to Danzig hoping to board a ferry to either Denmark or Sweden. Both of these countries have promised to help with orphans. I had originally hoped we could wait the winter out and leave in the spring but now it's becoming more dangerous trying to avoid the Russians. Their plan to deal with orphans is to shoot them—end of problem. If you care to join us I could sure use the help."

Rhena's attention is on Richard. He possesses a strength of character that she has not seen demonstrated in German men in her lifetime. She looks up at him rather sharply saying, "You do realize we're Jews?"

"My concern is not whether you are Jews but whether you have the stuff to help me get these kids out of here."

Rhena is sure she hears a truth in his voice that puts her at ease.

"Maybe we can help one another," is her response.

Sara wastes little time in gathering up what meager belongings she has and is ready to fall in with this little flock along with its self-appointed commander. She also finds something beguiling in this young shepherd. Not only is he enticingly handsome but has a transparency that is not regularly found in men of her age.

Short of throwing herself at him, she spends the rest of her day blinking her eyes as she hangs on his every word. He in turn is undeniably flattered with all of her female attentions. The striking contrast between her male clothing and her femininity makes her all the more attractive.

Wasting no time, Richard readily leads his latest additions to his camp. It turns out to be less than a kilometer away. They were just returning from a friendly farmer willing to share food. These are becoming less and less available as the Russian army continues to press westward making it all the more desperate that they put distance between themselves and this country.

Among those who were left in camp to stand guard is a young German named Reinie who has recently escaped a Russian slave camp. He's a vibrant young man determined to survive at any cost. This fits in well with Richard's mission and he is happy to have found another partisan of the same mind.

This being winter, they are foregoing the tents that are usually used under the protection of a thick summer foliage in favor of the many less detectable caves dotting the landscape. Some of these are large enough to stand and deep enough house three or four persons fairly comfortably.

Rhena and Sara are placed with a couple of younger girls in one of the larger caverns. Despite the austere conditions these young ladies enjoy putting feminine touches to their lodging.

Not being familiar with the camp's code of ethics regarding each other's privacy, Rhena in dismissing their cave mates as too young to be much of a threat and in their absence begins to rearrange the makeshift furnishings to allow her more space. The two other younger proprietors, already suspicious of these two new older roommates, on returning have their suspicions straight off confirmed.

One of the younger girls immediately explodes into an angry tirade. "Don't either of you touch my stuff!"

This explosive outburst catches Rhena off guard. Under more normal circumstances this kind of situation may challenge the disputers to show off their expertise in practicing a civilized, polite resolve, but when tensions are high as they have been for these two etiquette is left wanting.

Without a second thought, Rhena shouts back defensively in a voice tinged with guilt and embarrassment, "Don't wet your pants till the water comes little girl!"

"You'll find out who this 'little girl' is when she cuts your throat in your sleep!"

Both of these young women have been rocketed by these perilous times into a man's world of war and fighting. Both have adapted quite readily. Nonetheless both still retain a strong feminine ego and this in turn has caused one of these young women to disrespect the other's privacy.

Their explosive diatribe is quickly catching the attention of anyone within hearing distance. At this particular moment this includes Richard who along with Reinie, his second in command, are attempting to hold a conversation. It's Richard's pattern to nip these disputes in the bud. With a few well chosen words, he makes quick work of diffusing this situation.

Meanwhile Reinie finds himself face to face with a girl dressed as male wearing boots, pants, and a man's cap with beautiful flashing dark eyes.

He detects a sudden strange attraction toward this contradicting female anomaly. In some inexplicable manner here is a strange appeal about this "Polack-Jew." Her looks are more than okay but there's also a strength in her spirit that can't be hidden. She, on the other hand, shows no interest in him or anyone other than her immediate nemesis. And that's only long enough to provide her with a thrashing.

In spite of all of Rhena's attention locked squarely on her quarrel, Reinie is not dissuaded and he manages an introduction. She hears him but there is a pause as she finds herself way to ornery to shift gears. It's much to quick to even give an ear to what this infringing male is trying to say.

Taking advantage of this pause, Reinie with a wry little mocking grin says, "I like your decorating."

A combination of feelings of embarrassment, anger and some emotions that she can't define mount in her as she attempts to confront his teasing. Not finding it amusing, she lets loose with a rebuff of her own.

"Go to hell you Nazi shit!"

With that said, she turns on her heel and storms off in a tiff.

Reinie is like a bird dog on point. The brazen tenacity of this young woman has caught more than just his attention. He finds her strikingly alluring despite her attempt to blow him off. Within a few steps, he catches up with her, seeking to amend his first impression.

"I'm sorry. My attempt to be humorous was out of line. Please, please accept my apology."

Just the right amount of time has passed for Rhena to begin to realize the ridiculousness of her actions in this whole scenario. Suddenly speechless, she begins to clear her throat—not because there is something stuck but more as a way of pausing in hopes of coming up with words that will do something helpful to explain the last ten minutes of her life. The longer the time period lapses, the less sense it makes and the harder it becomes for her to rationalize her behavior.

"No, I can't accept an apology where none is due. If anything is true, it's that I owe everyone in this camp an apology."

Her embarrassment is clearly externalized in her blushed cheeks.

"I'm sorry I called you a Nazi shit."

"I'll settle for knowing your name," says Reinie with his wry little grin reappearing.

"It's Rhena Nowak, or Rhena Radinsky, take your pick," she says extending her hand.

Reinie grasps it. He would like to hold it longer but not wanting to come off as forward, he instantly releases after a well-mannered hand shake.

After a lifetime of repression from gentiles and from German gentiles in particular, she finds this kind of attention uncomfortable and pulls her hand back even quicker. Without any further conversation, she makes her way to the young girl she has just offended.

"I want to tell you I'm sorry for getting into your things. I don't know what came over me."

The young girl's name is Emma. She's still in tears over the loss of her lipstick.

Richard is standing by waiting for things to settle down. With his usual no nonsense approach, he pulls Rhena aside.

"I told you earlier that as long as we have a mutual goal and are able to aid one another in reaching it, that you are more than welcome to stay with us. But now I'm giving you a warning that if you ever pull another stunt like that you'll be out of here.

"Thank you for letting me stay. I guarantee this is a one-time deal. I still can't tell you what came over me," says a grateful Rhena.

CHAPTER 26

ALLEGIANCE TO WHAT

The one thing that remains true for this region is that things will not stay the same for more than a short period. The war is turning quickly in favor of the Allies. In this part of the world it means that the Russians are going to be in control. They have a horrendous reputation for seeking vengeance against anyone with even a German name. It seems that these Bolsheviks refuse to differentiate between ethnic Germans and Nazis. Instead all Germans are hunted down and either killed or sent to slave camps. Their penchant for Jews is a little better but not much.

Richard has been absent all morning on this early January day. The sounds of big guns can be heard off in the distance. When he reappears, he is in an obvious state of urgency. He's been on watch since early morning trying to make sense of what may be taking place. The most telling evidence is the hurried retreat of the Germans taking only equipment that can be moved quickly and easily. On this January morning the roads are full of them.

The recent thaw is making it much more difficult to maneuver some of the long cannons. They are abandoned along the roads left half buried in the mud along with the dead and wounded. At this crossroads it appears that every German soldier is on his own. His personal survival depends on his willingness to abandon the Fuhrer and make a break to Danzig.

His voice echoes through the whole camp as he mobilizes his young charges to gather up only their absolute necessities and prepare to break camp. His voice has the strain of an emergency to the point no one need ask "why?"

Within the hour everyone is gathered in a common area waiting for the order to move out. Richard takes only a few minutes to inform them of what is transpiring, warning each to be vigilant and watch out for one another. Soon this troupe of young vagabonds is on their way north to Danzig. They find they are far from being alone. The roads are not only full of retreating soldiers but also any citizen who perceives it will go badly for them if left to face the Russians alone.

Small groves of trees along the road are already reflecting the hopelessness of many of these war weary citizens. Many have chosen to hang themselves rather than have the Russian soldiers rape their woman and pillage their farms. In some cases it appears to be the entire family. It's a sad commentary for Russian dominance.

Situations like this bring out the best and worst in humans. The best includes sights of young people taking the time to assist those either too old or too young to struggle forward alone. The worst is those who are inclined to abandon family members to selfishly seek only their own safety.

Despite the seeming urgency, this seasoned ragtag partisan crew has developed a sense of calmness as they make their way through various conditions impeding their goal. As usual food, water, and shelter against the elements remain the ongoing problems for all of these fleeing pilgrims.

As the day wears on, Sara has found her way to Richard's side and Reinie has replaced Sara at Rhena's side. This shifting has met the approval of Richard but brought a level of defiance to Rhena.

"Why do I keep finding you skulking around my side?" she says with an unmistakably sassy tone to Reinie.

"Because you are the prettiest girl in this whole outfit," says Reinie with an air of confidence.

Rhena stops abruptly turning to look him directly in the face. "You're just like the rest of the German men I've had to endure. You see a pretty Jewish face that can be abused and then cast her into a crematorium at your will. Have you forgotten you're a German and I'm a 'sub-human' Jew?" Her resentments and contempt hang thick in her voice.

Reinie is taken aback by this accusation and takes only a moment to respond, his voice is indignant. "You are doing the same damn thing the stupid Russians are doing. You're blaming every German for the sins of the Nazis. That's unfair!"

"I didn't see any of your innocent Germans coming to the rescue of a single Jew!" shouts Rhena as her anger begins to mount.

"That's only because you've had your head in the sand and haven't paid any attention to those many Germans who sacrificed their own lives and the lives of their families to hide Jewish families from being discovered. We are far from all being Nazi supporters. Hitler's hangmen have snuffed out the lives of these brave, compassionate German families as well. Who in the whole world gives a damn what the Russians are doing to innocent ethnic Germans and their families living in Russia at this moment?"

This discussion reaches the ears of Richard as their voices crescendo into shouting mode. He is hesitant to enter the fray right away. Instead he listens with what appears to be a contemplative expression. A slight frown accompanying his demeanor gives the impression there may be a flood of thought behind it or that he's heard enough and wants silence.

The former may be be the case in this instance. He waits a few minutes until Reinie and Rhena have finished their say.

With a sigh and a scowl, Richard begins, "Both of you be careful where you place yourselves in these events. We are all dealing with impossible situations. There no doubt is evil wherever we turn. To excuse ourselves individually from its sphere will be to live in delusion. There is no way we can personally excuse ourselves from reacting to the pressures of our times. The truth is we are all capable of doing to another human what is being done to us, if for no other reason than to give credence to 'An eye for an eye' as a truth that we feel needs to be lived out in various vengeful ways, or for what we regard as a higher reason—that being to save our own ass. Either way, it demonstrates how void we really are when we claim to only do good."

Reinie and Rhena both listen unblinking as Richard pauses long enough to let his words have an effect. Not waiting for either of them to respond, he continues. Facing Reinie, he connects eyeball to eyeball. "You and I as Germans say we didn't commit the sins these Nazi have. But how many of us as a culture have closed our eyes and ears to the cries of injustices around us?"

Then turning to Rhena with the same intensity as with Reinie. "And you Jews as a culture have let your brothers and sisters down by refusing to pick up arms to defend yourselves and your families against those who would destroy every last one of you." Out of the 400,000 of you in the Warsaw Ghetto my understanding is that you could muster no more than 170 men and woman to try and protect the lives of the other 399,830 for one more day. That tells the world something. What's more, how many Jews attempted to save their own lives at the expense of leading their brothers and sisters to the door of the death chambers?"

The two of them remain somewhat dumbfounded as they review the shallowness of their own biases toward the other.

Seeing by their silence that he has the two of them on the ropes so to speak, Richard isn't finished yet. Not wanting to pontificate or sound moralistic, he chooses his next words carefully and certainly not to leave himself out of his assessment, he continues, "The problem with all of us is the evil forced on us is bigger than our ability to escape it. It has had its way with all of us in various ways—both in what we have done and also by what we have left undone."

The effect these words are having on Reinie and Rhena is obvious in how it has knocked the wind out of their preconceptions. Both have been given enough to clean up on their own side of the street without pointing the finger at the other's dirty gutters.

Meanwhile, Sara is so enamored by Richard that she hangs on his every word. It also is becoming obvious that Richard is enchanted with the attention this female is willingly awarding him. So much so that they spend the rest of the day delighted to be in the company of the other.

On the other hand, Rhena remains much more cautious with the attentions that Reinie is so freely giving. She has had little to do with males since her encounter many years ago with the German officer, remaining just as suspicious with this German's intentions.

Reinie remains undaunted as he resolutely continues to break down the defensive barriers this young woman has placed between them. They have both found a common ground in Richard's compassionate project for the well-being of his orphans. This takes their minds off their differences and enables them to share the chore of getting these children who range in age from eight years old to fourteen to safety.

The youngest of these is a brother and sister. She is nine years old and he is a year younger. They are from a Jewish family that had hidden the children with a Polish family. The Jewish parents were soon caught up in a German dragnet designed to rid the district of Jews and the Polish family feared being found out and deserted the children.

All of these orphans have similar backgrounds and have found a safe haven with Richard. Despite his interest in Sara, he hasn't lost sight of his goal to save these children. He in turn is pulling Sara into his fervent devotion to this cause. A great many motives may lead to this effort. In some cases it may be motivated by one taking on the guilt of a nation for compromising their ethics toward life. It seems that nations who rely on principles alone only adhere to them as long as they remains convenient, discarding them when they no longer suit their usefulness. In Richard's case it would not be for reasons of principle but rather a genuine God-given concern for the welfare of those who are too young to survive on their own.

In choosing his words carefully, Richard explains. "You may be a Jew and I may be a Christian but I believe that both of us have a responsibility to ensure that these little ones of God are not abandoned."

Sara contemplates these words for a moment. Already finding this man to be physically attractive, she looks up at his imposing figure staring down at her and contemplates the depth of his devotion.

"Do you really believe you can complete this mission?" asks Sara. The question begs more than a "yes" or "no."

"I don't believe I can accomplish much on my own but since you asked, I believe that as long as each one of us attempts to do God's will, the end result is His."

Although he has a captivating smile and is fearless in his struggle, he at times also wonders if he can accomplish this mission.

Raised in a strict Catholic household, as a boy his grandmother encouraged him to become a priest but his father was a career soldier and directed him toward the military. In these times he has found a use for each of these passions.

Looking into his eyes now, Sara, even if she had some doubts before, sees a strength that is rare. It's both compassionate and truthful. She discovers herself wanting to share in whatever this young man believes his mission to be. Richard also senses a comfort, a contentment, along with an exhilaration in being in her company. In spite of the intensity that these times bring, they both share a giddy lightheartedness that only comes when two people are falling in love. It's a beautiful reprieve from the ugliness surrounding them.

Reinie and Rhena have spent their day sharing their pasts with each other. Rhena's objective is to show Reinie the horrendous life she's had as a result of the German peoples prejudice against Jews.

Reinie, attempting to release himself personally from the accusation responds.

"I don't understand how you can cast all Germans into the same category. Most of us didn't participate in all those atrocities."

"Maybe you didn't participate but few of you did anything to stop, prevent, or even acknowledge that there was anything out of the ordinary going on," shoots back Rhena.

Reinie contemplates this thought for a moment when he recalled his own family's attitude toward the minorities living in Germany at the time. In all truth he has to admit that in spite of their non-participation in Hitler's "Final Solution" they did nothing to ensure the fair treatment of any of these marked people.

"I can't make any excuses for the German peoples' attitude. I just pray that mine will not be influenced by them as I grow older. But let me ask you a question along these same lines. My understanding is that many of you are hoping to return to Palestine. It's further reported that your people are being less than kind to the Palestinian people that inhabit that land. What do you say to this?"

Rhena is aware of the many Jews that hope to return to the land of their fathers and reclaim the land to re-establish a Jewish nation. She remains quiet as she contemplates the impact of this whole undertaking.

Reinie pushes further into this ongoing Palestinian outcome for clari-fication as his thoughts thrust forward.

"How is this much different than the Germans wanting a country free of those whose ideas will oppose them as a culture?"

Rhena listens with interest as Reinie lays out his question. Not able to sufficiently satisfy herself or him with an answer, she poses another. "This attitude is not much different from the Russians wanting all of you Ger-mans out of any country they intend to dominate. How do you feel about being kicked out of your home for no other reason than being a German?"

It quickly becomes Reinie's turn to mull over this question. In a few moments of thought, he begins to form his thoughts into words.

"I suppose it's human to gather around one's self like thinking people but how we propose to do this certainly takes more patience and thought than simply sending the non-like people to their death. I think this re-mains a weakness all humans have when an over-developed sense of losing something of value demands the obliteration of those declared to be the thieves. In other words Rhena, I believe this fault lies within all of us."

For the first time since she met him, Rhena is finding something to trust in this purported nemesis.

With the discipline of a military officer, Richard continues to move his beleaguered troupe of adolescents along the road to Danzig. As the day begins to wane, it becomes imperative they find some place to get out of the weather. The few days of above freezing temperatures have given way to a plunge way below. His immediate concern now is for shelter as the evening is bringing with it a cold wind. Others on the road are pull-ing their horse drawn wagons off to the side. These allow their occupants a place they can crawl into and ensure a nominal amount of protection.

Richard spots a lantern illuminating a window of a farmhouse across a field revealing a fairly good sized house and barn. Without hesitation, he begins to direct his entourage in that direction. His hope is to encourage its owner, in one way or another, to allow them to utilize some of his facilities for the night.

Upon reaching the courtyard of the farmhouse, he bids his dependents to huddle together in a most pathetic way in hopes that the landowner will have compassion and allow them shelter.

A large dog has announced their presence and brought with it the attendance of a ruddy-faced farmer. His scowl announces his immediate displeasure with these trespassers invading his domain. Closely examining this ragged collection of dirty faced adolescents, he soon realizes that of all the invaders that have made their way across his property during this war that these are the least threatening. Somewhat begrudgingly, he grants them a night's abatement from the weather allowing them access to his hay mow along with the strict condition they have no fires. Richard gratefully agrees.

All of them have been personally charged with the responsibility to ensure they filled their knapsacks with food and not with superfluous belongings. They also have grown accustomed to the rigors of going without. Each has an appreciation to conserve and to resist the temptation to fill their bellies today at the expense of being hungry tomorrow. The German penchant for order and discipline has so far successfully marked their trail to survival.

The plan is to get settled in while there's still daylight. It's a fairly large hay mow, just right for Richard's young partisans. Soon they are settled into their insulated beds. Reinie and Rhena are cautious not to bed down next to one another. To do that would be way too presumptuous at this stage of their relationship. Nonetheless they seek each other out to say good night.

"I can't tell you how much I enjoyed your company today Rhena," says Reinie smiling.

"For a German you aren't so bad yourself," says Rhena with the most lighthearted grin she's displayed in sometime.

"What do you mean by that?" he asks. His voice has an unmistakable tone of defensiveness.

"You Germans can be such awful people on so many different levels. I find most of you hard to understand. You have an antagonism toward anyone who isn't German, especially when it comes to marriage. On the other hand, many of your military people in charge of concentration camps will openly have a Jewish mistress and no one seems to find it scandalous. I find many of your values to be sheer hypocrisy," says Rhena with an air of finality.

"Like we discussed all afternoon, these are terrible times on so many different levels but you Jews have practiced hostility for everyone that isn't Jewish also," returns Reinie, hoping this is enough to silence this antagonist.

"Well that may be true enough but we don't kill them," says Rhena.

"Quite correct," mutters Reinie thinly. He realizes that the difference between a friendly discussion and an antagonistic discussion is knowing when to shut up—for him it's time.

On the far side of the hay mow, out of sight and ear shot of the others, things are developing differently. Richard and Sara are not willing to lie to themselves or to each other about their growing attraction for the other. Richard is consumed with her. His entire life has been in the company of males. He knows how the male minds work but admittedly is totally in the dark when it comes to females. As cold as it is, he can feel a trickle of sweat trailing from his armpit to his belt line. His whole body is quivering as though he's experiencing a chill, except in this case it isn't the cold that's responsible, rather it's nervousness. What he has been hoping to happen with Sara is beginning to come about, now he isn't sure what to do next. He has planned to be dashing with words, so smooth with his hands that her experience would be one of no regrets. Now he's consumed with passion and lust expressing itself in a nervous mess.

This night Richard produces a small bottle of cognac he has been saving for an important event. For the moment this event is the most important in his life. Uncorking it they both take a large swallow. Soon the warmth of the liquor along with their wish to continue exploring what they are starting results in them making their area as secluded as possible.

Sara in turn is not much better. Her life has been void of trustworthy males. Concentration camps and Ghetto fighting are not the usual places to find a love connection. Suddenly they both reach out grabbing the other. Sara as the willing participant allows herself to be thrown to the hay. Blinded by his own lust, he insensibly turns into an unmannerly lout as he tears at her clothing.

Sara gently stops him. She stands up. The barn is dark but there is still a glimmer of light left in the sky peeking through the gaps in the barn boards. Richard can see her as his eyes are adjusting to the dark. His breath is coming in shallow pants. She is taking her clothes off. There is barely enough light see her shape but enough to watch her as she returns to their straw sanctuary. They are both soon buried in their eros, desiring that this moment never end.

CHAPTER 27

VISTULA LAGOON

By all accounts the Nazi power structure did nothing but destroy the present as well as the future for the German people. It is apparent the Angel of Death has had full-time work claiming millions of victims through its vile programs. Now the tables have turned with another murderous regime, the Bolsheviks. The pawns in this wretched chess match remain the same non-combatants who merely want a peaceful life. The young who have no dog in either fight are hit particularly hard by both these despotic regimes.

Tomorrow comes sooner than expected as the sound of the big guns invades their night's safe haven. The sound envelops them like some evil shroud designed to cut their hearts and souls from their bodies. Before dawn has fully introduced itself, Richard is up and rousting his dependents. As usual, the younger ones are finding it difficult to be civil with each other and small squabbles break out over minor infractions.

It's noticeable that there has been a change in Sara. She is perceptibly quieter and more peaceful looking as she goes about her morning chores. The thoughts she's having are much closer to her heart than anything she has previously experienced, not to be seen as secretive but reflective.

Richard on the other hand is struggling with some compunction over his part in this change. Not quite sure where he should place his feelings. From his Catholic upbringing, a sense of guilt and self-reproach come with no effort, but on the other hand he is sure that his feelings for Sara warrant a special kind of bonding.

"Oh my Jesus, forgive me but at the moment I'm not sure that I'm clearly sorry for what happened last night, maybe later but not right now."

The night may have belonged to the two young lovers but the day is proving to be in the hands of those combatants who consider collateral damage to civilians as the price they are willing to pay to fulfill their twisted agendas. Civilian targets are not given a second thought as the prevailing thinking remains that "The end will justify the means." So be it. Civilians of all races and religions remain to this military as so much permissible waste and an expendable cost of doing war.

Their farm host suddenly appears at the entrance to this manger. He has a radio and has gained pertinent information.

"It's reported that the Soviets are making their way to Danzig. They're slaughtering everyone in their path. The only open area into Danzig is across the frozen bay of the Vistula Lagoon. If you plan on catching a ship out of there, it's reported the *Wilhelm Gustloff* is able to take 10,000. The rumor is that most of these are to be children," he says with authority.

The entire troupe is silent as the farmer states the urgency for them to get on the road. Richard is listening to his every word. He's beginning to realize the magnitude of this undertaking. Weighing their options, he orders them to be prepared to move out in five minutes. The whole group recognizes Richard's leadership skills including Rhena and Sara who have had to depend on their own abilities to make it this far. It's a welcome relief to let someone else make the hard decisions. So far he has not let anyone down. He seems to have that rare talent of perception to make decisions for the next move before it occurs.

Once on the road, they are met by every kind of horse-drawn wagon, all loaded with every belonging their owners are able to cram into the small space, thus making it necessary to pile things higher and higher. Some of these wagons have household furnishings piled three meters above the walls of the wagon along with family members jammed in between. They are all fleeing ahead of the hordes of Russian soldiers quickly breaking through the eastern front. Many of these fleeing are German soldiers along with their commanders who are deserting what is now referred to as "Hitler's Folly."

These are all ethnic Germans hoping to flee the retributions of Russian soldiers who have been given a green light to humiliate and degrade all German women who were thought to be the bearers of the pure race. The men are forced to watch as Russian soldiers rape and beat their wives, daughters, sisters and mothers. If they object they are beaten to death, or at best sent to the slave labor camps to be forced to rebuild the Russia the Nazis had destroyed.

With Richard's little brigade it's becoming a significant chore just to keep the young stragglers moving along. These children have become accustomed to one kind of exodus after another but this is the largest any of them have been involved with. It's full-time work to stay out of the way of these huge draft horses employed to drag all of this stuff, never mind the disposition of their owners. It seems these kinds of anxious situations put the needs of each wagon load in the way of another causing tempers to flair. Nonetheless they all continue to forge ahead making good progress.

Many of the villages they are passing through have already been decimated by disease leaving only a fragment of the population. Since there is no system for food or medicine, it's every person for themselves. This often has led to groups of bandits preying on what little these people have left. In this chaotic environment your worst enemy could even be your next door neighbor.

The distant sound and routine tremors of the big guns pounding away at the enemy all day have the effect of becoming mundane. They remain a hollow reminder of what could be in store for them if the Russians manage to overtake their escape efforts. In the meantime the problems for those on this road are those of an immediate nature, such as a broken axle or a horse throwing a shoe.

By the end of the second morning, Richard's entourage is within sight of the Vistula Lagoon. It couldn't come any sooner. Their food supply is running low as well as energy and morale. Some of the younger children are having difficulties staying up with the group. It's imperative they all stay together as the crowds of fleeing people are now in the thousands. Reinie and Rhena along with Richard and Sara have found themselves having to trade off carrying several of the younger children until they can recover enough to proceed.

To say there isn't chaos would be an understatement but nonetheless it all continues to move onward. The lagoon is frozen and already wagons and people on foot are stretched across its ten kilometer width. Richard casts a gaze across this sea of humanity all hoping and praying that they can get themselves and their families to safety. He finds himself beginning to mutter a prayer, "Dear Mother of God pray for us that Jesus sends His holy angels to protect us and give us the strength to bring this mission to a good end."

Sara overhears Richard's sighing at the end of this earnest prayer, taking him by the hand she draws it across her cheek. Her family had only been nominally religious. They would attend synagogue at Rosh Hoshanah or Yom Kippur, otherwise they remained only culturally Jewish. This prayer of Richard's struck her in an odd sort of way. She hasn't prayed in years but feels somehow fortunate to be in the company of one who does. She feels his strength and picks up her pace.

The shelling is becoming much more intense as they reach the shores of the lagoon. There are deserted wagons scattered up and down the beach. A horse drawn wagon is all but useless on the jagged ice and snow-covered lagoon yet many still attempt to cross with all their belongings. Many places where the current flows the water remains open and the existing ice remains thin and in some cases unable to support the weight of a horse and loaded wagon. Livestock wanders aimlessly, much of it agitated by all the confusion of the shelling. Richard quickly asseses their options. He sees a roll of rope under the seat of the deserted wagon. It's the type of rope a housewife uses to string a clothes line.

"This is going to have to do," he thinks. In another moment he organizes all of the children in order to wrap the rope around their wrists in such a way that in the event anyone should break through the ice the others could, with a group effort, pull them to safety.

The time has come when there is nothing left to do but to begin the trek across the treacherous and uninviting lagoon. Richard is in the lead with Reinie bringing up the rear. Sara and Rhena are mixed in with the children so if anyone gets in trouble, help is as close as possible. Within the first kilometer they encounter the devastation of panicked horses breaking through the ice with a family helplessly standing by watching their belongings sink to the bottom.

Richard stops long enough to assist the family. The poor horse is struggling to get out of the water and on to the ice. The result remains futile for the unfortunate beast. Richard assesses the situation realizing that there is only one option. "I have a rifle. Would you care to borrow it?"

The farmer answers Richard's offer with a most forlorn gaze. "I've never shot a horse before. Would you do it for me?"

Richard returns the gaze. He had shot a horse only once, when he was a Brown Shirt in the Hitler Youth.

It had broken its leg in a maneuver. Since it was his horse, he was in charge of its care and that meant its care in life and death. He stands in front of this thrashing, helpless critter whose fate is either a slow death by drowning or a quick shot to the head. Quickly making his decision, he uncovers his rifle from under his coat, takes aim and pulls the trigger. As quickly as the recoil from the rifle strikes his shoulder the horse is dead.

The family looks on with the same forlorn look that spells hopelessness. The farmer turns to Richard, taking his hand into both of his and tears in his eyes.

"Thank you, sir. I've seen too much death."

With that he turns back to his wife and gathers his children in the hopes of giving them some comfort.

If this were not enough to threaten the safety of this long line of wayfarers, the Russians have been bombarding the ice and blown holes that leave either open water or worse a thin layer of ice as yet unable to support any weight. To cause further devastation the Russian fighter planes are spraying the area, their pilots driven by hate and revenge. The shelling is intensifying as the crowds of these unarmed sojourners continue to defy the odds of surviving this unwarranted onslaught. There are scattered frozen bodies laying about stripped of their boots, coats, hats, and gloves, open and broken suitcases pillaged for whatever is useful for the still living. The debris is everywhere: some of it still breathes and has a heartbeat.

As the strafing continues, the screams of those hit by the bullets resonates across the ice. One of the children suddenly lets out a scream of her own. It's ten-year-old Anita. A bomb has just blown a hole in the ice throwing ice as shrapnel in every direction. A piece of ice strikes her temple causing a gash. By the time Richard and the rest of the group react, the child is dead. For a few minutes each of them tries to digest the freakishness of how their friend has just died. Tears are shed and everyone feels the loss especially the other children as each secretly hopes their friend will miraculously come back to life.

This is where the balance between benevolence for this departed child and the solace that can be given to one another has to be weighed against the heaviness of the circumstances. A conference among these survivors settles on Reinie reading a prayer from his grandfather's prayer book, leaving little Anita wrapped in her blanket that will probably be pirated by another in need coming up from behind. Time still remains at the core of their survival and must be used to benefit the longevity of all of these survivors. Everyone is aware that getting off this fragile ice as quickly as possible will significantly increase their chances of making it through the day. They're all aware that their immediate futures depend on it.

Unarguably the deserting German army has played a major role in marking the path across this harbor. A byproduct of its retreat is intermittent piles of brush used as points of reference to the trail. Nonetheless the fleeing civilians are still bullied by these soldiers trying to secure their own safe departure ahead of any civilian concerns.

All of Richard's group watch those on the trail with suspicion as these soldiers swirl past them expecting all civilians to yield to their progression. It's a bullying tactic that comes naturally after being an integral portion of their military training and now honed through experience to a level of perfection. It starts from the top down as their commanders have all secured ships in advance to insure their own safe retreat and now these leaderless combatants pull rank on anyone they can force into a subordinate role.

So far this insignificant group of God's children senses no danger from these deserters. All the same Richard keeps a wary eye open for any unexpected changes.

"Keep an eye on these guys. They're used to stealing food or anything else they want and wouldn't hesitate to snatch something from these kids," says Richard as three of the young scraggly uniformed men approach them.

"What should we do if they don't pass us?" asks Sara. Before these words are taken in by the group, an unshaven and battle worn soldier suddenly halts in front of them. He senses vulnerability in this group of children.

"We are in need of food and in the name of the Fuhrer we are commandeering your rations." He says this with an air of superiority that suggests this tactic has been employed indiscriminately and successfully in the past. It's obvious they create their own law.

Richard looks at the others and immediately they open their coats. They have surreptitiously concealed their weapons under their coats so as not to create any animosity among their fellow travelers. Their hands are gripping rifle stocks and pistol butts as these soldiers realize this is not going to be a simple heist.

"What the hell are you guys? Some sort of bandits?" says Richard.

By this time their weapons are pointed directly at this group of pilferers. This move has caught the men completely off guard. They quickly assess that they have encountered a group of seasoned partisans not about to surrender anything without a fight.

"You're armed!" the petulant soldier shouts. Their own weapons are out of ammunition but rather than apologize they merely place their hands in a neutral position, back away and forge on to seek more compliant unfortunates.

They all share a moment of relief, realizing they have just dodged what could have turned out to be an ugly and very different ending. Hopefully this experience will remain an isolated insignificant event and allow this brigade to move ahead. This encounter with these rogue soldiers has heightened their resolve to get off of this perilous environment and onto land where they only have one thing to deal with at a time.

The desperation of this kind of men always results in a subjective analysis designed to pull oneself to an advantageous position at the cost of someone else and their well-being. A show of a strong ability to protect oneself always ends with the desperadoes seeking weaker dupes. In this case it was more than a theory for Richard and his small but superiorly-armed militia it was a pragmatic determination.

In circumstances such as this where they all reacted in sync, Richard and Sara as well as Reinie and Rhena can't help but discreetly measure one another as a match. Richard and Sara have already moved forward with their relationship. They have found a kindred spirit within the other.

Rhena, on the other hand, remains aloof struggling with the old tension Jews have experienced in the presence of a gentile majority. She has a personal resentment because of the rape but she's starting to consider this budding relationship. She finds herself giving a little sigh particularly when it comes to Reinie's startling blue eyes and old young traits.

Reinie didn't grow up in a household that spent much time contemplating these issues. His background is Pietistic Evangelistic Lutheran where these things seemed more important among the theologians than among the parishioners. Consequently, his outlook is not as jaded when it comes to race.

"You did damn good Rhena," says Reinie.

"What? You sound surprised," says Rhena attempting to stay well within her barricade of emotional safety.

Being enamored with her clumsy attempt at keeping her emotions at arm's length, he breaks out into a smile that further aggravates Rhena.

"Why do you insist on presenting me with your shit-eating grin at everything I say and why do I find you standing right next to me all the time?"

"Because you're so damn pretty when you're mad and because we're tied together. Or haven't you noticed?" he says with the same persistent smile.

Rhena blushes, which in turn makes her even angrier at her vulnerability to this wonderfully strange German.

They continue their journey into the night. With the darkness, the continuous raining down of artillery shells and the air raids have ceased. The darkness and the absence of explosions gives an indication of the desolation this environment presents in its natural state. The only sounds that can be heard are the crunching of snow underfoot and an occasional echo resounding from an explosion lighting up the horizon. If it weren't for the peril of the times, this could be a romantic walk on a frozen lake.

CHAPTER 28

WHILHELM GUSTLOFF

By midnight they have successfully reached the narrow strip of land that separates the lagoon from the sea. Small fires are everywhere as these refugees are exhausted from the perilous trip across the frozen lagoon. They have determined that despite the high visibility of their fires, the Russians already know their presence and bomb them at will anyway, so a moment of warm respite is worth the gamble.

The need for Richard and his "wolf children" to keep to an indiscriminate time schedule is set aside to give these poor exhausted children a time to sleep. Meanwhile Richard has opted to forgo his rest in order to canvass the area for information. Sara is also determined to be at his side giving him assistance wherever she can. It's said over and over that there is a large ship that is selected for the evacuation of children named the *Wilhelm Gustloff*. Reports indicate it is at the port in Danzig. The normal capacity for this ship is 1,800 persons. For this mission rumors or reports suggest it's going to be crowding as many as 10,000 refugees to Kiel on the western mainland of Germany. For Sara leaving Germany altogether would have been a better option but for the present anyplace far away from the Russians is a good start.

Richard is trying hard to separate fact from fiction. Rumors are oftentimes passed on as reports and reports are often treated as rumors. The best he can surmise from a group of soldiers is that the *Wilhelm Gustloff* sails tomorrow January 30, 1945. It would be to their advantage to be on board early due to the onslaught of refugees. Richard and Sara return to their cramped camp site.

Reinie and Rhena have managed to gather enough broken boards scavenged from abandoned wagons and household furniture to build a fire. They have grouped the children around the fire placing them nearly on top of one another for warmth. The two of them have also made a decision to risk wrapping up together in the same bed rolls to share their warmth. It's twenty degrees below zero Celsius. Soon they are all fast asleep.

Richard's mind is turning so quickly that he finds it difficult to turn it off enough to even go to sleep. His thoughts continue to bang around before he finally gives in to the rhythm of Sara's light snoring as she lies with his arms wrapped around her.

Before daylight, Richard and Reinie are up and out scavenging enough wood to warm everyone before they begin the last leg of their journey to Danzig.

Currents of apprehension and fear continue to weave themselves throughout the community of refugees as the shelling in the distance reminds all of them what has brought them to this point. Some of these families are finding some of their older, weaker loved ones have not fared so well, having succumbed to the sub-zero overnight temperatures.

Those who are all accounted for and are choosing to shove on are on the trail as soon as food and toilet requirements are out of the way. The path continues to be littered with frozen corpses abandoned by those choosing to leave their dead and continue on with the living. There is a tension in those still struggling with what their morality and religion demand of them. Things like charity first are all but lost on this trail as the reality of living or dying comes with the slogan "survival of the fittest." These times don't lend themselves to the altruism women and children first.

"Today we stay together and follow the road. It'll be safer," says Richard.

Choosing not to abandon the rope, Richard's little group remains tied to one another snaking their way through the mass of refugees. Too many are risking their own and their families lives by struggling to preserve all their belongings in the hopes of re-establishing a semblance of their former life. Those that have one way or another detached themselves from their previous life are the young. They are traveling fast and soon find they are passing by wagon after wagon of these preservationists as they optimistically blaze toward a new life. For many of these younger people they have no legacy to try and preserve. Most are orphaned and have been in a survivor mode for a good portion of their lives. They are willing to go to any length to stay alive and find a life of their own making.

Groups like Richard's have found that they can hang onto a purpose so to speak, like saving these children. They have discovered by all joining together, adhering to their mission they have in turn preserved their civility and have saved themselves beyond merely a physical survival. These are the folks who are willing to lay down their lives for their brother. It remains a small brotherhood.

The morning wears on and this troupe, refreshed from a night of uninterrupted sleep, forges forward. They have a destination and a purpose. They are amazed at how quickly they are making time. The children are pulling their own uncomplaining. They have even begun to sing songs they all know and remember as they march along the trail. The peasants along the way gaze at them rudely wondering what the hell they could be so happy about and muttering under their breath for them to "shut up." Some of them don't even bother to look up, resentful that there could be happiness in this pit of despair.

On the horizon, the first tell-tale sign of civilization appears. It's smoke. Not smoke from bombs but the smoke from the chimneys of homes. Within an hour they are in the city of Danzig. Richard wastes no time finding the port. There are throngs of people lining the wharves waiting to be evacuated. The skies are gray this morning and there is an icy mist mixed with the smell of coal smoke hanging in the air. With a few inquiries, they soon find themselves facing the broad side of a ship larger than any of them have ever seen before. On the bow written in letters two meters long is the name *Wilhelm Gustloff.* The children are ecstatic.

"Is this the boat we get to ride on?" is the question resounding from a half-dozen of them at once. To hear their excitement one would think they are preparing for a holiday. Richard assures them that if they all stay together they could soon be on board.

Making their way to the main gate, they discover they can only take two adults with the children as the boat is already over capacity. It's quickly decided that those two will be Richard and Sara. Because of the urgency to get this ship going they are allowed only minutes to say their good-byes as the crowd continues to press on them. Tears of joy and sadness mingle with this farewell. Reinie and Rhena embrace all the children and Richard and Sara. All of them promise they will meet again.

Embracing Richard's shoulders with both hands Reinie manages a thank-you and adds, "This stupid war is stealing our time. Let's get out of it."

Richard, returning the embrace with a warmth that cannot be misunderstood replies, "No, no, let me thank you and Rhena. I never could have pulled this off without both your help. And yes we will get out of this war. Till we meet again."

Rhena and Reinie remain standing, watching as the little troupe disappears up the gangplank and onto the ship. There is no band on deck to greet them. There is only the hope that this is going to result in a positive life-changing experience.

There is an emptiness, a loneliness, a quietness that follows when something that humans value is taken away. This is where Reinie and Rhena are finding themselves even though they are in the middle of throngs of people. Still silent, they watch the last bit of smoke stack disappear in the mist.

CHAPTER 29

SWEET SORROW OF PARTING

It's bitter cold. The wind is picking up blowing in from the north. It's just the two of them now. It feels different to both of them. It's hitting them that they are still stuck here waiting for the Russians to plunder further on to the west. There is nothing of any significance to hold this fearsome horde back. What's left of the German army is making its way to Denmark or to the west German front. The Nazi hierarchy is already systematically making its way to prearranged conclaves in South America. The war may be coming to a close but the devastation it's caused prevails.

Due to the increasing cold biting wind, their focus on the ship, which is now out of sight, quickly changes. Looking around for some kind of shelter, Reinie spots a pile of abandoned bags left along a port building. The ship's purser had refused anyone more baggage than what one could carry, resulting in a mountain of household items left behind. He motions Rhena to join him behind it as it promises to be a way out of the wind. This is about as private as any quarters around here. In spite of its drabness they find a cozy spot to sit and share what little bread they have along with a potato.

"What do you say we explore this city a bit? I've never been to a city this size before. There has to be someplace we can get out of this weather, at least for awhile," says Reinie. He still has that infectious smile that keeps drawing her to him.

Nonetheless, Rhena's disappointment at not being allowed to board the ship is evident, coming out in her response as some envy and a lot of frustration.

"We may as well. We sure as hell aren't going anywhere sitting here," she says sarcastically. What had been keeping her going was the hope that this episode in her life would be behind her.

They begin to make their way into the city, passing through the bombed out shipyards. The streets are full of people from all over the region trying to gain passage on any kind of ship they can to evacuate themselves. This had been a free city under Polish rule but since 1940 the Nazis reestablished their dominance on the whole region including Danzig. The conquerors are now becoming the vanquished. They can't flee fast enough with the full realization of what is to become of them if the Russians find them here.

With Germans of all kinds milling around and Rhena being a Jew, she finds herself more nervous than she has been in some time. In hushed tones she makes her feelings known to Reinie.

"Don't worry about it. If anyone should ask, you are my wife. My Polish wife," he adds with his signature grin, "Besides at the moment all these officials are concerned with is saving their own ass."

There is little comfort in any of this as she draws herself in tighter on his arm. They find themselves being the only people who are going in this direction as they continue to push through the carts and wagons heading toward the port. The frustration levels are evident as parents are taking no nonsense from quarrelsome children, grabbing them by the collar for every infraction. Their faces have a mixture of panic and despair as their lives are once again thrown into turmoil.

They soon find themselves standing in front off a stately home with carts and wagons loaded with what appears to be everything this family owns. Neither of them has ever seen a home like this other than in pictures. The owner is a portly man. It's obvious he's had some important position in life from the way he directs his servants in their evacuation. His wife and children also appear to carry themselves effortlessly as only the privileged can. The family is loading itself into an automobile that carries a Nazi insignia.

The man turns toward the gawking pair and says in a matter of fact tone, "Don't stay too long. The *schweinhund* will burn it to the ground with you in it." With that said the man drives off leaving his servants to manage the wagons.

The wind is picking up as Reinie and Rhena stand speechless and alone looking at one another in front of this deserted villa. The door has been carelessly left open. Without a word their minds click together as they make their way toward the open door. The first thing they are hit with is the heat that continues to blow out of the opening. Cautiously stepping inside and shut the door behind them.

It's a luxurious home with many of the furnishings still in place. The warmth is so welcoming, had there been nothing but empty rooms it would have been enough. It's even equipped with indoor plumbing and electric lights. Neither of them have spoken a word as they cautiously move from one room to another.

Rhena is the first to make the observation that the family had in their haste left food scattered all through the kitchen. It's evident the family hastily ate a meal and left everything where they last used it.

"Reinie come here quickly," she calls. The excitement is evident in her voice as she discovers the soup is still warm in the pan and there's bread and coffee.

Quickly reacting, Reinie makes his way to the kitchen afraid of what he may find. Entering he stops in his tracks. He too is struck by the sumptuousness of the food. He has never seen a smile on Rhena as large as the one she's displaying this moment. Soon they are slurping soup and chomping on cheese and bread. It's a taste of heaven they are sharing together. The afternoon is beginning to wane as several hours have lapsed since Richard and the children sailed.

"I wonder if those kids are still as excited as they were when they boarded," questions Rhena laughingly looking out the window at those still making their way toward the port.

"They couldn't be nearly as excited as I am to be here with you," says Reinie. He has already made up his mind that Rhena is the only woman he could ever want to be with.

Rhena's time is running out on how to keep her safe distance. Her lonely life is beginning cave in to this one who is leading her heart in a direction she has never taken before. She sees this as a wonderful, beautiful thing on one the hand but also a dangerous thing on the other. Nonetheless when he takes her hands and draws her to him, she doesn't resist. Cupping her face in both his hands, he kisses her lips. It's like the world went away for the next few precious moments. It's the first time any sunshine has entered either of their lives in a long, long time. They savor the moment on this afternoon in January.

"You know we can't stay here too long," says an uneasy Rhena trying to make some conversation that will place her back in the world she's found to be miserable but at least predictable. This adventure does not possess a foreseeable good outcome in her mind. After all she still remains a Jew and Reinie a German.

"What are we doing Reinie? This can't work in any world you and I are from," she reiterates her anxiousness.

"A million worlds can come and go but none of them can change my love for you, Rhena," says Reinie pulling her closer once again. Hearing these words from him, she doesn't resist, sinking helplessly into his arms. She's falling for him in spite of herself. She's never known any man like him. He's completely turned her world around.

"You're turning the tables on me Reinie, you know that don't you? You're making me fall in love with you. You know I didn't want this to happen," she says closing her eyes making believe for the moment their hearts can make the world a beautiful place. If only it could.

In an attempt to regain herself she pushes him away playfully. "Did you see that big tub in the bathroom. That's going to be my world for the next hour. Don't disturb me."

Reinie's thoughts are focused only on Rhena as he listens to the sounds of the splashing water. She has stretched herself out in resplendence of the warm bath, rejoicing only in the present moment. It's as though she has found a world that left the horrors outside.

Opening her eyes at the sound of the door opening, she meets the stare of Reinie dead in his tracks.

"What are you staring at?" she says with a coy smile.

He in turn meets her smile by dropping his trousers. Standing naked, he enters the tub from the other end. Their legs are soon entangled as she splashes water in his face. "Get out of here you big lout," she says mischievously splashing more water at him.

He grabs her hands drawing her to him. Soon they are entangled in a happiness both have been waiting for and thought would never come. They leave each other breathless and lost for words as they make their way to a nearby bedroom.

The afternoon soon turns to dusk as they nap, make love, eat, make love, nap. Rhena has uncharacteristically dropped her guard all afternoon.

She has allowed herself to be vulnerable. It's both satisfying and risky for a girl who has lost everything she has ever cared for. They are paying little attention to the continuing flow of people passing by. The air raid sirens have been going off all evening motivating them to re-enter the world they had left behind for a short reprieve.

"I hate to leave but the way the Russians are pushing into the region, I think tomorrow is the last day we'll have to get out of here," says Reinie that evening.

They are still basking in their afternoon indulgence when they hear a terrible commotion outside. It's more than the usual hollering that goes on when people are trying to find shelter during the air raids. This is shrieking that seems to be affecting everyone. They can't resist and make their way out the door. Reinie grabs one of the shriekers, "What in God's name is happening?" he asks the hysterical person.

"The *Wilhelm Gustloff* has been torpedoed and has gone down with all on board!" Several are shouting the same message. Those who have put loved ones on board earlier are inconsolable, crying and shrieking.

Rhena is suddenly quiet. Coming back indoors she remains quiet. Reinie knows what this means. Rhena had become attached to the children, not to mention a long relationship with Sara. This is one more loss she is being forced to digest. He is not sure where this is going but he wants to allow her space and also to be available. Without a word she curls into a ball and soon they both fall asleep.

Reinie is awakened by the blast of a steam ship in the harbor announcing an arrival or departure. Looking at a clock staring at him from across the room it says 6 a.m. Wiping his eyes as he wakes a bit more, he notices that Rhena is not in the bed. Thinking she may be in the kitchen, he pulls on his trousers and makes a stumbling trip to the kitchen expecting to see her drinking coffee. Instead there is a piece of stationary on the table.

Picking it up, he begins to read.

Dear Reinie,

By the time you are reading this letter, I will have been long gone. Don't bother to look for me as I'm not even sure the direction I'm going. There is one thing I'm sure of and that is that everything I have ever loved has been taken from me. Now I find that I have fallen in love with you. I am willing to go the rest of my life alone, imagining that you are still alive than suffer the ache of knowing you are dead. That is more than I could bear.

Thank you for loving me,

Rhena

CHAPTER 30

LOOSE ENDS

The plane touches down. The stewardess makes her way through the aisle assisting where she can to aid an orderly deplaning. The sleeping old man feels a gentle touch on his shoulder.

"Sir, we have landed and I need you to wake up. Sorry."

The old man thanks the stewardess and quickly checks for the yellowed sheet of paper he had been holding on his lap. Satisfied it's safe, he purposely refolds it along its ancient creases and replaces it in his breast pocket. Safely on the ground, bags in tow, he hails a cab and heads for the hotel.

The sixty-something year old man has parked the Lincoln Town car in the parking ramp adjacent to the hotel. Turning toward the elderly lady sitting next to him, he is aware of how her talkativeness has turned to silence in the last hour.

"Ma, we don't have to do this you know."

She remains pensively silent. Her mind is elsewhere.

"Go stretch your legs for a few minutes, I'll meet you in the lobby in a bit," she says definitively.

Pausing only long enough to give his mother a concerned look, he closes the car door and does what she says.

Within a few minutes she lets out a long sigh and begins to make her way to the lobby. Her son is there waiting as is another interesting older gentleman across the room. For a moment she stops and stares but for only a moment as she has caught his attention. Now it's his turn to stare. Without breaking their gaze, they slowly begin the trek toward each other. So many thoughts in such a short distance. Meeting in the center, their hands grasp. For the moment they are only aware of each other. Tears begin to well up in both their eyes followed by a little nervous glee.

Turning to her son, she says "Eric, I'd like you to meet your father. Reinie, I'd like you to meet your son."

THE BEGINNING